# THIS COULD BE FOREVER

**Also by Ebony LaDelle**

*Love Radio*

# THIS COULD BE FOREVER

# EBONY LaDELLE

SIMON & SCHUSTER BFYR

New York   Amsterdam/Antwerp   London   Toronto   Sydney/Melbourne   New Delhi

An imprint of Simon & Schuster Children's Publishing Division
1230 Avenue of the Americas, New York, New York 10020
For more than 100 years, Simon & Schuster has championed authors and the stories they create. By respecting the copyright of an author's intellectual property, you enable Simon & Schuster and the author to continue publishing exceptional books for years to come. We thank you for supporting the author's copyright by purchasing an authorized edition of this book.
No amount of this book may be reproduced or stored in any format, nor may it be uploaded to any website, database, language-learning model, or other repository, retrieval, or artificial intelligence system without express permission. All rights reserved. Inquiries may be directed to Simon & Schuster, 1230 Avenue of the Americas, New York, NY 10020 or permissions@simonandschuster.com.
This book is a work of fiction. Any references to historical events, real people, or real places are used fictitiously. Other names, characters, places, and events are products of the author's imagination, and any resemblance to actual events or places or persons, living or dead, is entirely coincidental.
Text © 2025 by Ebony LaDelle
Jacket illustration © 2025 by 2&3
Jacket design by Lizzy Bromley
All rights reserved, including the right of reproduction in whole or in part in any form.
SIMON & SCHUSTER BOOKS FOR YOUNG READERS
and related marks are trademarks of Simon & Schuster, LLC.
For information about special discounts for bulk purchases, please contact Simon & Schuster Special Sales at 1-866-506-1949 or business@simonandschuster.com.
Simon & Schuster strongly believes in freedom of expression and stands against censorship in all its forms. For more information, visit BooksBelong.com.
The Simon & Schuster Speakers Bureau can bring authors to your live event. For more information or to book an event, contact the Simon & Schuster Speakers Bureau at 1-866-248-3049 or visit our website at www.simonspeakers.com.
Interior design by Tom Daly
The text for this book was set in Adobe Caslon Pro.
Manufactured in the United States of America
First Edition
2 4 6 8 10 9 7 5 3 1
CIP data for this book is available from the Library of Congress.
ISBN 9781665948678
ISBN 9781665948692 (ebook)

To the black sheep everywhere

# Part One
# First Sight

# CHAPTER ONE

## Deja

Diamond don't play, and that's why I love her. My big sis, but I call her my little fried green tomato: tough exterior but a complete softie underneath it all. We habitually barter clothing and skin care, and I could use her fashion tips right now because nothing I own feels right enough to bring on this trip.

"Excuse me, is that my shirt?" my sister asks, entering our bedroom.

"Uh, no," I lie, stuffing her coral halter into my suitcase. I know I ain't right.

"Hmm, whatever." She gives me a look, sensing my stress levels. "That's why I'm finna keep that new face toner you made," she says as she rummages through the random airtight glass jars full of creams and oils atop my wardrobe, where my experimentation with facial products and exfoliating scrubs has gotten out of hand. I call it my junk pile, where my family and friends come to pick through whatever skin care concoctions are left.

See? *Softie.*

I'm headed to College Park, Maryland, through my Onward Bound program to visit my number one school of choice: the University of Maryland—a school I chose after reading all the brochures, attending every virtual Q and A with students and faculty that I could, and comparing financial aid offers. But even after all that, I still felt uneasy, and I realized I have to visit the campus for myself; I have to get a feel for the school and make sure it's the place for me before I accept their offer of admission.

Another reason I love Diamond? She always knows when to step up as a big sister and save me, even when I don't know I need to be saved.

"I just, I don't know." I pace back and forth across our bedroom, throwing random toiletries in my bag as I do. "Am I being weird for going to visit just to be . . . *sure*?"

"Girl, no! I wouldn't want to move to a place without seeing it first either. Why you think I haven't moved outta here?"

I gaze out our window overlooking the pasture and the family garden, where I've spent much of my time cultivating my little facial cream experiments. The midday sun is beaming through our window, giving me a clear view of the newly ripened apricots on our tree. I've devoted hours out there to planting eucalyptus, roses, and lavender bushes, and to helping my parents harvest cucumbers, oranges, mint leaves, and other foods that are key ingredients in the homemade products my family consents to testing.

I hesitate. "I'm just . . ." I stop walking back and forth, take a deep breath, and sit on the edge of my twin bed. I know I'm capable, but it doesn't mean it's not still scary as hell.

My sister takes a long look at me, like she's able to read every single one of my thoughts. She crosses the room. "You nervous about going?" I relent and nod my head. "Aww, baby." She plops down next to me. "I'm coming with you."

"No, I'm fine." I force a smile, looking past her at my section of the room—filled with a collage of beauty and skin ads, vintage photography of Black beauty idols I bought from local and online thrift stores, and a time line of pictures from the last four years with my high school friends—afraid if I look at her my eyes will reveal my truth: panic. Diamond and my parents always complain how being an adult is overrated. I'm starting to agree already. "I know the bank doesn't give you much time off, and . . ."

"Oh, stop it!" she says. "The way they be carrying on in there, I'm about to look for another job anyway." She rolls her eyes. My sister complains about working at the bank twice a day—before she goes to work and the moment she gets home. "Plus I need to check the place out too. Gotta make sure my Dej is safe." She gives me a look I've never been able to refuse. "Lemme come with you."

"Okay," I mumble, silently thankful, and lay my head on her shoulder. She rubs it. "But I'm paying for your bus ticket," I say, "aaaannd, you know I plan on vlogging this, so you have to verbally agree to let me record you."

She huffs, knowing my word is final. "I'll put you in touch with my lawyer." I roll my eyes at her. "I can't remember the last time I got outta the Carolinas anyway. Who knows, maybe I'll meet my future husband. Can you imagine?" She releases her grasp and does a strut as she walks to our closet, flipping her Marley twists. "Me with a fancy professor or doctor?" She does a little shimmy, and I shake my head. Then she begins pulling outfits off the hangers.

We both know she'll never leave. She loves it here, at home, with our family and community.

I'm the adventurer, she's the glue.

Diamond huffs as she crouches on our bedroom floor, pulling her suitcase from under the bed, the zipper getting caught on the frays of her sky-blue comforter.

"Why don't you put the suitcase on the bed?" I comment.

She scrunches her face at me, a look full of disdain. "Oh, no, honey, you know *we* don't do that. I'm not putting this nasty-ass suitcase on my duvet. Queen taught you better than that."

Our grandma. *Queenie would scoff at me just for rolling a suitcase coated with germs on her clean floor, let alone putting it on her bed.*

"When we get back, you finna help me take these twists out," she continues.

"This is why mine is nonexistent on my head. Minimal maintenance. You know I hate taking out hair," I say, rubbing my hands through my short, coiled mane. "You better ask Dominique."

"But you know Dominique is a little asshole," she responds, patting her itchy scalp while seated on the floor, separating clothes to pack. I laugh.

Yes, my parents were *those* parents who gave all their children names that start with the letter *D*. In order, it's Diamond, Darius Jr. and me (people mistake us for twins because we were born in the same year, but my mom got pregnant with me right after Darius was born so we're the same age for a solid two months), Dominique, Deandre, and finally our little three-year-old sibling, Damarion. My parents call him a gift from God, but we know that's code for *he was unplanned*. I know that for sure 'cause after he was born, Mama went to the doctor and got her tubes tied as soon as she could.

"Just bribe her with snacks. That's how I get her," I tell her, secretly going over the packing list in my head.

"I used to change her funky diapers; she owes me," Diamond responds, rolling her eyes.

"That attitude is the reason why no one in this house will take out your twists." I giggle.

Diamond smacks her lips. "Straight up? Ma and Poppa making all these boys is the real problem. The struggle of being the oldest girl."

It's my turn to roll my eyes. The oldest child has such a superiority complex, but I can respect it. She is coming to Maryland with me after all, which makes her the best oldest sister ever. I don't know how I would have survived without her.

Frustrated with the choices from our shared closet, Diamond begins to pull everything she owns out of our mahogany wardrobe. She puts together outfits and holds different pieces up to her torso in the mirror beside the wardrobe, picturing what they would look like on.

"It's *just* three days," I remind her, as if I wasn't just doing the same thing.

"Did you not hear me when I said I might meet someone?" She continues stuffing more clothes in her suitcase, and I note a few shirts I might borrow as they make their way into her bag.

I shake my head, suppressing a laugh, relieved that for this trip at least, I won't be alone.

Greyhound has a straight shot from Fayetteville to DC, but they only have two slots a day, which means we can't miss our bus. And of course, with Diamond—who kept packing and unpacking up until the last possible second—we almost do. Like, have to run two blocks in random Fayetteville traffic to get to it. But as mad as I am, it's also hilarious. We're tired and sweaty when we get on the bus, and I make Diamond promise, on camera, that she'll buy me a Slurpee when the bus makes its first stop.

Unfortunately, shortly after the ride begins, the driver announces the AC has stopped working. The sun beams through the bus windows and gives us no reprieve after the Olympic-style running we've just done to catch our ride. We're sticky and sweaty and gross.

After the rest stop, my sister and I finally feel better, the slushies cooling us down and sending us on a sugar high as we talk nonstop for the next few hours, crash for the final two, and wake up to DC's city lights.

This is nothing like North Carolina with starlight shining across a deep, pitch-dark sky. Here, the night is illuminated by the lights from buildings throughout the city. A car honks, and it startles my sister awake.

"We're here," I whisper to her, pointing out the window.

She looks out the top window for a minute, trying to take the city in. "It's loud and bright here." She scowls, rubbing her eyes. I can tell that's code for *this ain't for me*.

I take out my phone to record this moment. "I know," I say, feeling at ease as a sense of belonging wraps around me. "I love it."

# CHAPTER TWO

## Raja

I step into the tattoo parlor, still reeling from yesterday's conversation with my parents that plays in my mind on a loop. All the words I could've, *should've* said. What I had planned to say to better translate my desires and dreams into words they could understand. I told them I was moving into an apartment close to campus this summer, and they weren't thrilled about it. *You need to stay focused,* they said. *Home is where you belong.*

Before I pop my backpack into my locker in the break room, I check my messages.

My older sister's name comes up.

RANI: How did it go?
ME: It went.
RANI: Sounds about right. They weren't happy when I left either. I don't think they like this idea of kids moving away for college, and you're local so they don't see the point.

RANI: Plus you're moving in like a couple weeks. That's a big shock to their system.
ME: Yeah, I know. But the alternative was telling them months in advance and having to hear it the entire time.
ME: Anyway, you coming home this weekend?
RANI: I wasn't . . . but I can make an exception for you since our parents are being . . . typical.

I smile. I could use her right now.

"Raj, what's up, bro?" Van, my mentor and the owner of the shop calls out, bursting through the back.

I shrug my shoulders.

"You finally told your parents, huh?"

"Yeah," I respond, rubbing my wavy mane. "And it didn't go over too well."

"What's not well?" he inquires, following me out of the break room back onto the tattoo shop floor, my second home. This place gives me so much peace—not only am I surrounded by talented tattooists who have similar goals, but I've been accepted in a space where I get to do my own thing. While at my parents' place, my sketchbook is hidden underneath my bed, here it's welcomed. Mostly it's on the front desk in between appointments, laid out on the worn black leather sofa in the break room, or nestled in the open chair I like to sit and draw in during slow periods throughout the day. I get my best work done in between job tasks, and the crew gives me feedback on my portfolio. Contrary to what my dad believes, I don't mind constructive criticism.

"Constructive" is the key word.

I go to the front to begin checking inventory for the day. "They told me my grades are guaranteed to suffer because girls and parties will cloud my priorities. 'Why waste money, Babu, when you could live at home?'" I say, imitating my dad. "And then I heard my mom mumble something in Nepali about me basically flunking and moving back in before the semester ends anyway."

Van laughs, knowing too well what I'm going through, being first-generation Sri Lankan and all. "They're projecting, but they're actually afraid you'll leave and never come back."

"I mean . . . they should be?" I mutter, shrugging my shoulders again. Van chuckles. "Wouldn't it be nice if, instead of all this passive-aggressive bullshit, they'd just . . . say that?"

"You're asking for too much, Raja," Van tells me.

"But for real, Van, I don't get it. I *am* keeping it local. Hell, this is as close to home as a college kid can get. All my friends are gone away for school, and I'm starting a new school a mere twenty minutes away. How do they not see that?"

"It's not what they're used to," Van says, hearing out my frustrations like he often has, ever since I met him a few years ago at a tattoo convention and we bonded over a shared pain of parents not understanding us wanting to do anything other than the predetermined career paths set for us. It took his parents years to accept that he wanted to be a tattoo artist, to understand that being a doctor, lawyer, or engineer wasn't the only "respectable" career choice out there. That there were different paths to being successful. "Our parents expect us to stay in the house with them, get married, and move our spouses in too. It's about building little communities here and preserving the culture. The fact that both you and your sister decided to move out is scandalous."

"I hear that. But also, what about the culture here? This is what most of my classmates are doing. They go *away* to college and go live *on* campus. I don't want to be away forever, but I do need to live a little. I'm not trying to have my college experience feel like thirteenth grade."

"They'll come around," Van says. "One of the hard truths of being first- and second-gen. Nothing came easy to our parents, so nothing can come easy to us. They're trying to teach us true fortitude the best way they know how."

I sit on one of the stools and crack my knuckles, meditating on what Van just said. Deep down, I want to believe that he's right. That one day, I'll get my parents to hear me out, to begin to understand.

When I met Van, it was one of the few moments I stuck my neck out and went after what I wanted, secretly of course. I'd been following him online for years, and he was generous even then—detailing how he lines and shadows his work. I didn't want to be a weirdo and start popping up in his shop, so about a year ago, I saved up enough money from my other side gig, reselling sneakers, and went to a local tattoo convention at the National Harbor to get a dream tattoo, one that was inspired by my graduation trip to Nepal a few months back.

As he inked away, Van and I went from keeping it casual to going all in—we talked about where we grew up—he in Vienna, me in Silver Spring—our family dynamics, and everything else. I was getting a pretty intricate design on my shoulder and upper arm, a Ganesha tattoo with white, blue, and pink lines surrounding its crown and tusk, which required a few hours of his time. After a little while I found myself getting lightheaded; Van gave me some water and sat with me as I waited for my head to stop spinning.

"You got some balls requesting a tattoo this intense," he said.

"I know," I said, then pointed to my backpack. "I have some coconut water in my bag." *I came prepared.* He nodded and opened my backpack for me. That's when he saw my portfolio. I didn't have a plan of when or how I was going to show Van my sketchbook, but it definitely wasn't when I was close to passing out.

"You an artist?" he asked, handing me my carton of coconut water.

I shrug. "Tryna be." I was sweating bullets while trying to act cool on the outside and feeling even more lightheaded—because of the tattoo *and* because my idol was seeing my work for the first time. But after reviewing my work and hearing about my desire to infuse my art with a combination of my Nepali and American heritage, he understood at once. During the second session of the tattoo, I met the rest of his crew. They saw in me what he did, and in some ways they began to feel more like family than my own parents.

Van and his crew offered me an apprenticeship on the spot, and I've been working here ever since.

Outside of shadowing him, I also run the register, help close and clean, and handle general tattoo shop maintenance, which I don't mind since I want to have my own someday. I'm learning this shop inside and out. My high school was one of the most diverse schools in the whole state of Maryland—that was the first time I felt like I found my people, and in some ways, I was sad about graduating. Many of the chosen family I had come to love over the years were moving away—to other schools in other states. But I felt stuck, wanting to stay here but still wanting to find a crew. I almost felt like I made the wrong decision, until I found this shop. Figuring out college didn't feel as overwhelming, knowing I had a place like this to come to.

I think about how thankful I am to have found this place, my feet propped up on one of the shop chairs, sketching another permutation of a lotus mandala tattoo. I know, I know, a little too on the nose considering its meaning, but something about the circles and geometric symmetry with the petals settles me. Our shop is on UMD's campus, so spring breaks and summers are our offseasons, with nights like tonight usually running slow.

Usually.

Imagine my surprise when two beautiful girls walk in, and I fumble to unprop my legs on Van's tattoo chair and act like I work here.

Both girls are wearing matching jackets, radiating laughter and joy. My eyes go from the girl in the jeans to the girl in a jumpsuit. In an instant I notice every bit of her: a smile so wide it warms her entire face, her perfectly shaped profile as she points to some of the sketches on the wall, the way she walks over gracefully to an image she likes, moving like she's levitating. I should have popped up, greeted the two ladies, asked if they had any questions. But I physically can't move—my breath light, my pulse throbbing—and all I can think is: I'd bet she'd look stunning in a saree.

So yeah, Van and this parlor have given me everything I've ever wanted.

Including the chance to talk to a goddess, who just walked through the shop's door.

# CHAPTER THREE

## Deja

*Earlier that day...*

My tour guide spits out random information as a few potential classmates and I walk across the lush University of Maryland campus, admiring the students and faculty as they go about their day, excited to be immersed in this world. I've been dreaming about this moment for far too long. The chance to finally step out on my own, budding from the shadows of a small town and a large family, to pursue my dreams of being a cosmetic chemist.

A moss-green color sweeps over UMD's campus, which is incredibly serene. It's almost like a different world from the bustling nightlife of DC that we saw as we got in last night. Which I kinda love—when I want the fast life, I can party in the city, and when I want to focus on my studies, I can hide away on campus. I'm feeling a little more at ease already.

The school's signature welcome sign is an *M* located in a traffic circle built in the late seventies, which was planted by the facilities team and features red and white petunias raised by the horticulture department. I learned this all while researching the school, and it was another plus for me. "Excuse me," I interrupt the guide. "How many flowers are in the *M* sign?"

"Great question!" she shouts enthusiastically. "Our landscape workers plant about eight hundred and fifty flowers twice a year, and it takes five of them to do this in one full day. You'll notice the red begonias, but as you can see there are still some flowers that haven't quite bloomed. Those are our yellow pansies and they'll begin blooming this fall."

"Thank you," I say. Guess not all my research was correct. I read petunias, but now pansies are the new plants, which I like even more since they have the same yellow-golden hue as sunflowers. My excitement tiptoes in, and suddenly I imagine witnessing those yellow flowers blossom during my walks to class.

There were a few other colleges I looked at, both historically Black colleges and predominantly white institutions, and while my heart was initially set on attending an HBCU, UMD was offering me a full-ride scholarship plus room and board. Spelman also accepted me, but I didn't have the same financial aid options, and as much as I wanted the Black college experience, I'd seen the student loan debt my sister accumulated after being away for only one year. Still, it didn't stop me from complaining to my Onward Bound counselor about how I was a Southern girl and the city life seemed like the most. "DC is the mid-Atlantic," she said. "Still some Southern vibes there. Where do you think the go-go sound came from?" *Oh*. That got my attention, and so I agreed to check the school out.

After touring the rest of the campus and seeing the student union, cultural center, recreation center, and more, I head back to McKeldin Mall, the go-to meeting spot to convene with some Onward Bound students for an informal meet and greet. I've never been more thankful for a program like this, which helped me and other students like me with tighter financial constraints prepare for college. We all connected on Slack when one of the students mentioned visiting campus for spring break with family members. It inspired some of the other students to come check it out, hoping it would help with our decision-making.

Two of the incoming students are already on the lawn when I pull up. I sort of feel like I could spot Chloe in a crowd based on the pictures of her big, curly wigs, but the color is different from her avatar so I'm not quite sure if that's her. Regardless, I push through my nerves and walk over to them, hoping one of them will recognize me instead. "Deja!" they practically say in unison, and I wave nervously, unsure how to respond.

They get up to introduce themselves.

"I'm Chloe!" the girl says, standing up so fast I almost get whiplash. And for such big hair and personality, I'm surprised at how little she is. Chloe comes up to my nose when she stands, which is a noticeable difference from my five-five frame, with caramel skin and locks swaying in the wind. She's got on a matte lip and bedazzled sunglasses that overpower her face, but she takes them off before practically jumping on me to embrace. "Sorry, that was a lot," she says after she lets me go. "I can come on strong sometimes."

I chuckle. Chloe and I have been pretty engaged in the Onward Bound channel as two intended chemistry majors, so it's nice to see her personality be the same in real life.

"And I'm Ramiro," Ramiro says, going in for a hug after Chloe finishes. "Nice to meet you." Ramiro is much taller and lankier than us both, with a tapered haircut and olive-color skin. His smile reveals dimples that just don't seem to end. I can already tell he'll be breaking some hearts on campus this school year.

"Nice to meet you both," I respond, relieved to find out that the chemistry we have in our chat translates well in real life. We all sit back down on the lawn, and I look around to see students lying on the grass reading, lounging in hammocks, or riding scooters along the pathway. We talk a little about our trips, comparing notes like a study group. "This is such a vibe," I say, looking around at the campus.

"Right?" Chloe replies. "Enough to make a decision?" I look at her and she smiles.

"I'm strongly considering," I reply.

"Okay, what's stopping you, then? We need more of us"—she points to her and Ramiro—"at this school, so tell us your concerns and we'll address them right here and right now."

"You two are definitely coming here this fall, then?" I ask, eyebrows raised.

Ramiro nods. "Yeah, me and Chloe decided today we're going to accept, and we need you to combine forces with us."

"Combine forces?" I ask.

"The color coalition," he responds, motioning his hands like he's unleashing superpowers. We all crack up. While Onward Bound's program is full of students from all different backgrounds, UMD, by comparison, is starkly white, and that's becoming more apparent the longer we people watch.

"I'm learning Ramiro is just as crazy as I am," Chloe says, still giggling. "So what's your issue, then?"

"Honestly," I say, looking around, "not much. Meeting up with you two already makes it better." They both look at each other and smile. "I . . . I don't know. I'm just afraid to make the wrong decision."

"We all feel that way," Ramiro says. "I don't think it will fully feel right till you're in it. What's your gut saying, though? Like when you consider your main reasons for going to *any* college, does this work? Does this school check most of your boxes?"

I nod, without hesitation. "Yeah, it does," I say, deep in thought. "I needed my tuition and everything paid for first and foremost . . . and a school close to home so I could go back easily when I'm homesick."

"Those are pretty big needs, and it already checks them off," Ramiro says.

"And you seem to like the campus," Chloe responds. "Ramiro and I already saw some pretty cute upperclassmen."

That bright smile shows up on Ramiro's face and I laugh again. "Just remember," Ramiro says, "you can always transfer. But don't psych yourself out either."

Social media makes college admissions look so easy. Someone sits at a computer, opens their acceptance email, and reads it aloud while their parents lose it in the background. There's tension until they are all able to process the news at the same time—that they've been accepted into their dream school, and after the initial celebrations and hugging and crying, they begin chronicling their life as they prep to move to campus. Their parents seem to know everything—not only did their folks help with the application process, but they run all the errands to get their dorm essentials and travel with them to campus on move-in day to get them settled.

For me, though, my parents are depending on me to figure it all out. They trust I will, but sometimes the hardest person to trust is yourself.

'Cause I'm all in my head right now.

I look around again, this time with new eyes.

I could see this.

Meeting Chloe and Ramiro on the lawn in between classes, scoping out campus cuties, taking Friday night trips to DC to hang. My sister can come visit when she's up to it, and I won't have to pay high airline prices to go see family.

Greyhound might not be ideal, but it's cheap and gets me here in one piece.

"I think this is it," I tell them. "I'm going to accept." Chloe squeals, and Ramiro fist-bumps me. Then we take a lap around the turf, envisioning our future lives together.

My sister and I walk through College Park, the streets packed with pedestrians, and I'm euphoric. All my fears are gone—well, most of them anyway. I found my school. The campus is beautiful, the other Onward Bound students and I got along so well, and now Diamond and I are going out to celebrate.

We started the night with dinner at a local dining hall and ate with Ramiro and Chloe and her family, who were all incredibly nice. I think Diamond felt more comfortable knowing that there were two people I could lean on while I'm here. She's such a mama bear. After we parted ways with them, Diamond and I decided to stroll through the campus town, observing students mingling and getting a feel for the city as we catch up on our days.

"I've been talking this entire time, but I want to hear about your day," I say.

Diamond opted to sit the campus visit out, which worked for me since I wanted some alone time. I love my sister to death, but sometimes she projects her fears of new places onto me. Drifting off to sleep last night, I began to wonder myself. But being on campus today helped me realize I can't let her opinions sway my decision in any way. This is a choice I'm making for me.

"Stayed in bed and watched *Love Is Blind*."

I laugh, shaking my head at her.

"Then I went downstairs and hung out in the pool. Best sick day I've ever had."

"I thought you used vacation days?" I asked.

"Sholl did. Told them today I was sick and had to rest before we traveled." My sister is a MESS. "How much did you pay for this hotel anyway? It looks *expensive*."

"Onward Bound got us a really good discount," I reply. "So don't expect this type of luxury every time you're in town. We'll be sharing a twin bed and cuddling next time you visit." My sister snickers, and I sigh, blissful. "I'm so happy right now, I feel like I need to do something . . . wild."

"You talkin' crazy! Like what?" she says, giving me the same look Ma gives us when she's judging.

"I don't know," I utter. "But I need to do *something* to commemorate this moment."

My sister rolls her eyes and buttons up her jacket. "The temperature sure does drop at night here," Diamond chimes, rubbing her hands together.

I giggle, taking note of a few restaurants and places I want to hit when I'm back on campus later this summer. "Di, it's in the seventies, relax."

She grabs her phone out of her purse and pulls up a weather app as proof. "It's sixty-eight!" she proclaims, putting the phone in my face. That's when I look past my sister's shoulder and notice the tattoo parlor across the street. A devilish grin creeps across my face and Diamond gazes at me, then looks back.

"Deja . . ." she says, reading the neon sign.

"Oh, come on Di . . . please?"

She shakes her head vigorously. "No, 'cause I'll have to sign off on it and you know if Mama found out, she'd kill me!"

"Since when have you been afraid of anyone?"

She rolls her eyes, so I know I got her. "You must be crazy if you think I'm not afraid of *our* mama."

Okay, maybe I don't got her.

I grab her arms. "Diamond, this is a big moment for me. And just think, every time we see this tattoo we'll think of this night. Together. You being with me when I made my first big-girl decision." I widen my eyes and flutter my lashes. "Please?"

"Why are you so damn dramatic? 'This night, together,'" she imitates in a Shakespearean accent, then keeps me on edge five seconds too long as she considers the idea. "Okay. . . ." I squeal and jump like a kid playing hopscotch. "But! I'm taking the lead here," she demands, putting her finger in my face. Here she go with the oldest sister talk. She points to the shop. "We are gonna go in there, and if anything looks sketchy, I'm dragging our Black asses back out, you hear me? And I don't want to hear no lip!"

I stand straight like I'm saluting. "Yes, ma'am!"

Diamond laughs. "You're so wack, come on!"

We cross the street and enter the shop and I already dig it. The walls are painted a steel blue, with multicolored framed images scattered throughout the front. A Punjabi/hip-hop mash-up plays in the background as my sister and I walk in, and everyone greets us with genuine smiles, including a Black girl with a mermaid-green bob. I can tell that immediately makes my sister feel better. My excitement dissipates a little when I see the crazy cool design on the thigh of another Black girl she's tatting, which looks sophisticated enough to make me believe this will be her last client of the night. Guess I can't go to her.

My sister and I point out a few framed tattoo designs we like on the wall, then head over to the counter and flip through their design book until I hear, "Can I help you?"

Both hands are on the counter, and as I draw my eyes upward, I see two arms full of tats. Some of the tattoos look tribal, and there are a few cherry blossoms sprinkled in, a large elephant-like tattoo, and words scattered throughout in a language I don't recognize. His arms are inked with blacks and pinks and reds and greens, and the designs are so impressive, I can't look away. It doesn't help that his biceps look nice, too.

The guy clears his throat and I jump.

"Oh, sorry!" I say, my gaze traveling quickly from his arms, to his sleeveless shirt, and finally settling on his face.

A cute one at that.

His eyes are a deep sienna brown, surrounded by the best-looking eyebrows I've seen on a guy. Thick and perfectly arched, but you can tell it's all natural. Probably never got his eyebrows threaded a day in his life. His eyes meet mine with a soft gaze as he waits for me to say what the hell I'm doing here. A nervous smile appears across his face, which seems right considering I can't stop staring. His mustache and stubble are cleaned up pretty nicely, and his rich black mane is faded on the sides, with a little more wave up top. I sort of chuckle, noticing we have matching hairstyles, my coils shorter and tighter.

My sister pokes my thigh underneath the counter, bringing me back. "Sorry for staring," I say, scanning the area for something to focus my attention on, "but um . . . what language is that on your arm?"

"This?" he says, flexing his arm so that I can get a better view as he points at the words. "It's . . . it's Devanagari. My native script."

"It's really cool," I say.

My sister puts her arm around me and looks at the cute boy behind the counter. "What's your name?" she inquires.

"Raja," he responds. "Welcome to the Salon."

"Interesting name," I blurt out, immediately regretting it when it registers that he might think I meant *his* name. "I mean the name of the place . . . not yours. . . ." Maybe I should just shut up.

Raja shrugs. "I feel you. Very unoriginal. I petition for a new name every week in our staff meeting." His nervous laugh turns into a chuckle, and I let my wide smile overtake my face.

He also has a sense of humor.

"Nice to meet you, Raja," Diamond says, her smile matching mine. "My little sister wants to get a tattoo, and since I'm her guardian, I'm paying for it. You free?" Diamond thinks she's *slick*.

Another man walks up to the counter next to Raja, slightly shorter and way more outgoing. "I'm Van, the shop owner. And Raja is a budding new artist here." Van passes me a different portfolio. "Check out his work and see what you like." I quickly glance at Raja, whose now-panicked eyes narrow in on Van. Instead of acknowledging Raja's unnerved look, Van smiles, pats Raja on the back, and goes back to what he's doing.

I look through his book, instantly falling for his pieces. His style is quirky with a bit of grit, and there's something unique and endearing about every piece he creates. I notice certain tattoos from his own arms in the book.

"What are those?" I ask, pointing to the picture and then to his arm. "They look familiar."

"You've probably seen them at the top of the Himalayan mountains in pictures and stuff," he says as he looks up at me. Smile crooked, eyes playful. "They're prayer flags."

On the outside I nod and smile, but inside my stomach is tensing up, my leg is shaking, and Diamond has given us very little space, but I feel her lurking, watching me and Raja interact. She knows me better than I know myself.

She senses the pull.

I survey his face, trying to find a hint of insincerity, something to make me believe that I didn't just walk into a tattoo shop and become smitten by the first man I saw.

'Cause I can't possibly be on campus for one day and already have a crush.

# CHAPTER FOUR

## Raja

Quickly I move my hands away from the counter and casually try to stuff them in my pockets. Because they are shaking, violently. People have been impressed with my work, but I've never had to ink someone . . . I'm into. My eyes are set on this gorgeous woman in front of me and I'm barely able to stand it. My nerves are cranked up to the highest setting. I am gonna *kill* Van when she leaves.

Why would he give her my portfolio? My tattoo is going to look like a kindergartner drew it, and it'll completely ruin my opportunity of ever having a chance with her.

Why is he trying to end me like this?

There's no way I can tat her up with my hands quivering like a wet dog. I wouldn't trust me if I were in her shoes. I wasn't even trying to tat her; I wanted someone *else* to give her a tattoo so that *I* could ask her out on a date. She'll never let me take her out now.

Something about her, this whole encounter, is throwing me off my game.

The easy part is always meeting a girl. The hard part usually happens when a girl wants to be introduced to my parents and I adamantly tell her no. That's when a breakup of some sort occurs, and whether it's me or her, I find it best to end it rather than come face-to-face with my dad.

I'm a soon-to-be freshman, going to an entirely new school. Which means new classmates, new friendships, new ways to meet people more like me. Of *course* I want to date. But if I'm bringing someone home to my parents, I'm making a statement. That it's serious and I plan on having her around for years to come. Truthfully, no girl has ever been worth the headache. It's just easier that way.

But no girl has ever made me this nervous either.

*Okay, Raj, you gotta calm down, bro. Do some deep breathing. She's engaged with you and . . . maybe flirting a little?*

At least I think she is.

Even if she's not flirting with me, she's *definitely* eyeing me.

Like, staring longer than normal, right?

What the hell is happening? I'm usually so much better at reading body language, a trait I learned early with my parents— it's not what they say, but rather how their bodies tell on them. How they'll avoid eye contact when shielding something from me, or fidget from worry. I could be a special agent the way I'm able to pick up on mannerisms. She's pulling at her short curls while flipping through my book, and I feel like that's telling me she's a bit bashful, but it's easier to pick up on cues when I'm not a nervous wreck myself.

And then she looks up from my portfolio and says the words I didn't even know I needed to hear from her until she said them.

"You're good . . . like, *really* good."

For a second my breath leaves my body and I want to pass out right here.

Instead, I shrug. "Thanks, still new at it, but I'm trying."

She closes the book, then tilts her head and locks eyes with me. They twinkle and invite me in, like a warm hug. "You do any tats on the fly?"

"Of course I do," I manage to get out without stuttering. I clear my throat. "What do you have in mind?" *Please* let it be something easy.

"Your lotus flower drawings are pretty nice, and sunflowers are my favorite. Can you do that?" I simply nod, and she continues. "My melanin is poppin' though, so you gotta promise me you'll make it show." She smiles.

*I'll do whatever you want.*

"Huh?" she replies, startled.

Oh shit.

Did I say that OUT LOUD?

"Uh, I said I can do whatever you want," I quickly utter, praying my man Hanuman bails me out of this one. I blabber on to recover, "Vicky over there taught me how to tattoo melanated skin. Plus I've tatted a few brown and Black folks with similar complexions. I have practice."

"That's right, sis, you in good hands!" Vicky yells from across the room and winks at her. Why are they all embarrassing me like this?

The girl of my dreams giggles, and that smile simmers the tremors in my hands.

*Say something, Raj.* "I . . . I realize I didn't catch your name."

"Deja, Deja Martin," she replies, and extends her hand. I pull my hands out of my pocket to shake back, but my phone falls out instead.

*Fuck*, why does this girl want to shake my hand of all things?

"You okay?" she inquires with concern, peering over the counter as I pick up my phone.

"Yeah, I just . . . uh . . . was just finishing up my dinner in the break room," I say, my hands getting a little clammy. "Guess I'm still hungry."

"I don't need you messing up my tattoo, Raja," she responds with some snark in her voice. My kinda woman. "Why don't you go finish eating? I'll be here when you get back."

"Okay" is all I say as I walk away from the counter, not wanting to take my eyes off her for one second. I rush into the back and splash water on my face in the bathroom as I hear Van yell, "Have a seat, best one in the house," before coming into the break room.

"What seat did you give her? I don't even have a chair!" I demand.

"Mine," he says, assessing me like a judgmental auntie. "Bro, why are you shaking?"

"Help!" I yelp at Van, and he grips my arms as if to shake some sense into me. "My hands are clammy like my cousin's. This is what I get for always making fun of her."

"So the universe is conspiring against you now?" Van asks

with a slight sneer. I know he's being an asshole, but I still nod. "What's *really* wrong with you? First thing that comes to your mind. Go."

"I saw her, and all I wanted was her number. Then here you come with my portfolio, telling her I'm an '*artist*,'" I say, using air quotes, "and now it's over. She's never going out with me."

"Why are you being so melodramatic?" Van shakes his head, letting go of my arms. "I really thought something was wrong with you for a second. Bro, it's a flower. Which is, like, your *favorite* thing to draw. You *are* ready. Use the time to learn more about her!" He looks back at the break room door, almost like he can see through it, and smiles. "You're just nervous 'cause she's stunning."

"Yeah, duh. How am I supposed to concentrate with her staring at me the entire time?" I say, and we laugh. I start pacing and cracking my knuckles.

"Do you want to go out with her or not?" Van asks, and I pout, but nod. "Then you need to get it together and get out there before you ruin your chance. Come on, time for a mindfulness check."

I groan. "You're really gonna make me meditate right here?"

"It's not like I'm asking you to do yoga, chill out." He puts his hands in his pockets. "Close your eyes and check your breathing."

I roll my eyes before I close them and do as I'm told. Aama and I used to do this when I was younger and I would pull up yoga videos for her on YouTube.

I stopped once I started high school and began my own rebellion era, but this is so centering. My body is fully relaxed.

I open my eyes and Van is smiling, his hand on the break room doorknob. "You ready?"

I nod. I hate when he's right.

# CHAPTER FIVE

## Deja

"Did you try and shake that boy's hand?" Diamond comes over and whispers to me, and I peer up at her, my laugh uneasy.

I might as well have curtsied.

"Yeah. And said my full government name too," I manage to say, humiliated. What a dork move. "Di, what am I *doing*?"

"Looking like you just interviewed for a job," she replies, and I giggle. Then she leans in closer, making sure no one in the shop hears her. "Girl, that bronze statue of a man is cute. Giving me Oscar Isaac energy."

I cover my mouth to keep from laughing hysterically. "Stop being racist. Oscar Isaac is Latino."

"Oh, shut up, I'm not being racist. He still looks like him." Then Diamond looks at the break room door and back at me, questioning herself. "Right?"

I have to turn around to hide my amusement. "No, you're right, he kinda does. Especially his chiseled jaw and those thick eyebrows . . ." *A rich head of curls, killer smile . . . I could probably keep going.* "And here I thought we'd find *you* a potential bae in DC," I say.

She looks at me and grins. "At least one of us might. And it should be you, Dej. You just accepted your admission here." She cups my chin and I melt.

"I swear, if I meet one more guy who has better eyebrows than me, I'm gonna scream," Di mumbles as Raja and Van walk out the break room. Diamond scoots back over to the waiting area, and Raja comes right over and gets his equipment ready. I'm sitting in the chair trying to make some contact with him, but he's laser-focused on preparing for the job, and then on drawing my sketch. For some reason, watching him work makes him . . . a little more attractive? Okay, a lot more attractive.

Also a problem.

God. I barely accepted my admission and already a deviation from the plan. But maybe it's not a bad thing . . . it could be a pastime to take me away from my studies. I can't solely be consumed by school, I need balance. At least that's what all the forums have been telling me. *That's how people flunk out,* I try to tell myself.

That's why Diamond dropped out.

Raja rolls his chair over and studies me. "Where do you want the tattoo?" he asks, his voice almost quiet.

I take off my jacket and point to the inside of my left wrist. "Here."

"Wrist-taker," he says, and chuckles.

I give him a sarcastic laugh. "Uh-oh, are you that person? Dad jokes?"

"Guilty." He shrugs, then relaxes his tight shoulders as he settles more into his chair, the ink already lined up on his tray. "Dad jokes are some of the most underrated ones. At least you didn't say you wanted a lower back tattoo."

"Hey! No tramp stamp shaming over here," I respond defiantly, and he laughs, then sighs in defeat.

"You don't understand, it's all UMD students ask for . . . I'm tired of seeing ass cracks," he whines.

I laugh, failing to come up with a good rebuttal. "Well, you shouldn't talk bad about UMD students, 'cause you're looking at one."

"Oh." His eyebrows rise. "You're a Terp like me, then?" he asks, looking equal parts impressed and something else I can't place. He gestures for my wrist and wraps his fingers around it. Knowing that we'd be going to the same school and feeling his touch at the same time sends a chill through me. You'd think with his black gloves on, my body wouldn't react, but now my hand quivers. "You okay?"

"Yeah, must be the temperature drop." I'm lying through my teeth, as Granny would say. "Still getting used to DC nights."

"Can't have you having poor circulation. May I?" I nod, and he takes off his black gloves and extends his hands out for me to hold. He cups both hands over my wrist and rubs my lower arm. Okay, definitely butterflies. "What year are you?" he asks casually. "I assumed you were around my age."

He's been hard to read up until this point, but maybe there *is* interest. Which makes the undertones of my skin redden. "If your age is around seventeen, then I am. I *just* accepted my admittance here. Like, today," I answer proudly.

A smile spreads across his face, and it's the calmest I've seen him since I met him. I want him to smile more often.

"Congrats, that's big!" he says, putting his gloves back on, then wiping my wrist with green soap. "And you're getting a tattoo to celebrate?"

I nod. "Thank you, it's a big deal for me. Being the first in my family and all."

Once I approve his sketch and he applies the transfer paper to my skin, he inserts a cartridge needle into his tattoo machine and begins dipping it into the ink.

Before he draws on my skin, he looks up at me and says, "Well . . . I'm happy I get to share this moment with you." My breathing grows a little heavier. I can tell he means it.

"I am too," I reply.

"Wrist tattoos sting a little," he tells me.

"I have a pretty high tolerance for pain. I can take it," I respond, the buzz of the tattoo machine suddenly causing me to tense up.

"Okay, but if it hurts don't hold it in. Tell me, okay?" I barely flinch when the needle pierces my skin. Barely. Then it sends what feels like an electric shock, but not the romantic kind. Instinctively, I try to draw my wrist back and he stops.

This one did sting.

"Already starting on the wrong foot. You lied to me," Raja scolds me. Rather affectionately.

"Sorry," I mumble.

"Let's give you a minute, and this time take a deep breath and release before I start again, okay?" I nod. "Time to take some breaths." I do as I'm told and feel the incision again, this time less painful. "You might think it's cold here now, but get ready for the summer," Raja says, bringing me back. "The humidity will make it feel more like home for you." He wipes with a paper towel and then is back to inking.

"Oh, good, more my weather!" I say excitedly.

Raja shakes his head. "It's too hot for my taste. I sweat out all my clothes."

"You ever try natural deodorant?" I ask him. "Maybe it's the ingredients in the one you use."

"You into that stuff?" he asks, hands steady, eyes focused on my wrist.

"Yeah, I like to play around with . . . ingredients sometimes" is all I say, suddenly shy.

"I use a few natural things, but deodorant was a no for me," he says. "I knew it wasn't working when I went to hug my mom and she asked me if I showered."

I practically choke with laughter. "One, your mom is savage."

He stops tatting as he waits for my laughing to subside. "Tell me about it. Brown moms show no mercy," he says, chuckling himself.

"Two," I say, still snickering, "your body is acclimating. You gotta give it time to work. And maybe try it now instead of the summer? You know, work up your body's tolerance."

Raja nods his head. "Noted," he says, switching up the ink color. He looks up at me for a moment. "Also, you gotta stop making me laugh or I'm going to mess up your design. I need to make sure you like it."

"Okay," I say, and he's gone again, back down to inking me.

Watching him work is really like watching a painter filling

in the lines of their piece. I'm probably not as concerned about the tattoo as I should be, sneaking glances between Raja and his work (okay, more Raja), but I'm enjoying our chat. Every new petal forming on my arm is a reminder that the session is almost over, and I can't help but feel a little melancholy. Whenever I catch myself staring at Raja for too long, I eye my sister, who's sneaking glimpses in between watching videos on her phone.

Well, she's no help. At one point I could have sworn I saw her steal a video of us, and if she posts it anywhere, I'm going to end her. Between my conversation with Raja and sneaking glances back at Diamond to make sure she's not embarrassing me, I'm in shock when I notice Raja finishing up the last details.

"Well, I'm done," he says, looking at me nervously, wiping his finished product.

"That was fast," I say.

"I know," he responds, sounding slightly disappointed. "Anything else you want me to clean up?"

I stare down at the tattoo. The way it glimmers on my skin is golden. He got the appearance of the petals just right, somehow mixing the yellow with my complexion to produce the right amount of depth in each leaf. The brown of my skin is infused perfectly with the flower's dark center, adding shades of black to create more texture for the flower's core and stamen.

I'm breathless. "Wow, you really do know how to work with dark skin. And you're so good with flowers."

He smiles, looking at his work, satisfied. "Your skin is the perfect hue. A great canvas."

Oh, he's *all* the way feeling me.

He clears his throat again. A nervous reaction I'm now realizing. "I like drawing plants. There's something soothing about them. Every year I go visit the cherry blossoms and practice my skills. Even with the crowds, it's a great place to think."

"I do the same with sunflower fields," I reply, smiling back. "I mean, not draw them, but go visit them. They're big in North Carolina. When do cherry blossoms reach peak bloom here?"

He looks shocked. "You've never seen them in person in DC?" I shake my head. "Oh, you're in luck! They bloomed this week. I could take you!" He pauses, looking like he spoke too soon. "You know, only if you want to go. No pressure or anything. I don't even know when you're leaving town...."

"I'd love to," I respond, trying to prevent him from canceling my dream date before he's finished asking me. "We'll still be here tomorrow. Just tell me what train stop to get off at and I'm there."

He shakes his head, then stares intently into my eyes, the most confident I've seen him since we walked into the shop. "You're wildin' if you think I'm going to let you get on a packed Metro full of tourists. I'll drive you around *my* city. It'll be fun," he says with a smirk, almost like trouble. Definitely my speed. I feel my stomach flutter. "I can pick you up at your hotel . . . unless you're afraid I'm a stalker or something."

My insides feel so warm, until I remember I'm here with my sister and tomorrow is my last full day here. I told myself I need to get her out of that hotel, because if she had it her way she'd never leave. "I really should spend some time with my sister. Can I meet you here later on? Like, three p.m.?"

He nods. "I'd like that." He gently adds solution and tattoo balm to my arm. It smells incredible, and familiar.

"What's this tattoo cream?" I ask.

"It's some organic stuff I bought. Put the whole shop on. It's made by this Punjabi guy I found online."

"So, you do use natural stuff," I say.

This man wants to take me to see flowers on a first date? He's into natural products too? What's *happening*? He's about to put a bandage around my tattoo, but I ask him to hold on so I can show my sister.

"Got it," he says, and smiles. "I'll wrap you up front. Make sure to use fragrance-free soap or body wash when you shower and follow up with an ointment like this one. You should be able to get some at the pharmacy nearby until you get home and"—he chuckles—"you know, concoct some shit."

I snort. "Whatever!" I say, then soften my voice. "And okay." We sneak each other a quick glance as I grab my things and head to the front to show my sister while he cleans up his station.

She gasps. "It looks sooo gooood. I should have gotten one!" Then she calls out to Raja. "Hey, hey um . . ."

OH MY GOD, Diamond.

"Raja!" I hiss, giving her that *don't embarrass me in public* look.

She mouths "sorry" to me before addressing him. "I'm sorry. Raja, this is dope!"

He clasps his hands together and does a mini bow. So humble. "Thank you," he replies, then finishes putting his equipment away.

Diamond looks back at me. "I'm surprised he was able to do *anything* the way you were eyeing him."

I pinch her arm. "Diamond, shut UP," I say in a hushed tone. "I was not *that* bad."

She can't stop laughing. "Damn girl, that hurt. And yes. You WERE. You looked like you were ready to slob him down like a baby suckin' on a pacifier." I put my hands to my face, completely embarrassed and praying no one heard her over the music. "But don't worry, I got it all here. . . ."

She goes to show me a video and I snatch her phone so fast. "Di, I swear to God if you put that up anywhere . . ."

"Hey," Raja says. I snap out of my tussle with Diamond, turning around all coy.

"Oh, sorry, I forgot to pay. Coming now." I give Diamond a death stare and walk to the counter. She throws me a sinister smile back.

"You okay?" he inquires, putting his hand out so he can bandage me up.

"Yeah, yeah," I respond, and this time the moment he touches my wrist again I calm down. "I'm still just so shocked at how good this tattoo looks! How much do I owe you?"

He half whispers and edges closer. "It's on the house," he says.

"No, no, no, I can't accept that," I whisper back firmly. I get close so that Van doesn't hear, but closing the gap gives me a whiff of his scent—cedar, a little bit of jasmine, and some amber. Smells divine. "Let me pay you. Your work is too good not to pay you."

"You're going to be here tomorrow at three, right?" he asks.

"Of course!" I say, thirsty as ever.

*Calm down, girl.*

His finishes his wrap and looks at me, doe-eyed. "Then that's payment enough. Van's cool with it. It's our way of saying congrats on such a big decision."

I feel like I'm in an art gallery somewhere, and an up-and-coming artist just painted a masterpiece and gave it away.

To me.

Melodramatic? Maybe. But he's proud of his work and he's proud to give it to me. And it's good.

I can't stop smiling, and after staring a beat too long, I look over his shoulder at Van. "Thank you for the acceptance gift," I say. He looks . . . slightly confused for a second? Maybe he forgot, or maybe Raja hadn't told Van about the family and friends discount he just gave me. Either way, he went along with it.

"Of course, and congratulations once again! Make sure you tell all your new college friends about your experience here."

I nod. "I absolutely will. See you tomorrow, Raja."

"I'll be here," he replies. Raja stands at the counter until I walk away. As we walk out the shop's doors, he throws up an awkward wave and I give one back, trying to keep it cool.

The moment we hit the corner of the shopping plaza, Diamond and I look at each other and exhale. I still feel like I'm floating.

"Ooooh! Deja and Raja, sittin' in a tree . . . ," Diamond chants, and I burst out laughing. "You know our Queenie would say stay away if she saw him, right?" she says.

"Why, 'cause he's not Black?" I ask, full of curiosity.

"No, 'cause he's inked up," she responds. We both laugh. "She'd probably quote the Bible and say something like 'he's nothing but trouble. And not the good kind.'"

"I would have to respectfully disagree," I purr, his smile reappearing in my head.

He's the kinda trouble I wouldn't mind at all.

# CHAPTER SIX

## Raja

It's 2:53 and I'm so nervous. Is she coming? Did I come on too strong? Not strong enough? I tried to use my superpower of holding in emotions to play it cool, but I've also learned that when I overcompensate, sometimes it can come off... cold. It's a strange feeling to be enamored by a girl I've only met once. I've never felt something like this so quickly. I don't know her, I don't know her family; hell, I don't even know her major. But we connected so well, it's like I've known her my whole life. The closest thing I can compare it to is a classmate who went away for the summer and blossomed, and I'm meeting this new version of her. Except I'm literally meeting her for the first time.

Does she have me thinking in flower metaphors? I laugh and shake my head.

I'm turning into Shah Rukh Khan.

Van walks in while I finish up some callbacks. "I thought you weren't coming in today?" I ask.

"I wasn't," he says. "I just came by to make sure you're good."

"Oh yeah, I'm real good," I reply. Too quickly.

Van laughs. "Raj, I know you," he says. "You're lying."

I sit on the stool behind the counter, leaning my head back against the wall. "Van, I'm kind of a mess."

"There you go," he says, patting my shoulder. "Talk through your feelings." He's so annoying when he turns into Zen Master Van, but I need it today.

"What if she doesn't show up? What if I misread everything? What if . . ."

"Okay, okay. One, you need to calm down. I opened a Pandora's box, didn't I?"

I nervous chuckle. "Yeah, sorry. I'm on edge today. Also, man, I put money in the register for her tattoo. I'm sorry I made an impulse decision like that. . . ."

"It's okay," Van says. "I know you were trying to impress her." I sigh a breath of relief, until I notice him opening the register and handing me the bills I just put in there. "I don't need your money."

I stand from my stool. "Van, no! Don't reward my dumb behavior!"

Van laughs. "Bro, you're starting to sound like our dads." I laugh at that one. "I was eighteen once. And she's a gorgeous and enchanting girl. I'll allow it this one time. But don't go giving every cute girl on campus free tattoos. I got a business to run, Babu."

I laugh at his imitation. "Deal."

He pauses, then says, "She's coming."

"You say that so confidently. How do you know that?"

"I just do. It's the only reason I'm okay with you giving her a free tattoo. I saw the way you two were interacting. There's something there . . . and I think she's just as curious as you are. She's coming," he repeats, and goes to the break room to chat with Ty, who just got in.

Please be right.

When Deja doesn't walk into the shop by 3:01, I sulk (I know, I'm pathetic), and four minutes after the hour I assume she's stood me up, but at 3:07 I finally notice a girl outside taking pictures . . . and my heart stalls.

It's her. She walks in all breezy, wearing shorts that show the most beautiful brown legs I've ever seen, a halter top, and a UMD baseball cap with matching red lipstick.

God, she looks amazing.

"Rocking the gear already, I see," I say as soon as she opens the door.

"You know it." She smiles and does a little profile pose, and impulsively I snap fake pictures with my fingers. We both chuckle, and she goes from silly to serious in two seconds flat. "Sorry I'm on CP time, my sister decided she needed to shower as soon as we got back to the room and that's why . . . wait, do you know what CP time means . . . ?"

I shake my head aggressively. "Nope. Don't do that," I reply.

She lets out a hearty laugh. "My bad." She looks down and her cheeks turn dark red. "Just checking." Then she looks back up at me with a cunning smile. Almost as if she's . . . relieved. *Good,* I think. *Starting this date off right.*

"Nice playlist," Deja says, riding shotgun with her face practically out the car window, taking in the scenery and letting the pleasant gusts and sunrays hit her face. "Did these speakers come with the car? 'Cause my mom's speakers don't sound like this in her Toyota."

I laugh. I'm driving Deja around in my silver Corolla Cross, a car gifted to me thanks to my family's dealership hookup. So naturally, since my entire family owns Toyotas, I had to customize my own car. Another hobby. "Thanks! I had to change them; the old ones were trash." The playlist in question is from a local DJ from Trinidad who mixes the best mash-up of everything I love—hip-hop, Bollywood, reggae, and bhangra.

"So, what's the plan for today, Raja?"

"I'm giving you a proper DC welcome and showing you around."

She looks at me. "That gave me absolutely nothing."

I laugh and simply say, "I like to wing it, but you'll find out soon enough."

I'd drive around with her all day if she let me.

Once we get off I-395 and hit Maine Avenue, she gasps. It truly is a sight to see. The Tidal Basin is surrounded by pink trees in full bloom, and it looks ethereal. Tucked between the cherry blossoms are some of DC's iconic monuments—the Thomas Jefferson Memorial, the Martin Luther King Jr. Memorial, and the Washington Monument. One day I plan to visit Japan and see these petals in their full glory, but for now it's nice to know I can drive fifteen minutes from home to get something similar.

"This is breathtaking," she says.

I smile. *So are you.*

"Yeah, it's the best view in the city." I turn down a side street and park in my secret location (aka the best place not to get a parking ticket), then grab my black backpack out the back seat.

"Why does it look like you're about to go to class?" Deja jokes.

"Oh, we're clowning, huh?" I say, and she laughs. "You'll thank me soon enough. Follow me." We walk the two-mile stretch as Deja and I slowly get to know each other. That's when I find out she's from North Carolina. She tells me about her siblings and parents and how excited, yet nervous, she is for college. How she feels like so much is riding on her success.

She has no idea how much I can relate.

Deja shares some facts about UMD's campus, and I'm shocked at how little I know considering it's been down the street from my home my whole life.

"Did you, like, read your welcome packet front to back?" I ask, suppressing a laugh. Buwa would love her.

"Well, some of it, yeah." She giggles, then gives me a look. "So I like to be in the know, okay? But then the rest I got from my tour guide. She was pretty amazing."

Not to be outdone by her guide, I drop a few cherry blossom facts, damn near desperate to impress her. I explain that the trees were a gift from Tokyo in the early 1900s and there are close to four thousand trees planted along the Tidal Basin. "See this one?" I graze the flower, lowering it ever so lightly to show her. "See the color?"

She nods, the pearl-colored leaves popping out of the tree, moss trickling down the stump.

"It's a Yoshino cherry tree. These cover about seventy percent of the Basin. But these"—I lightly pull a branch right next to it—"are from the Kwanzan cherry tree, which covers about twelve percent of this area."

"You had all those facts in your head and were acting like you didn't?" Deja responds, smiling.

I shrug, smiling back. "Okay, now your turn. Tell me everything you know about sunflowers."

"I won't tell you everything, but I'll share *some* today."

"And *some* on another day?" I inquire.

She glances at me and shoots me a smirk before planting her eyes back on the pebble pathway. "Let's see . . . they're native to the US . . . they need plenty of sun to live. Um, what else. They are actually thousands of tiny flowers."

"I mean . . . I knew that," I respond.

She rolls her eyes. "Oh my God, were you a straight-A student when you were little? You just seem to have everything packed in that head of yours. Now I see why it's so big," she mutters, snickering.

"I deserved that," I manage to get out while laughing. Deja has no problem matching my sarcasm, and I'm eating it up.

"Had to see if you could take it." She smiles, seemingly pleased with my reaction. We stop to admire a girl posing in a cherry blossom–themed quinceañera gown and a few other tourists climbing up trees to get the perfect shot. "So, back to being a straight-A student," she states.

"My dad wishes," I blurt out. "A solid-C student. But there were a couple times I came home with straight As. I just hated being told *how* to learn. I learn my own way," I say.

"It seems to be working for you," Deja states, and I blush. Her optimism is cute; maybe some of it will rub off on me today because I sure could use it. "Oh! Sunflower oil has anti-inflammatory properties, so I use it in some of the things I concoct." She pauses. "I feel like this is a battle of the flowers. You know, like battle of the bands? Have you . . ."

I throw my head back and groan. Loudly. Deja cracks up laughing. "Are you going to do this to me *all day*?" I ask. While Deja tries to sway me on why A&T's band is easily better than Howard's, performance-wise, I explain to her why I won't get into that debate, but I mention a couple of my friends who will be attending school there in the fall who would eat this discussion up.

"Will you have a lot of friends here for the summer, or will they move early to live on campus like me?" Deja asks. My heart jumps at the possibility of her being here before the semester starts.

"All my closest friends are leaving early," I respond, solemn. "Either they have internships or are going to visit family for the summer or are moving early."

"I'm sure it'll feel pretty lonely for you," Deja says, and I'm surprised by her directness.

"Yeah, I guess you're right. I will miss them. It's like I'm away for school in some ways since all my friends are leaving me." Deja and I both chuckle at my statement. "Even with my Howard friends, Jamaal will be in Ethiopia for the summer to help with the family business, and Marcus is doing some community work in LA for a class credit. I'm proud of my friends, though. They're out here making big waves." I pause. "Like you."

Deja smiles at me and the moment feels frozen in time like a painting, the scenery behind her vibrant with ducks swimming close to shore for scraps and families riding paddleboats along the Potomac River. She takes random videos and pictures along the way, telling me she plans to show them to her sister and the rest of her family when she's back home. I love how connected she is to her family. She seems so close to them yet is still taking this big leap to move away. My family might drive me crazy sometimes, but I couldn't see myself being too far away from them for too long. Maybe that's where tradition takes root in my bones. I can't wait to travel for spring breaks and study abroad programs and eventually tattoo conventions and work stuff, but when it's time to come back, Maryland will always be my home base.

I wonder if Deja would live here after she graduates. I can't believe I'm already thinking about Deja's future in Maryland.

I chuckle to myself as we walk to 14th Street to grab a bite from one of the food trucks. After we decide on tacos and order our meals, Deja and I walk across the lawn.

"Hold this," I ask her, handing her our food and plopping my bag on the grass.

I pull out a blanket and she snickers. "Okay!" she says. "Mr. I-like-to-wing-it. I see you with the planning."

I do a fake bow and she giggles. I like making her laugh. "If that's what you want to call it. . . ." She smiles as I lay the blanket out and help her sit. I also pull out a jar of the tattoo balm she raved about at the shop.

After she gets on me for giving away too many things for free, she takes a look at the ingredients. "Oh, they put sunflower oil in here."

"So you're big on skin care and stuff?" I ask, biting into my chicken taco.

"Yeah, I love natural skin care anything. It's all I try to use."

"I could tell when I was tatting you," I say. *Crap.* "I mean, your wrist was so soft, and your face is super clear." I really should just stop talking. At least I didn't say supple, which is the initial word that came to mind when I first touched her skin at the parlor.

"Thank you," she says, blushing. "It's actually what I'm going to school for. I created my own natural skin care line, so I want to go to school to learn more about ingredients and make it better."

"Damn, that's sick," I say. "I'm impressed, man." I pause. "I mean, not that you need my validation, but I'm just saying. It's . . . fearless."

"No, thank you. Sometimes I feel crazy saying that out loud. It's nice to know some random boy I met in a tattoo shop thinks I'm onto something." She chuckles nervously. "Makes my dream feel less crazy."

I'm the one that feels crazy. This girl has her shit *together*. Even if she's nervous about moving to a new city, you can barely tell. It's like she's figuring it all out as she goes and making it look effortless. In some ways she reminds me of my buwa and what he did—first Nepal, then India for school, then the States. Getting out of a smaller town and moving to the big city to make something for herself. She has no idea what she's doing, but even still she chooses to take a leap. I want to be that confident talking about being an artist, but saying it out loud like that is so . . . daunting.

It means I have to live up to it, and I don't know if I ever will.

"More people should dream like you. Plus, your skin looks great. Like really, I'd buy fifty of whatever you're selling." Raj, *shut up*. I watch as kites drift above her, almost disappearing into the powder-blue sky.

She laughs. "Seriously, I can't take all these compliments. You're causing ya girl to blush."

Okay, I'm not bombing too much. "What made you get into it?" I say, trying to sound like a normal human and not an infatuated puppy.

"I had horrible acne," she says, sipping on guava soda. "And with my family being so big, my parents couldn't afford to take me to the dermatologist or buy me anything from Sephora or Ulta or any of those places. So I started to research on my own and use plants and stuff from my family's garden. Once I learned how to mix ingredients together that worked on my skin, I started plotting my own little area and growing things." I notice her eyes are shining the brightest they've been as she talks about her passions. "Like, for example, sunflowers. They leave your pores unclogged and help heal wounds, which is why they're a commonly used ingredient for tattoos."

I nod. "That's pretty cool, and I see battle of the buds is still on." She laughs, which is good because I'm stumped on more facts to impress her with. "Who taught you all this?" I ask.

"Mostly my grandma." She almost hesitates when she says it.

"Is your granny maintaining the garden while you're away?" I ask, thinking of Aama's garden and how much effort she puts into hers.

Deja's light dims a little. "Nah, she died of melanoma right before my senior year. Wow." She pauses. "It's gonna be the one-year anniversary soon."

"I'm sorry, Deja. We just lost my baba a couple years ago.

And he was the patriarch of the family, so it was pretty wild to see him go. It felt like my last strong tie to Nepal."

"I'm sorry too," Deja says, her hand finding her way toward mine, causing the air to leave my lungs for a second. "It's hard losing a grandparent."

"It is," I say, finding my breathing. "I mean, he was ninety-eight, so I couldn't ask for a better situation. He lived a *looong* life."

She almost spits her drink back in the can from chuckling, which lightens up the somber moment. "I'm sorry, I didn't mean to laugh," she says, her face guilt-ridden. "But also, it didn't help with you saying it like that. What a long life! I can't believe he almost made it to one hundred, I don't know anyone as old as he was."

"I did it to make you laugh. Had to lighten up a pretty morbid conversation," I say. "The thing about Nepal's records at that time was there were none—Baba wasn't born at a hospital. But based on what my family knows, they came up with a date. He honestly could have already been one hundred."

"I think my mom is talking about doing something for the anniversary," Deja says, and her voice trails off.

"Still too fresh to think about it, huh?" I say, and she nods. "In Nepali culture, you shave your head and travel to see family as part of our honoring. My dad went to Nepal for, like, a month after Baba died, which is unheard of considering he never takes off from work."

"Did you shave yours?" Deja asks me.

"Pssh! Didn't you just make fun of my big head? You think I'm crazy? I prayed and told Baba I can honor him another way, but the hair has to stay." Deja is practically laid out on the blanket laughing. "I'm joking, culturally my dad and his brothers are the only ones expected to do it."

She wipes the tears from her eyes, then says, "I love how silly you are Raj, even the dark humor. You can keep the dad jokes, though."

I put my hand to my heart like I'm wounded. "But you still laughed at them."

She rolls her eyes again, then pauses. "I hate that I'm even admitting this, but I have to be honest, the first time I really understood Nepal and its culture was when I watched *14 Peaks*."

I burst out laughing, which I think startles her. "You know how many people who aren't South Asian have told me that?"

She sighs. "I'm sorry, I couldn't hold this in anymore."

"Don't be. Nims is the shit." She laughs as she nods in agreement. "Nepal is a small country, so we don't get too much attention outside of white people climbing the Himalayas. I'm glad he switched the narrative."

"Me too," she says. "All these people claiming they were the first to climb the mountains with the help of the Sherpas. And I'm like what the hell do you think the Sherpas were doing then? Twiddling their thumbs?"

I laugh, like, hard.

Damn, I like her.

A LOT.

"Sorry," she says. "My sisters and brothers and I were just . . . shocked. Like, look at how no one is acknowledging this? It's the same stuff white people have been doing to Black and Native people here for centuries."

"Columbusing it," I say.

"Oh, I'm definitely Columbusing that phrase," she responds, and we both chuckle.

"There's also a lot of political unrest there," I continue, "with bordering countries trying to take our land and all."

"Oh, Raja, I'm so sorry," she responds, then sighs. "It's not right that other places can just come in and take countries as they see fit . . . or people, in my ancestry's case."

I let a long sigh slip out of my mouth, then pause, trying harder to find the words. "I wasn't born there, so when I go, I feel so different from the people, but they're still *my people*. And weirdly I feel like myself when I'm there too. It's a strange feeling. But yeah, slavery, indentured servants . . . this world's obsession with power over land and people is something else." Deja agrees by snapping her fingers, and then we both watch a dad chasing his daughter around the grass, her giggles infectious. Which takes us away from our heavy conversation and causes us both to warm up again.

She looks at me. "I'm having a really nice time, Raja. Today is beautiful and makes me feel even better about moving here."

*Perfect.* "The date isn't over yet. I have one last place to take you."

"But the sun is about to set," she says, "and there can't possibly be a better place to view it than here!"

I give her a look, brows raised. "Last I checked, didn't *I* bring *you* here?"

She giggles, throwing her hands up in surrender. "Okay, let's go." I throw our trash away, and she dusts the blanket of excess grass, folds it up, and neatly packs it in my backpack.

Then we walk over to the World War II Memorial.

We sit on the steps and take our shoes off, ready to dip our toes in the fountain. As the sun sets along the horizon, we stare at the calm of the sky, the elegance of the sunset creating a mood of serenity between us. The lights slowly cut on, highlighting the luminous fountain, and the breeze gives us a slight mist of water, cooling down the air. Beyond the fountain we get a glimpse of the Lincoln Memorial, with the Washington Monument behind us.

I take my jacket and drape it around her shoulders, which she doesn't object to. I sit my Jordan 1s between us.

"These are the second pair of fresh kicks I've seen you rock. You a sneakerhead?"

"Not since junior year, but I used to sell them online. I'd use bots and grab 'em when they dropped and sell them to sneaker apps."

She pauses, thinking. "Oh, those are like the apps my brother is always on when he's tryna convince my mom to buy him some. But she always told him if he wants shoes, he's gonna have to wait until he's old enough to buy them himself."

"Sounds like we have the same mom," I say.

We giggle simultaneously, and then she looks out at the water. "You work at the tattoo shop and sell sneakers and upgrade your car for fun? You're such an artist."

I blush. "I wouldn't say that, I just like creative shit."

"So, that makes you an artist." She stares boldly at me, the glow in her eyes peering into my soul. "Say it."

I shake my head as a reflex. Which trips me up. Why *can't* I say it? Why am I so afraid to admit it?

She raises her wrist, then points to it. "So this isn't art?" I stare at it, surprised at how much more I like it now that it's settled into her skin. I go to graze the tattoo with my finger but stop myself, knowing better than to touch it with unclean hands, but wanting to relive the feeling of holding her arm and feeling her heartbeat accelerate through her wrist. Realizing in that moment that her body was reacting to me in the same way I was reacting to her.

Still, I can't say it, and I watch her observing me, sensing my reluctance. "It's okay," she responds with gentleness. "We'll get you to say it one day."

. . . *one day*.

She smiles with sincerity, then switches the subject. "So . . . why do you have so many side gigs? Is it to pay for your tuition?"

"No," I say. "I'm saving up to own a shop. My dad is already paying for my tuition since I'm going to school for what he wants."

"And what's that?" she inquires.

"Mechanical engineering," I reply dryly, watching the stream of water spill out of the fountain.

"You sound *sooo* excited about it," she replies, still watching me carefully.

"In most Nepali families I know, they'd damn near denounce you if you said you wanted to be a tattoo artist."

"I get it. Being a tattoo artist can be taboo, *especially* if you come from a religious background," Deja adds. "I saw you have an om tattoo. Do your parents practice Hinduism?" I nod. "If you don't mind me asking," she says, timidly, "do they even know about your dreams to own a shop?"

"Nope," I say, slowly shaking my head. "That wouldn't go over well. So I'm just getting my degree, and then I'll open a shop once I graduate."

She pauses. "But that's such a waste of money when you know you don't want to be an engineer."

Well, shit. She's right.

"I . . . I just know my parents. They'll refuse to speak to me if I change my major. They can be difficult sometimes, but they're the only family I got." And I leave it at that.

She drops it, thankfully. "I actually get that," she responds, "but I hope you can tell them how you feel before you graduate. That's a big secret to carry."

I sigh; *if only*. "Thanks. We'll see about that," I say, trying to mask my pessimism—and failing. "So, what does one major in when they want to get into skin care?"

"I want to be a cosmetic chemist."

"Got it, chemistry," I say.

She nods, taking her feet out the water and then wiggling her toes to dry. She brings her knees to her chest.

I feel like I was too curt with her about my family, that I should give her a little more. "My family would love you. That's the dream—doctor, lawyer, or engineer. The trifecta of brown success."

She suddenly gets a little fidgety. "I bet your parents wouldn't like it if they knew we were here together, though, huh?"

Well, that comment backfired. I sigh. Conversations like these are usually when my dates start to wind down, when I habitually shut down and find a way to call it a night, but after the day I spent with Deja, there's no way I can do that. I want to see her again, and she doesn't deserve to be lied to.

But explaining this part to most Americans never seems to go well. "No, because . . . they want me to have an arranged marriage."

"A what?" she says, her brain not properly processing what I just said.

"Arranged. Like, set me up with a girl from Nepal."

"Wait, wait, wait. So would you even *meet* her? How do you—"

I stop her in her tracks. "Let me say this now. I never want an arranged marriage. Ever. This is what *they* want."

Her tightened shoulders loosen up and she nods.

"But," I continue, "it's hard to say, to be honest, since the term has evolved. My parents met once right before their wedding. My grandparents met on their wedding day. I have cousins who've been set up and had good experiences. They got to choose suitors, which means they met up and got to know them and then picked from the pool of who their parents deemed to be eligible candidates."

"Oh, more like a blind date, or the show *Indian Matchmaking*," she says.

"And I'm getting on you about asking me about CP time and battle of the bands," I respond.

"Mmhmm," she says, smiling for the first time in a while.

I breathe a sigh of relief. "Yeah, you can say that. It's just added pressure because they want it in a certain caste. A friend of the family's child fell in love with a guy who was in a, quote, unquote, 'lower caste,' and it became this whole thing."

She pauses. "Damn, by social status? That's elitist."

"Who you tellin'?" I say. "Like, even if there was a, quote, unquote, 'acceptable suitor,' you mean to tell me I'll be judged based on a girl's last name? I hate it."

"So . . . have you ever brought a girl home?"

Fuck.

I rub my head. "Not really."

"Not really . . . or no?" she asks boldly.

I look her in the eyes. "No. Never." It gets heavy, fast. We sit there in silence, looking at the lighting illuminated upward to highlight the names of the dead white presidents who ran this country. A country that, for as messed up as it is, allows for this moment: a son of an immigrant boy sitting here with a breathtakingly beautiful Black American girl, explaining to her my family's ancient-ass caste system and cultural expectations that have plagued me since birth, hoping she doesn't ask me to drop her off and never contact her again.

It's only our first date and she already has me decompartmentalizing, telling her things I've never told a girl before out of fear she'll reject me. For some reason, being around her feels so natural, and her honesty makes the things I try to hide force their way to the surface. Plus she seems to be getting my situation in more ways than I would have expected.

I knew whoever I dated would not stand for certain practices tradition requires, but that also requires me to stand up to those very traditions if I want to be with her.

It's terrifying.

When we get back in the car, things are slightly awkward. We make small talk until we arrive at her hotel, and then we both play the cat and mouse game. I'm hoping that after I opened up, she'll ask me for my number; if she doesn't, it means she doesn't want to continue this.

"I had a good time," she says, somewhat hesitant.

"I really did too," I reply quickly. Eagerly. Damn near desperate.

With a clumsy pause, she says, "Okay, have a good night."

My chest feels like someone popped a balloon with a safety pin. "You too," I say.

She gets out of the car and shuts the door, then leans back in to say, "I think cherry blossoms might be one of my new favorite flowers. Night, Raja."

And walks away.

# CHAPTER SEVEN

## Raja

I completely misread her.

She was into me, even after our conversation at the memorial. Cool, I blew it.

I'm such a dummy for not asking Deja for her number. I cursed at myself the entire time driving home, but the alternative would have been begging the concierge to call Deja's room. I'll pass on being the weirdo who security escorts out of their hotel.

I turn my headlights off as I pull up to my parents' home and sneak in through the basement window, knowing if my parents catch me, they'll demand to know where I was and who I was with. At eighteen. This is why I have to move out. They'll do this my whole college career if I stay here.

Once I'm in sweats and in bed I grab my sketchbook and do what I usually do when I'm faced with my difficult reality: distract myself. I start by sketching more cherry blossoms and then afterward, I search for images of sunflower fields online and begin drawing those. Before I know it, the night has gotten away from me and bright red and orange hues beam through my window, reminding me I'm on the schedule to open the shop and should take advantage of the few hours I have left to sleep, kicking myself for all the stupid spring break decisions I've made.

I haven't finished any of my schoolwork.

I met a girl, took her out.

And didn't do the one thing I needed to do, which was get her number to keep talking to her while she's back home.

I drag my defeated self into the shop like a zombie, and the entire shop swarms me. "How did it go—oh," Van says after reading my body language.

"Uh-oh," Tyler says.

"I don't wanna talk about it." I mope, throwing my backpack down to grab a broom.

Vicky pats her chair. "Nah, don't sweep. Come sit, we need to talk about this." I sigh. When Vicky says we need to talk, everyone knows it's not a suggestion. I acquiesce and sit in her chair. Van and Tyler crowd around. "What happened?"

I tell them what happened on the date, explaining the conversation I had with Deja about my parents' views on dating and what happened when I dropped her off. "I thought I scared her away talking about the arranged marriage stuff, until she said the whole cherry blossoms thing . . . and then I felt like a complete dumbass." The crew nod their heads in approval, and I roll my eyes. "Thanks for the support, greatly appreciated."

"I can see how you'd be worried about how she took it," Van says. "But even if you're starting to like this girl, you're not marrying her tomorrow, Raj. She probably wasn't even thinking that deep into it. Just absorbing a completely new culture."

"Did you online stalk her?" Vicky asks.

I shake my head. "V, I'm not a stalker."

She eyes me. "Don't be high and mighty. *Everyone* looks people up now."

"I don't know, I guess I didn't want to find something I didn't like. I just didn't bother."

"You're better than me," she says. "I look up *allll* my dates before I go out with them. People out here acting as posers. I have to protect myself, especially as a woman."

I nod. "True."

"Well, I found her," Tyler proclaims, and my heart skips. How did he find her so fast? "I just want you to know, Raja, you're pretty stupid for not pursuing her."

"I know that, Ty," I bark. "Thanks for the reminder."

"No, look," he says, shoving the phone in my face. I replay a travel video of Deja's trip to DC—her mad dash to make the bus station (which makes the shop snicker), in the hotel room with her sister, a video of the shop (which I'm assuming she took when I caught her outside before our first date), and . . . a video of Deja in the chair getting her first tattoo.

This must be what she and her sister were bickering about

before she came up to pay for her tat, since the video was recorded right where Diamond was sitting. I'm inking her, and there's a moment where we both lock eyes for a second too long, then nervously chuckle as I go back to drawing her tattoo.

"Ohh, that look . . . !" Vicky coos. I roll my eyes again, praying they don't see my cheeks redden. The burning connection we shared still gives me a rush.

"Right?!" Tyler responds.

Van nods. "Yep, I kept seeing glances like that between you two all night."

"Damn, I can feel that chemistry coming out from the phone. Y'all are sexy together!" Vicky says. This blush I can't contain.

I'm glad her sister caught it because, watching us interact, we're completely captivated with each other. We do look good together.

So obviously I feel like even more of an ass.

I click on her profile and am shocked to see the number of followers she has.

"Fifty-five thousand followers? She's a freakin' influencer!" I proclaim.

Ty nods.

"Oooh, let me see!" Vicky says, snatching the phone while Van looks over her shoulder. "Damn, this girl is just giving me all kinds of Black Nubian goddess-ness." I smirk. Yep, exactly what Vicky said. "She kinda looks like that girl from that movie . . . what's that movie? *Queen and* . . ." Vicky says, snapping her fingers to jog her memory.

"*Slim*? You mean Jodie Turner-Smith!" I say . . . a little too eagerly.

"Have you seen it?" Vicky smirks, knowing me well.

"No," I respond.

Vicky laughs, hard. "Someone has a crush, you know her *full* name!" she says, pulling Jodie's picture up for the rest of the shop to see, to which everyone nods again in agreement.

"I mean, it's crossed my mind once or twice," I say in a failed attempt to clean up my passionate response. Then I whisper to Vicky, "Of course I remember the names of my dream girls."

"Mmhmm," she says, nudging me. I laugh. "Who else?"

"Priyanka Chopra, Amita Suman, Rihanna, Lucy Liu . . ."

"Lucy Liu?" Vicky responds. "What do you know about Lucy the baddie?"

"*Kill Bill* is a cult classic," I say. "I like watching these old movies I'm just learning about, the ones you all grew up on because your parents watched them too. My home was Zee TV until I started hanging at my friends' houses."

"Hey," Van says.

"Oh yeah, *our* homes," I reply.

Vicky laughs. "Well, at least we know this boy doesn't have a fetish. He clearly doesn't discriminate."

Ty falls out laughing. "He sure doesn't!" he says.

I shrug. "Vicky, come on. Beautiful is beautiful."

But everyone's moved on. "Speaking of, she has a beauty line of skin care called Queen!" Van says, scrolling through her videos with the phone now in his hand.

"Lemme see," I say, and Van hands me the phone. I look back at the screen and watch a video of Deja explaining her products. So that's what her concoctions are.

"Names have meaning. And so, I named my skin care line

after my granny, Queen. A woman who always gave me the confidence to be myself and be proud of my rich Black skin," Deja explains to the camera, "who used her hands to produce food for me and my family and taught us to do the same, who used herbs to help those who were turned away from hospitals or didn't have access to health insurance. And like her, I wanted to learn how to plant ingredients that were healthy for my skin, just like she grew crops that were healthy for our bodies."

What a girl. Names having meaning? She's into gardening hardcore like Aama? My family would love her if they got to freakin' know her. My mom's always bugging me and Rani about coming home to help plant and prune our backyard, but I hate being outside in Maryland heat during the summer months. I'll melt away.

Vicky sends the video of Deja to herself through Tyler's phone. "I'm definitely supporting. Gonna buy something now. Raja, you *have* to DM her! This girl is amazing, hell, I wanna date her!" The shop laughs. "But I do want to be her friend now." She slaps my shoulder and begins organizing her station with me still in her chair. "Don't mess this up for me."

I'm laughing. "Nope, I can't message her. I don't want her to think I'm suddenly interested in her because of her 'platform,'" I say in quotes.

"Agreed," Van says. "She's coming here for school, so find her on campus. What's a couple months?"

An eternity.

But glad Van sees my point of view.

"Ughhh!" I utter, handing Tyler back his phone and then letting my head fall to the back of the headrest. "You're right. I should wait. But Vicky, let me know when you put an order in. I don't want her knowing I'm stalking her through you, I guess, but I need my skin glowing like hers for when I see her again."

"You can try, but her melanin is next level. Your skin won't look like hers."

She's certainly right about that.

# Part Two
# Budding Romance

# CHAPTER EIGHT

## Deja

I'm outside with my dad and siblings, working on the family garden. The early June heat is slowly dissipating as the sun begins to set, and my father's helping me pull some plants up and repot some essential items like hibiscus, chives, lemongrass, rosemary, and basil—things I can keep alive in my dorm room in Maryland until I start my farm job. One of my biggest yeses to UMD was finding out the produce from the school's farm is used in the dining hall. Since I'm moving in early to take a couple of summer classes, I looked into the farm, got in touch with the director, and immediately asked for an internship opportunity. Get to learn the land early before the classes start, which will give me a leg up.

I'm thankful Chloe agreed to be my roommate because I couldn't imagine trying to explain why my room is overrun with flora to anyone else. I knew Chloe and I would work just fine when she expressed she's excited about my plants because she "doesn't have a green thumb to save her life," but wants to learn through me and be one of my beta skin care testers. I told her however she wants to learn is fine by me, but if I realize she sucks at plant care, she's promptly getting cut from duties. This green thumb comes naturally to me, and I can't have anyone killing my plant babies.

As we're opening the earth, I think of Queen. The twilit sky always makes me think of her. Queen and I would watch the sky at dusk as I'd vent about the kids in school, talking to the one lady in my family with the same deep brown complexion as me, who understood my frustrations. Growing up in the South can be tough for someone with my skin color. I was constantly picked on, and while I was thankful for my big sister always standing up for me, I felt alone in a house where no one could fully understand my struggles, except Granny. She was always the one I felt I could share my world with because she experienced her own share of discrimination and bullying, far greater than I ever did, and yet she had the confidence of a goddess. As a young child I never understood where her poise came from, but my grandmother sowed it in me, and as we gardened and compared stories, my confidence budded like each new leaf budding from the soil—rich with nutrients, armed with courage, and ready to withstand any harshness that came my way. I always felt beautiful, and what sucked the most was being around playground kids that didn't validate me the way the people in my home did. It was unfair, and quite frankly I was so over it at first, I asked my parents to homeschool me, but Queen pushed back with every complaint I had. "Chile, life ain't never been fair to nobody who looked like us." Early on it was important for me to be like her—proud.

*Dark like the night sky and proud of it,* she'd say. A common phrase used to degrade us, she reclaimed the word as a source of pride, and even gave me the nickname. She'd talk about her skin being the color of dark chocolate and dried peppercorns and wild blackberries. All things sweet, sometimes with a little kick, and satisfying and rich in flavor. There was a hardness to her, living a life I'd never understand, and yet her beauty was undeniable. Bob-length hair, the black and white of her mane blended together like marble, a round face with wrinkles from days when the sun became unbearable, and the prettiest pearly whites from a lifetime of using baking soda and charcoal on her teeth. I'd laugh at her, sitting on the front porch, listening to the grasshoppers chirp in the distance. Looking up at the blackness of the sky filled with twinkling stars, staring at the vastness of it all. How unassuming it looked, knowing there was a whole universe out there. Even before I knew what the sky was full of, how it was only a small part of a much larger universe, I knew I wanted to explore, to find answers. To leave the South and venture wherever, to see what's out there for me to learn and grow from.

The sky also reminded me of us. Intimidating, intriguing, captivating. All at once.

She'd wrap her arms around me, our skin glowing under the moonlight. I'd hear the breeze whistling through the trees, the night air giving us a reprieve from the Carolina summer heat; I felt safe and whole in her arms. "People finna talk about you, Night, but know it's not you. It's them. I reckon they see darker skin as a curse 'cause of what they been taught, what lies been passed down to them about us." I see a little hurt in her eyes. "Know where it comes from. And don't internalize it, promise me."

"Yes, ma'am," I'd say.

My thoughts are interrupted by my dad and younger brothers bickering over the yard work.

"It's hot!" my younger brother Deandre complains. "Why I gotta be out here doin' this?"

"You like to eat?" my dad scoffs.

Deandre groans while I laugh. "If I had a quarter for every time you say that, I woulda been rich by now."

"Bruh, you're eleven!" Jr. says, turning from his task and shaking his head. I chuckle again.

"Boy, if you don't quit carrying on! And pass me that shovel over there!" my dad says, trying to suppress his own laughter to make a point.

I smile watching them, sitting on the grass in dusty overalls I stole from Jr., a sports bra, and an Adidas bucket hat. My dad calls my outfit farming couture compared to his staple—a frayed straw hat that he's worn out but refuses to let us replace.

I've spent so much time thinking about getting away from a family that constantly feels on top of me, but now that it's almost time to leave, hearing my father and brothers' bickering and seeing Dad's silly straw hat helps me recognize just how bad I'm going to miss them. I'm probably one of the few people who don't mind a roommate for that reason; I'm used to always being around people and having to find ways to carve my own space in a big pond. If not, I would have drowned.

"Y'all got the rest of my corn?!" Mama yells from the kitchen window.

"I got it, Ma!" I yell back, brushing dirt off my overalls as I grab the corn stalks in the basket near my pops.

A blast of scents hits my nostrils at once as I walk up to the back porch and open the screen door. My mom is in the kitchen throwing down on my farewell meal—neck bones, fried okra, black eyed peas, macaroni and cheese, corn on the cob, cornbread, and collards. "Set them on the table so your sisters can get to shucking," my mom orders as she somehow manages to taste, flip, add seasoning, and reorganize pots on top of the stove and in the oven.

"Yes, ma'am," I say.

She drops a bowl of water with baking soda on the table. "And make sure you soak 'em in here."

My sister Dominique groans. "Where's Diamond?" she scowls, snapping the peas like she's snapping Diamond's neck and chucking them in the bowl.

"Aggressive much?" I respond as I set the corn down. Then I put my finger to my lips and slowly move the bowl of peas to my side of the table. My mom has strict orders that I'm not to do any dinner preparations since I already have enough on my plate with getting everything together for DC. I love how even though my mom doesn't know *how* to help me academically, she makes up for it in other ways as only she could. She's giving me exactly what I need, but with any house full of siblings, extra attention on one child can sometimes mean resentment from others. Especially Nique, who would rather do yard work than any sort of housework. I decide to snap the peas for Dominique since it's easier than peeling off that damn husk, and the monotonous task is calming.

She smiles and whispers, "Thanks, love you," before finding a reason to excuse herself (bathroom break) and darts out the room.

"That girl's got five minutes to get back here or I'm comin' for her and Diamond," Mama says.

"Oh, she's banking on it," I laugh, still snapping peas.

My mom pulls the towel from the oven's door handle to wipe her hands, and she gives me that look she's been giving me for the last month in moments where it's just us together—her gaze sorrowful, her lips tight like she's hoping her mouth will hold back the tears forming in her eyes.

"Maaaaa," I whimper. It's all I can say to keep from letting out my own tears. I'll give her credit, she's been finding ways to keep busy with tasks, like this dinner, to mask the pain she feels about me going away. I don't know if my mom ever expected me or any of my siblings to leave home, and after Diamond came back, I'm sure she took that as a sign we'd be one big happy family forever. It's how it's always been. My parents were born and raised in Fayetteville and then raised their kids here.

She comes over to my chair and hugs me from behind, her arms and hands dusted with flour, and kisses the top of my head. "I know, I'm tryin', Sunflower. It's just hard." I place my hands atop her arms and look up at her.

"I'm going to miss you too," I hoarsely manage to get out, a stream of tears running down my cheek. Life suddenly feels so overwhelming, and I look up at her and whisper, "Mama, I think I'm scared."

"It's okay to be afraid at times like this," she says, eyes bright with pride as she rubs my head. "Means you doing something courageous. And one thing I know about you, Dej, you've always been gutsy, but smart too. Keep at it. It's carried you this far."

I release an exhale. Of relief and of acceptance. "Yes, ma'am," I utter.

"Hell, you were making decisions right out the womb, bossin' everyone around old and young." I let out a hearty laugh while my brothers run in the house, released from their outdoor chores and thrilled about it. My mom's face goes rigid. "Go wash up for supper," she calls out as they run through the kitchen. "And you know betta! Don't be tracking dirty shoes in my house!" And just like that, the brief peace my mom and I shared is gone, replaced by barking orders as she struts down our long, unleveled hallway that my dad, his brother, and some great-uncles helped build with their bare hands when I was a toddler.

It's always been this way, and I sigh again. But just when I think the moment has passed, Mama walks back in the kitchen and places her hand above the cast iron skillet, making sure the golden cornbread covering the skillet's bottom has cooled. Before I know it, she's cutting a small piece and sliding it across the kitchen table. "I made it burnt on the edges, just like you like it."

"Bless you," I reply, and she winks.

"Let me go see about these girls, 'cause the rest of this food ain't gonna fix itself. Eat that before anyone sees it." She lightly slaps me with the hand towel she's still holding and heads to the back to find Dominique and Diamond.

I chew the first bite and smile. I'd never tell Mama this, but it tasted even better when Queen would make it with sweet milk, as she called it, and a touch of sugar sprinkled on top.

I catch my emotions building up as I eat the cornbread. Off to a new place, needing that last bit of reassurance I'd always get from someone I looked up to, and she's not here. She's not here to help me when I need her. Queen had the most courage I'd ever seen, and I could use an ounce of it right now.

Diamond and I sneak away into our room after dinner and games, trying to steal as much quality time together as possible before I'm away. Through our paper-thin walls, we hear Nique and our brothers roughhousing in the next room over. We conclude Dominique has once again won a play fight over Deandre since we hear him repeatedly crying "get offa me!" to Nique.

"You ready for Nique to take over my side?" I ask, giggling. Now that I'm taking off, it's the guys versus the girls. Jr. and Deandre are in a room, which means Dom is now with Di, and the baby of the house gets his own room so Mama and Poppa can finally get some privacy again, as they say.

Diamond shakes her head in distress. "Absolutely not."

I crack up.

"First of all, I can't believe Ma and Pops told me I have to pay rent if I want my own room."

"Well . . ." I say, hunching my shoulders.

"And she's such a tomboy!" Diamond huffs. "She's gonna terrorize me and this room. And it was just starting to feel calm in here."

"*Just?* I'm the peaceful one."

Di rolls her eyes.

"She needs your big sister touch," I continue. "She's about to hit puberty soon. She's not gonna want to have her period in a room full of boys."

Diamond shrugs.

"Look," I say, "I know you and Nique don't always see eye to eye, but she's easy. You and her clash cause y'all just alike—ready to fight, but always to protect the ones you love."

"Well, she must really love herself, 'cause she will fight anyone that tries to mess with her."

". . . or family," I respond, casually reminding her of the times Nique got detention for standing up to Deandre's school bullies. "They're wrestling in there now so she can teach him how to defend himself if he has to. You, on the other hand, would just fight all my bullies off for me."

Diamond smiles. "But you were so liked at school by the time I left you didn't have to fight anyone."

I laugh. "You're right, I'm a lover, not a fighter." My sister is a lot of things, but the main thing is a protector.

The first time my older sister fought someone for me was when I was in third grade during recess. I wore this cute canary-yellow number my mom got for me, an outfit I adored as soon as I spotted it in the store—a sleeveless yellow dress with a tulle bottom. The first time Mama slipped the dress over my head, my skin radiated, the richness of my mocha pigment popping out like the center of a flower.

The next day my mom plaited my shoulder-length hair, and I rode on the school bus with Diamond, excited to show off my new dress. But Jasmine Barnes, a light-skinned girl with woolly, sandy-colored hair and matching freckles, surveyed me like a street cat on the prowl the instant I stepped on the bus, and once we were in class, she circled me like prey. When the teacher stepped out, Jasmine proclaimed in front of the entire classroom that the dress color was too bright for my skin and called me "darkie." By recess half of my class was chanting that word, and I tried to get as far away from everyone as possible, finding a little corner on the playground to shelter.

When Diamond noticed me sitting on a swing moping, she forced me to spill the tea and point out the culprit. She grabbed my hand and marched right up to Jasmine. "Don't you ever call my sister darkie again, ya hear me?"

"I'll say whatever I want," Jasmine huffed. "It's a free country."

Diamond's eyes went lifeless, and I knew what that meant. I tried to step in, but she shooed me away like an obnoxious fly. "It may be a free country, but you call her that one more 'gain, you're gonna have to deal with her big sis. I'm warning you."

"I don't care if you're darkie's sister-brother-mama-or-daddy, I ain't—"

And before I knew it, a loud pop ricocheted through the playground, and Jasmine was on the ground crying her eyes out.

As all the kids crowded around us, I tried to pull Diamond away before a teacher came over. But she was as strong as a bull and impossible to move, hovering over Jasmine and yelling at the top of her lungs. "And I'm not gonna tell you again. Don't mess with the Martin girls. Especially this one," she said, holding my arm up. "You just mad you could never look as good as Deja does in this dress!"

The teacher on duty finally managed to slice through the crowd of students, yanked my sister by the arm, and dragged her to the principal's office. Before she reached the building, she looked back at me and blew a kiss. I blew one back and smiled.

She was right. Jasmine could never.

My bullying was short-lived after that day.

"*Definitely* not a fighter," she huffs now, picking at a loose thread from her duvet.

"Go easy on her," I respond, then smile. "Everyone can't be a darling little sister like me," I say, connecting my index and middle fingers into a heart shape.

Diamond's grin goes from angelic to sinister, and I'm not feeling it. She's found a way to deflect the conversation back to me. "So, I haven't been askin' 'cause I didn't want to annoy you, but . . . you goin' to the tattoo shop when you get back?"

I huff and sit next to her on her bed. "Di, I've been going back and forth about this, and I honestly don't know what to do. I mean, he was cute, but I'm not tryna look desperate. Maybe he doesn't even like Black women."

Diamond smacks her lips.

"I'm serious," I say. "You know how non-Black men try to get at us for one night to fulfill whatever sick fantasy they have? Maybe that's what it was?"

"Please," my sister replies. "Black women are poppin'."

I chuckle. "I never said we weren't, I'm saying maybe he liked flirting with me, but I'm not someone he'd bring home."

She shakes her head. "Nah, 'cause straight up? The way he was looking at you? The *free* tattoo you got? The *full-on* date the next day? I don't think it's a fetish. I think he's into you!"

I sigh, somewhat relieved. "Okay, okay!"

Diamond huffs. "Girl, I've yet to have a *boyfriend* do that for me."

I laugh some more, then whine. "Well, why didn't he ask for my number, then? And why didn't he DM me or *something*?" I roll my eyes. "I'm easy to find."

"'Cause boys are dumb," she says simply.

"You can say that again," I say, sulking.

I've done everything I thought possible to shake my thoughts of him, and it seemed to work while I wrapped up my senior year—I went out with my prom date a few times (but that faded quickly), hung out with my family and homegirls, prepared to *upend my life*—but the closer I got to my move-in date, the harder it became *not* to think about Raja. I even tried to look him up myself and couldn't find him. Figures that the guy I'm into is nowhere to be found online.

She grabs my hand. "Look, I don't know why he didn't press it, but maybe he panicked. He did say some heavy shit," she says. "But what I *do* know is you won't know if you don't try one more time. So, put on a push-up bra, go to the shop, and have him touch up your tattoo or something."

I scrunch up my face. "A push-up bra? What is this, *Bridgerton*?"

"You're right," she says. "Your legs are your showstoppers anyway."

"I'm not going back there, this already feels like too much," I say. "As Queen would say, 'This a hard row to hoe.'"

We both laugh until our sides hurt.

"Queen was a wild woman," my sister says, still cackling. I stare off for a second. I'm trying not to get my hopes up, but I pray I bump into him. Just once, God, and preferably when I'm looking the cutest I've ever been.

It's the wee hours of the morning, the sky stained with pinks and reds as it slowly lights up our family plot. We may not have much, but one thing we do have is this here land. If we have nowhere else to go, we always got this plot to come back to, Queen would say. I'm conjuring all her words of wisdom while standing on our land, near her tombstone, trying to hold close every lesson she's ever given me. I don't want to fail, but I also refuse to let shame stop me from coming back to North Carolina if things don't work out in Maryland. I always have this plot to come back to, which says a lot 'cause some people don't even have that, and Queen's parents bought these acres before they knew me to make sure of it.

Our plot of land, passed down from my great-grandparents, stands at about twenty-five acres. And for a small house packed with family, we use every bit of it to stretch our legs when things feel too cramped—me in the garden, my father managing the chickens, my siblings racing across the hills to our pond. This plot belonged not just to us, but to my father's brothers, who moved up north and never looked back. Except when Queen passed away and it was time to cash in. My dad was ready—he and Mama saved up and gave his siblings cash to buy them out. As far as my dad was concerned, he handled the upkeep, and they didn't. The land was the family plot, but also our own to do what we wanted.

I take one last stroll to the part of our property a little

closer to the woods, our grave site. It may seem strange to have a grave site behind our house, but for us, that's the way it's always been. Our families bought this lot and intended to stay here, forever.

Most people fear death, fear the unknown, and watching Queen waste away from cancer was the first time I saw what those fears are made of. My brave granny, for the first time, had moments of looking terrified. It hurt my heart to see her that way, but it also helped me understand the inevitable. *Fear will always consume us if we let it,* Queen told me one day, laid up in the back room, tired of worrying about what was preordained for her future, wanting to cheat death just a little longer. I took her to our enclosed front porch and carefully sat her on the swing. We rocked for hours like old times, my neck straining from holding itself up, acting like I was resting my head on her frail shoulder, afraid I might break her.

"Chile, don't be fakin' with me. I know what you doin' rubbing that crick in your neck," she said, and I laughed.

I gently brush away a little bit of hay and weeds from her tombstone and replace the roses laid across her site with sunflowers. He never tells us, but considering how freshly manicured the site is and the half-wilted roses sprawled across the base of the headstone, it's clear Poppa comes to visit often. "Fear always consumes us if we let it," I recite to the forest, to my grandma, wherever she is. It wasn't until she faced death that I felt I could understand her the most. It's when I could ask her the rawest questions and get the sincerest answers. It was another way I recognized how she and I were alike.

*"You really think there's a heaven?"* I asked her one day while she was lying in bed, too sick to have me carry her to the front-porch swing like normal.

*"I sure hope so, baby,"* she sighed, *"but I'd rather believe on this here earth and find out in the afterlife than know about it now. Sometimes, ignorance is bliss. Life is hard and believing got me through. Believing helps me to feel like I'll see your grandpa again. And if there is one, he's there waiting for me. All dressed up."*

*"Ready to take you out on a night on the town,"* I whispered in her ear.

*She smiled. "I tell you what, baby, yo granny gonna look as pretty as a peach too when he see me."* Her lips curled into a weak smile as I rubbed her cheek. *"All you can do is hope, Deja,"* she whispered softly.

*"Ma'am?"* I said.

*"All our people do is hope. I hope there's a heaven. I hope your grandpa is up there, and I hope to see you change the world."* She paused, catching her breath. Her voice was more faint these days. *"My granny bought our freedom. My ma bought this land. In a time when that was unheard of. But we hope. Look what it's done for the Martin family thus far."*

My eyes watered, feeling like this talk was one to prepare me for what I didn't want to imagine, a life without her in it. *"Queen . . ."*

*"Shh, hush up, chile, when your granny talkin' to you."*

*"Yes, ma'am,"* I said, sniffling.

*"I gotta say this now. I know you ain't gon be a healer like me. You wanna go to college and learn that medicine."*

*"Queen, come on. It's nothing wrong with learnin' science."*

*"I reckon you right,"* she said, then started coughing. I rubbed her

back for a minute, then finally got her propped up enough to fetch some water.

When I brought some back, she drank it, then settled back into her bed and didn't miss a beat. My grandma was determined. "But you my legacy, chile. I helped people around here, but look what I got to share with you." Tears were streaming from my eyes now. "It's like I birthed you myself, even defiant like me too. Just as stubborn about what you love. Never lose that, but protect it, okay?"

It felt like Queen was using the last bit of energy she had to tell me everything she could about life. "I know you gonna do well, Night. Whatever you do, you carry that legacy of the women in our family. You protect your family. And you help others. That's what healers do. There are many ways one can heal," she said. "You got to find yours, ya hear?"

I nodded and hugged her. I know now I had to be crushing her, but she didn't move an inch. Instead, when I pulled away, she wiped my tears, pointed to her cheek for me to kiss it, and told me to run off so she could nap.

She drifted off to sleep that way.

Over the next few days she was in and out of sleep, having brief spurts of consciousness with Dad, with Mom, and with my siblings. But eventually we had to accept what was truly happening. What we didn't want to admit.

And that was our last conversation before she drifted away for good.

I feel the tears falling as all these memories overtake me like they always do when I visit her burial site. I wipe them away, feeling Granny's presence, forcing me to say what I gotta say.

"I'm sorry I haven't visited sooner. I get so emotional when I come here," I say, looking around. "But I always feel so close to you when I come, which is weird since you're technically not here, right?" I wipe my nose with some tissues and smile. "But if anyone would find their way back to me, it's you, Queen. I can't believe it's about to be a year since you left us, but what an imprint you left on me. All I can think about is how to channel you when I go to Maryland. How to be strong and brave and . . . honest. That's what I want the most. To be honest with myself about if I'm overwhelmed, if I'm homesick, if I hate it there. I don't want my pride to force me to stay to prove a point." I sigh deeply, hearing one of Queen's teachings whisper to me in the wind.

*"You don't have to prove nothin' to nobody but yourself."*

Our rooster begins to crow, which means Poppa will be up ready to pack the car. He wants to get to Maryland and back in North Carolina before the day's end, and I know for a fact it's because he has no intention of being in a crowded city longer than he has to. He barely likes driving through downtown Fayetteville.

Somehow one last visit and one good cry has me a little more ready. It's time to be a big girl and do the thing I set out to do. "Love you, Queen," I whisper, as I head back to the house.

*"Love you more, Night,"* I hear her sing in my ear.

# CHAPTER NINE

## Raja

"Namaste," I say as I walk into the house, prayer hands above my head. My mom gives me a big kiss on the cheek, the number one sign she missed me.

"Make sure to take those bags with you when you leave," she says, motioning for me to take the Aldi bags filled with home goods next to the front door. "Chora, you already looking skinny, eh?"

I roll my eyes, without her seeing of course, because I'm not senseless. Yep, guilt. Sign number two. "I've only been gone for two weeks, Aama."

She sighs loudly and puts her hand on her chest. Here come the dramatics. "You're breaking our hearts, Raja. Why don't you come back home, huh? You'll never stay focused in a place by yourself."

I wouldn't say I'm the *best* at speaking Nepali, but I understand it well enough to keep up with Baba when he rambled on about stories from our homeland. But sometimes the way me and my parents don't see eye to eye makes me feel like we've never spoken the same language.

"Listen to your mother," my father says, coming out to the living room to greet me, and I silently chuckle. My dad is the only person I know that can wear sweats with a button-down shirt at home as loungewear. This man eats, sleeps, and breathes work, so I guess being the most comfortable in his work clothes suits him.

"Namaste," I say, bowing my head to his feet, then coming up to sniff the air, some of my favorite smells lingering. I drift to the kitchen to see what Aama's made, and to change the subject. Quickly. "What's for dinner?" I ask, lifting a pot lid and smelling the steam, knowing my mom will be thrilled to talk about tonight's menu.

"Dal, aloo ko achar, cauli, saag, roti, and khasi ko masu for you," she exclaims proudly.

Goat meat for me? She made the works. Which means there's an announcement of some sort. My parents will find a reason to call me and my sister over and relay the latest family gossip in a way that's so over the top, you'd think life as we know it is over. But these discussions also serve as reminders for what we shouldn't do: shame the family name.

"Rani bahini!" I yell as Rani rounds the corner to our family room. She rolls her eyes and gives me a hug.

"Stop saying that! I'm the big sister!" she huffs.

"But you're the *short* big sister," I reply as I squeeze her tighter, her face coming up to my chest.

"You're not even *that* tall," she says with a sneer. She's got the most adorable face, but people don't know how much of a jerk my sister can be at times.

She's gotten thick skin from being around my humor all these years.

"Rani, don't even go there," I say. "I'm practically a foot taller than you." I hear my mom chuckling in the background.

Rani playfully pushes me off her, and then her face goes serious. "What's going on?" she asks in a hushed tone, her eyes darting to the dining room, where my mom is setting up the table with her porcelain plates.

"I was hoping you knew," I whisper back. "How've they been?"

"I came home this morning, and Mom was in the room talking on the phone for hooours. The only reason she got off was because she told Padma didi she had to go and cook."

I lean my head against the wall and fake hit it repeatedly. "Family drama," I utter, and Rani laughs.

"Yep, I think tonight we're finding out who disappointed whom," Rani suggests.

"Well, at least Mom sweetened the pot by . . . sweetening the pot," I say, laughing.

My sister shakes her head. "Oh my God, you're getting worse with the dad jokes the older you get."

"Make sure you both take off for Dashain this year. We can celebrate now that we've done puja for Baba's passing. Rani, Padma didi will ship us an outfit."

My sister smiles and nods, slurping up the last of her dal. My mom knows how to force us to listen: she feeds us.

Baba's anniversary has passed, and in tradition, the first year is for mourning, which means we didn't attend any weddings or major Nepali events last year, and now that the mourning period is over, we can continue with holidays as normal, the first being Dashain.

"But don't take too many days off," my dad says, looking at me. "You don't want to get behind on your schoolwork."

"Don't worry," we both say in unison. Buwa has always been a stickler for grades and Mom reminds us of all the holidays, but Rani and I know that's what they both want the most, for us to stay tethered to their world. Our family's lineage. I didn't realize how much I'd miss holidays, weddings, and other community events until it wasn't an option. When I was younger it was annoying as hell, but now? I find myself carrying a bit more pride. Maybe that's what getting older means, appreciating the things you once loathed.

My mom gives a loud sigh. "So, we have news," she says, clearing her throat. My sister and I look at each other, mouths stuffed with food, trying not to laugh. *This* is the part of tradition I *do* mind. "In addition to Dashain, we have a wedding to go to in October. Lakshmi will be married."

My sister and I both utter celebratory responses while my father's brow creases, and my mother's worry lines form around her mouth.

"Okay, and that's great . . . right?" I ask.

"Yeah," my sister chimes in. "A wedding to go to after over a year of missing out. You both love that!" Then Rani looks at me, and before she can catch herself, she murmurs, "And it gets everyone off my back."

"What was that, Rani?" my mom asks, mortified at what she *might* have heard. Rani freezes. I look at her, surprised myself that she let that slip out her mouth.

It's so not like her, but Rani's loose lips are just an indicator of how over it she is. There's not enough respect in the world that can stop you from reacting to someone trying to enforce a marriage you're not ready for, particularly to a person you're not in love with.

"Another open bar!" I quickly howl, and put my hand up in the air for my sister to high-five me. She cracks up laughing, but since I'm under the drinking age, I get a stern look from Buwa.

Deflection successful.

"This is a serious matter, Raja," my dad interjects. "Her parents didn't choose him."

I feel my sister tense up, and my temper rises. I jokingly called Rani "little sister" in Nepali when I was younger and began to outgrow her in height, but moments like these are probably the true reason the bahini joke stuck. Our culture expects the children—and as we grow older, women in particular—to comply with whatever the head of the family says, and in situations like this, my sister feels so powerless. Instead of bending the rules like I do, Rani will always try to find a compromise.

To appease my parents but still stick up for herself, Rani found a compromise with them with her own career—the doctor title for my parents' happiness and the psychiatry degree for her own. She wants to eventually get into cultural therapy and be part of the change of undoing the stigma of therapy in communities like ours.

"Can I see a picture of him?" my sister asks.

"Yes, Chori, your cousin sent me pictures," my mom says, pulling it up on her phone.

My sister wipes her hands with a napkin and takes it out of our mom's hands.

I peer over Rani's shoulder. "That was a Facebook post, Aama. She didn't send it to you directly." My mom shrugs her shoulders like, *whatever*, and I turn back to the phone to find Rani's hands shaking. When I take a good look, I can understand why: this dude looks like us. Well not really, but enough.

"He's Nepali?" Rani asks before I can.

"Yes," my dad says, "but of a different caste."

*Goodness.*

"Dad, he's hella Nepali. More Nepali than me." I keep scrolling through his pictures, at all the weddings he posts and Mount Everest treks he's done. He even hosts a momo bar crawl in Queens once a year. Dang, I need to get to know this guy, I want in on the crawl. Lakshmi's been holding out, but for good reason it seems. "What does his last name matter?"

"It means everything," Aama says, her bangles waving in the air for emphasis. "We're from an upper caste."

"Okay," I say, wanting to push it further. "But she's in love with him, right? Doesn't love mean something, too?"

Most kids I know in the States have a childhood memory of a favorite song, or maybe a movie, or words of affirmation from a parent that elicit a positive emotion. Mine was a childhood full of critiques. My parents' affirmations were *finish school without distractions*. And so, in my own ways, I learned to rebel.

*Why play Xbox when you should be studying?* Guess who became a gamer?

*You don't need friends. You need to be in the books.* So I hopped around friends' houses in high school while my parents were working long hours.

*Don't spend your money on superfluous things.* I became a sneakerhead.

Girlfriend?

Dad: "We barely even have a word for that in Nepali." End of story.

Mom: Introduces me to every "lovely Nepali girl," rattling off our entire résumés before I can say hello.

All of it awkward.

While my mom is focused on finding me a wife at the ripe old age of eighteen, my dad wants to talk career plans and nothing else. When you come from dirt roads and sharing one pair of shoes between brothers, it kind of puts you in that state of mind. What did I do instead? Lean all the way into girls and used my charisma to learn the art of talking to them, one of the few things I felt I had control over in my life.

My dad has had enough. "It isn't about love; it's about bringing two families together. Making sure they are trustworthy and will look out for Lakshmi. . . ."

"It's about bringing two *elite* families together," I say, and it comes out a bit too smug. I know I'm in trouble the moment it escapes my lips.

"That's enough!" Buwa says, his voice steady but full of power. "We are having this discussion because Rani knows after graduate school, we will begin the process of finding her a husband. She should not be like Lakshmi and should be obedient to us. That's my guidance to you, Rani. You both must understand, this is the way it's always been. Your mother and I were set up that way."

Rani looks at me with real fear, and I know why. I've met her boyfriend, Sam. They met in her program, and he's one of the sweetest guys I've ever encountered. Perfect for my sister, but she's too afraid to bring him around until she's sure he's the one.

Because who wants to bring someone into the fold only to break up like a normal relationship and have your family judge you like it's the biggest mistake you've ever made, when all we want to do is date and find the right person for us?

"And look where that got you two," I mumble, stuffing my face with dal bhat to stop talking back and failing miserably.

"What did you say?" my mom responds, voice low and brows lowered with fury.

Rani kicks my foot under the table. Her signal for years when my anger boils up, ready to explode from everything I'd been holding in. It's her way of telling me if I react this way, it won't end well for me. And while she's usually right, today I feel like taking the risk. Not just for her, but for selfish reasons.

Deja.

I haven't stopped thinking about her. These ninety-one days, yes, I counted, have been the most difficult. Ninety-one days of waiting to see if the spark I felt months ago was authentic, or a fluke. I find myself counting down until the moment she's on campus, when I can bump into her and hopefully undo the damage I did after a perfect afternoon. I keep telling myself maybe it wasn't real, maybe I'll see her, and she'll do something to annoy me, and I'll find myself less inclined to pine for her in the way that I do, but deep down I know that's a lie. You can't meet a girl that special and then turn your feelings off, especially when said feelings came out of nowhere.

If I can't stand up for my cousin and my sister, if I can't stand up for my own blood, how the hell am I going to stand up for a girl who has no problems standing on her own? If I ever had to bring her around, I want her to know how committed I would be to her and how no one, and I mean no one, would disrespect her.

Look at me, already envisioning myself proclaiming my love for her to my family, and I don't even know if she's the real thing.

Look at me, ready to give it a try.

"Aama, Buwa. I love you both. Don't you want Lakshmi, or us, to be happy? This is a normal thing in the States. We shouldn't have to sacrifice our happiness in the name of tradition. We should *at least* be able to pick who we marry, even if we're being set up!"

"Enough of this, Raja, you're upsetting your father," Aama says, her lips tight.

I look at Rani, and her face begs me not to say another word, so I don't. I silently finish the rest of my food, and when Aama asks if I want to stick around and watch a movie, I sit there watching my dad stew in his anger.

Sitting next to me, Rani whispers, "Go, I'll be all right." She understands I need to leave before this blows up any more than it already has. "Excuse me." I get up from the table quickly and grab my things.

My mom isn't happy with my decision to abruptly leave,

especially with her missing me. "You're leaving already . . . ?"

"Let him go," my dad intercedes. "He has it in his head he's a grown-up now, so let him be one."

That one cut.

Mom's food was so good tonight, and I miss it. I miss home. I want to be able to pop in and out, be present with my parents without bearing every one of their burdens. But the more I'm away, the more I realize I can no longer tolerate being complicit in this, just because that's the way it's *been*. That reasoning isn't enough for me. So, no leftovers for me tonight. In less than a month I'll be a college student. If I want respect, I must fight for it. I quietly grab the Aldi bags and hear my parents bickering in the background as I close the front door.

I was hoping for seconds, but since I wasn't able to take home leftovers, off to Wendy's I go to get a ten-piece nugget meal.

The Salon's summer hours are pretty dead, so the next day I'm the focus of conversation.

Van starts it this time. "How many days left?" he asks, smirking as he's counting his books in the back of the parlor.

"Two," I mumble, darting my eyes his way.

Vicky squeals. "What's the plan?" she asks.

I shrug. "Run into her?"

"So unoriginal."

Ty comes walking in the door, hands typing away on his phone. He gives Vicky a look and they roll their eyes in unison.

What is this, the roast of Raja Sharma?

"Raja, you're basically chasing a celeb."

"No, I'm not!" I declare, laughing, then freak out. "Wait, is she considered that? Her personality is *so* not that."

Vicky laughs. "Don't listen to Ty, he is just trying to grow his follower count like Deja. He's low-key been obsessing over her."

"Ty, don't be a pest. It's one thing if I chase her away, it's another if you do it," I proclaim.

Ty laughs. "I won't. Scout's honor," he says, putting two fingers in the air. I've never seen a Boy Scout salute in my life, so I respond with *The Hunger Games* salute instead. The shop laughs.

"Well, Deja might not be a celebrity, but she's doing big things," Vicky says. "How you been, Raj? You seem extra preoccupied lately."

"I don't know." I shrug. "My cousin is getting married, and it's not arranged, so the Sharmas are throwing a shit-fit. Then my parents told my sister she'll need to be a good daughter and let them choose her mate. I ended up calling them out on it."

Vicky lifts an eyebrow; she's heard stories about Aama. "And they didn't slap you silly?"

"No!" I say with defiance. ". . . surprisingly." Vicky and Ty crack up. "My sister was there, and they were drilling her about all the things she is supposed to do, and I just couldn't stand them talking over her like that. No one even let her speak. About *her* life! Does she not get a choice?"

"Humph," Vicky notes. Vicky and I are about five years apart, and she's had to figure things out in a way I never could imagine. Lost both her parents to a fire when she was young and was in and out of foster care until she found foster parents in high school who ended up adopting her. They couldn't conceive so they poured love into other children, and Vicky told me she learned so much from their love story, and she's taught me a few things in the process. "Raja, I know you feel like shit, standing up for your sister. But misogyny needs to be called out. Period. And it needs to be called out from other men. It may be for selfish reasons, but you're doing something good."

I smile. There it is. I knew Vicky wasn't going to give me a pass without calling me out on my own bullshit.

The shop door chimes again, and everyone is surprised when they turn around but me. Big sister is here.

"Rani!" Van says, and he skips to the front for them to embrace. "How are you?" he asks her.

She shrugs. "Hangin' in there. I came by to kidnap my brother for his lunch break," she says, lifting up a bag of food that I can already smell from here. Last night's leftovers. She loves me. She whispers to Van as I approach them, "I brought you some, too. I would have brought more, but I didn't know it would be a full house."

"What's shakin', Rani bahini?" I say, giving her a hug, not wanting to let go.

She looks up at me. "Nothing, I just wanted to come see you. You free? I'm about to make a department store run if you want to come with."

As Rani says this, Vicky pulls out her purse, ready to go on her break.

"Errands it is," I say.

"Oh, I was runnin' there too! Can I roll?" Vicky asks, and we both nod. "I'm taking an early lunch with Raj and Rani!" Vicky calls out. Van gives us a thumbs-up, still deep in crunching numbers—he likes to do it the old-school way to keep his math skills sharp—and even more thrilled now that he has Aama's leftovers as lunch.

"But Raja's driving," Rani giggles, and I roll my eyes as I take the food into the break room and grab my car keys.

Rani and Vicky both grab separate shopping carts, and I stand there, confused. "Do you both need those big-ass buggies? What about a basket?"

Rani laughs. "You know you can never leave here with just one thing."

"It's a department store, Raja," Vicky adds. "You always have to be prepared."

I'm regretting this trip already, but I know the real reason Rani asked me to come is so we can talk, so I fight the urge to wait in the car. I walk with them down each aisle as Rani picks up some things to take back to our parents while she's home for the summer, and Vicky buys new beauty products. We also rehash last night's dinner.

"Did I make it harder on you?" I finally ask.

She shrugs. "The pressure is already on, Raja. I'm home for the summer, and Aama has already showed me suitors on Facebook that they want to set me up with." She sighs. "I should have found a way to stay on campus."

"Aww, Rani!" Vicky says, hugging her. "I can't imagine what that must feel like!"

I can imagine, because unfortunately I've witnessed it as a child. If it's only gotten worse, I feel deeply for Rani. "How about this: This summer you crash with me when it's too much, okay? I'll make you a key."

"Really?" she squeals. "Can Sam come over sometimes too?"

"Yeah, but there will be rules . . . ," I respond, my eyebrow raised. Rani pinches my shoulder and I jump.

"Okay, good, I'm going to buy some extra stuff for your place, then," she replies, dropping body wash into her cart. "I might come over this weekend if Dad's anger doesn't die down."

"How mad is mad?" I ask Rani.

"Preeeetty pissed," she responds, her voice full of discomfort.

"Yeah, that's what I figured," I say, cracking my knuckles while Vicky looks at mascara. She and Rani get distracted trying to decide whether she should get waterproof or not (who knew that was an option), and I stand there adrift.

"Why the sudden change of heart?" Vicky asks me, and I'm confused for a second until I realize she's bringing back up the conversation from the shop. Me facing my parents.

Rani's eyes twinkle. "Is this because of that girl you met? During spring break?"

I shrug. "Maybe a little. If I run into her, I can't say the same BS that I said last time." I puff out my chest. "I need to sound like a man who knows what he wants and how to fight for it."

Rani and Vicky both look at me, impressed. "Okay, so do you have what you need to plan a romantic evening at your apartment if she gives you another shot?" Vicky asks.

"She's right, Raj," Rani replies. "Your place is a straight-up bachelor pad." And suddenly Vicky is telling Rani all about the night Deja and I met, and they are chatting and moving at lightning speed, throwing things in the cart as they mosey down the aisles.

"It's called manifesting, Raj," Vicky says. "It's better to be prepared."

"I guess you're right," I say, browsing aimlessly while they stock up on decent-looking plates, cups, and other things for my new place.

Rani drops satin pillowcases in the buggy, and Vicky nods in approval.

"I have pillowcases at the house, Rani."

"But these are better for my hair and skin," Rani says.

"And I'm sure Deja wouldn't mind them if she slept over," Vicky says, and Rani smirks.

What is this secret girl code? I roll my eyes and let Rani and Vicky walk ahead of me as they go down the hair aisle.

Rani picks up some shampoo and conditioner and shows Vicky. "You like this brand?" she asks her.

Vicky nods, and Rani drops them in the cart. Then Vicky grabs a headscarf and a few other hair items that my sister definitely doesn't use.

I give Vicky a look. "Vicky, I know what you're doing," I say, taking the scarf out of the cart and placing it back on the shelf. "I don't even know if I'll get her number, let alone if she'll ever spend the night at my place."

"I don't know, Raja." Vicky slows down her cart. "I have a gut feeling. If you two make it, there's hope for all of us." The crazy part is Vicky is so sure, she's even got Rani eating this up too. "So what's the plan, then?" she asks as I push Rani's cart while she grabs more items.

"I messed up," I confess. "So I'd like our next interaction to be . . . natural. Buying her an overnight bag doesn't quite feel natural, though. . . ."

Vicky laughs. "And that means what? You're going to just wait for fate to intercede?"

"My patience won't allow that," I say. "I'll give it a week. Maybe two. Then I'm going to find her in the chem building and let it happen naturally from there."

Vicky and Rani smile. I knew they'd like my plan.

"If you don't wanna step to her, that's one thing, but don't you dare not step to this girl 'cause she intimidates you," Vicky says. "You understand? You step to her like you would any other girl, and if she bites, then she's feelin' you! If not, your ego will be bruised, but you'll bounce back. Point-blank, period. I just feel like these new men don't know how to approach women anymore!"

Rani slow-claps.

Blame it on the internet. "I know," I say boldly. "But if she rejects me, I'm not going up to any more women *all* semester." I shrug as Rani and Vicky groan together, knowing I mean it.

Before we head to the front to pay, Vicky takes us on one more detour. "You got washcloths at home?" she asks, pushing her cart through the home goods section.

I start laughing and roll my eyes. "Yes . . . but I need more." I pick out a set of deep yellow Turkish washcloths. Vicky gives me a look as I throw them in the cart.

"She got you down bad," Vicky says. "I approve."

And with that, all three of us head to the front of the store.

# CHAPTER TEN

## Deja

We pull up to Johnson-Whittle Hall, my father and I both awestruck by how beautiful the building is. The hall, which honors two African American students and the racial barriers they broke, is one of the more recently built dorms on campus, created as another way to preserve the culture and history of Black students at this school.

Once a campus ambassador pulls up with a rolling bin and introduces herself to me and Pops, she guides us to my dorm room. Chloe is on a family vacation and won't be here until Sunday night, which means a few nights to myself to organize and claim the side of the room with the best natural lighting. I settle on the bed closest to the window and set up my shelf on the sill while my dad builds another shelf that will live across the room in direct sunlight, and a smaller one for my low-light plants.

"It's cramped in here," my dad says, turning a screw into my IKEA Billy bookshelf.

"Please, Poppa. This is still bigger than Di's and my room," I respond, placing my aloe vera plant on the shelving above my desk.

"Really? Maybe it's the city that feels cramped, then." He shrugs and stands the bookshelf up. "There you go, Sunflower. Where you want me to put this?"

I motion for him to place it in the corner and watch him grunt as he moves it across the room.

"Your pops ain't as young as he used to be," he says, and I laugh. He stands and looks at his work as I begin to place my plants and books on it. "I feel quite old now."

I turn around and see my dad with tears in his eyes, which causes me to freeze, stunned.

My dad is a passionate man, but crying is not his natural response when he's sad. I've barely ever seen him cry, and I'm sure it's because Queen and his gramps taught him ain't no point in crying over spilled milk. He'd repeat that same mantra to my brothers, and it was the one I hated the most. He'd tell Jr. or me to brush things off or toughen up, and when I'd challenge him, he'd tell me it's to get us ready for a world that isn't kind to us and doesn't care about our emotions. I don't know if it was the best parenting tactic, but unfortunately, it was honest.

Right now, though, with his second daughter leaving home for good, he's letting his emotions show.

He comes up to me and hugs me tight. "You ain't moving back, are ya?"

My family is happy for me, but it took my poppa a while to accept it. My dad doesn't understand my sense of adventure. He doesn't get why I would leave everyone I know and love, when there are good schools like UMD "right here in our backyard," as he said it, and when an urban life won't let me foster a farm like I get to do down south. He knows how much I love farming, but he doesn't understand the other things I love too; not to mention he's afraid what the city might do to a young Southern girl like myself. So many stories of naïve kids coming back to the South because things didn't work out or they got caught up with a city boy. I had to remind my dad that's not everyone's story, and part of taking a risk is giving it a shot. Finally, after months of reluctance, my dad offered to drive me to Maryland. A peace offering.

I sigh. "I'll never say never, Poppa, but at least not right now. Ask me in four years."

My dad lets out a hearty laugh and squeezes me tighter. "Yeah, I don't even think you'll stay here for much longer after ya graduate. There's so much you wanna see. Always been that way." He pulls away and looks at me. "I see so much of Mama in you right now."

"Really?" I respond, astounded. Queen always stayed in North Carolina. I guess I never stopped to consider why.

He shakes his head. "I used to wonder what Queen would have been like if she had the same opportunities you got today. But I know now, 'cause I see it in you." Tears began streaming from my own eyes. "She put everything she had into you, Deja, even if you didn't have her for long. I reckon you have everything of her, right here." He points to my heart, and more tears shed. "Even if you call me and your mama and we don't know what to do to help ya. We'll try our best, but you know who taught you. She prepared you for this, ya hear?"

I wipe away my tears. "Yes, sir." And that's my poppa. Hits you with the juggernaut of feelings when you least expect it, but when you need it the most.

"The beds are longer," he says, lying down on Chloe's bare mattress. He stretches his legs out extra wide and puts his arms behind his head, and I lie down next to him, snapping a goofy selfie of us to send to the family chat, missing the hell out of him already.

I'm really trying to receive my dad's lesson on Queen prepping me, because two hours into unpacking, things go awry. It takes me a while to realize the AC in my room is barely working, and opening the window only lets more humidity in. Great. After I go down to the front desk and ask them how to put in a service request, I go back upstairs and wait for an update, feeling a little defeated when I realize I might not get one tonight. *It's fine,* I think to myself. *I know what it's like not having AC in the summer. We didn't install ACs in our own home until middle school. I can handle this.*

I accept my fate and try to finish packing before a sad attempt to take a cold shower before bed, itching to get out of this sweaty tank top and leggings. Things are looking up as I notice my side of the room is starting to feel like my own space as I pack up all the boxes and trash to throw down the chute. It's not until I toss my bag down that I become paralyzed in fear, realizing that the access card to my room accidentally went down the chute with the rest of my trash.

I rush back to my dorm room, praying the door is unlocked and after discovering it's not, I'm greeted downstairs by a note that says they've stepped away. Being on campus for summer classes is a far different experience than being here in the fall, I can already tell. Less help. *Okay, not a big deal,* I think. I decide to sit and wait, until the television downstairs lets me know thirty minutes have passed and I realize at this rate I might be waiting all night.

With nothing to do but be in my thoughts, I decide that if someone were to ask me right now how college is going, I'd say maybe I should reconsider this whole thing and go back home.

The only solution my mind keeps going back to is the one I'm dreading the most. My phone is in my dorm room so I can't reach out to Ramiro, Chloe, or anyone in the program, and the longer I wait, the closer it will be to closing time. I swallow my pride and take the walk I remember. Well, I guess my prayers were answered . . . sort of, because while this is not my best look, I just might be running into Raja tonight.

I muster up some courage and open the door to the tattoo parlor. And those beautiful, amber-colored eyes look up at me, pleased.

# CHAPTER ELEVEN

## Raja

*Thank you, Hanuman.*

I can't believe my luck; I feel like I'm in a Bollywood movie. My cousins would eat this up. I remember Deja telling me she would be back with Onward Bound's summer program two and a half months before the start of the fall semester, so I did my research and if my calculations are correct, today is her first night in Maryland, and she's here with me.

Probably not feeling her best, though, as I notice the sweat dripping from her forehead and her outfit covered in what looks to be dust. Still, her tank top and pants hug her figure, and I don't want to look like the guy who's being a creep when she might need help, so I quickly try to focus on Deja's face. That's when I see the look of dismay in her eyes.

I come from behind the front counter and meet her halfway. "Hey," I say. "You okay?"

She's shaking a little, distraught. "Hey, Raja, how are you?"

"Better now," I respond, my gaze intense.

She lowers her head and a smile tiptoes across her face. "So, I wasn't crazy," she almost whispers, but her eyes pierce into me, demanding an answer.

"No. I was just a coward," I admit. "When you walked in just now, I felt like my dad, thanking the gods like he does each morning," I pause. "Just happy to see you again."

She gives herself a quick look over. "Even with me looking a hot, sweaty mess?"

"I mean, you look hot in every sense of the word . . . so." I shrug and she chuckles. Two for two. "What's going on with you?"

She pours out the entire day, from the moment her dad dropped her off until her crushing realization that she dropped her key in the trash chute.

"Damn, you're having a rough go," I say, noticing Van making his way up to us.

"Tell me about it," Deja mumbles, pouting. "I don't know what else to do."

"Hey, Deja," Van says softly. "Bad day?"

"Very," she says, and waves. "Good to see you, though."

"You too, but no one is as happy to see you as my man Raja is." My cheeks redden. "Sorry, man," Van says, looking at me, not sorry at all. "We got a couple hours till closing and it's dead, so Raja is yours this evening."

Deja gives Van a look of deep appreciation. "But how does this work in a tattoo shop, does someone take his shift? Will Raja's pay be docked?"

I can't remember the last time a girl I've dated has looked out for my well-being in this way. The level of courtesy, even with her own inconvenience, is so admirable, my heart can barely stand it. "Deja, please," I say, chuckling at how concerned she'd suddenly become. "Don't worry about any of that. Just let me help you. I know you'd do the same for me if I was stranded in Fayetteville somewhere."

She smiles. "You know it."

I elbow Van and whisper, "Thanks, man, I'll make up the hours next week."

Van nods with pride, secretly pleased with my answer. I still got to show up and work.

Deja uses my phone to message Ramiro online before we pull off, letting him know she's safe and with me and to reach out when he's back at the dorm. She giggles and sighs, somewhat defeated.

"What's wrong?" I ask.

"I just checked his stories. He's at a gay bar. I don't think he'll get this message anytime soon." Deja puts the phone in my face, and I chuckle. Ramiro has a cowboy hat on and is dancing to Beyoncé.

"Oh, they are having a great time!" I say, "Do you want me to try and figure out what bar they're at? I can ask the shop, they're good at finding . . . things on social," I say, not wanting to reveal how quickly Ty and Vicky looked her up.

Deja laughs. "No, it's okay. Let's see if he responds first. Unless you have something else to do."

"You're the reason I got off work early, so you have me for the evening. . . ." I clear my throat to clean that up. "For however long you need me."

"Okay." Deja blushes, her shoulders tight and her hands between her thighs in the passenger seat. I love that I get to see her in her most comfortable clothes, because she looks so good. How did I get so lucky tonight?

"So. What do you wanna do?" I inquire.

Deja makes a big sigh. "Can we go back to your place?"

OMG.

Did Vicky and Rani really manifest this? Women are the greatest gift to mankind.

Deja looks at me with fear in her eyes, and I realize my reluctance is beginning to make her think I'm not feeling this arrangement.

"It's *A GREAT IDEA!*" Great, definitely let that slip out instead of keeping it to myself.

"Okay?" She giggles, eyeing me with curiosity.

What's up with my intrusive thoughts coming out lately? "I mean, I'm sure you want to freshen up or something."

She smiles and nods.

The mugginess in DC wraps around your skin like a sleeve, so I'm sure a nice shower would do. I have an idea. "I left something in the shop, I'll be right back."

She nods again. I jump out the car and run into the store. A white lie. I really need to talk to someone.

"You leave something?" Van asks.

I shake my head and tap my phone button to make a call. Van shrugs, knowing all too well I'm scheming something, and goes back to inventory.

*Pick up, pick up.* "Hello?"

"Rani bahini, help!" I say, pacing in the lobby, feeling Van's eyes on me. "Deja is locked out of her dorm and might stay over and Vicky isn't here and I need advice."

"Yaaaaaaaay!" Rani replies, giggling.

"I don't think Aama and Buwa would approve of your enthusiasm for a girl staying over," I say, chuckling. And blushing.

"Oh, please, I've seen you sneak girls out the house before."

*I really thought I was quiet. . . .*

"That sucks for her, but I know you love it! What can I help you with?"

"She wants to shower. She could borrow my clothes no problem, but . . . would it be weird for me to offer to buy her some . . . underwear?" Rani bursts out laughing. I don't need her being an asshole right now. "It's not funny, Rani. This has got to be the weirdest shit I've ever asked a girl. How do I make myself not sound like a creeper?"

Rani is losing her breath from laughing so hard. "Raja, you have to admit this is the funniest predicament ever. What size do you think she is? I'm a medium."

"She's short like you, but her butt . . . well, I don't look at yours, Rani . . . I hate everything about this conversation." I lower my head in defeat and hear Van suppressing a laugh in the corner.

Rani's chuckles finally simmer. "I cannot remember the last time I laughed this hard. The reason I asked is I bought brand-new underwear that I left at your apartment, so she can have a pair. So you won't even have to pay for her panties, Raj."

"Ew to all of this," I say. "And you did save my ass, or I guess Deja's. . . ." We laugh again. "So, thank you. I owe you."

"I know," she responds, and I'm assuming she's giving me the smirk we both inherited from our mom. "Also, use one of the satin pillowcases in the bag for her. Now don't make her wait, byyye!" And with that sweet yet firm goodbye, I'm ready for my night with Deja.

# CHAPTER TWELVE

## Deja

Raja opens the door to his place and I gotta say, I'm impressed. He's got a studio apartment with a decent-sized living area with a couch I recognize from the IKEA catalogs, a wall-mounted TV, and a matching set of speakers. He even has his bedroom area partitioned off with a natural, rattan weave divider. Not him being a man with refined taste.

"Mind if I look around?" I ask.

"Yes, but one rule. Shoes come off at the door. You're in an Asian home."

I give him a look, unbothered. "Oh, don't worry, I had a lot of practice with that growing up myself," I say, slipping off my Crocs and rubbing my feet on his plush area rug as I take in more of Raja's enclave.

He's such a chill person, but you see his personality come alive in here, where he's able to creatively express himself. There's lighting above his kitchen cabinets, and his floor lamp is glowing a shade of deep purple. He's got some wrapped canvas paintings hung up on his walls like in an art gallery. Subtle drawings of flowers adorn his walls, and I take a closer look at some of the smaller pictures that look similar to what I saw in his portfolio.

"This place is niiiice, Raja."

He shrugs. "It's a studio, so it's small...."

"But it's *yours*. I've never had my own room, let alone my own place. And it has a balcony. You know how many plants you could grow out there?"

Circling the rest of his studio, I notice his desk is actually a drawing table, with sketches scattered on top. I pick up a drawing of a sunflower. "I love this one too," I say, comparing it to the one on my wrist. The details are even more pronounced.

"I'm trying to get better at it," he says, hands in pocket. "I've never really drawn them before, but after I met you I got a little obsessed with perfecting them. Now I wish I could redo your tattoo."

I swat his comment away. "Please, it's perfect. All your pieces are unique."

"I just want to make sure it looks half as good as the person wearing it," Raja says, with the sweetest closed-mouth smile.

This boy really knows how to make someone blush when he wants to. I walk over to his window, attempting to mask my flushed face. "It's also nice having an apartment on the top floor."

"Yeah, feels like I got a penthouse," Raja replies. My eyes are drawn to a wall filled with more drawings, near the corner by his bed, tucked away just enough by the partition that if you weren't looking hard enough you might miss it.

He's got all types of Hindu deities and figures, landscapes of what looks to be Mount Everest, sketches of monuments around DC, including the WWII Memorial, and wildflower drawings with such intimate detail, I feel like I'm in a field with them. Some are drawings, and a few were even created with watercolor. He comes up behind me as I continue to study his work. "You paint?"

"It's a new thing I've been doing since I moved here," he says. "Now that I don't have to hide it."

"Another hobby?" He nods. I turn around and look him dead in his eye. "Raja, these are . . . you're talented, man. This is just as much an artist's studio as it is your apartment."

He gives me the cutest nervous laugh and his head tilts to the side. "Thank you."

I can't help but wonder who else has seen this. "Has your family been over?" I watch him tense up and I'm afraid I already pushed a button, but slowly his stiffness dissipates.

"No, my parents haven't been over yet," he responds, looking down at his feet. "As a kid I always drew things, but at a certain point anything that wasn't getting my C grades up was a distraction. So I mostly drew in my room when my parents watched their shows. Most of these pictures," he says, pointing, "were from those sketchbooks. My sister knows; she even helped me put some of my art up. Rani always had me draw things for her when we were kids."

I can't let what he first mentioned go by. "Have they not come over on purpose?"

He nods, his shoulders dropping ever so slightly, but I notice it. He's carrying something. "They don't want me to have my own place, so coming over . . ."

I sigh. "I understand a father's pride all too well." He nods again, relief in his face for my understanding. As loving as my dad is, I've seen his stubborn side come out when he feels the slightest bit disrespected. And going away to school went against what he wanted. It was a hard conversation to have, helping him understand that going to UMD isn't disrespectful, it's living my life.

He hesitates, but then lets the words come out. "I'm sorry about not asking for your number, Deja." So that was what he'd been building up the courage to say this whole time. I could sense his anxious energy.

"Why didn't you?" I ask.

I've been waiting for this conversation. We stare each other down for a second, and I hope he just gives it to me real. I don't want this guy to play games.

"I was scared," Raja admits. I relax a little. "You were so . . . easy. Like easy to talk to!" he says, his eyes going big. I crack up and he calms down again. "And engage with. I felt like I could be myself around you." He pauses. Hands still in his pocket. "Then you hit me with some real-ass questions and . . . I don't know. I wasn't ready to answer them, I guess. I wasn't ready to be honest with myself."

Wow, I'm at a loss for words. "You've been thinking about this since we last saw each other, huh?"

"Every day! I needed to know what to tell you. I guess after going through all my normal excuses, I realized none of them would be acceptable to you . . . except the truth." He shrugs.

"Which is fair to ask for. I just felt dumb admitting it to myself because I fumbled. Hard."

"Well," I smile, "Queen used to always say, the truth will set you free. I brushed it off when she said it, but it's true. It's tougher to be honest with yourself than anyone else. You can't hide from yourself."

"Your grandma say that last part, too?" he asks.

"Don't Columbus it," I respond, and Raja laughs hard. "I sorta did, though. It's a lyric to an old-school song Queen liked. She always sang that part with extra soul."

"Well, in the spirit of . . . souls, and confessions, I have another one." He sighs loudly, then continues. "I'm only an apprentice at the shop. Van and everyone went along with it because they could tell I was . . . into you."

"I want a refund!" I demand. "Oh, wait—" We both crack up.

"Sorry to break it to you, but that's not happening," Raja responds.

Since he's being so sincere, I guess it's my turn to share. "That's funny you say that, 'cause my sister was in there rooting for us too. Look at this." I pull up the video of me and Raja sitting at his chair—or whoever's chair it is—playing tag with our eyes until we both finally lock them on each other, and grin. Raja smiles while watching the video, until he realizes I'm looking at him and attempts to act normal again.

"This is cute" is all he says, playing it cool.

Too cool.

"Oh, that's all? You don't have another confession?" I ask.

"Actually, I do," he says, and I lift an eyebrow. "Everyone at the shop already showed me this. I kinda saw your vlog."

My eyebrows furrow and I give him a small shove.

"Dang, you *did* grow up with a house full of brothers!" he says, regaining the little balance he lost. "You're strong."

"So you knew where to find me, but you never messaged me?!" I ask, feeling testy.

"It's Van's fault!" Raja blurts out, and I give him a look. "Well, it was both of us. We had the same idea. I didn't want to look shallow, like I only wanted to date you because you were an influencer or whatever." I humph, crossing my arms. Without saying another word, Raja walks into his bathroom. "I'm assuming customer service was slow with it being your senior year and all, because this took forever to ship," he says, cheesing with my custom mask jar in his hand.

I'm what you might call an itty-bitty business owner, and I usually sell my skin care on a third-party marketplace, thankful for the feature to temporarily close your shop when life becomes too much. But juggling senior year responsibilities while taking mass amounts of orders to save up for college stretched me way too thin.

"Whaaat?!" I smile, not believing my eyes. "You bought some of my stuff?"

"Yeah, I bought a few things. It smells nice, too. I told myself I'd use it when I moved in, but I haven't had a chance to yet."

I stand proud. "Well, I guess that means I have to do a tutorial."

After advising Raja on how to wash his face and getting on him for using his body wash as a face cleanser, I slather the mask on me first to show him how it's done, then him next. I have him sit on his couch, and as I continue to rub the mask across his chin full of stubble and brush his cheeks, I see why Raja hasn't given much thought to the type of soap he uses. His skin is flawless, with barely a blemish or mark. The bit of stubble on his face makes him look more mature, but he's got skin as velvety as a flower petal. It's rather annoying if I'm being honest.

And for all the reservations I had about Raja, I love that he's making this situation easier for me, 'cause God knows my sister and I have watched enough investigation shows to know a girl going to a guy's house when she's only met him once? That could be a setup. "When I first got here, I thought, you know what? This kinda feels like the beginning of a horror movie."

"I went from being a nice guy to a serial killer, huh?" Raja asks as he sinks into his couch, head leaning on the sofa's back. "Normally I would be offended, but I am *veeery* relaxed so I can't care less about my name being dragged through the mud right now. Five-star review already."

I smile. "That's the eucalyptus."

"I like it," he responds, eyes still closed. "But you didn't answer my question."

"I wouldn't take you for a serial killer, more like a super-villain," I reply.

He laughs and his mask begins to come undone.

"Don't laugh, you're breaking the mask," I say, laughing myself.

"You need to take your own advice. Here." He pulls his phone up to show my face, and after debating for thirty seconds about whose appearance looks the worst, we take a selfie to compare.

"Not all superheroes wear a cape, all villains wear a grin."

"You're an A$AP fan?" I ask.

"You knew that way too fast," Raja responds.

"I have a house full of brothers and paper-thin walls," I say.

"More like a Rihanna fan," he replies, fiddling with his fingers. Of course, a childhood crush. "I just think Riri deserves better."

"Does any of this have to do with her brown billionaire ex-boyfriend?" I inquire.

"Hey, representation matters," Raja says, and I'm cracking up. "I was just waiting until I turned twenty-one to approach her. So, why a supervillain?"

"You just seem like the type. You're smart, you come across as way too likable and trustworthy, and you're clever. But I woulda still pegged you for a serial killer, since you're not really online like that."

"As a supervillain I can confirm we also don't like social media. We are the antiheroes of the world. Misunderstood," he says, eyes still closed and hands folded in his lap.

I giggle. "Yes! And stay thinking what you're doing is for the greater good!"

Raja opens his eyes. "I don't know, Deja, your humor is darker than mine tonight. You thought I was a serial killer and then . . . came over."

"Absolutely not!" I retort. "I said when I first came in it gave scary movie vibes, but I trusted my instincts and decided it was safe. You gave it a name."

Raja looks at me, with sincerity. "You are impossible, Deja Martin."

Three hours later Ramiro still hasn't messaged Raja; meanwhile, Raja and I have eaten the pizza we ordered and passionately ranked our favorite superhero shows and movies, deciding that *Power Rangers* is an underrated classic, regardless of how bad the CGI aged. Like me, Raja didn't grow up on cable, so Roku introduced us to the group of misfit teens fighting to save our planet. Another piece of my heart budding for him.

It's my first night in a new city and I've never been alone before, and with my dad leaving just as quickly as he got here, it's nice being around someone who makes me feel a little less alone my first night. "Raja," I say, "I'll sleep here, but how about I sleep on the couch, and you sleep on the bed?"

He shakes his head. "I won't allow it. Plus I sleep on my couch more than the bed. I haven't even slept on those sheets."

I laugh, looking over at his steel-gray duvet with taupe-colored sheets. They also look soft. "So you made your bed and it's been like that the whole time you've been here?"

"Guilty," he replies, chuckling. "Three whole weeks. My version of adulting."

I shake my head. "Okay," I relent, both of us sitting next to each other on his bright red couch.

He looks at me. "God, you must be exhaaausted."

I nod, not even trying to fight it anymore. I did drive to a new state, unpack half my dorm room, and walk to a tattoo shop in Crocs and Maryland's August heat. "I didn't want to seem like a rude guest 'cause I'm having so much fun. But right now, I don't even have the energy to move. And I still feel funky. I barely wanted to sit on your couch."

"You don't smell as bad as you think you do," Raja says, and we both giggle. "But you should shower if you want." Raja gets up and grabs some shorts and a T-shirt for me. He also hands me a bag wrapped up tight.

I sense Raja's unease until I open the plastic bag and burst out laughing. "Tell your sister she is the absolute best. You can tell she's the oldest," I say, chuckling, trying to ease Raja's discomfort.

"You two have the same sense of humor I see," he says, still bothered. "You know where the towels are."

I come out the room, and immediately my heart jumps. Raja is fluffing up a pillow that's now covered with a satin pillowcase. "Raja, satin pillowcases? Is this part of your lure?"

"This doesn't help my serial killer case, does it?" he asks, his arms hanging in defeat. I cross my arms and shake my head, dying to hear his excuse this time. "Rani bought this for when she comes over and told me today to put them on for you. So, I'm doing what I'm told."

"She's a smart woman," I say.

"She is," he replies. "Always has been my voice of reason."

I'm noticing that he's—very slyly, I might add—looking me up and down. He hesitates, then shakes his head. "I was trying to keep my mouth shut, but how do you look better in my own clothes than I do?"

"Thank you," I say, playing with a curl before stopping myself. It's usually what I do to calm my worries, but right now it just looks like I'm being flirtatious, when I'm in fact a nervous wreck. I went from not talking to Raja for months to sleeping in his bed on the first day I live here, and if he uses the same fabric softener he does for his clothes, I will simply melt into his sheets.

There's another part of me that wants to melt in his arms, but I brush that feeling aside.

"Umm," Raja says, cracking his knuckles. "You, um . . . want me to put on a movie or something? Help us fall asleep?" It's nice to know he's just as freaked out as I am about this.

"Sure," I half whisper. He queues up *Power Rangers* and I grin as I snuggle under his duvet.

"You get this comforter from IKEA too?" I ask after secretly sniffing his sheets to confirm he did in fact use the same fabric softener.

"The duvet insert, yeah. The duvet cover? From T.J. Maxx. My mom goes there all the time to find Buddha statues and other knickknacks. I go with her to test out towels and sheets."

I giggle. "I never would have expected T.J. Maxx for Buddha statues."

"She likes to look at the price tags to see what she's saved."

"She knows those prices are inflated, right?" I ask him.

He pulls the cover over his chest as he lies down on the couch. Finally, he looks at me. "Yeah, but I don't want to crush her spirits, it's our bonding time. Plus, every time I go with her, I sneak something for my apartment."

We both laugh. "You are so ridiculous, Raja . . . wait a minute. I'm sleeping in your bed, and I don't even know your last name!"

"Sharma," he says, yawning. "Raja Sharma."

*Deja Sharma does have a nice ring to it,* I consider. *Go to bed, girl,* I tell myself as I drift off to sleep. I'm impossible even to myself.

# CHAPTER THIRTEEN

## Raja

If it weren't for Deja half snoring in my bed, I would have awoken in the morning thinking I dreamt the whole thing. Instead, I look over and can't help but grin—she sounds adorable. Deja's lips are partially pursed, and she's balled up under the covers like a kitten, which makes me think she's not waking up anytime soon.

Good, it gives me time to figure out food, since I have yet to buy groceries. It's pretty pathetic, really. I scope the Aldi bags my mom packed me a few nights back. Aama's care package is filled with clementines that thankfully haven't gone bad, a set of teacups, and a jar of homemade masala. Bless her for being in a giving spirit. She also packed a Costco-sized box of black tea bags, and I decide black tea is a good substitute for the coffee I don't have, and both will hold us over before I grab breakfast for Deja and drop her off.

I boil the water and steep the tea, and as the steam rises from my mom's ceramic cups, Deja slowly begins rising from my bed like the Sleeping Beauty she is, stretching out her arms as she yawns awake.

"Morning," she says, rubbing her mane as she rises for the day.

"Good morning," I say back, and I love seeing her when she wakes up. "How did you sleep?"

"I was worried the city noise would keep me up, but I guess last night I was too tired to notice. You know, I can't remember the last time I slept in a bed that wasn't a twin. This was glorious." She rips the covers off her and drapes her legs over the bed.

*You look nice when you first wake up,* I think. But this time, I also allow myself to say it out loud.

She smiles even brighter. "Thank you," she says, making up my bed. If she wasn't here, it would have stayed like that for three more weeks. "Did Rani happen to convince you to get another toothbrush?"

"I put one on the counter in the bathroom."

"Thanks," she says, and is in and out by the time I stir honey and lemon in her tea. I also set some of the clementines on the counter for her.

"Caffeine in the morning your thing?" I ask her, holding up a cup.

She shakes her head. "I'm not a big tea drinker. Queen had me mixing things when I was younger and . . ."

"What did your grandma do?" I ask.

"She was, uh . . . a healer," she says, scrunching her lips together rather shyly. "I know folks think it's, like, a weird thing, especially up north, but I learned a lot from her, and um . . . it inspired me to do my own thing, so I did skin care. But if I could do that and save some lives too by adding sunscreen into my products, then I'll be half the badass my Queenie was." I look at her, stunned. And fucking intrigued. Who is this girl? "You okay, Raja?"

"You ever heard of Ayurvedic medicine?"

"Vaguely. It's like a tradition of herbal medicine that started in India, right?" she inquires.

"Yeah, Nepal is big on it too. It's supposed to be a type of therapy that incorporates herbs, meditation, a special diet, and all that. My baba, he used to practice it on the people in our village."

Deja gasps, her eyes the widest I've ever seen them, and puts her hand to her heart like she can't take this news. "He was a healer too?"

I smile and nod. Slowly. "Yeah. He was." We both look at each other in shock for a moment. "It's amazing you're still so connected to it. I've heard about it all my life and brushed it off because my mom never trusted Western medicine. I've tried for years to explain that they should both work congruently."

"I agree," she says. "I think for our families, though, they didn't have many options, so of course they depended on this heavily and questioned everything else. Queen wanted to be a medical doctor, but no one was gonna give her that opportunity. And Black folks in the South at that time were barely getting proper medical care. I mean, Black folks *still* don't get proper medical care in this country." I nod in agreement. "I'm trying to merge both, at least for skin care. The things herbs can't do, science can."

I nod. "I've asked my mom more about Baba's past with Ayurvedic medicine, but it's not something she talks about."

"If he was anything like Queen, he was probably trying to practice his own version of doctor-patient confidentiality," Deja says. "It was something she asked me to practice, and she barely let me in the room for intense or super emotional cases. I'm thankful she shielded me from that stuff, though."

"You're probably right," I say. "Also, I think it's a thing in my family in general. They just don't share certain things about life in Nepal. I think it's a way for them not to relive painful parts of the past, but knowing more about the past would be so helpful for me. Especially when I go back to visit."

Deja sighs. "I understand in some ways. Even with me, I could never go back to the areas of Africa I'm from and be accepted with open arms. So, home for me is here. And I just happen to be an earthy girly, but it's in my culture and yours. I like taking care of the little world around me. Even if I don't know exactly where I come from on this big planet, I can appreciate where I am now."

"You're clearly a morning person 'cause . . . I just got so much from you, and you never told me why you don't drink tea."

We both burst out laughing.

"I just got excited!" she exclaims, her hands expressive, still in disbelief. "Okay, so, because she was a healer, she would mix teas for people when they had a stomach bug or an infection, and she had me steep it for a client once and I still tried it, even though I knew better; had my stomach in knots for hooours. I've been scarred ever since. My ten-year-old behind thought I was about to die, and Queen is telling me to calm down."

I'm still laughing, envisioning this older woman who reminds me so much of Deja, it's like she's been reincarnated through her. "She sounds like so much fun. I wish I got to meet her. Old people love me."

Deja snickers. "Whatever you're brewing smells good. I'm willing to try it," she says.

I pass her the cup and hold my breath. I never imagined life with a girl who doesn't drink tea until this very moment. Could this work? I mean of course it could work, she's everything. But I would need to find a way to convert her. . . .

"Mmhmm, Raja, this is good!" Deja blurts out, blowing on the tea to cool it down enough, eager to drink more. I exhale. She continues sipping and walks around some, like an old woman herself. "Lipton tea. My mom drank these all the time, but who woulda thought adding a little honey and citrus could make it taste like this."

I blush. "Yeah, I've got some practice, but Lipton is a sleeper. I use it to make chia, too."

"Is that like chai?" Deja inquires, leaning on the counter in the kitchen, still sipping out of her mug.

"Yeah, it's the Nepali word for chai, or tea." I pull the masala jar out of the cabinet, excited to see Deja's reaction. "Smell this."

Deja takes one big sniff, and I swear it looks like she's smelling the freshest bouquet of wildflowers.

"So you steep this with Lipton and milk?" she asks, still sniffing the small jar. I nod and she raises her hand. "Okay, sign me up when you make this, this might turn me into a real believer."

"I absolutely will," I say, feeling so touched she's this interested; it's nice to date someone open to trying new things and experiences. She's peeling a clementine and smiling so bright, I almost forget she's got to leave soon. She's mesmerizing. "Oh, um . . . Ramiro finally messaged me, and I told him you're safe. He said he's around all day, and I'm sure your RA is easier to find. So, I can take you back. I can also get you food if you're . . ."

"You've done more than enough, Raja. Thank you for last night, and everything."

I nod. "Wasn't a problem at all."

I'd do it again and again.

# CHAPTER FOURTEEN

## Deja

I groan as I wake up from a nap, my body stiff from loading and unloading the car and moving boxes and trash around the day before. My mind and heart, however, are feeling two completely different yet extreme sensations.

I sigh. I'll figure out Raja . . . later. I shake him from my thoughts. First, I gotta make a plan for the rest of my summer.

Okay, one. Print out a calendar of my class and internship schedule, which begins next week. Two. Begin posting content on my social accounts to show my school and product launch progress.

As I learn about Maryland's soil in my fundamentals of soil science class, I'm hoping I'll be able to quickly learn what plants work best and how to modify my skin care products. My customers know I'm in college, in a new state, so they trust what I'm able to do and have been supportive and patient with me. Learning to run a business is rewarding, but it's also exhausting. Which is why until I find the best ingredients regionally and try them, a summer pause seems wise. I wanna live a little, too.

Chloe doesn't get here until tomorrow evening, and after letting Ramiro know I'm safe and that I'll check in on him later and telling the Martin group chat that I passed out early so they'd stop blowing up my phone, I take the longest hot shower of my life. I huff, thinking about how annoyed I am for dreaming about him when I just saw him. *It was all a setup to get me over,* I think to myself. Never mind that I was the one who went to the shop asking for help, or suggesting that we could go straight to his house.

I just need to point a finger at something to help me figure out why I'm feeling these feels. Last night was even more perfect than our first date, and Raja is looking finer than the last time I saw him, but now that I'm here and seeing him and feeling how intense the attraction is, I'm worried.

I barely know the guy, and yet I'm so drawn to him.

What if I really fall for him and meet his family and . . . they hate me? Then what?

It's more about subjecting myself to a family who wouldn't treat me the way I should be treated—the way my family treats me, the way Raja treats me. It's why for so much of my little-girl childhood, I thought I should only date a Black guy because I didn't want to date a man who would compare me to European beauty standards.

It's a different type of complexity when it's another person of color, and yet seeing beauty ads for bleaching cream in Asian and African communities has shown me all I need to know.

Like I learned in my world history class, the stains of colonialism are everywhere.

Just because I would walk into any family setting with confidence, doesn't mean I want to be met with resistance. Do I want to be a poster child for my race or get beat down by their judgment of me? Do I want to be the one to have to educate them on the prejudices they may have been taught about my people? If he's being treated this way, imagine how they'll treat someone who is a walking representation of all the ways in which their son is rebelling—a Black American woman who fails their brown paper bag test?

Just thinking about all this gives me a headache, and we barely exchanged numbers a few hours ago.

Still, when I think of just me and him, all those other thoughts drift away. My heart knows what it wants.

Frustrated that this has already taken over so much of my thoughts, I decide I've done enough moping around about it, and that it's time to get myself together for the day. Three. Eyebrows, a top priority. I put on the adorable wildflower-skinned wireless headphones Jr. got me as a going-away gift and head toward a place nearby with good reviews to start my self-care.

"Your eyebrows look so good!" Ramiro tells me when he's finally back from the dead. We're walking back from the smoothie shop so that he can get some fresh air and fill me in on the night's festivities.

"I'm more of a fresh-faced, short-hair chick. So I can't play about my eyebrows."

Miro rubs his finger over his brow. "I might be going to them next. You get a referral discount?"

"No, but I'll definitely be asking," I respond, and we snicker as we stride across the campus, taking in the late afternoon breeze.

"Thank you for forgiving me. Last night was a *night*!" he says.

"It's okay, I wouldn't have had the night I had." I blush thinking about it. "And thank you for this," I say, holding up the smoothie Ramiro treated me to, even though I told him a million times last night wasn't his fault.

"What happened last night?!" Ramiro and I end up strolling until we get to Frederick Douglass Square, sitting on a bench as I give him the rundown on everything.

"I really like him? But I don't know him. This feels so weird."

Ramiro nods his head. "I get it. That was my high school boyfriend: as soon as I saw him, I knew." Miro's eyes are looking dreamy just saying it.

"What happened to you two?" I ask.

He smacks his lips. "He cheated on me two months later. I hate him."

I howl. "Miro, this is not helping."

"I'm sorry, you should know by now my love life is flighty like me. But you seem like you're a relationship girly so I love this for you!"

"Yeah," I say, looking across our campus yard. "Except I've never really been so invested in a guy like this. Especially with all the stuff with his family."

Ramiro sinks into the bench. "What's going on?" he asks, his face tense with concern.

I think of what my campus guide mentioned about the bronze statue in front of us. The Frederick Douglass memorial was built to show how Douglass was a role model for social justice.

DC is such an interesting place. The ancient architecture and history here are surreal considering how this country was made, with historic buildings like the Capitol and the White House all built by enslaved folks, and now we have these monuments that honor the very people who oppressed us. The same feelings crop up inside me when I think about the South, when only recently half a dozen Confederate statues have been removed from the state I lived in, with many more still standing.

So it's nice to also sit here and witness the honoring of someone like Frederick Douglass, born right in this state, or see the Martin Luther King Jr. Memorial. It reminds me of what's possible.

"Like, how much will his family not like me, you know? Every race has biases, but when it comes to interracial dating, it seems like Black girls always get it the worst," I say. Miro nods. "Will it be because I'm Black, and darker skinned? I feel like it's no different from the colorism I dealt with growing up, and to think I'd have to deal with that with his family is enough to make me hesitate. I don't want to live that nightmare again, especially because I don't have any issues whatsoever about how I look." I do a little shoulder shimmy. "I know I'm easy on the eye."

"Mmhmm, talk that shit," Ramiro says, slurping on his smoothie in one hand and snapping his finger in the other. He lowers his voice. "It's in Dominican culture too, Deja. It's fucked up. But I also won't let anyone in my family stop me from something real, and if this is real, Deja? Maybe just go with the flow. You know the color coalition got yo back if we need to roll up on anyone!" I fall out.

I spend the rest of the night with Ramiro and some of his friends, who all conclude I'm at the start of my own love story. Whether or not I believe them, I'm just happy to have found hilarious and wonderful human beings my first few days on campus. I feel like Queen is watching over me, because the last twenty-four hours have been some of the best of my life.

# CHAPTER FIFTEEN

## Raja

I open my door and almost trip over the sandals and sneakers scattered in my entryway, all while a room full of girls pine for SRK on my television screen. Lakshmi's engagement has everyone in my family on edge, and my cousins are feeling the pressure, getting chastised by their parents to remind them of what they shouldn't do, how they shouldn't be like Lakshmi. Poor Lakshmi. She's hearing it from all sides.

So Rani asked if she could plan a hideout slumber party at my apartment, and they're four hours and two bottles of wine in when I come back from working a late shift. I shake my head when I walk in the door.

"You all should be ashamed!" I say, pointing my finger at them.

"Oh, shut up, Raja uncle," Bina says, mocking me. "We all needed a glass to take the edge off today."

I laugh. "I don't know what kind of math you're doing, but I see two bottles on that table."

"There are seven of us here," Rani says. "You're lucky we managed to save you one glass."

"Damn right. You're my supplier," I tell Rani, and she throws a pillow at me, laughing.

"Stop saying that! It's not true," Rani announces to the room, like anyone in here takes me seriously.

They all laugh. "No one ever believes him," Naima chimes.

See? "So, what happened?" I ask. Sipping wine in a plastic cup after a hard day of work, asking about the latest family gossip—definitely feel like Buwa right now. Only thing I'm missing is a reclining massage chair.

"Someone overheard Gandira didi make a nasty comment about Akhil's family being Christian Nepali."

Deja's family is Christian. Can add that to my list of why I'm terrified of having her meet my family. At this point, I'm using Lakshmi's wedding to better understand what I can expect. Boy, am I in for a treat.

I down the rest of my wine, and on an empty stomach at that, so I don't mince words. "Lakshmi, did you worry your parents would disown you?" I ask, maybe too bluntly, but I hope she can sense my own desperation. I want so badly to stop by the house and take Aama on a T.J. Maxx run, or even crack jokes with Buwa and his brothers. But my parents and I haven't really talked since the dinner, and I worry our relationship dynamic won't be the same the more I stand up for myself.

She sighs. "There is that fear in the back of my mind, you know? Like, yes, they want everything, but also, they don't want much. Just to keep things as close to where they come from as possible. But because I fall in love on my own and I want to marry this guy whose family happens to live a few villages over, it's suddenly an issue." She shakes her head, her long tresses waving. "But as strange as it sounds, somehow, I still get their point of view. Doesn't matter, though," she says, sipping more wine before she continues. "I love him. We'll marry, and if they disown me, so be it. I've built up the courage for this moment." Her voice goes from being loving to ice cold, and I hate this for her. I hate this for all of us. She should be able to celebrate one of the happiest occasions of her life.

But while I'm feeling sorry for her, my sister and cousins look at her in awe, the first woman in our family to defy the orders of not just her elders, but elder men—her own buwa, my dad's eldest brother, and the man who has become the helm of the family since my other baba passed away years ago. There are levels to this act of defiance.

"You make it sound so easy." I mope, looking into my empty cup and feeling just as hollow about how this might play out.

"In some ways it is, and in some ways, it isn't. It's not easy in that I can't believe my family is giving me such grief, all because I love someone who loves me for *me*, and not for how we can elevate each other's status. I want to be more than a trophy wife, and Akhil makes me feel like that. He listens to me, he understands me." She pauses, blushing. "He's just my person. So it might sound crazy, Babu, but sometimes love just makes everything else . . . easier," she says, and Naima and Rani squeeze Lakshmi's arm.

"Gag," Bina says, and we all double over laughing. Bina's in her second year of high school and is generally over most things, until she's not. But Bina's cynicism also gives her this acute ability to notice changes in us before anyone else. I suspect it's because she loves to call us out on it to force us to talk. I also suspect she forces us to talk so we all can learn how to navigate this first- and second-generation Nepali-kid world together. She gives me a sly look. "What's her name?"

"Whaaat?" I say with a nervous chuckle. "What are you talking about?"

"There's a third toothbrush in your bathroom, so that means one for you, one for Rani, and one for . . ." Bina gives me a look, then takes another sip of her wine.

"You don't need to know her name just yet, just know I gave this incredible woman a tattoo, and I have no idea if she'd ever consider dating me after hearing all this drama."

My cousins and sister look at me, eyes swoony. "What's your concern?" Reya asks.

"She's a family girl. Which is great because she understands how important family is to me. But she also doesn't know how *our* family is. I feel like the only way to get her to get it is to bring her around. And that's when I freak out and have these internal battles where I try to tell myself I'm going to leave her alone because I'm afraid that subjecting her to this environment would end us." I let out a loud exhale, happy to finally get this out. "Then there's the other part of me that sees her, and selfishly I just can't get enough." Rani, our resident therapist, rubs my shoulder.

"It's bad, Raja," Bina says.

"Shut up, Bina." I mope, and she snickers.

"It's silly to bring her around, though, right? I don't want to marry her today, but I could see myself getting really serious with her. What if we become college sweethearts or something? Marriage would still be years away."

"You're right, Bina!" Reya chimes in, aghast. "Raja babu, we've never seen you like this, so you must like her."

"Something about them," Rani replies, "they just have . . . that instant connection thing. It's obviously going fast, but it feels like love at first sight to me!"

"Was it a one-night stand?" Bina asks.

I cough up air. "No! Why would you think that?"

"Because that still doesn't explain why she's got a toothbrush over here," she says, straight-faced.

Fair point. "She accidentally locked herself out of her dorm and had to stay over. We just stayed up and watched *Power Rangers*."

"Aww!" both Reya and Lakshmi say.

Bina shakes her head. "That's cute, I guess," she replies, as deadpan as ever.

"Look, as someone who is in the thick of this, let me offer you a little more wisdom," Lakshmi says. "It's obvious you're attracted to her, but make sure you like her and *actually* get to know her. And if you still are into her, then yes, it means it's moving forward and she should learn about our family dynamics early. Because watching Akhil go through this is torture." I nod, and she comes over and shakes my hair messy.

"What Raja hasn't said is he met this girl months ago, he took her to see the cherry blossoms, and then she came back into town to go to UMD and they *still* have strong feelings for each other. I think you should rip the Band-Aid off and ask her if she wants to meet our family," Rani says, and I'm shocked.

Is she saying this because of Sam, or is it because she knows her little brother and has never seen me this smitten? Maybe it's a combination. "So what if you probably won't get married for another ten years? Let Deja decide if she wants to be a part of this now, because no one in our family has brought a Black person home before. I can't imagine this will be easy for her."

It's my turn to run my hand through my hair. Rani said the thing I've been avoiding.

I have seen relatives bring home darker-skinned Nepali and Indian suitors, and they seemed to get the worst of it. So I have *no* idea what to expect with bringing home a Black girl. From anyone.

Lakshmi, silent this whole time, gasps out of nowhere. "I got it!" she says, looking at me with trouble in her eyes. "How about you invite Deja to the tika-tala?"

I shake my head furiously. "No! You want me to invite Deja to your engagement? Absolutely not!"

"Why not?" Lakshmi asks. "It's perfect. It's my event so I control the guest list."

"Pssh!" I say, and everyone cracks up.

"You get what I'm saying: it's still my event. Kind of." We all chuckle again, knowing too well engagement and wedding guest lists include people we've never met, but have talked to our parents at least twice in their life. There's no other way to make sense of a five hundred–plus guest list. "Look, only if you want to. But she'll meet everyone immediately and she can gauge how comfortable she feels. Everyone in this room can help. I mean, there's already the religious drama, let's really keep them on their toes!"

Rani and the cousins laugh. "Lakshmi, you're drunk," Rani says.

"Slightly. But mostly tired." She plops back down on the couch, then looks at me. "I'm with Rani, rip the Band-Aid off now so you don't have to deal with this drama later during a time that's supposed to be the most joyous."

I see the hurt in her eyes and feel bad for her. "Just because I bring Deja in now doesn't mean my parents won't hold it over my head until the day of the wedding."

Everyone chuckles. "True," she says, "but you won't know until you try."

I give in and show my cousins her social media account and they all squeal, ready to follow her on the spot as they listen to her talk about many things they've been trying to push back on in our own community. I make them promise not to follow her until they meet her, and so we tweak the plan. If all continues to go well, then I'll invite Deja over to meet my cousins here, where they'll warm her up to family customs. Then they can follow her on social media. But first, they agree, I need to see for myself if this is the real deal. And I'm giving them a front row seat to witness it. After all, it's not like I can get dating advice from Buwa, so I'm letting the hopeless romantics in my life show me the way.

# CHAPTER SIXTEEN

## Deja

I know I'm doing this thing backward, but after seeing Raja and sleeping over at his apartment my first day back, I decide to slow things down with him while I figure this out. Call me old-fashioned, but isn't it weird for us to have such an intense bond off the jump? I don't know if this is my gut telling me to run or just straight-up fear, but until I figure out what's what, I need to cool it. That doesn't stop our late-night texting, though, which Chloe catches on to very quickly.

"Are we gonna talk about how you've been texting all hours of the night for the last week and a half? Do you plan on seeing him, or do I have to keep waking up to giggles and your phone's bright-ass screen?"

"Was the ambush necessary?" I ask as I slip off my shower shoes and put on my fuzzy slippers. Note to self, dim my phone's screen. I plop on my bed and rub my legs down with shea butter, thinking about Raja's and my texts.

He explained that he's bad at this dating thing and started to ask me questions. Maybe it's his naïveté, but I've never had someone be so inquisitive. He asked questions to learn about my interests and likes, more about my chem major and soil science minor, and he straight-up told me his own dreams. I hadn't sat up with anyone like that since Queen, and it felt nice to bounce crazy theories and goals with a kindred spirit. It's like we felt so comfortable around each other, we barely had time to put the walls up like most people do at the start of a relationship.

Chloe gets her bathroom caddy ready as she heads in next. "I'm just saying, it's obvious you're avoiding him. Just go hang out with him already!" Chloe does a dramatic eye roll, then smiles at me.

"It's not juuust me," I say, telling the half-truth. "He's been busy with family too and working more at the shop. You know he already took off to help me and he's paying for his off-campus housing and . . ."

"Blah, blah, blah, excuses, excuses, excuses," Chloe says, her fingers opening and closing like a hand puppet, her acrylic nails making noise in the process. "Dej, this is all a front because you're on edge about crushing on him so hard."

"For obvious reasons," I tell her, plugging in my steamer. Chloe has given up on showering—at least for the moment—and has instead sat at her desk chair to grill me.

She pauses. "I get it, but you had the perfect night together. He didn't even try anything! Do you know how freshman guys are? Complete assholes. They all want sex and nothing else."

"I know," I mumble, and my insides warm. He's being a perfect gentleman. "But you should see how he looks when he's talking about—" My phone buzzes and I look at the screen, expecting it to be nothing important, but my heart jumps when Raja's name pops up as my notification. "You spoke him up!" I tell her as I show her the phone.

"Look at your goofy smile," she laughs. "I have my internship at the lab today, so please take advantage of the alone time and invite him over." Chloe puts on her extra-large, kaleidoscope-colored shower cap and heads to the communal bathroom.

> RAJA: What are you up to today?
> ME: In my room studying for the most part, but I was gonna grab some breakfast from the dining hall.
> RAJA: If you want to keep studying, I can pick it up for you and stop by for a little bit.

It's like he read my mind. I text him my order immediately with a caveat.

> ME: Okay, but don't think I'm not paying you back.
> RAJA: I won't argue this time. ☺

I put my phone down and smile as I search my closet for today's look. I can't be as raggedy as last time, so I'm going for casual chic—denim shorts with a crochet tank and hoop earrings.

Raja gets here earlier than expected and Chloe is in our room putting on a full face, so I meet him in the dormitory's community space while we wait for my room to free up.

Downstairs, a few students are watching television and talking, but we have the couch area mostly to ourselves.

We sit down on one of the gray couches and eat the lunch Raja brought as he admires the windows.

"There's a lot of natural light in here," he says.

"Yeah, I wish I could capture more of it in my room," I say. "I should warn you, I might have a few plants in there. I'm currently trying to figure out how to keep them all alive."

"I could add some LED light strips on your shelves," he whispers. "Give your plants the light they need."

I sit there, stunned. Raja has quite literally solved my plant dilemma in a matter of seconds. "Bless you," I say, happy for the help.

He laughs. "It's so easy," he says. "If you can keep plants alive, you can learn this."

I put my hand up. "Everything ain't everyone's ministry."

"That sounds like a grandma statement right there," he says. It's then I notice that the skin under his eyes is a darker hue than his light brown complexion. His bags tell me he's under more stress than I realized.

I'm about to ask more when Chloe comes down, looking as fabulous as ever.

Raja gets up immediately as she strides over to us, prepared for the grilling. "You must be the infamous Raja," she says as she holds out her hand for him to shake. Either Chloe is doing that to make fun of me, or she's choosing to be formal. Either way, I chuckle.

"Pleasure to meet you," he replies.

"Same to you!" Chloe gives me a quick look of approval.

"You two have fun today, but not too much fun." I roll my eyes. So inappropriate.

"Best behavior, Ms. Chloe, I promise," Raja responds, and she chuckles.

"Please, boy, just call me Chloe. I'll see you later!" she says, looking at me, and walks away. "Smooches!"

"Smooches?" Raja inquires.

I laugh. "We've been rewatching *Living Single*, and she's trying to revive some of the sayings."

"She's funny." Raja smirks.

I pause. "You wanna go upstairs now?"

He nods. "I'm down."

# CHAPTER SEVENTEEN

## Raja

I feel like I've been transported into a botanic garden the moment I walk into Deja's dorm room. I step out of my shoes and am immediately drawn to her window, filled with all types of plant life. I study the flowers, imagining adding these plants to my sketchbook.

"If I'm a supervillain, then it's only right I'm dating Poison Ivy," I say, and Deja cracks up.

"Wasn't she a biochemist too?" I nod and Deja shrugs. "I'm surprised Chloe hasn't kicked me out yet, but she says she loves it." Deja paces, watching me explore her room.

"It's . . . soothing," I respond, touching the leaves of her hibiscus plant. "They seem to be thriving here."

"They are!" she says, perking up. "I'm crossing my fingers it works out. Between my internship at the farm and my class, and hopefully finding a community garden where I can plot my own stuff, I'll have my business back up and running by fall."

"What's the farm you're working at?"

"I'm commuting with some other students to intern at the school's food farm, like, thirty-five minutes away. The dining hall uses the food they grow."

"What? No way!" I exclaim.

She nods. "It's one of the things that drew me to the school," she says proudly. "You think I'm gonna eat a whole bunch of processed food? Get outta here."

It's my turn to laugh. "You have an amazing green thumb," I say. "Reminds me of my mom. People come over and are shocked to find this thriving garden in the backyard of a random Silver Spring house, but farming was her family's primary source of income, and I already told you about my baba." I pause then, thinking about how much Deja must miss her own farm. "I'm sure she would love the help, too. And with soil science being your minor and all, maybe you could learn about planting on Maryland soil from her."

Deja stands there with a half-nervous smile. "Yeah, that could be nice," she says, wistfully. Okay, maybe I ease her into the idea by discussing what my cousins told me. But not yet. "So, Raja, you okay?" she asks me, and it's my turn to freeze.

*What gave it away?*

I shrug and do my usual I'm-unfazed-when-really-I'm-losing-it-on-the-inside routine. "I'm fine," I say.

"Don't lie to my face," she calls out, and starts combing through her top dresser drawer, full of so many products I can't keep up. She pulls out a tiny mask.

"But how do you know?" I ask.

"I do now." She smirks, walking over to me.

"I can't believe I fell for the oldest trick in the book," I respond, shaking my head. She chuckles.

"No, your face told on you." She passes me a hand mirror and points to my cheek. "Look at the dark circles under your eyes. That only comes from one thing."

"What?" I ask.

"Your blood vessels being dilated. As more blood flows to your eyes, the color darkens underneath them, and your skin starts lookin' baggy and puffy."

I look at her, amazed. "You really are about this life?"

"Come on, why are you shocked?" She rips open the packet like a present, and pulls out two wet, leaf-like things. "The body will tell on you."

"That looks like those swimsuit pad things."

"You mean the bathing suit inserts?" I nod, and Deja's laughter fills the room, which makes me the happiest guy. I want to always make her laugh.

"I'm not even gonna ask how and why you know that," she says, still chuckling. "You've never seen an eye mask?"

"Come on, hasn't history shown you anything?" I inquire. "I have no idea what I'm doing."

"It's gonna clear up those bags and dark spots. That and rest."

"What's in it?" I ask.

"If I tell you, I'd have to kill ya," she responds, slightly distracted as she looks around for something. Deja grabs a few items, then lays a throw blanket over her quilt. She looks at me. "You should lie down while these are on," she says, and before I can object (which, why would I?) she grabs my hand and leads me to her bed.

My palms begin to sweat again and I pray they don't slip from under hers before we make it there, which seems to be taking forever.

Less than two weeks since Deja and I have been in the same orbit, and not only has she slept in my bed, but here I am heading straight toward hers . . . and not for the reasons I would have hoped, to be honest.

I'm instructed to lie on my back. I take a look at all the images on the wall next to Deja's bed and notice some lavender, hibiscus, and rose plants hanging on a wooden board, affixed by rope.

"What's that?" I ask, pointing to the DIY rack.

"It's a flower and herb drying rack. My poppa made it for me." Then she smiles. "Now close your eyes." I do as I'm told, and she applies a cotton swab of something underneath my eye. Whatever it is, my skin sucks it up like a towel to water.

"What's that?" I ask, enjoying this impromptu pamper day.

"Rosewater," she replies.

"Do you use the dried roses up there to make it?" I ask, enjoying her soft hands on my skin.

"No, I use fresh roses for this. I dry the rest," she says, rubbing my skin upward with a few swift finger motions. You'd think my body would be calm with this spa-like experience, but I'm having heart palpitations from her touch.

*Can you do this all the time?*

"Mmhmm," I say as she adds the last of the rosewater to my skin, and I'm not mad I accidentally blurted that out.

The thing is, even if it's not what I hoped, it's what I want. I absolutely want Deja to sit beside me like a doctor tending to a sick patient and dress me up in eye pads that look like half-moons; I want to talk to her about all my problems . . . and listen to hers, too. I want her to give me a facial every day if she wants to. It's more than just wanting to make out with her—I want to know her, and for her to know me. Like Lakshmi said, I want to be her person.

Finally, I feel a cold, slimy substance over my left eye, then another on my right. After controlling my urge to jump out of bed from the shock of its consistency, the coolness of the ingredients lulls me.

I heave a deep sigh. Between the smell of fresh flora, the hum of the fan, and Deja's warm skin touching my face, I could go to sleep right now. "This feels like heaven," I say. But if she happens to lean in for a kiss, I won't refuse either.

"Good," she responds. "'Cause you have to lie like this for fifteen minutes."

"Oh, I'm passing this test with flying colors, then." Deja laughs, and I feel the weight of the mattress lift, her body now off the bed, and a tinge of sadness hits, realizing I might have missed my chance. Until I hear some music playing. Rihanna. I chuckle.

"Something to dream about," she says, sass in her voice. But she has no idea that, even with my eyes closed, the only face I'm seeing is hers.

I open my eyes, feeling someone close, and see Deja's beautiful face over me, removing the eye masks from under my eyes.

Deja smirks. "Afternoon, Sleeping Beauty. You took my statement literally."

"The easiest fifteen-minute nap I've ever taken," I say, and we both chuckle. "Did you poison me?"

"I only give my victims the good poison," she responds, eyes flirty.

"I think that's an oxymoron," I reply. "I guess I'm tired. That eye stuff was everything."

"Thank you," she says, her eyebrows shifting. "I know we just ate, but you want a snack? Or! Do you want some tea?" she asks, her face full of life. "I just warmed up some hot water in the pot."

I've never had a girl I've dated ask me if I want tea with this much passion, especially since Deja wasn't drinking tea a mere few weeks ago. I can't resist her any longer.

I nod, but when she goes to get up, I interlace my fingers around hers.

"Wha—" she attempts to say. And before she can finish, I go for it. I can't have this be like last time. I can't miss my chance.

# CHAPTER EIGHTEEN

## Deja

Raja leans into me and touches my chin. He pauses before our lips connect, as if to give me a chance to pull away if I'm not ready. But I lean in closer instead, an invitation.

The soft pecks from his lips cause me to melt wholly into him until his lips are interlocked with mine, his arms pulling me in closer. We continue kissing and I feel my chest rise and fall on top of his, causing my blood to boil with passion. Finally, I pull away and sit back up. Our breathing is intense, and I see the rhythm of our chests matching, pulsating in double time. He takes my hand and kisses it, twice.

"I would say I hope I wasn't too direct, but . . ."

"Not at all," I respond. Feeling the change between us, all the built-up tension we've had over the last few weeks . . . last few months, rather. This hypnotic pull we have has only been heightened, with all of our awkward affections creating these small magnetic bonds, pulling us to each other. Making our emotions impossible to ignore.

"Of course I want tea," he says, eyes locked on mine. I slowly get up from the bed, not wanting to show how woozy my body feels, tingling all over from his sweet lips.

I catch him eyeing me as I pour some loose tea into two tea strainers, both of us struggling to figure out what to say next.

"For a girl who just got into tea a few weeks ago, you sure did go all out," he says as I squeeze honey into mugs and steep the tea with boiling water.

I smile. Humor has always been our thing. "I found an herb shop nearby that had some flavors I thought you'd like. It even inspired me to play with blends."

I make some slight adjustments to the recipe, including shaving some ginger and adding hibiscus, and Raja joins me on Chloe's fuzzy rug. Our bodies still buzzing, we awkwardly clink our mugs together and he sniffs the turmeric tea blend.

After a few sips of my own, I use this chance to call him out again. "You wanna tell me how you're doing now? Or do I need to poison you with truth serum?"

"After that kiss, I'll tell you anything you want."

And he does. I'm sitting cross-legged listening to Raja's story about his cousin Lakshmi's wedding drama and feeling my anxiety rise more and more hearing about all she's facing. Lakshmi, who is like a sister to him in so many ways, is actually marrying a Nepali man, and it's *still* an issue? Simply because of his family's name? And religious background?

The Martins are your typical Southern Black Baptist family in that our grandparents were the churchgoers, our parents went to church on major holidays (usually Christmas and Easter), and my siblings and I are figuring out what that means for each of us. Seeing Raja immediately made my heart flutter like it always does when I see him, but hearing stories like this makes it sink.

I don't want his family looking down their nose on my family because they practice Christianity. And my family isn't a walk in the park either—I don't want them rejecting Raja because his family practices a religion they also don't understand. I'm coming in with an open mind, so we all should. But who am I kidding?

Nothing about this will be easy.

Raja and I sit for a second in silence after he gives me the rundown on his family drama. I don't have much to say. "You've barely touched your tea," I utter.

I'm dying to know what he thinks.

He takes a sip and nods his head proudly, and I feel content. "I love it," he says, and I smile. "Sooo . . . I have another confession," Raja says timidly.

*Oh, goodness.* I eye him. "Okay, Usher. What is it?"

It takes him a second to register, but once it does Raja almost spills his drink from chuckling. "I have the radio to thank for that reference." We snicker some more, and then another pause. "I . . . uh, might have told my sister, and my cousins, who as you can tell by now are basically my sisters . . . about you."

My heart is back to fluttering. Except this time, I can't tell if it's angst or adoration. "Should I be worried?" I ask, then regret that that's the first question that comes out of my mouth.

Raja laughs. "No, they already love you. I kinda showed them your business account. I had to force them not only to *not* follow you yet, but not to buy anything, because how crazy would it look to have twenty-two cousins with the last name Sharma following you at once?" It's my turn to laugh.

"How many, uh, sister-cousins do you have?"

Raja gives me a nervous smile. "Sister-cousins, huh? I like it. And I'm joking, it was only six that came over."

"Only six?!" I proclaim. "That's only a basketball team and a little of the bench! Or a whole army right there. Especially if they're going to drill me like war generals."

Raja is crying laughing. "And throw some kukris in each hand?" he says, pointing to the two curved blades crisscrossed on his upper arm.

I cannot stop laughing. "I'd be down to watch a crew of female Nepali assassins any day. I just don't need to be the target."

"Yo, a FEMALE GORKHA crew?!" he responds, his voice getting louder.

Raja explains what Gorkhas are, known to be fearless warriors who are fiercely loyal in serving their country. Typically men, they use mixed martial arts and kukris in combat. "My baba told me a general who served with the Gorkhas once said, 'If a man says he's not afraid of dying, he is either lying or he's a Gorkha.' So," Raja says, clearing his throat, "there's another part to this. They want to host a momo night at my new place. Momos are basically Tibetan dumplings. They said it's a housewarming, but they were just at my place the other night! I think it's just an excuse to have you over." Those big brown eyes gaze at me, pleading.

While this could go real south, real fast, a part of me is curious. What if it isn't as bad as I think? Maybe his elders are the difficult ones, but his sister-cousins could be the bright side I need to give me some hope in all this.

If his cousins watched my videos online and weren't turned off by them, maybe they are exactly the kind of girls I need to meet. Maybe they get me more than I think.

On the flip side, what if they don't? What if it's awkward and they're eager to meet me so they can judge me? I'm not the same girl who used to get bullied back in the day; it's harder for me to hold my tongue nowadays, and Queen told me that would come with age. I don't want to step into conflict.

I'm probably overthinking all of this, but I don't want to answer just yet. "Can I think about it?" I simply ask.

His face looks dejected, but he nods. "Take all the time you need," he says as my phone rings and my dad's picture pops up on the screen. I haven't even begun to think on how he might react to Raja and me, so I press decline.

"Thanks, Raj, I just want to make sure . . . ," I try to say, but my phone buzzes again.

"He's called you twice, it's okay to answer," Raja says.

He's so considerate. I quickly answer the phone. "Poppa, everything okay?" I ask, and Raja takes our cups and carries them to my sink.

"I can't call you 'cause I miss ya? I wanted to see how my . . ."

I hear a loud thud, and then Raja yelps, "Craaap!" When I look in his direction, Raja is squeezing his elbow from banging into my bookshelf.

"Deja, who was that?" my dad says, and while he's not on

speaker I know Raja must have heard him because we both freeze.

There's no way to avoid this. "Um, Poppa, it's just a friend . . ."

"What kinda friend? Let me speak to him," Poppa responds, not really asking.

Raja comes closer to me and attempts to say something through the phone. "Hi, Mr. Martin, I'm Raja . . ." And I mouth "no, no, no" to him, not ready to have this conversation with my dad. At least not in this very moment.

"Raja?!" my dad inquires. "Where your people from?"

I cut them both off. "Poppa, I'll call you back and explain, but please, I have to go," I say. "I love you!" And with that, I hang up. Great, now I can add my dad being mad at me for hanging up on him to the list of things we'll need to discuss next time we talk. Instead, I focus on Raja. "Okay, so one, when he says *your people*, it's literally what we say to each other in the South. It's not . . ."

"I get it," he responds. "But I can also tell he *was* trying to figure out where I'm from based on my name."

I nod. "He was." Now it's my turn to be nervous. I'm in my head about conflict with Raja's family, but my dad's call brought another dimension to our already complicated dynamic: the Martin family judgment. Just like his cousins, my sister and mother will be fine. But the men? I'm not so sure, and today confirms it. "Are you okay?"

"Yeah," Raja says, although he's clearly a little shaken up himself. "Looks like we're gonna feel this on both sides, huh?" I nod again, not sure what else to say. He grabs hold of my hand. "I'm still game if you are. Nothing about how I feel has changed. This kiss confirmed that. Even your dad can't scare me away." I nervous chuckle, hoping he means it, and squeeze his hand tighter.

After we talk for a little longer, Raja decides to head home and get some rest before his shift tomorrow, and I've gotta be up early for my internship in Upper Marlboro. Something tells me that him being here has been one of the few bright spots in some serious adult decisions he's had to make with his family. He hasn't told me everything, but he doesn't have to.

I can sense the weight he's carrying every time I see him.

Before we walk to the door, I stop him. "Thank you for coming over," I tell him.

"Anytime," he says. "Seeing you always makes my day better."

I blush, then lean over and kiss him on the cheek. It's warm to the touch and smooth. He's been listening and using my products, and while I feel special, I truly wonder if we could ever work. It doesn't change how sweet he's been and the way he's opening up to me—the very thing I was afraid he wouldn't be able to do. I just want to make sure he understands how much this could backfire with his family . . . and now I have to also consider how it might backfire with mine.

Raja's head goes down, trying to shield his face reddening. "At this point, if you said no to the momo night I wouldn't even mind. I got a kiss from you today, twice." He can't stop blushing. "My sisters can meet you six months from now for all I care."

I laugh. "Oh my God, Raja. It wasn't a no, more like 'I'll think about it,'" I say.

Raja looks at me deeply, his eyes showing longing. He sees what I'm hiding, too. "Like I said, in a few weeks, in a few months. Anything for you," he says, his lip curling into a smile. He looks so damn cute when he does that. We walk down together to the lobby, and I check him out as we awkwardly say our goodbyes.

I feel bad, but I just don't feel comfortable making a decision immediately, and I hope he's okay with that.

I'm on my bed researching Ayurvedic medicine and thinking about whether or not I should accept his invitation, waiting for Diamond to get off work to FaceTime her.

"Dej!!!" Diamond yells, her big smile bursting onto the screen. She's helping my mom prep dinner in the kitchen.

"Oh, is that my baby?" My mom's being all extra in the background, like Di didn't just say my name. Still, it makes me smile. My mom pops up behind Diamond. "How are you, my sunflower?"

"I'm good, Mama," I say, hiding my angst. Meanwhile, Diamond is eyeing me like a church usher.

"You eatin' all right?"

Just like a mom. "Yes, ma'am," I tell her.

"Deeej!" I hear Jr. in the background and his grin pops on the screen next to my mom.

"Good," Mama says, her eyes squinting as she looks closer into the phone. "You don't look like you've lost any weight, so keep it up."

"What's good, Sis? You like it out there?"

"Yeah," I say. "I've been tryna call you, buttface. Where you been?"

"Football practice been whoopin' my—"

"Ayee!" Mama said, subtly slapping Jr.'s arm.

"I know, I know, watch your mouth," Jr. imitates, then puts his face closer to the phone and whispers, "ASS." I burst out laughing and my mom pops him again. "I gotta go, love you, I'll tell you all about it later!" And Darius rounds the corner and throws up a peace sign. What he's yet to tell me about is how his summer training is going. But he still texts me randomly to check in, and sometimes will send me money from his summer job just 'cause, so it shows me he's putting his head down and working hard. Just like our poppa.

"Love you back!" I yell as my mom continues to size me up, making sure I'm not hiding anything from her. She pauses, then smiles herself. "Well, I know you called Diamond, so I'll let you two get back to it, but I miss you. Call your mama sometime, okay?"

I cackle. "Mama, I just called you two days ago!"

She laughs too, and pouts. "I know, I just miss ya."

"Okay, y'all save this lovefest for when y'all talk again. I'm going to the room," Diamond says.

"Love yooou, Night!" Ma calls as the phone leaves the kitchen.

"Love you too!" I yell back, but I can tell Diamond is already down the hall and about to turn the corner to her and Dominique's new haven. It's been a minute since I've heard someone call me that, and I smile. A feeling of longing wraps me, and I wish Queen could hug me right now. I wish she could tell me what's right, what life taught her to do.

It's already looking different—Dominique has all her favorite soccer players on my side of the room, and the windowsill, usually filled with plants, only has the one or two I made Diamond keep for proper circulation. What I can't see on FaceTime is the lavender bush I planted near our window so the smell could linger into our room as we drifted to sleep. For now, I have to settle for a diffuser with an essential oil I made, but nothing beats the real thing.

Diamond closes the door and plops on her bed. "I see those worry lines tryna pop up on your forehead. What's up?"

I spill. I give Diamond all the details about our most recent date—if you'd technically call it that—and am thoroughly entertained by her reactions. She's giggling like a mad woman, giving me eye rolls whenever I say something she doesn't approve of, kicking up her feet and giving me kissy faces when I tell her I locked lips with him . . . you know, just EXTRA.

"How are you *just* now getting into tea? Goodness, and you work with herbs? I don't understand," she proclaims, after telling me all the things I need to loosen up about.

"You know I almost died! Remember when I was curled over and Queen was over me, just yelling at my ass?" I retort, and Diamond laughs.

"I'll never forget it," Diamond says, smiling and also wiping tears.

"Now that I'm getting into teas, I think I'll start mixing my own."

"Good! You can mail me some." We look at each other, cheesing all goofy. "I miss you, Sis," she says, and means it. "And you were right, Dom is not as bad as I thought she'd be. I'm learning a lot about her. She's like a perfect little combination of me *and* you. But *way* more of a tomboy."

"She is," I say, missing Diamond too, and Dominique. And everyone. Since Dom and Deandre practically live outside, she's a hard one to catch and by the time she's indoors, she's getting ready to eat and go to bed. But when Di was away at school, Dom moved into the room for a semester and we began our pillow talks. I learned then how much Dom was like me, someone with a budding blueprint for her life. She wants to play sports professionally, and the way I've seen her play with our brothers, she absolutely could. I told her to keep at it, because she could get a full-ride sports scholarship for college. And she listened to my dreams of skin products and farming, and it inspired her to do more work in the yard. She was too young to appreciate Queen, but I sensed she wanted to be close to her through me.

I ask the question I've been avoiding. "Has Poppa said anything about . . . anything?"

"No, should I be concerned?" she asks.

"Yeah," I say, shaking my head. "He called me after our kiss and heard Raja's voice. Raj tried to introduce himself, but Poppa could tell from his name he's not Black. I rushed him off the phone."

My sister shakes her head and huffs. "You know how our dad is," she says. "He's going to avoid you since he can't control the situation."

I slouch on my bed, thinking about the silent treatment my dad has given us over the years when we didn't comply with certain rules, which almost felt worse than telling us off. "He's been doing this to me for years, Di. We do so well, and then he acts like this."

"He can't take hearing your truth. Trust me, it was worse

when I was a little girl. I don't know why he has so much trouble hearing us out sometimes—it's not like his mama or wife didn't prepare him for this. But now that I'm older I realize it's 'cause he's watched us grow from little seedlings." I sigh, defeated, but Di smiles so bright. "I'm proud of you, Deja. You doing it. You are figuring it out as you go, but so far you seem in a good headspace. Much better than I was."

"Am I?" I ask.

"Oh yeah," she says, sinking back into the bed. "You know me, I like being at home. I was overwhelmed, and then the one place I go to decompress I don't have anymore? It was too much for me. But you, you wanted this since you were little. Always inquisitive. Always jumpin' in Pa's truck to go somewhere. And then when you asked Auntie Betty if you could spend a few weeks in Detroit and came back full of stories, I knew."

"I love you, Diamond. You are *such* a good big sister. Thank you for always sharing everything with me." A tear forms in my eye.

"I wish I told you about college sooner, but girl, I was embarrassed. I thought somethin' was wrong with me. I want you to learn from my mistakes, Deja. Like in real time." We both giggle. "So as your big sister, I need you to do something for me."

"What?" I ask, tense for what's to come. "Diamooond . . . ," I whine.

"Aht aht aht, wait," she says, putting her finger up to the phone like Mama puts it up to our face when she's had it up to here with us. "If you go to that party, you will meet every single woman who is important in Raja's life and what they stand for. . . ."

I try to contest. "But Di . . ."

She puts her hand back up and I shut my trap. "They will tell you everything you need to know, because if family is important to Raja, then there's a reason he asked you, Deja, even if it's a little . . . messy right now. If his sister and cousins are anything like us . . . ," she says affectionately, "then they will have Raja's back, and they will have yours because they'll see you for who you are. But the sooner you do this, the sooner you'll know. And at some point, me and you need to brainstorm what to do with Poppa. I'll butter him up for now. Okay?" My shoulders slump; I don't feel like it.

"One thing Deja is gonna do is make a sound choice. You just gotta face it, girl."

God. I needed that.

# CHAPTER NINETEEN

## Raja

I can't stop thinking about that kiss.

Her plump lips were so delicate and soft on my lips and cheek, I don't ever want to wash my face again. Which Deja would kill me for.

I can't say I wasn't spooked out about her father, or even disappointed she didn't immediately say yes to the momo night. I know, I'm greedy as hell, but even if we haven't said it, we both know it. It's an unspoken truth. The passionate kiss confirmed any doubts I might have had about how she's got me spellbound.

I'm bummed about it, but that's not what's eating me up. I'm more concerned she might not want to date me because she's afraid of how my family might treat her, and honestly, I wouldn't blame her. Because who wants to be part of a family that doesn't accept them based on nothing but . . . colonialism? How do I even fight that? And now that I've had my first encounter with her dad, I can relate to Deja even more because how will I react if her family doesn't accept me? What *would* have been his reaction if I told her father where my family is from?

Nothing matters, though, because the kiss confirmed it all. I have to still try, so first, I warm her up to my side, and then maybe she can do the same for her folks. In my heart of hearts I know if she agreed to meet a few of my family members, she'd know I have some female Gorkhas in my camp who'll protect us if necessary. If I can just convince her to do this, I think she would feel better about it. I need to find a way.

I open up my text exchange with Deja, when three dots appear on my screen.

She's already texting me!

Hey Raj, if momos still stand I'd love to try some. Dumplings are my shit.

I smile. She's so silly.

ME: It always stands. Pick you up this Saturday at five?
DEJA: No this is still your housewarming. I got a ride.
DEJA: See you then.

There's a knock on the door, and while tonight's housewarming party is supposed to be about me, we all know it's really about the woman of the hour, this mysterious girl I've invited over for my sister and cousins to officially meet. I've never done this before so the energy in the room is bursting. They're ready to love her.

I put my hands together, begging. "Can you all please at least act like you're doing something instead of standing by the door? This looks weird." They're bunched together in the middle of the room.

Rani laughs. "We do look like creeps. 'Look at us! We're not scary like our parents! Be our *frieeend*!'" The rest of the cousins laugh and go back to prepping in the kitchen. Rani is the worst, though, fluffing a pillow while she eyes the door, smiling.

Rani is such nice a person, it's not natural. But I like to remind her she was selfish enough to steal every nice piece of DNA our parents combined to make us, so how nice is she really?

I open the door to Deja's breathtaking smile, her lips slightly glossed. The black kohl—or whatever the Western word is—on her eyes is subdued, but it gives her an edge. I like her fresh faced, but seeing what a touch of makeup does to enhance her features suddenly does something to me.

I need to figure out a way to kiss her again before the night's over. But I'll need to get my sister-cousins out the apartment first, which is another kind of impossible.

"Hi, are you gonna let me in?" she asks, smiling.

"Sorry, you just look good." I shrug like, *I got nothing else*. She bursts out laughing.

"You're so cute," she says, affectionately touching my cheek with her hand.

"Aww!" I hear voices behind me. Five distinct "awws" if my ears heard correctly. They've been watching this whole time.

"It's not our fault you're standing there looking at her like a creep for five minutes. We needed to check in on this poor girl." Deja laughs. "Namaste, I'm Reya," my cousin says, scooting her way toward the door and noticing a tote bag full of products on the floor. "Ooooh, what's that?!" Reya asks.

"Oh!" Deja says. "Raja told me you all were interested in skin care stuff, so I brought over some products. A few soaps, some essential oils . . . and I'm playing around with tea blends, so I threw some of those in there."

This is almost too easy. "Thank you," I say. She rubs my arm lovingly.

"Oh my Gooooood," Rani says, squealing. I give her a look like, *Rani, cool it!* She mouths "sorry" and giggles and patiently waits to be introduced.

"Reya didi, why don't you take those into the kitchen so Deja can take her freaking shoes off at least," I say.

Reya laughs and shoos me away while she takes the bag. "Thank you, Deja!" she yells. "I'm almost finished making chia, so you try our tea and we try yours."

"Aww, I love that!" Deja yells back, untying her shoelaces. I can't stop chuckling. Why is she fitting in with them so well, and why are they both so loud?

"Thank you, Auntie!" I yell back to Reya just to mess with her, and the whole apartment giggles.

"So, 'namaste' *is* a way to greet people, huh?" Deja whispers to me, sliding off her other shoe.

I smile. I like her so much. "Yeah, it is."

Deja huffs. "Then why do yoga classes always say it at the end?"

I laugh. "Exactly," I reply, "cultural appropriation at its finest." Deja just looks at me, rolls her eyes, and we chuckle, a silent understanding.

While everyone is busy smelling and testing Deja's products, I pull her to the side, quickly taking advantage of a fleeting moment where the cousins are so absorbed in Deja's brilliant products they forget about us. She leans back against my wall, and I lean my body to the side of her, shielding her face.

"Another confession."

"Oh, goodness . . . Raja, I am not your priest, bruh."

I put a fist to my lips to hold in a laugh. "I'm sorry, really. But we are opening up and being honest, right?" I shrug, hands in the air. "Isn't this what you want?"

She smiles. "Okay."

"Okay, so I know you're wondering why I'm wearing a long-sleeve shirt in the summer and the AC is cranked up? I'm actually sweating like crazy."

Deja does the unthinkable: sniffs my armpit.

"At least you don't stink," she retorts, holding in a laugh. And I don't even fight mine this time. Before we know it, we are laughing so hard our sides hurt.

"Stop being gross and come on, Raja bhai!" my older cousin Kasmitha yells. I know that voice without having to turn around.

"Wait a minute, I'm trying to see if she has any questions!" I yell back.

I look back at Deja, and she has a smirk on her face. "Yo, I don't know whose family is louder, yours or mine."

I smile. "It makes sense that you are fitting *right* into the chaos." I get serious and lean in some more. "Listen, half of the cousins don't know about my tattoos. So that's why I'm in this," I say, grabbing my loose crewneck. "Can you not bring it up tonight?"

Deja eyes me suspiciously. "Are you scared they're gonna judge you?"

"No, I'm scared one of them will accidentally tell *their* parents. Who will then tell my dad."

Deja's exhale is so big, it feels like it's enough for the both of us. "But everyone in here knows about your job, right?" she asks, still giving me the courtesy of a whisper.

"Yeah, so do my parents. But I added more ink this summer. I initially promised them I'd only get a few, but we took a trip to Nepal for my graduation, and I started sketching and got inspired. . . ." Deja just shakes her head at me, smiling. "Do you have any questions?" I ask.

"When do you plan on telling everyone?" she asks.

"Can I get a pass about telling everyone about you *first*?" I plea.

She smiles and puts her hand on my chest, which immediately relaxes me. "Okay," she says, and then whispers closer to my ear, "I'm glad you told me, though, because if they asked me how we met, I'd have to tell them I couldn't stop looking at your sexy arms . . . with the nice art on them." She leans back, blushing, and I could kiss her in that very moment, but I know better. I must contain myself. "You said Reya 'didi' next to her name? I thought it was just Reya. And they called you . . ."

". . . bhai," I say. I'm feeling euphoric, having her closer to me, hearing her voice whisper in my ear about how nice my arms look, reminding myself to go to my apartment gym TOMORROW. Deja's also picking up fast, asking all the right questions. She's a sponge. "It's what they call me. Sort of like brother. Like I said, we don't really call our cousins "cousins"—more like brother and sister."

"Oh, that's like sir and ma'am," Deja says.

"Ehh sorta, except we have terms for older and younger people too to show respect."

"Oh, okay," Deja responds, eyes a little wider than before. I grab both shoulders.

"It's a lot, don't worry. We learn one day at a time. I'll teach you."

"How much of it do you know?" she asks.

"Not a lot," I reply quickly. Deja covers her mouth to giggle. "But my dad always says you don't know a concept unless you can teach it to someone else. So, if I don't know, I'll find out," I say. "Now come on, I know you like your scorching hot chia. Don't want it to get cold."

# CHAPTER TWENTY

## Deja

This man.

Raja and I head toward his kitchen where his cousins and sisters are huddling around the counter, waiting to be introduced.

The smallest of the bunch, only a few inches shorter than me with a face similar to Raja's, comes up to me first and hands me my cup of tea.

"Hi, I'm Rani," she says with enthusiasm, which makes me smile in response. "Sorry, my brother has never brought home ANY girl for me to meet . . . and I've caught him sneaking a girl out once . . . but *nothing* since then!" I lose it and laugh, then immediately look at Raja, who is red in the face. Rani covers her mouth with her hands, the rest of the cousins giggling. "Let me start over. I'm Rani," she says, laughing right along with me. "I see one of the reasons why my brother likes you. You seem to share our odd sense of humor."

"It's nice to meet you," I respond, and take the hot cup from her hands. "Raja sings your praises."

"I don't know about right now," Raja interjects, and another cousin pinches him playfully. His family feels like mine—big, welcoming, and warm. And his sister-cousins in particular are my type of crew. "Oh! So, you know how we were talking about the phrases we use to show respect?" Raja says, and I nod. "Well, Rani is my big sister, but she's short in stature so she's my Rani bahini."

The room erupts in groans. This must be one of his dad jokes.

"Don't listen to him. 'Bahini' means 'younger.' But I am his older sister," Rani says.

Raja quickly rattles off names and I say hi to so many faces.

Raja's counter has been covered with aluminum foil, and his sister-cousins are filling what look to be dumpling wrappers with vegetables and meat before pleating the momos and dropping them onto the foil. Another family member is watching a pot simmer with tomato paste, and I watch her add cilantro while also plucking the momos from the counter to steam them. They're multitasking in here like my own ma, all while greeting me with smiles and eager faces of people genuinely interested in meeting me.

I take my first sip of chia, and all the aromas I smelled last time I was here burst in my mouth. I can't stop sipping.

"And once you're done with that, our first batch of momos should be ready," Kasmitha says.

"Batch?" I say, counting what looks to be thirty or more momos on the counter.

"Oh, it's a whole production. I'm Bina, by the way . . . there's a lot of us, so we'll remind you," Bina replies sarcastically, and I chuckle.

"I'm one of five so it's always funny when my parents call us everyone's name but our own," I respond.

Bina rolls her eyes, smiling. "It's so annoying!"

"And as part of Raja's housewarming celebration, we are doing a momo and wine pairing, with the finest selection of Barefoot wines." Kasmitha swoops her hand below the counter to highlight the collection.

"And where did you all get this?" I ask, giggling.

Bina and Kasmitha laugh. "We never reveal our sources," Bina says.

"Got it, no snitches in this house," I say, and they all laugh.

Reya raises her hand, guilt on her face. "I'm the second eldest cousin and should have better morals"—Rani and Kasmitha groan—"but sadly I don't. The best I can do now is make sure everyone is sober before they go home, which is why they're all crammed into my car. I supply the liquor but babysit everyone." Raja clears his throat. "Okay, *we* babysit everyone. Since Raja has grown out of his rebellious phase, he likes to act like he's our baba."

"I have some practice," he says. "I'm trying to get them to learn from my mistakes. You know, be better than me."

"Does it work?" I ask, looking between Reya and Raja.

A *pfft* noise escapes Raja's lips. "No! They just take my mistakes and find smarter ways to do it."

"Like, organize a designated driver and all that?" I ask, and we all laugh.

I watch them take the momos out the steamer pot and add the tomato spread in a smaller bowl. "So, we serve what's called a chutney. That's what all of these sauces are," Raja says behind me, pointing to the green and red sauces also on the counter. "This one," he says, pointing to the red chutney, "is hot, but if you can handle Reya's hot-ass chia, then you can handle anything."

Everyone in the room laughs, and I playfully push Raja. "You know that's not how that goes," I say. "And I do like spice, thank you very much. I'll try a little of both."

"Perfect," Raja smiles. He grabs a plate and adds some momos and a few dollops of each sauce for me to try. "You are the guest of honor, so you have to try it first."

"But this is your special night," I say. "You should eat it first."

"Oh, please," Kasmitha says, waving Raja off. "We don't care what he thinks. We want to see if you like it."

"I told you this was never about a housewarming," Raja leans over and tells me.

I smile and take a bite. The scallions, green peppers, and mushrooms burst in my mouth.

"This is so bomb! Are those scallions and mushrooms I taste?" I ask, stuffing my mouth with another dumpling.

"You know all these flavors, so you cook?" Raja looks at me, impressed.

I silently giggle, thinking of how my sister made fun of my tea debacle. "Not at all, I just know fresh ingredients when I taste 'em."

Raja smiles. "Of course you do."

"We picked some from Aama's garden," Rani interjects. "My

mom would kill to have a daughter who actually cares about that stuff." She shrugs.

"My mom would kill to have a daughter who was interested in cooking," I tell her, still stuffing my face while everyone serves themselves. "Out of three daughters, only my sister Diamond likes to cook."

After everyone has had a hearty helping of food, we sit around the television, some of us on the floor and others on the couch, and I have them put on their favorite Bollywood movie. I smile at their banter with Raja—they initially want to put on *Dilwale Dulhania Le Jayenge*, Lakshmi claiming it will remind her of love again, while Raja begs them not to force him to watch another romance. But once they explain to me that this is a classic Bollywood love story, Raja knows he doesn't stand a chance.

Forty-five minutes into the movie and I'm just as mesmerized by the singing and dancing as the sister-cousins in Raja's life, because one thing I love is a good musical. *Dreamgirls*, *Little Shop of Horrors*, *Glee*, you name it . . . if it was on the television and had singing and dancing, Diamond and I would watch and rewatch it. Every single time.

My phone buzzes with a message from Chloe, and I whisper to Raja.

"Chloe and Ramiro said they're at a boring house party near your apartment complex. They asked if I needed a ride since they're about to go back to the dorm."

"Tell them to come over, we have plenty of wine!" Lakshmi says, and Raja nods, agreeing with Lakshmi's idea.

I text her and they're at Raja's door in less than a minute.

After friendly exchanges, Chloe pulls out mini Fireball shots from her purse that we all share, and the cozy housewarming party becomes something else entirely.

While the sister-cousins, Chloe, and I watch the movie, Ramiro and Raja compare notes about their favorite action movies after bonding over *RRR*. We're all chatting so much, the movie begins to watch us as Bina and Lakshmi collude with Chloe to play truth or dare, and the thrill-seeker Chloe obviously chooses dare.

"I dare you to eat this," Bina says, pulling out a container of tablets, a mischievous smile forming on her lips. Chloe extends her hand out and accepts her fate, looking at me right before she pops one in her mouth.

Her facial expression goes from fully confident to full-on regret. She covers her mouth with her hand and runs to grab a napkin, everyone else at the party practically on the floor. After she spits a few times in the napkin, she sticks her tongue out, whining.

"I thought you liked me!" she says, and Bina gives her a big bear hug, chuckling from a successful prank.

"I do like you," Bina says. "This is great for digestion."

"I should have warned you," Raja says. "Bina likes to pull that prank on any and everyone."

"Hajmola," I read aloud, then scan the ingredients. "This is definitely great for your stomach," I say, then take a whiff of what's in the container and promptly pass it to Raja.

"Great to know my poops will be regular," Chloe responds, voice flat. Truth or dare gets canceled almost as soon as it begins, and after Rani shares with me the moment her brother surprised her with tickets to see *The Wiz* in DC a few years ago for her birthday, we put it on. He and his family laugh as Chloe and I sing along on the couch using Raja's remotes as microphones. As the room is bopping and humming to "A Brand New Day," Raja leans toward me on the couch. "Do you want more food?"

I look at him and smirk, making sure no one hears me. "Only if you get some too."

He smiles. "You got it, but trust me when I say eating more is always encouraged in my family." He looks at me a beat longer than normal, his eyes telling on himself. I hear contentment, with a touch of relief in his voice. He's pleased and more relaxed.

I'm glad Diamond pushed me, because she was right. This whole time I thought seeing Raja with his family would change him, turn him into someone unrecognizable, but seeing him with his sisters and cousins showed me quite the opposite—this is the most comfortable I've ever seen him. Having Chloe and Ramiro over is the icing on the cake.

Tonight I'm seeing the best, most relaxed version of Raja, and I know. I can do this. I can give it a shot.

# CHAPTER TWENTY-ONE

## Raja

As my cousins pack up their belongings—including the cooking supplies and a couple bottles of the Barefoot wine—I spot Deja whispering in a corner with Chloe and Ramiro. Deja catches me looking and calls me over.

"They're about to order a car. I could stay and help or I could leave with them. I didn't know if you were taking Rani home or something."

"It's up to you," I say. "But everyone's got a ride, so I got you. I have no problem taking you back."

"Mmhmm, I bet you don't." Chloe smirks.

"I can take you home if you're over him," Reya yells from the kitchen, a mischievous smile creeping across her face.

"I said I'm taking her home!" I yell to the whole apartment.

Everyone gives Deja their goodbyes, which means tons of hugs, lots of gratitude for the gifts she's brought, and sharing of social handles so they can begin ordering her products. I swear it takes thirty-five more minutes for them to say goodbye, but finally Deja and I are alone, and the apartment is ours again.

Serene.

We just look at each other for a second, dazed.

"Sensory overload, huh," I finally say.

Deja giggles. "No! They really are lovely!"

"The fact that you used the term 'lovely' means you're lying. I've never heard you say that."

Deja laughs. "Okay, one, you don't know me that well."

"Enough to invite my family over to meet you," I say.

She looks at me, bashful. "I mean it when I say they are lovely. I was nervous and just trying to learn everyone's name at once and keep up with everything happening . . . and then Chloe and Miro showed up. So yeah, lots of fun and I guess . . . sensory overload." Her shoulders droop a bit.

"Deja, I'm breaking generational curses by saying this— you're too hard on yourself." Deja laughs, which lifts my mood. "If I were in your shoes," I say, "I'd probably feel the same, right?"

She nods. "Oh, just you wait," Deja says, cackling a bit too hard. Now I'm nervous. She looks at the sink full of dishes. "Want me to start here?"

I let out a loud sigh. "Orrrr . . . and hear me out . . . we sit on the couch for a second and get to it after we take a break."

Deja's head nods, a look of relief on her face. I snicker. Poor thing is exhausted again. But this time instead of worry lines, I've seen nothing but smile creases all night. Before she sits down with me, Deja goes to put the sour cream container in the fridge, perplexed by its weight.

"Open it up," I say. Deja sees it's stuffed with momos and

begins to laugh uncontrollably. "One thing you should learn about my family: We use any old container as Tupperware. AND they will curse you out if you don't bring their sour cream container back."

Deja and I plop down on my couch, our heads leaning on the backrest toward each other, the tips of them almost touching. I flip through the channels, trying to find something worth watching before settling on an episode of *X-Men*.

"Your sister told me she really liked me," Deja says, filling the silence. "Do you think she meant it?"

"Rani is the sweetest thing living. If she didn't like you, she would have kept her mouth shut."

Deja laughs. "I like her too. Something about her energy." She lifts her head and looks at me. "Reminds me of yours."

"Thanks," I say, wanting to lift my head up but too tired to. "I'm glad I have some of her in me, because it feels like she took the best traits." She's opening up and I want to talk to her about this so bad, but I've been so busy cleaning and picking everyone up and going to Patel Brothers to buy ingredients I've never had to buy before that this boy is pooped. I don't see how the aunties plan anything; it's all too much.

Deja stops and smirks. "It's funny how you see yourself, Raj, versus how I see you. You are one of the most thoughtful people I've ever met. At least, so far."

"Deja . . ."

"It's your turn to hear me out," she says, her voice stern. "You didn't know me at all, but you gave me a free tattoo, you let me crash at your place, you had me meet your family because you know how important family is to me, you quietly explained everything to me tonight, you listen to me, but you also pick up on what makes me comfortable and act on it . . . you're always thoughtful, Raja."

"But am I thoughtful when all of this is a selfish ploy to get you to like me?" I ask jokingly, but also not. I want her to want me, so I'm doing whatever it takes to win her. I spent months trying to scrub her from my memory after spring break and it was impossible, so I must try, or Deja will forever be the one that got away. I can't spend the rest of my life comparing every girl to her.

"Is it part of your diabolical plan?" she asks me, a little playfulness in her voice, then she gets serious. "Come on, Raja, we all have our selfish reasons for doing stuff, but you could be selfish and still not do half the things you've done. All this required work from you, with little or no payoff, but you're still doing it. And I kinda like it," Deja says, blushing. "You're wining and dining me like how my grandpa courted Queen. It's like . . . a little old school, but in all the best, nonpatriarchal ways."

I shrug with a smile. "Meanwhile, I'm making this up as I go along. I can't really ask the men in my family for dating advice."

She grazes my cheek with her hand. "You're doing it your way, and I like it just fine." We both nervously chuckle. She's got me wanting to go in and relive our last kiss. But she *just* complimented me on my apparently stellar, nonpatriarchal courting skills, so I can't let her down now.

Instead, I grab her hand from my cheek and hold it. That seems right . . . and respectful. But I still get to touch her soft skin. "Thank you, Deja. I'm still getting used to the whole compliment thing."

"I can tell," she says, leaning her head back against my couch's backrest, this time her head facing me. "You're awkward as hell every time I give you one."

I laugh and we collectively exhale, not saying anything else and not needing to.

# CHAPTER TWENTY-TWO

## Deja

I awake trying to reorient myself and remember where I am. And then before I can adjust my eyes, I smell it: the fabric softener Raja uses in his sheets and pillowcase, a mixture of eucalyptus and fresh rain shower. I'm lying on Raja's couch. At some point last night, Raja and I must have passed out and instead of waking me, Raja got me a pillow and comforter and let me sleep on the couch. He knew if he woke me up, I'd insist on going back to my dorm. Queen is probably looking down on me, shaking her head at the number of times I've slept over. She wasn't one of those grandmas to call me a heathen to my face, but I've had judgmental family members who have for less, like for wearing a crop top or sneaking into parties with Diamond.

Still, *I'm* shaking my head at the number of times I've slept over.

I get up to head to Raja's bathroom and glance over toward his bed to see a bit of sunray hit his face, which doesn't bother his snoozing in the least bit. *Boys really can sleep anywhere*, I think, recalling how my brothers would be passed out all over the house growing up. He's even handsome first thing in the morning, which is both parts pleasing and irritating. I sneak to the bathroom to brush my teeth and make sure I don't have any eye boogers, and come back to him still sound asleep, the shy dawn light suiting him, making his amber skin and bedhead curls glow.

After a failed attempt to go back to sleep, I read some lecture notes on my phone for a while and then silently get up to turn on his hot water kettle.

I hear ruffling in Raja's direction, and the sleepy slowness of his sweet eyes begin to open, making my blood heat up as well.

He smiles, one eye open and the other closed from the sunbeam hitting his face. "What time is it?" he says, his morning voice deep and husky, and beautiful.

"Close to seven," I reply. "Did I wake you?"

He shakes his head, still stuck. "I'm just trying to figure out who gets up this early for fun . . . besides you."

I laugh. "My body is trained from years of getting up in the morning to water our garden." He looks so exhausted from yesterday. "You don't have to get up. Hosting is no joke."

"No, it's not," he says, yawning again. He excuses himself to the bathroom, though, and I hear the faucet run as he brushes his teeth. "I have a new respect for the weddings they plan," he says as he comes out of the bathroom and chooses the couch to lie on instead. "I could barely plan a housewarming party. It was nice to have them all here blessing the place before my wild college parties."

I giggle. "Oh, so you plan on making this that type of bachelor pad?" I ask, eyebrows raised. "Also, where are your cups?"

He points to the cabinet from the couch. "The one next to the microwave." He's not a morning person at all but trying as best as he can. "Maybe second semester." He shrugs. "This semester I might take it easy, especially if I'm switching majors. I got to buckle down on my studies."

"Wait, what?" I gasp, dumping the citrus-infused tea bags I made into the hot water.

"I thought a lot about what you said. It's not definite, though, so don't get excited, but you're right." I look at him, still in shock. "I *am* wasting money. I'll probably get cut off, so I need to find a way to pay for college first. I'm at least meeting with an academic adviser and see what options are available to me."

"I'm proud of you, Raja!" I smile so hard. "It's a start. Take it from me," I say, squeezing honey into our mugs, "you have to take all of this one day at a time. Or you'll never get anywhere. Onward Bound really showed me that. There are so many extra steps if you're the one handling your college stuff on your own. But I can send you a few things that helped me."

"That would be really helpful," he says as I bring a cup to the couch, sitting on the edge. "Is this a thing too? Falling asleep every time we're around each other?"

"It does kinda seem like this arrangement has been naps and caffeine," I say, scooting closer. "Try it. I poured some cold water in yours so you can drink it immediately."

Raja smiles. "I do the same," he says, and takes a sip. "Damn, this is good! What's in it?"

"My favorite type of flavor, citrus! Orange peel, lemongrass, hibiscus, a splash of peppermint oil, and I steeped it with Lipton for the caffeine. You seriously like it?"

"Yeah, a LOT," Raja says, shocked. "Especially coming from someone who only tried Lipton a few weeks ago."

I laugh. "I'm a fast learner," I say, "and also cheap."

"I'm not one to monetize every single hobby you have but . . . you should sell this one," Raja says in between sips. "You have a squad of Sharmas who will support." He takes a big gulp before putting his cup down.

"You finished already?" I ask, surprised.

"I did," he responds, staring at me. This time I put my mug down and initiate the kiss. Starting slow and tender, I wrap my arms around Raja's neck and kiss him closer and deeper. Last night sealed it for me. He planned a perfect evening, all to make me feel comfortable about things out of his control. I think I'm ready to be his something more.

# CHAPTER TWENTY-THREE

## Raja

"Where do these go?" I ask my mom, bringing back a few kitchen items I borrowed for my housewarming. She motions for me to place them in the cabinet underneath the stove.

When I stand up from bending over to put Mom's pots away, I notice the cute little bag of Deja's teas on the counter. My chest gets tight, and for a second I can't breathe.

"Where . . . where did you get those?" I ask my mom, pointing to the tea bags.

"Your sister tells me she met a nice friend of yours?" My mom's eyes are extra expressive.

I sigh. Why would Rani do this? It's one thing for me to let her meet Deja, it's another for her to tell my mom—who is ready for me to get married the moment I am handed my degree—about Deja.

"Oh yeah, a classmate. She makes teas for fun, and I gave some extras to the sister-cou . . . I mean to the girls."

Aama shrugs, but still gives an inquisitive eye. She's not buying my lies. I hate that I'm doing this, but I have no idea what Rani told Aama, and I wasn't exactly ready to have this conversation.

First shot at introducing the idea of Deja to my mom and I friend-zoned her.

After stewing for hours, I finally FaceTime Rani, who went to Baltimore for the weekend to hang with her college friends.

"Rani, what did you do?" I ask when her smile and deep dimples pop on the screen. Her grin quickly turns into a look of confusion and slight annoyance.

"'Hi, Rani didi, how are you today?' 'I'm fine, thanks for asking,'" my sister imitates, then relents. "I brought some things home from your housewarming and she started unpacking my bags before I could protest. She's obsessed with the tea and asked where I got them. All I said was that you have a nice girl in your life and she makes these great teas and is into gardening. I even gave her one of Deja's oils and she's been using it in her hair."

I groan. "I'm sorry . . . I just went home and Mom started asking all these questions about Deja . . . I felt blindsided."

"I'm trying to help, Raj. I really think we should try to casually bring up people we date. And since our parents are passive aggressive, my thought was that if I said something without you there, they could tell me how they *really* feel and I could call them out on it. Plus, Aama was pretty intrigued when I told her Deja likes to garden. Any way to make connections with our parents is a plus."

I'm not buying that that's all she said, though. "Anything

else you tell her?" I ask, still tense. I hear her, but I still feel like I should have been included in that decision.

"I told her how beautiful and funny and smart she is. How considerate she was to bring tea over for us. But not just that, the way she looks at you. Raja, you know Aama is secretly a hopeless romantic. I think she'd be open to you finding a love you get to choose." Aama is definitely a hopeless romantic. But "secretly" is the key word. If I declared my love for Deja to Buwa, she would stand by any punishment he gave me.

A love I get to choose. It sounds so simple when she says it like that, and yet that's not my parents. "And you?" I ask.

"What about me?" she responds, somewhat defensive.

"You haven't brought Sam home. Why are you forcing me to bring Deja into all this? Why not make Sam go through all this instead?" I snap.

Rani pauses. "Maybe I shouldn't be forcing it, Raja. But I don't want you to make the same mistakes as I did." There's some space between words, but I don't say anything. When we were kids, we used to build a fort in our rooms and sit underneath it for hours. In the pillowy darkness of our fort, Rani would confess things to me she wouldn't dare share with my parents. She was one of the first girls in my life to show me my privilege as a guy. So I try to give her space when she's thinking out loud, and I always make an effort to hear her out since she feels like so many don't. "I know how much you saved and how hard it was for you to move out. But you did it, and I was so proud of you for stepping out of your comfort zone and standing up for yourself. And then I met Deja and she's so easy to like, and I can already see the way she brings out sides of you

I've never seen before. Seeing you two together . . . I know you feel crazy for liking her so fast, but you two just seem . . . to fit."

I find myself getting choked up. "The younger Sharmas have always had each other's backs," I get out, trying to suppress my own emotions.

"Always," she begins to sniffle. "But yeah, Sam has been pressuring me about meeting our parents and every time he's asked, I've found an excuse. When I told him about the wedding, all he could say was 'see, this is why I should meet your parents.'"

"How did you take it?" I ask her, knowing that was a trigger for her.

"Not well. I told him he didn't understand how different it was for women in immigrant households. He told me he'll never learn if I don't let him." Her voice begins to crack. "And I want to tell him that's easy for him to say, he gets to go back to his peaceful home and I have to deal with the backlash." She pauses. "But he's also right, Raja. Confronting them feels impossible, and it just felt easier to walk away from the relationship than to stand up to our parents. I'm not proud of it, but I told him I need a break."

Wow.

All this time, Rani and I were doing the same mental hurdles, just separately. And because I never brought a girl around, it never allowed us to have this type of conversation. "Rani, I'm so sorry. Being a girl makes things much harder."

She rubs her nose. "It's okay. I forced it on you in that moment because you're the golden boy who gets everything in the family. But hearing your distress now over the phone, I realize how wrong I was. Deja is Black. As much as we may not want to admit it, our own cultural views of castes are pretty messed up, and I'm sure our parents will probably categorize Deja in a way even they are too afraid to admit." I nod vigorously through the phone, thankful for Rani being able to break it down in ways I've had a hard time comprehending myself. "Deja is a Black girl, and in America's caste system her people are grossly mistreated. So I understand your hesitation; you want to protect her from someone saying or doing something ignorant."

My eyes go big. "Rani, it's my worst fear. For an uncle to say something inappropriate and then Deja tells me she doesn't want to date me. Look at Manaak uncle, for instance. We all know how he is. He says ridiculous stuff to everyone! He just has no damn filter!"

Rani is giggling now. Good. Might as well laugh at our pain.

"Well, this also brings us back to why I told our parents. Raja, Deja is a take-charge girl, and if you want to keep her, you need to take charge of your own life. This is where you start, this is your power. Men have more respect in our culture, and it's unfortunate but it's true. Use it to your advantage and stand up for Deja if you care for her."

I sigh deeply. "You're so right."

"It's why you need to start with our parents. We avoid people like Manaak uncle at all costs." It's my turn to snicker. "You won't need to worry about him because she'll barely see him. But she does need to know where our parents stand and see if she's comfortable with their views. She deserves that."

I nod my head. This advice is solid. "And maybe I can use this moment to help you too. Maybe if I do this, it will be easier for you."

She smiles. "That's sweet, but on the flip side it's probably easier for me because Sam is white. For someone like Sam, he's fine. As long as he can support me, I know Buwa and Aama will be okay. But for women it's completely different. And because Deja is a go-getter, she should know the cultural pressures that might be thrown on her when she *is* accepted. She needs to know everything."

I rub my forehead, trying to contend with everything Rani is throwing at me. "Nothing about this feels easy. But it's nice to have a magnificent big sister to help me figure all this shit out. Thank you for putting me in my place. Buwa should be proud of the education you're getting."

She laughs. "Always," she says. "Also, you can thank my Caste and Race class in college for that. You should consider looking up a similar class this year."

"I will. I promise," I say. "I can't wait to talk about it with you."

Deja is a lot like Rani, with one of her best traits being her refusal to tolerate bullshit. I've made enough excuses for enough girls in high school, but I can't go into freshman year doing childish things. If Deja was down to meet my cousins, maybe it *would* make sense for her to meet my parents first before the tika-tala. But not right now, because let's be real . . . I also don't want to scare Deja away until *we* know each other a little more. And I still haven't decided if inviting her to the engagement party will help or hurt.

Now that my cousins have given her the rundown, I'll let Deja decide . . . but later. Our dating is progressing, and I have no plans of ruining it with overbearing parents. At least not until the time feels right.

# Part Three
# Summer Love

# CHAPTER TWENTY-FOUR

## Deja

As we approach the first official day of summer in late June, the summer heat creeps up. I'm shocked at how muggy the DMV area gets in the summer, but being outside doing yard work will get you acclimated to sweltering temperatures quick.

Chloe, on the other hand, is not handling it as well.

"I thought New York's humidity was bad," she says, pulling one of the eucalyptus washcloths I made out the fridge to cool us off, as well as her handheld fan. As I'm reading about the latest trends in skin care, trying to decide how to apply what I've learned in the last month to my own concoctions, Chloe falls on her bed and puts the cold compress on her forehead.

"Are you going out with us this weekend?" she asks.

"Saturday, yes. But Friday I have plans," I say, bashfully hunching my shoulders.

"Boo! You suck," Chloe says, laughing. "You were supposed

to be hanging with us every weekend and now you went and got a man."

I laugh. "He is *not* my man!"

"Well, you are spending quite a lot of time with him like he is," Chloe says, shifting from lying down to sitting up. Chloe is not one who can be idle for too long, and being hot isn't helping.

"Even if Raja wasn't in the picture, you aren't catching me out two nights in a row. I like the fast and slow life equally."

"You're greedy is what you are," she says, and we both laugh.

"Back to what we were talking about. He may not be your man, but you're spending time with him like you want him to be. Am I right?"

I chew on my thumbnail, trying to mask my smile. "I don't know, if I'm being honest. I just know every time I hang out with him, I keep thinking maybe I'll find something wrong him, but it's the opposite. The more I learn about him, the more I like him."

"Aww!" Chloe chimes. "Seriously, Dej, that's the sweetest thing I've heard you say about him. Guys nowadays don't know the meaning of quality time, and look at you two. So romantic." She clasps her fingers together like a Disney princess.

"Really?" I ask. "You think it's romantic?"

"Yes!" she says. "My ex-boyfriend always had football and track practice, but barely had time for me. So I knew when he went to college he definitely wouldn't. But my momma always said men make time for things that are important to them. And the problem is we out here dealing with a lot of boys."

I wave an imaginary fan in the air. "Well!" I fake shout, and we giggle. "Raja does make time for me, but it's also the summer and a lot of his friends went away to college. Maybe he's just hanging around me because he's bored."

"He's from the area, he's working to pay for his living, he's juggling family responsibilities too, and is still *choosing* to hang with you," she says, using her fingers to call out each rebuttal. "Open those eyes of yours. He's infatuated with you, and I have a strong feeling you feel the same."

"Is this healthy?" I ask, and she cracks up laughing.

"Why are you overthinking this? We're basically eighteen and living our life. Girl, if you wanna be infatuated with that cutie for the first semester and another one the next, who cares? Just be direct with them and yourself . . . and live your life. We can't know what we want in a guy if we don't test a few," she responds, moving the handheld fan closer to her face as she closes her eyes.

I shut my laptop, realizing I'm not getting anything done anyway, and consider what college life would be like with Raja as my person. At what point would his family accept me if we got together? Would it be when we made it official as boyfriend and girlfriend, or would they not even respect that? Would they only come around when we were engaged, or worse, after we married? What if I married him and they never accept me—could I be okay with that?

And when will my own father open up? Is there a possibility that he might take just as long as Raja's family, afraid that I've made the wrong decision for myself? It's always these moments—when most girls daydream about a future with the guy they're dating—that instead of thinking sweet thoughts, I go into panic. It's probably why I have a hard time considering that, for as quickly as Raja and I are connecting, it also feels weird to have this lingering truth hanging over us.

At some point, our sweet, fun, and thrilling honeymoon phase will come to an end, and we'll be at a fork in the road. Do we make this the real deal or chalk it up to a summer fling? Every time someone mentions him, my brain gets dizzy with excitement and my heart flutters, but I also need to be sensible. I have too much to lose with school and my goals.

I need to see where he stands. Like, for real. Maybe I'm a girl who loves the idea of love, or maybe I'm a girl who knows what I want, and I want this . . . or maybe it's a little bit of both. But maybe, I'm just a girl willing to trust her gut.

Either way, I can like someone . . . and they can like me . . . and still lead me on. So the question is, how serious does Raja *actually* want to be with me? Like boyfriend/girlfriend bring-me-over-to-his-folks' serious or let's-keep-it-a-secret-on-campus-for-two-years serious? Because I will not stand for the latter. I get that his culture makes it hard, and I couldn't imagine standing up to my parents in the same way Raja has to stand up to his, but I am a family girl at heart, and if I cannot spend time with him and the people he cares about the most—if that has to be separate and yet we all live in the same state, then why are we a secret? It's not just avoiding his parents' home, but everything else. Just like Raja has to hide the rest of his tattoos from his cousins out of fear it will get back to his parents, I'm afraid he'll hide me that way, too.

Still, I won't force him to do something he's not ready to do, so I'll wait to see what he does and how long I can last.

He doesn't make me wait long.

# CHAPTER TWENTY-FIVE

## Raja

The server hands us the menu. "Hi, Raja, haven't seen you here in a while, how are you?" she asks.

"I'm doing well, Mrs. Johnson, just got busy with moving and stuff. I haven't had time to be reckless with the boys."

She laughs, one hand on her hip. "Got a good head on your shoulders now that you're headed to college, huh?"

"I'm trying to have one." I smile, eyeing Deja.

"How reckless is reckless?" Deja asks, giving me a look back.

She places her hand on my shoulder. "Don't worry, sweetie, it's all harmless fun. He and his friends liked coming here after a night out. But he seems to be staying in for the moment."

"He must be conserving his energy for first semester," Deja replies, which has us all laughing. She and I give each other an extra look, thinking about our housewarming shenanigans.

"I like this one," Mrs. Johnson tells me, pointing to Deja.

"Well, here are your menus," she says, handing us each one, "and here are the kids menus."

"Kids menus?" Deja asks.

I laugh, slightly embarrassed. "Every time I come to IHOP, I ask for a kids menu and crayons so I can doodle."

She smiles back. "You are such a kid at heart."

I shrug. "I know."

"And since you're his plus-one for the morning," Mrs. Johnson chimes in, "I figured sharing is caring. Let me know when you both are ready to order."

"Thank you," I tell her, and she gives us a nod before taking the next table's order.

"Let's place a bet," Deja says. "A coloring contest. Whoever loses pays for the next date."

"If this is your way of making sure I let you pay next time, Deja, don't worry. I couldn't care less who pays for it."

Deja cracks up laughing. "Rude," she says, rolling her eyes, rather flirtatiously. "You don't know what skills I got. I used to take art class junior year and got an A-plus, okay?"

I just pop my knuckles. "Let's see." To throw her off, I try to set up the diner table like my artist desk, putting my crayons in order based on color, ready to prove her wrong.

Mrs. Johnson interrupts the glare Deja gives me at my sad attempt to intimidate her, but once our orders are in, we go back to drawing, quiet in each other's presence for the first time. Even *this* feels natural. I watch a determined Deja coloring to her heart's content, even asking to borrow my red crayon as she continues to work. I hide my doodling behind the ketchup and mustard bottles, hoping she doesn't notice what I'm doing, but it's clear very early on that Deja is choosing not to look my way.

As Deja is midway through coloring her picture, I finish mine up. My hands are doing that weird shaky thing when I finish, so instead of handing her the paper, I move the condiment caddy over and slide the paper to her side of the table.

# CHAPTER TWENTY-SIX

## Deja

Not only do I stop coloring when I see Raja's menu, it almost causes me to squiggle outside the lines.

It doesn't matter. He won. Raja, being the rebel he is, didn't actually color in the picture on the menu, but drew his own—a sketch of a sunflower. That's why he was hogging the yellow crayon.

It's just one flower, and while I'm almost finished with my entire picture, I can see how this image took the same amount of time it took me to color in the lines. With three crayon colors, he's managed to draw a beautiful flower by playing off the white of the paper, lightly shading with the red crayon to give the flower its airy feel, and using the green crayon for the stem and leaf. And next to the flower is a note. *Will you be my girlfriend?* Underneath the question are two checkboxes—yes and no.

I can't stop giggling, in a state of shock. "You cheated!" I say.

"Rules are made to be broken." He smirks. "Plus, I knew by your shit-talking you could color well, and you made it clear earlier you wanted to pay for date two. I had to ensure nothing got in the way of that. I'm a feminist ally, after all." Raja beams, proud of his answer.

I check the yes box and slide the menu back to him as Mrs. Johnson delivers our meal. "Why are you smiling like you just popped the question?" she asks him, and Raja and I both look at each other in horror. It's nice to know that even if this feels like it's going fast, we both are clear that's a little *too fast*.

"Not quite," I chime in. "No marriage proposal at our age."

She chuckles. "My husband and I got married at your age. Been together ever since! You never know," she says as she nudges me and walks away.

Raja faces me. "Well . . . that took a turn. I felt like Mrs. Johnson turned into Aama." He nervous chuckles, his hazel eyes round and big, full of concern.

"Welcome to being a woman," I say. "Marriage and motherhood are forced down your throat as soon as you turn eighteen, and for some girls even younger than that."

He pauses. "Damn, you get it too?"

"Absolutely," I say, snacking on my fries before they go cold. "You hear it your whole life in the South. You know how many of my aunts and uncles told me going away to college is good 'cause I'll come back with a man? Not 'you'll find your dream job,' or 'you'll have an experience of a lifetime' . . . you'll find a man. I can't imagine what the girls in your family go through."

# CHAPTER TWENTY-SEVEN

## Raja

I always knew it was a lot, but not like this. As a woman, to be told your life is defined by the man you marry, and then the added pressure of not getting to decide who that person is has got to be scary. Truth is, if I get my career to a place that makes my dad happy, I have a better shot at convincing them to let me marry on my own terms. For my sister, it doesn't feel as attainable. I can't deny it, I have the better outcome as a man, and it just makes me feel sadder for what Rani is going through. And what Lakshmi must be facing right now. I think about all this as I'm picking at my pancakes, not knowing what to say, so all that comes out is, "I'm sorry."

"For being a man?" Deja asks, laughing a little.

"Yeah, I guess so." I shrug. "And for having it easier, I guess. When it comes to this. No one ever told me to find a wife in college. If anything, I'm told to wait until I settle in my career and one will be 'chosen for me,'" I say in air quotes. "I'm basically told to get my career in order, and maybe have some fun here and there, depending on which uncle is giving me advice. But I'm sure if I wait too long, they'll be breathing down my neck soon enough."

Deja shakes her head. "I think all men get that talk about college to be honest. Two different conversations for boys and girls." She pauses. "I bet it's all your mom and aunties ask your sister-cousins about, huh?" Deja says matter-of-factly.

I nod. "Even my dad. *Everyone* asks my sisters. All the time," I admit.

"Yeah, that's about right." She bites into her turkey burger, shrugging her shoulders. "So. Did you plan to ask me out like this?" I'm thankful to her for lightening the mood back up.

I shook my head. "When you told me cherry blossoms were your new favorite flower, I knew I messed up. I wasn't risking it again. Then I started drawing sunflowers to perfect them, when really I just couldn't stop thinking about how much I like you, and, I don't know. I didn't want to start the semester without you being my girl. College is a new start; I want to do this thing my way, and the right way. You feel so right, Dej."

She gives me a sheepish grin. What I didn't have in me to tell her—yet, anyway—was that it was eating away at me that I didn't ask for her number because I was fearful, and I'm tired of letting fear dictate my life. Fear not just about her, but about my major and standing up for myself. Seeing Deja at the housewarming reminded me of why I was drawn to her, because of how daring she is. And if being around her made me want to be more fearless, then it was something I had to pursue.

But this honesty thing is getting me somewhere. At least I'm not lying to her anymore, and it makes me want to not lie to myself either.

# CHAPTER TWENTY-EIGHT

## Deja

It's a sunny Sunday afternoon and we're sitting in high-top chairs at a pizza spot in northeast DC, eating while Raja screams at a foul called on a Nationals player. This is becoming our new thing, Raja introducing me to his favorite spots in Maryland and DC.

"You watch baseball?" he asks me, picking at a pizza slice.

"My brother used to play, and the family plays softball all the time. It's pretty fun! We'll probably play it at the family reunion in a few weeks."

Raja looks . . . disappointed? "Oh, how long are you gone for?" he asks, seemingly trying to play it off, not doing a good job.

"For, like, three or four days," I say. "Usually they do this on Fourth of July weekend, but this year we're doing it around the anniversary of Queen's passing."

"That's sweet," Raja responds.

"Yeah. I just feel like I'm juggling so much already that going seems like a lot. . . ." I stop. "I don't know, I just think I'm overwhelmed with everything. And I had to put my business on pause to catch up on my studies and it's just . . . not how I envisioned this summer going."

"Hear me out. You do have a lot going on that's exhausting. But maybe you are also-sorta-kinda feeling a way because Queen's anniversary is coming up? Like actual sadness?" Those eyes, so deep and expansive, look right through me with a tenderness I can't escape.

I let a small sigh escape my lips. "A little," I reply, still attempting to suppress my feelings. I didn't know her anniversary would pull up emotions I buried, trying to distract myself with school and living in a new state.

"I think more than a little," he repeats, completely focused on me. "Grief hits us all differently. For our family's one-year anniversary we traveled to the motherland and paid respects to relatives. But we also do things like fast and remove meat and salt from our diet so that our blood pressure doesn't go up."

"It's good you all are looking out for yourselves in the grieving process, too. That's unheard of," I say.

"I mean, yeah, that part is cool. But also there are some parts I don't love. I'm sure it's the same for you."

"Yeah, I love how the community comes together. So many people had love for Queen and our family was fed for months before and after she passed. People would just come over to clean or sit with us and share stories about what Queen meant to them. But for me, it's the drama that comes with death that I hate," I say, finally releasing things I've been holding in.

"The family fought for almost a year before she was even in the ground, divvying up who deserves what and arguing over funeral costs because some of them wanted this grand, dramatic gesture to celebrate Queen. Which, I get it, she deserved a beautiful homegoing, but she also didn't ask for the family to go into debt doing it. It always feels like the most dramatic family members are the ones with the most guilt for not spending more time with the person while they were alive. Funerals are not for the dead, they're for the living." It comes out of my mouth before I know it, the thing Granny would say when my father was attempting to get her estate affairs in order.

"They absolutely are," he agrees, taking a large bite of his pepperoni pizza.

"Thank you for being a very welcome distraction. And just showing me around—it's nice to experience a new place with someone who knows it inside and out. Especially now when campus is so dead."

He shrugs. "My life has somehow always felt like it's in a waiting pattern. Even now, I'm waiting on friends to come back, on starting classes, on saving to buy my own tattoo shop, on having tough conversations," he says. "I'm always waiting to achieve something. Meanwhile, you're over here working hard for your goals but also living your best life in the now. It's admirable; helps me see I can live my life that way too."

My insides warm. "Thank you," I say. "No time like the present. Even now, do you feel like you're waiting? Or are you just enjoying a day with me?"

He smiles. "The latter."

"Sometimes, Raja, it's not about waiting for the perfect time, but finding those moments in the now. Even if it feels messy or you don't feel ready. It's what I love about gardening. It's so grounding. What a plant looked like yesterday, what they'll look like tomorrow, is totally out of my control. But I can take care of it and foster it and help it grow, and also appreciate where it is in its life cycle," I say, putting my greasy hand on top of his.

"Thank you, old wise one," Raja responds, and I smile. Then his smile turns coy. "Well, since there's no time like the present..."

"What is it?" I ask, slightly uneasy.

He puts his other hand over mine. "Lakshmi has extended an invitation for you to come to her engagement party on July third."

Another reason why he was bummed earlier—he thought I'd be out of town. This is it, now or never. "Okay, sure!"

"You sure?" Raja asks, suddenly anxious. "I don't want to force it, and you seem very nervous about the whole thing still."

I try to play it off. "I'm just thinking about what I will wear...."

"Don't worry about that," he says. "The cousins will hook you up. They'll pick out your saree."

I laugh. "I thought I'd be lying in bed depressed for the Fourth 'cause Chloe and Ramiro are driving home for the weekend. But I still have my internship duties...."

"Now you get a little business *and* pleasure."

I smile at him. "I like that."

A long breath escapes his lips nonetheless, which concerns me. Why does he still look pensive? "I don't want to blindside you, though. My parents can be... interesting. They can either be super blunt or very comfortable sitting in awkward silence."

"Bluntness I can handle. You haven't met my family," I say, shoving a fry into my mouth.

Raja nods his head in approval, chuckling a bit. "Okay, okay. But still, Rani had a suggestion that you might not like, but seeing as you like Rani, I thought you'd hear her out...."

I give him a look. "What is it, Raj?"

"It might be best to do a family dinner beforehand. Think of when you met the cousins; now multiply that by fifty. There's going to be so much happening at once at the engagement party. I want you and my parents to have a private moment to get used to one another before the tika-tala instead of meeting for the first time in such a public place, in front of their whole family." He grabs both my hands and pulls me closer to him.

"I don't know what I'm doing, Deja, at all. No one taught me how to do this, and I'm still *trying* to be a respectful son. I'm making this up as I go along and getting advice where I can, but one thing I do know is if something is said or done to offend you, I need you to tell me. I want to have the tough conversations right then, right there." He pauses. "I'm trying to rip the Band-Aid clean the fuck off."

I know casual dating is taboo in Raja's family, so on the one hand I'm proud of him for wanting to do this, and also pleased that he wants to do this early to let me decide for myself.

But while it probably *is* a good idea to have dinner with his parents, his sister-cousins spoiled me. I'm now dealing with the heads of the house. What happens when our differences show between cultural and religious views, and I have to defend myself while also still trying to show respect to an older generation? And if they don't respect me, then what? It would be shitty to turn down Lakshmi's invitation considering I had a great time with her and the rest of his girls, but I don't think going to her engagement will be as enticing if something happens at his parents' house.

It's hard *not* to think about that when racism is something you're forced to learn and understand at a young age as a Black person in this country, when the world around you tries to remind you of the box you're supposed to stay put in. Every Black child remembers their first racist encounter, the moment their innocence begins to dim, when the world shows them its true colors. That feeling, no matter how prepared you are to experience it, is soul crushing.

The idea of dating this great guy and visiting his parents only to face discrimination is terrifying. I don't want it to taint what Raja and I have.

"Do you think they'll say something like . . . racist?"

He shakes his head forcefully. "No, no . . . but they may have biases. Biases that are layered, and honestly, Rani has been the one helping me see them in our family. This is less about you and more about how it's traditionally been done. Since I've never done this before, and it goes against everything we've been taught, I just don't know how they'll respond."

"Spell it out for me again: How is it traditionally done?" I ask, trying to remind myself how different being an immigrant is from being American-born, but also trusting my own instincts, the things Queen taught me to be mindful of as a Black woman in this world.

He sighs. "Typically, families ask around. Your parents choose someone for you. This someone is based on family values and career and . . ."

"Status? Education? Skin color?" I ask, knowing the answer.

He nods. "All of that. If one is left out, then it could be considered a fail. I come from a higher caste in our system, so we are supposed to marry into that class."

"Like a royal family," I mumble, already exhausted. But he's being candid, and I'm looking into strong yet fearful eyes and trying to put myself in this world I'm having trouble understanding my own place in.

I'd be nervous too if I defied my parents' orders. How would they react? From what I read online it can be as extreme as disowning your own child, with horror stories of some kids never talking to their parents again. I can't imagine. I want to ask Raja what he thinks the repercussions would be for *him*. I can't picture having that fear as a possibility. I also don't want him to detach from his own family for me. But I'm trying to be optimistic about this meeting and speak positively, so I don't ask. Today.

Instead, I give a long exhale. "Okay," I say. "I'll do it."

# CHAPTER TWENTY-NINE

## Raja

My dad is on the couch in the family room, reading a newspaper when I let myself in. He hasn't looked up at me yet—not because he doesn't see me, but because he's avoiding me. I haven't exactly been the apple of his eye lately. But I think about the post Rani sent me from a brown therapist online about how to confront your parents about a new relationship, and I'm going for it. I'm tired of the double life.

I clear my throat. "Buwa," I say, sitting on the couch, "we have to talk."

My dad's death stare isn't one I enjoy, but I stand my ground. Mom walks in and I motion for her to sit next to me. Hopefully she can be the voice of reason here.

I take a deep breath, and exhale, releasing my words with it. "I have a girlfriend."

My mom jumps a little in her seat, I'm sure putting my "friend with the tea blends" and "this sudden girlfriend I'm announcing" together. Instead of responding, she looks to my dad for his response. His approval. She looks like she wants it as badly as I do.

Deafening silence for what seems like forever. Finally, I can't take it.

"Dad . . ."

"This is a complete waste of time," he says coldly. "Worry about school. And what's this I hear about you having a party . . . ?"

My mother gasps. I'll worry about which one of my sister-cousins opened their mouths to the parents later. "It was just a housewarming party. It's a thing Americans do when they get a new place."

"I thought that was for buying a house?" my mom replies sarcastically. "Not a rental."

I silently groan. "Aama, it's not reserved for just being a homeowner. People do it all the time for apartments."

She brushes me off. "You must come back home. It's better for you." The burns never cease to amaze me from these two. I sigh.

I wish they could see how much I compromised—I stayed in-state for school so that I can be close to home. I need some *breathing room*. I just need to get away so I can come back a man worthy of my parents' respect. They claim I need to earn it, but I can only earn their respect through their preapproved dreams. The vision they had for our family was moving to America to provide a better life for my sister and me. But once they got here, their dreams seemed to be stuck in a loop like old film, only envisioning certain achievements for us. I want to dream up new dreams, yet still gain their respect by *imagining my own*.

Pray for me.

I don't know how to address their adamancy about me coming back to my childhood home, so I bring our conversation back to the topic at hand. "I'd like to bring Deja here to introduce you all, so you two can get to know her. It's important to me, like, *really* important to me." I'm begging at this point.

"Is this Deja . . . ?" my mom inquires.

"Yeah," I say. Then silence for a second. *Raja, don't back down now.* "She's Black."

"From Trinidad?" I see what my mom is doing. Trying to find a connection between our cultures as best as she can, thinking of the Trini-Indians we met at a family friends' wedding recently who had the biggest showing of Black and brown people at a gathering that we've ever seen.

"No, Black American," I proclaim.

Aama has worry lines forming on her head, which concerns me. Silent treatment from both parents won't do me any good for a dinner like this. "Does she eat Nepali food?"

My shoulders relax. If that was her only worry, we're good. At least for right now. "She's already had momos, and loves them," I say proudly. My mom clasps her hands together, filled with excitement.

"Well, yes. We should have her over for dinner. Don't you agree, Bibek?"

My dad makes a noncommittal noise I can't quite read, and I allow Mom's enthusiasm to take over the conversation while she asks me what she should cook, letting me know as soon as Rani is back from Baltimore they'll get to work planning the menu. I suspect Aama herself has taken advantage of Buwa's quiet disapproval, filling the room with plans so he can't change his mind, secretly curious to meet a girl she shares interests with. But I can't stop eyeing my dad, ignoring the rest of the conversation, letting his passive-aggressive stance speak volumes. My insides are screaming for me to cancel the whole thing, but there's no going back now. Time to face this storm head-on.

Deja's in the passenger seat, her legs shaking, as we drive to my childhood house.

"Deja are you . . . okay?" I ask her, worried I'm not reading her well enough, and trying not to turn back around. Maybe her body language is warning of possible danger looming ahead.

"Yeah, I'm good," she says. "I have to pee. It's, like, the thing that happens when I'm super nervous."

"Aww, you're like a cute puppy," I say, holding in my laugh.

"Not now, Raja!" she yelps, half scowling, half smiling.

"Sorry," I say, and shut it. I do enjoy when she chastises me endearingly.

We park in the driveway and Deja takes a deep breath, looks at me, and then smiles.

"You ready?" she asks, exhaling. Her eyes are filled with wonder, distress, and hope all at once.

"Deep breath," I say. "Here's something Van taught me: A mindfulness check. Inhale and exhale." We both close our eyes, open them in unison, and smile when our eyes meet.

She's a rider.

My mom comes flying out the kitchen as soon as she hears

me unlocking the door. "Babuuuu, hi!" She leans in to give me a big wet kiss on the cheek.

My mom can be affectionate but not like this. Is she . . . excited about meeting Deja?

"Mom, this is Deja," I say.

"Oooh! Hi, Deja," she says. I watch her for any signs of judgment, but so far all warmth.

"Namaste, Mrs. Sharma," Deja responds, extending her hand to shake. My mom violently shakes Deja's hand back, her bangles jangling so loud it sounds like Tupperware falling out of the cabinet.

"Okay, Aama," I say, playfully squeezing her shoulders to stop her. She won't stop looking at Deja, her head slightly bent in admiration, and knowing my shallow-ass mom, all I can think is *she loves this girl because she's beautiful*. She's worse than I am.

Aama looks like she's pondering what to name our first child.

Rani walks in the room and gives Deja a big bear hug before I introduce Deja to my dad, who stands there, face emotionless.

It's stale and professional, like someone who is polite, yet uninterested.

This is where I find my irritation beginning to fester. His strategy tonight is to be detached to Deja, all because he's upset I didn't do things the way *he* wanted me to do it. All for control.

Instead, I ignore his demeanor and introduce her. "Buwa, this is Deja."

"Namaste, Mr. Sharma," Deja says, and shakes his hand. While my mom's handshake was overly enthusiastic, Dad's handshake barely seems to have any give. He shakes her hand lightly and fast, and then quickly becomes disengaged, opting to go to the family room and continue watching the news.

"Don't go too far, dinner is almost ready!" Aama calls out as Dad walks away.

I look at Deja, who just shrugs, and the only thing I know to do is rub her back to reassure her. I know she can't read minds, but I'm hoping she knows this isn't personal, that most of the kids in my family have experienced similar types of treatment from parents when they defy orders. Either way, the calm and grace she's exhibited is admirable.

Mom looks at us. "I'll make chia after dinner since Rani told me you like it, no?" Deja smiles and nods, and my mother doesn't know it, but I'm thankful to her for showing grace herself after that weird exchange.

After I show Deja to the bathroom, I watch as she takes in the surroundings of my childhood home, grinning when she looks at the wood-paneled walls. "I see our houses share the same walls," she whispers, and I chuckle.

"Yep, house hasn't been upgraded since before I was born," I confess.

"Our house was built right after I was born, but it hasn't been updated since," she says, smiling back. I show her the dining area, designed with a wooden china cabinet and matching dining table set, and then walk her around the rest of the house. My room has already been changed to Aama's storage, filled with a sewing machine, threads and threads of fabric, and other random keepsakes atop my bed. When we come back to the dining room, my mom is shuffling back and forth to set the table.

"Babu, move these," Mom says as she hands me a metal

bowl filled with mangos, bananas, and clementines.

My mom motions for us to take a seat while she screams my dad's name five times in English and Nepali before deciding to drag him to the table herself.

"Meet my family," I whisper to her while Rani finishes setting up the table on Mom's behalf.

I pull out a chair for Deja to be seated, and as I sit next to her she whispers, "I mean, they pulled out the fine china for this occasion. Somewhat promising?"

She shrugs and I cough to keep from laughing as Mom and Dad enter the room, Aama sitting across from me and Buwa at the head of the table. Thankfully Deja has Rani to look across at if anything goes down tonight. Like Van said, positive thoughts yield positive results. Or something like that.

Mom has made dal, chicken, tarkari, masala chickpeas, eggplant achar, and bhindi, all served with rice and roti. As Deja and I serve ourselves I briefly explain to her what each dish is.

"Is that okra?" she asks, pointing to the bhindi.

"Yeah," I nod, and I look over at my mom, who seems happy that she knows. They start buzzing about the eggplant dish and how Mom grows it out back and then begin discussing all the things they've both grown. Deja tells my mom about her family's farm. Even Buwa can't help but be impressed, listening to advice they each give each other, and my mom gives Deja tips on the best plants to grow in this area while Deja talks about what she's learned so far from her Introduction to Soil class. She even promises to share some of her notes with Aama.

"What are you in school for?" my dad suddenly inquires

while slurping his dal, and I know what that means. Deja's knowledge of vegetation has impressed him.

"I'm a chemistry major and soil science minor," she tells him.

"Lovely!" my mom says, biting into the bhindi. She's being so over the top, but I guess it's better than the alternative.

"What would you do with your degree? Work in a lab?" my dad asks.

"I guess I'd be doing some of that, but I want to own my own skin care company. I'm studying to be a cosmetic chemist."

"Oh?" my mom responds, this time her voice falling flat. Rani and I look at each other, eyes wide. *Uh-oh.* I hold my breath, hoping my parents' bluntness doesn't come out in a way that offends Deja.

"Yeah, remember the tea and oil I brought back that you liked, Aama?" Rani says. "And she makes lotions, too."

"So, you are in school for science to make teas and lotions?" Mom asks.

Rani tried.

I'm looking at Deja to see her reaction, and she wraps her fingers around mine under the table, letting me know she's okay. "Yes, ma'am," she says. Then, after taking a slurp of dal, she continues, "A lot of skin products don't cater to the needs of melanin-rich skin specifically. Or they're not affordable. Or they have ingredients that are harmful for your skin. I'd like to make affordable, natural products that cater to people who look like us."

"It's more like products for sensitive or acne-prone skin, like your face and eyes and neck," I chime in. "And also, protection against the sun."

"But not bleaching cream, more like sunscreen!" Rani chimes in. Thank goodness she caught that.

"Ahh, so you can help me with my wrinkles, no?" Aama says, touching her cheeks.

We all laugh—well, everyone but my father. "Maybe one day, but that's the goal," Deja replies. "But I know your dad studied natural medicine, so I'm sure you already know lemon oil can help prevent wrinkles if you just use it before bed."

My mother beams. I forgot how much Deja knows about Baba, and Mom loves it. "Yes, we use lemon oil for many things, even for cleaning." My mom smiles and so does Deja.

"What does your college track look like?" my dad interjects.

Deja doesn't miss a beat, and I sit there, shining. "I'll study chemistry in undergrad, and then my graduate studies would be in cosmetic science. But for undergrad I'll be taking classes in microbiology, organic chem, pharm chem, and a foreign language, just in case I get a chance to work abroad. I'm also interning at the school farm this summer. It's why I'm in Maryland now."

Rani chimes in. "That's so exciting! So you could take French or something to study abroad in Paris for skin care?"

"Yeah," Deja says, "or Chinese or Korean. I don't know if I'll be any good, but it's worth a shot."

"You seem very bright," my dad replies dryly, and Deja quickly hides the annoyance in her own face. Backhanded compliments are my dad's specialty.

"Thank you," Deja says, chewing on the last of her roti. Deja's mirroring my dad's energy, and I don't blame her.

Deja looks at me, and I can sense the gears in her head

turning. "Your son is very talented, by the way. He gave me a tattoo," Deja proudly announces, showing her sunflower wrist. My mom grabs it from across the table.

"That looks very nice," Aama says, surprisingly engaged about my tattoo work considering she also thinks it's a waste of time. "Raja liked drawing the bride and groom during ceremonies and would gift them to the couple. I still have some of his pictures."

My sister and I look at each other in complete shock. Mom never told me she kept any of my work.

Deja eyes me and Rani and gets the hint. "Well," she says, trying to break through the awkward silence but not force it further, "I'd love to see them one day. I looked through his portfolio and knew he was the perfect artist to do this."

"Babu has talent," Mom coos. "We knew he'd be a great engineer." I cringe, thinking about the next big conversation I'll have to have with my parents.

Still, Deja comes to one dinner and has my mom complimenting me on my artist skills when she'd barely acknowledge them before—that's progress. "I agree, your babu is incredibly talented." She looks my direction and grins, and I match her. My mom looks at Deja endearingly, and for as cold as my dad is, Deja saying something in his native tongue causes his face to relax, if only for a moment.

Deja just has a way with people.

This continues to happen throughout the rest of the evening, my dad having spurts of conversation about career and school, but any time we come back to Deja's and my relationship status, he becomes insufferable, the tension sharp like shattered glass. Somehow, Deja pays my father no mind, transferring her bubbly energy to those showing love back: my mom and Rani.

"You know, Gandira auntie was soooo disappointed in Babu when she found out about his criminal interests," Aama says as Deja settles into the family room, and she and Rani come around with the fine china cups Deja mentioned, my least favorite for chia. My index finger is too big for the cup's tiny-ass handle, there's no insulation for hot drinks, and Mom's chia is scalding, so holding it for too long always burns my hand, which is my moneymaker. I set my chia right down.

Criminal interests? What the heck is Aama talking about?

I whisper to Deja. "I'm sure you picked this up, but 'babu' is used to address a younger male in an endearing way, like the baby of a family."

Deja nods, trying to cool the chia she's been desperate to try since sniffing Aama's masala ingredients a few weeks back.

Rani's and my eyes meet for a moment, and Deja's eyes go big as she sips her chia. It's too hot, and I watch her take the tiniest sip ever, knowing that even for her, my mom's version is lava. Her tongue didn't stand a chance.

"What is Mom talking about?" I ask Rani as she sits on the other side of Deja on the couch.

"Gandira auntie caught Nijar with ganja in his room," my dad replies.

My mom nods in agreement, and I look over at Deja who is clearly trying to suppress a laugh. I don't need to translate.

"Didn't Baba grow a cannabis farm in Nepal to support the family?" I ask.

"That's different." My dad shoos me off, not wanting

to discuss further. "We did that out of necessity so you kids wouldn't have to. He shouldn't use it for recreational activity!"

I want to explain to my parents how the US criminalizes marijuana use; how if Baba had grown it here back in the day, he would've been in prison like many others selling for survival; and how their extreme distaste perpetuates the problem. But I'm already trying to get them open to the idea of my new girlfriend and my new career. One issue at a time.

Instead, I grab my cup, hoping it's cooled down, and drink chia to shut my ass up. These are the arguments that have lived inside me, ready to spill out lately, but now that I'm admitting these emotions exist, Van told me I must learn how to channel them properly. I have to still show honor and respect to my parents while finding a way to release my truths. Easier said than done.

I need to pick my battles, and my battle tonight is making sure Deja feels as secure as possible so that she can be comfortable around my family.

My dad changes the subject, firing another question at Deja. "Have you thought about working in a regular lab?" he asks.

Before I can say anything, Deja answers. "Doing what?" she ponders, still sipping chia.

"Pharmacology, biomedical engineering, pathology," he responds, and even though my mom was just asking Deja for the fountain of youth earlier, she's nodding her head now in agreement with my dad. Traitor.

"I thought about being a biomedical engineer. And then I realized someone is also making the skin products we use, and that just spoke to me more. I like learning the science and data, and also the creativity of it." I'm in a trance listening to Deja stand up to my father without her even realizing it, showing him that she's smart enough to pursue whatever she feels in her heart, and driven enough to make it work her way. "When my grandmother died of melanoma last year, that's when it all clicked for me. I guess I felt like she did so much for others and neglected herself. It felt like it was a sign. Being here this summer, I can already tell this is exactly where I should be."

"You're so young to be so sure about your life and future," Buwa says. Is this another comment about to turn left, or am I just on edge?

"I heard you had to make adult choices even younger," Deja responds. "But you didn't fold under pressure. That's admirable. I'm looking to be that person in my family too. I want to be an example."

My dad goes to open his mouth, then shuts it. Which tells me he was going to try to use this as a teachable moment, and Deja's generous compliment backfired in his face. You can't cheat karma. "Thank you," he says. Deja nods, then goes back to sipping her chia.

I know my girl. She took that as a silent win. I chime in to try to lighten the mood. "Yeah, Deja is good. She put an eye mask on me that looked like a bra. Changed my life."

Rani giggles, but my parents' faces are deadpan.

Tough crowd.

"That, and the fact that you use moisturizer on your face now," Deja says, looking at me. She's really trying to tag team with me and Rani here.

"Well, maybe your good grades will rub off on my son and

motivate him to be better in school. I worry he isn't," he says, like I'm not *right here*.

"The semester hasn't even started yet," I say. "How do you know I'm not motivated?"

"You moved out, Raja. That wasn't fiscally sound. You could save more money staying home and commuting."

I try to count to ten, but screw it. "I moved out for my mental health too, Dad."

Rani gives me a look like, *maybe right now isn't the best time for this*, and Deja's eyes go wide as she continues sipping her tea.

"Mental health," my dad scoffs at me and again disengages, turning up the volume to watch his favorite reality singing Zee TV show, like he hasn't seen it a thousand times already. The rest of us continue to make small talk while my dad awkwardly sits in the room with us, his silence making the air more and more uncomfortable to be in. I've finally had enough and announce that Deja and I are leaving. My mom pouts, but hands both me and Deja some produce from the backyard before we leave. My dad barely acknowledges our exit.

We drive most of the way from Silver Spring to College Park without talking. Finally, I can no longer take it.

"What are you thinking?" I ask her.

She looks over at the driver's seat. "I don't know," she says. "I didn't feel like your parents hated me. It actually seemed like they liked me? Or more like your dad was fighting it."

I laugh, but when I look at Deja, she's not.

"I'm sorry," I say, "that's probably the perfect way to describe him."

"That doesn't help much," Deja mumbles, scratching her head.

I put my hand on her leg. "Deja, I'm sorry my dad was acting weird. But he'll . . ."

"Come around?" she asks. "That seems to be the theme. I understand when parents are skeptical as soon as they are given a reason to be, but I don't get being skeptical just 'cause. Do you think you know *when* your dad would come around?"

"I mean, I guess I could ask you the same question. Have you talked to your dad?" She looks at me, guilt-ridden, and then eyes the road.

"No," she finally utters. "It's been harder to reach him since I've been away. He never wanted me to leave in the first place."

I shake my head, realizing how similar our dads can be. "Deja, I've been fighting on and off with my dad since high school, trying to get him to see me and it's been . . . a long journey. I don't have an answer." I crack a smile. "Maybe when we get married in ten years?" Hoping to lighten the mood. Deja isn't having it.

She sighs. "Yeah, that's probably the only way." She looks out the window and we drive the rest of the way in silence. When I drop her off, she gives me a dry kiss on the cheek and tells me she's picked up a few more hours at the farm this weekend but will text me when she's free. I know what that means. Code for: I need space, I need to process. *Great*. But if it's space she needs, I'll give it to her.

# CHAPTER THIRTY

## Deja

As the new kid at the farm, I've been tasked to do the thing most gardeners hate: pulling up weeds. But right now there's so much technical jargon the student farmers have been applying to the work here from what they learned in class that I feel behind, and I don't mind doing a task I know I can do well: removing the obstacle that's preventing the plants from growing and thriving.

I also use weed-pulling as a way to release my own emotional deadweight. I call it a day to clean house.

A day after rain is a great time to pull weeds, and the morning dew is dropping onto my skin, cooling me down as I work. The birds are singing and the sky is clear, and I feel at home. The house my parents built was for us to sleep in, but the garden was my real room, and that land was my home. And though I'm not in the Ville, it's always in moments like these when I hear Queen's voice, and now my own.

The school has tons of gardening tools to use, but I find using my hands and a trowel to be most therapeutic, my headphones crowning my face because I don't want to hear myself, or Queen, today. I'm tired of being strong and having to figure all this out. I just want to vibe out and relax outside with my shovel and soil, get a little dirty, and watch new life emerge. Maybe it'll inspire me like it always tends to do.

But Queen's voice doesn't have to be in my ear for her to be heard. She uses Diamond instead.

I'm relaxing in bed when I look at my screen and see a picture of me and Diamond at a beach along the Outer Banks coast, posing in our swimsuits and giving the camera our best as the golden hour hits our skin. It was our last sister getaway before I came to Maryland. I let the phone continue to ring until it stops. I've been doing this for the last few days now.

Diamond for sure is over me. I just don't know what to tell her . . . or Raja, for that matter. How do you say something doesn't feel right when it's so hard to put your finger on exactly what? I'm giving it until the end of the weekend before I reach back out to Raja to let him know that maybe going to the engagement party right now is a bad idea.

Also, maybe *this* is a bad idea.

I guess when I met his parents, I was afraid it would be one big thing that would set me off, make me believe this relationship wouldn't work. But instead, it was lots of tiny things that seemed to add up, the small jabs that chipped away at Raja's armor. I felt him when he said he moved out for his mental health, because as much as I love my parents, having a father *still* trying to tell me when to date and how long to be out for at eighteen gets tiring fast. And I didn't have him telling me how to live every aspect of my life. My dad understood that at a certain point you've got to let your children grow up, no matter how hard that may be. Diamond also likes to remind me that she had it way harder than I did as the oldest, and for that I'm thankful—that I didn't have to be the one to take that heat.

My phone keeps buzzing and I check: five new text messages from Diamond, including a voice note. Over the past few days she's gone from threatening me to telling me she's going to ignore me (her version of being hurt), but this voice note hits me different. The sisterly guilt.

*Deja, I'ma be real here. I'm worried about you. You haven't called me back, and Mama said she hasn't talked to you either. This ain't fair, Dej. I love you, and whatever happened, you should be able to talk to me, not shut me out. If the tables were turned, you'd be so hurt.*

Damn it, she's right.

Then, to add salt to the wound, she texts:

If you don't answer by tomorrow, I'm booking a bus ticket to come see you and rolling right up to your dorm.

Instead of responding, I lean my head against the wall and FaceTime her.

She answers with a scowl. "Nice to know you're alive," she greets me coldly.

I concede. "You know you couldn't get past the front desk if you barged your way into my dorm, right?" I smile, hoping to soften the blow.

It doesn't work. "You think some college student is going to stop me from seeing if my sister is okay? Please. That's what wellness checks are for." She pauses. "You're an asshole, you know that, right?"

"Diamond, look. I'm sorry, I just . . ."

She puts her hand up to the screen, then stares off into space for a second. I know that look, the same look that Granny used to give us and that Poppa inherited. The look of carrying the weight of something that makes you so ashamed, you bury it until a trigger brings it back to the surface.

A tear drops from her eye. "Deja, when I flunked out of school, it wasn't something that happened in one day. It started as a depression that just . . . spiraled. When I felt overwhelmed, I would shut down. And for me that meant going to my dorm room and sitting in the pitch black until my roommate, Steph, came home. It was the only thing I felt like doing. But I didn't want Steph to think I was crazy, so I started skipping classes to have alone time, and my grades suffered. And once that felt impossible to change, I just stopped caring. That's when my depression hit an all-time low. I was fine staying in bed all day and all night. That's when Steph called Mama."

I'm stunned. This is the first time Di is talking about this with me. When she came home and I tried to pry, she told me to let it go, that she just wanted to forget it ever happened, and so I never brought it up again. The shame on her face was enough to know how bad it hurt. "Deja, not hearing from you like that, it . . . scared me. I didn't know if you were suffering from the same thing, and I'm, like, this is the one thing I *can* help her with, and she won't let me in."

"Di, I'm seriously so sorry," I respond, hand to heart. "I shouldn't have boxed you out like that. I didn't know how to talk about what's been going on between me and Raja, so I just took more shifts at the farm until I was able to sort it all out in my brain. It all felt overwhelming. I needed to be able to control the things I could control until I could figure out a better solution."

"You're not an island, Dej," Diamond states. "I might not be able to help you with school stuff, but you know I've dated enough losers to help you with boy stuff."

I chuckle. "That *is* true," I say, and laugh some more when Diamond gives me the finger. "This is just . . . different."

"His family?" she asks, and I nod. I tell her the entire story, and Diamond listens intently, nodding occasionally, and by the end of the story putting her hand to her chin to ponder.

"It's *a lot* to deal with," I tell her. "And I know you like him and all that, but part of me feels like I'm facing way more than I ever planned to. I'm only seventeen. Should dating someone be *this*—"

Just then Mama bursts through the door. "Is that my baby's voice?" she asks, damn near frantic. I've been avoiding her as well.

My eyes go big and Di's expression shows no remorse as my mom's face pops on the screen. "Yes, ma'am," I say, lowering my head in shame.

"Chile, where have you been?!" she asks, eyes practically bulging out their sockets.

"Mama, I'm so sorry," I say, voice low. "I just didn't know what to do."

My mom scoots on the bed next to Diamond. "Watch your big booty!" Diamond responds, and that makes my mom's anger dissipate, and she chuckles. My mom puts her arm around her oldest.

"Don't hate on all this junk in the trunk," Mama says as she uses her hips to scoot Diamond over. I laugh, missing them something terrible. "I was listening in on this conversation . . ."

"Ma!" we both exclaim, mad she broke our code.

She puts her hands up. "Look, I ain't sorry when my daughter goes missing! I have a right to know what's going on, even if she don't tell me!" My mom hesitates, looking past Diamond's screen at the bedroom door. Then she lowers her voice. "Don't tell your father, but you know your granny was about to be set up too?" Mama says calmly, and Diamond and I gasp.

"Come again?" Diamond says with her mouth agape, looking right at my mom.

"Mmhmm," Mama responds, nodding her head. "Remember the Robinson family?" Diamond and I nod our heads in unison. "Well, the kids all came up from a good home, went to school, and were God-fearing folk. Your great-pa tried to force Queen to marry one of the boys, and she went missing."

Diamond and I are breathless.

"Who was it?" I ask. Mom tightens her lips like she's sworn to secrecy. "Come on, Mama! Is the guy they tried to set Queen up with even alive?"

"No, he passed not too long ago."

"Who could it . . ." And then my eyes start dancing, losing it at the possibility of my own theory. "Pastor Robinson?" I ask. My mother nods slowly. Pastor Robinson's white church was perched atop a hill around the corner from our land, but I never considered why Queen preferred to go to church across town. Or why First Lady Robinson would give every single Martin woman the evil eye anytime she saw us. Pastor Robinson must've told her.

"Not these family secrets coming to the surface!" Diamond says. "What the hell, Ma?"

My mom clears her throat and gives her a disciplinary look, followed by one of remorse. "I know, I know. I just felt like it wasn't my business to tell while she was alive." She kisses Diamond on the cheek and says, "But watch your mouth." Time stands still for me until I hear my mom's voice. "Dej, you okay, sweetheart?"

"How long was Queen gone for? Where did she go?" I manage to get out.

"A month, maybe two. She never said where she went. All I know is it felt like an eternity for her pa, and he went lookin' for her. Wherever he found her, she said she ain't coming back unless she can live her life *her way*, and he agreed. She came back home, and no one spoke a word about it."

I thought Queen told me everything, but if she and her dad came to an understanding, then maybe their deal meant keeping it between them. There were a lot of things kept between us that I never shared with Diamond and Mom. Why wouldn't she do the same for others? Still, a tinge of jealousy creeps in, knowing she shared secret parts of her life with other people that even I don't know.

Great-Grandpa was one of the most stubborn men alive, I heard. For her to challenge him and have him relent gives me a bit of hope for Poppa and Raja.

"When did she tell you?" I ask.

"Two months before she passed," Mom answers. "She said when you're close to dying, there's no point in holding all your secrets. She made me promise not to tell your dad since he and his grandpa were so close, but only him. I reckon she figured y'all might need to hear this story at some point in your lives." Mama laughs. "But I bet she couldn't even begin to imagine this would be why, bless her heart."

I shake my head. This feels like a blessing, or some sort of sign from her.

My mom clears her throat. "I know this ain't my business . . ."

Diamond huffs. "Mama, you barged in here and made this all the way your business. Please share with the class."

Mama lightly shoulder-checks Diamond and we chuckle. ". . . but y'all been talkin' 'bout this boy since you came back from your spring break trip."

"Mama, you've been listening for this long?" I ask, mortified. *What else does she know?*

"Yes! It's not like y'all were whispering, these walls are paper-thin!" Mom proclaims. "Anyway, I know it's hard, baby. If it's too much, then it's too much, but life is hard. And love is *always* a fight. Now, is this a harder one? Probably. But let's not forget how this family acts too. His family ain't the only family in this relationship who can be difficult. You both are in a relationship, aren't ya?"

I give my mom a closed-mouth smile and she laughs. "Maybe" is all I say. "Has Poppa asked about my dating life?" I ask.

Poppa has never been a fan of the boys Diamond brought

home, so I took that as a sign—don't bring anyone to meet him unless you're serious, 'cause Poppa's callous demeanor will absolutely drive him away. Whoever my man is has to be ready. So the only guy I brought home was my ex, and Poppa had no problem interrogating him about his intentions. Let's just say I still have PTSD from it.

"No," my mom responds. "Is there a reason why he would?"

"I'm afraid to bring him around," I finally admit, not wanting to reveal just yet what's going on with me and my dad to my mom. I don't want to cause unnecessary fighting between them.

"I know you afraid, but you need to. If you and him doin' all this in the name of love or like or whatever y'all call it, then our family needs to meet him too, so both his family *and* our family can respect it."

Damn, she's right. It's not like I've announced to my family that I'm dating a non-Black guy, which I'm sure might not go over well for some of my uncles . . . and I already have an idea of how my dad is feeling. "So what are you saying—I should even the score and invite Raja to a family function?"

Diamond and Mom nod. "And I know just the thing," Diamond says. "The family reunion."

"The one in a few weeks?!" I exclaim.

"Yeah, why not? Mama's right. You two have been dating for over a month and you're a couple now."

"But it's new," I say. "I mean, we're still getting to know each other. We've only been on a couple of dates. . . ."

"A couple?!" my sister exclaims. "You two have seen each other practically every weekend and at least a few more times during the week. And he still works on the weekends!"

"Bless yo heart," my mom says, laughing. "You do need help with this." That causes me and my sister to fall out. She gives Di's leg a love tap. "Well, I'm gonna let y'all decide this part. Fixin' to finish supper. Love you, Sunflower."

"Love you too, Mama, miss you. I promise I'll call you in a few days."

"You better," she says, before literally pressing her lips up to the phone and walking out.

"Eww, Ma!" Diamond says as I watch her use her shirt to wipe off Mama's germs.

Now I'm wondering, Am I ready for this?

"I mean, if I decided to invite him, I'd have to ask him, like, this week. I just don't know. . . ."

My sister's face suddenly changes, and she gives me a nervous grin. "So that part. You don't have to worry."

"And why is that?" I ask, the tone of my voice sharp like a scalpel.

"I . . . uh . . . I might have mentioned he should come?" my sister responds, the inflection of her voice going up like she's asking for permission it's too late to get.

"It's simple," I demand. "You either asked him or you didn't. Did you call or text that man and ask him Di? Yes or no?"

"Okay, fine!" she retorts. "I DMed him yesterday to check in on you and he told me what happened. I might have mentioned it would be nice to see him there too."

I'm not thrilled Diamond asked, but she had a right to reach out to him if she was as worried as she said she was. I would have too. "What did he say?" I ask, my curiosity piqued.

"He said if you wanted him to go, he'll go." She bites her

lip. "I was wondering why he was so cryptic, and now it makes sense. Bruh was hanging on a hope."

"Humph," I exclaim. I didn't consider as much what this must feel like for him, to think you might have lost someone you like because of your family, the one thing you can't control.

But in this moment, I do. What if my dad starts carrying on when he meets Raja? How will I react? I've never given it much thought until now since I'm forced to, and I gotta be honest—I don't like the feeling.

"So, I'm assuming Mama listened in already, but have you told Poppa?" I ask.

Di chuckles. "No, not yet. Not until I heard from you." She studies me. "You're worried about Pops and his brothers, aren't you?"

"Of course I'm worried. They're cowboys. I don't know what they'll say or do to him."

"I think he'll be able to handle them just fine. And I promise I'll always be close by . . . since technically this is my fault."

"Technically . . . ," I chime in.

She smiles. "It's yours, too, for ignoring us!" she quickly retorts. I roll my eyes but don't disagree. "This is honestly a good thing, Deja. You need to see how he handles himself around our family. He won't survive if he can't keep up, but based on what you told me, he seems scrappy. He might come out of the reunion with a slightly bruised ego, but if he handles himself well, like Ma said, he'll have everyone's respect."

I nod, a bit more convinced. It's time to level the playing field. I need to know how my family reacts, and so does he. Raja needs to know what he's up against too.

"I hope he has a backlog of jokes, 'cause he's gonna need it if they get to roasting him," I mumble, already worried about how they'll annihilate Raja if they sense any weakness.

My sister cracks up. "If they roast him, it would be out of love."

"Yeah," I say, "but they show no mercy." We both chuckle some more.

"You said you find him funny!"

"But dark humor is a different kind of humor. I don't know if everyone will like it. Especially any religious takes."

Diamond laughs some more. "I can't wait to see this!"

Glad to know our appearance will be mainly for Diamond's amusement.

# CHAPTER THIRTY-ONE

## Raja

Rani's face pops up on my screen.

"Hey, I saw you called," I say, chomping down on a burrito bowl in the break room. "What's up?"

"How are you? How's Deja?" she asks.

"We're hanging in there." I shrug.

"I bet," Rani says. "Aama has a care package for you *and* Deja. She told me to make sure you get it." Figures. Mom is siding with me, but in secret. "And I talked to Buwa."

I chuckle, almost choking on my food. "And how did *that* go?"

Rani sighs. "I'd rather not get into it, but the conversation ended well. He's requested we both come home for dinner this week."

I suck my teeth. "It seems pointless, Rani. We never talk about anything. Or if you try to talk it's considered disrespectful. We can't question anything; we're supposed to just do it and live miserable lives forever," I say, pouting.

"Raja, that is so extreme," Rani replies.

"Is it?!" I am frantic, almost. Tired. I can't believe I'm being punished for being the most content I've ever been. It's the wildest thing. "Deja's incredible. Why are they acting like this? Like, really? And I don't want to hear 'because that's the way it's been.' Does that make it fair?"

"No, it doesn't," she says immediately.

I practically slam my plastic fork down on the table. "I just can't shake that maybe . . . just maybe . . . things would be different if Deja wasn't a Black woman."

"I mean, I hate to even say this, but let's say people in our family do subscribe to the whole model minority thing. On paper, Deja's got it," Rani says.

"Yeah, unless you factor in her family's socioeconomic status or her race or skin color. I don't know, Rani, it's definitely one of the three. And they know nothing about her family's finances, so I'm just saying."

Rani looks at the screen empathetically. "Maybe it's none of it, or maybe it's a tiny bit of all of it. And there are also other things, Raja, like you working at the tattoo shop and moving out." She pauses. "Sometimes I can't tell with our parents. But he does want to see you."

"Can I be real, Rani? It's a little passive aggressive to send an invitation to your own son through your daughter, no?"

Rani chuckles and so do I. "A lotta passive aggressive. You know that's our parents' love language," she says. A real laugh escapes my lips as I pick at my rice. "Raja, let me give you some big-sister advice. Adults can be so stuck in their ways, it can feel almost impossible to get them to change. Especially adults as stubborn as our father. This is an olive branch," she says. "Take it."

I huff. "Fine."

*That's interesting—who's here?* I think as I pull into my parents' driveway and see a car I don't recognize.

I open the door and immediately freeze.

*Oh nooo. God no, no, no, please!*

But it can't be. If this is what I think it is, custom says our family would have to go to *their* house.

There's laughter and aunties and uncles and my gut is telling me things I'm not liking: that my dad has no intention of apologizing for anything about Deja this evening, but quite the opposite. He's on that bullshit.

I try to steal a couple more seconds and do a quick mindfulness check at the front door, my breath the only armor I got before going into battle.

I turn the corner to our dining room to face my gut punch, my parents sitting on the couch next to another familiar Nepali family, and their daughter. My age.

A whole fucking setup.

Rani's there too, frozen. And when she looks up at me, she jumps to her feet, ready to calm the storm likely to spill over. My heart feels like he crumpled it in two. This feels like utter madness, my parents ignoring something that feels as real as the rage I feel now.

"Rajaaa!" she says with an awkward smile. She wraps her arms around me and whispers, "I didn't know."

"I know," I whisper in her ear as I embrace her back. Then I mutter, "I'll be good. But if they say one thing about Dej . . ."

"I got you," Rani whispers.

Dad gets up. "Raja, you remember Manaak uncle and Sita auntie, ho?"

I nod. "Namaste, Dr. Manaak . . . uncle and Mrs. Bhatta."

"Ahh, fine grip!" Manaak uncle says, voice loud and quite annoying at the moment. He's doing nothing wrong except being overeager in the moment he's been waiting for his daughter's entire life, but I really don't want to deal with this right now. And it doesn't help that a woman who I presume to be his daughter is staring at me like I'm the worst thing that's happened to her. Almost disgusted? Damn, I know it's bad, but come on, help me out here. "Raja, this is my daughter, Bhumi," he says, motioning for Bhumi to get up from the sofa.

I extend my hand out, hoping to ease the tension. "Hello," I say, trying to figure out if we've met before or not.

"Hi," she says dryly, and accepts my shake.

"Bibek, let us help you in the kitchen so they can get to know each other, ho?" And our parents just get up and . . . walk away. Rani looks at me, not sure what to do, and I motion my head for her to follow, letting her know I'm okay. She gives me a quick smile and walks to the kitchen with the rest of the adults.

I settle on the couch, and Bhumi slowly sits back down, twiddling her thumbs. We remain silent for a moment and then I look at her, hoping my eyes show sympathy.

"You don't remember me, do you?" she asks, and it takes me a second to register.

"Wait . . . you're *that* Bhumi? Ninja Turtle Bhumi?"

"Yep," she replies, a light chuckle. "Lots of things have changed since then. Like being promised to a man who doesn't even remember my face." She looks away, mumbling.

It all makes sense now. Bhumi came over a few times as a preteen, and I assumed they were bringing her over as a playdate for Rani. But somehow, they'd always find a way to put us in a room together, and when I offered her the option of playing with my Nintendo, she accepted, then beat my ass in the *Teenage Mutant Ninja Turtles* game I'd just saved up enough money to buy. My little boy ego never forgave her for that day. "Bhumi, I'm sorry, I just . . ."

"It's okay," she responds, rather quickly. "It's not like I want this either."

I pause for a second, understanding. "Um. How long you two been together?" I ask.

She looks at me, shocked, and then her whole body relaxes and a sweet smile spreads across her face. "About six months," she whispers, still afraid our parents might hear us. "We met at the community college. We both were taking precollege courses together."

"Oh, a power couple. I was barely making it senior year," I say, and she chuckles. "What's his name?"

"Her," she says, and I put my hand to my face.

"Ooooh!" I respond dramatically, and she chuckles. "What's her name?" I whisper even lower. This is a different type of struggle.

"Gita," she whispers back.

"Oh shit, this is getting better. She's brown! Your life is about to be a movie." I cover my mouth with my hand, but Bhumi doesn't care and is crying laughing.

"I must say, Raja, you surprised me, you're not so bad! Better than the sore loser I remember," she says, and I roll my eyes. I deserved that. "What's the name of your special someone?" she whispers back at me.

"I'm still a sore loser, thank you very much," I respond. "And Deja," I say, instinctively smiling.

"Oh my God, look at your goofy grin," she replies. "If you don't mind me asking, what's her background?"

"She's American, Black. From North Carolina. Goes to UMD," I say. "She has her own skin care business. Helped me stand up to my parents."

"They've met her?" she asks, intrigued.

I sigh. "Yeah, and this is how it went. They invited you and your parents over."

She rolls her eyes something vicious. "I'm proud of you for trying to bring her around this early. That takes a lot of courage."

"Thank you," I say, still feeling a bit defeated. But hopeful.

"Sounds like between the two of you, she's the real catch!"

I choke on my spit from laughing so hard. "Not you coming to steal my girl! Bhumi, I thought we were getting cool!"

Both our parents come into the room, overjoyed, and Bhumi and I stop chuckling immediately, knowing our parents are taking this interaction the wrong way.

"Aama, Buwa. Raja has someone he cares for deeply, and so do I. Can we go home and talk about this?"

I blink a few times, afraid I just dreamt this exchange. Wow, that was the most honest and efficient way of telling them. Salute.

Rani gasps in the background, then covers her mouth.

All our parents stand there, collectively aghast.

"You've raised a lovely woman," I say, trying to lighten the tension. "Bhumi and I were talking about games we both love to play!" I shake her parents' hands, and they sort of turn around and say goodbye to my parents before walking out. It's the most awkward moment of my life. I turn to Bhumi. "That was . . . frank."

"You brought your girlfriend over here, the least I can do is acknowledge that someone I care for exists," she replies. "It's a start."

"I'm proud of you, too," I say, and she smiles.

"Well," Bhumi says, breaking the silence. "I should go."

I give her a thumbs-up, and she, Rani, and I chuckle. After we exchange numbers to introduce our real girlfriends to one another and I give Bhumi Deja's online code for her skin care products, because I am a supportive boyfriend after all, we part ways.

I close the door and my shoulders droop, prepared for the hardest battle yet, the aftermath. Standing up to anyone feels so much easier when you feel like you don't have to go at it alone.

Rani is right there when I look to her, ready for combat. She pats my back and escorts me into the room, her pats reassurance enough that I can do this.

My parents are on the couch, letting the television watch them when I come in. Everyone's still in shock from what happened, so I try to channel Bhumi's directness to get to the point. "Dad, why would you try to set me up with someone knowing I'm in a relationship?"

"Relationship?" my dad says, his selective memory doing what it does.

"Yes, relationship," I reply. "I don't want to be set up, I want to find love myself. And Aama, you knew about this?" I say, turning to her. "I thought you were on my side with all the care packages." Her eyes are filled with guilt. Good.

My dad looks at my mom. "You brought them food?"

"Of course I will feed my son, you see he's losing weight? And Deja appreciates my garden!" Mom says. A small win.

My dad waves my mom off. "You shouldn't have brought her until you were serious."

"I am serious," I say.

"You haven't taken *anything* serious," my father responds, voice stern.

"Buwa, I'm the most serious I've ever been in my life," I say. "I realized I'm wasting your money on a career I don't even want to do. That's why . . . I'm switching my track and double majoring in business and graphic design." I stand tall. I tried leading with business in the hopes it will soften the blow coming.

"If you were serious, you wouldn't be majoring in graphic design!" Dad snaps.

I feel my blood boiling like a kettle, but instead of reacting I slump on the couch and put my head in my hands. My mom is to the left of me, and my sister sits down on my right.

"I know I haven't been the easiest son. . . ."

"You're right! You give me nothing but trouble!" my dad fusses.

"Do you think she's the reason I'm this way?" I ask defiantly.

"She is influencing you somehow. I fear it's getting worse . . . and what will people think?"

There's the real reason, hidden under everything else I'm

doing wrong. It's not just my major, it's not just me moving out. But everything all at once. And because my dad can't imagine me making a decision of this magnitude on my own, he's got to blame someone. In his mind Deja must be filling my head with craziness, because why else would I defy them this way?

"What do *you* think of her, Dad?"

"I already told you what I think. I think . . ."

"No," I ask. "Of her. What was your impression of *her*. Did you feel a bad energy? Did she say anything disrespectful? Outside of her wanting to be a cosmetic chemist, she is a chemist, right? What is your real issue with her, then?"

"I don't have an issue with her, I barely know her. I have issues with you and your decision-making," my dad deflects.

"Dad, I'm making my own decisions. Deja isn't swaying me. If anything, I found someone who finally gets me."

"And what do you mean, 'what will people think?'" Rani opens up. "Because she's not Nepali or South Asian? Because she's Black?"

"No, of course not!" both my mom and dad say in unison.

Rani looks at my dad. "Then what is it? You haven't answered the question. She's a lot like me, she's funny, sharp, insightful, friendly. . . ."

"This is how it's been done!" Dad's voice booms. He's had enough.

I've had enough, too.

Like Rani said, adults as stubborn as our parents are impossible. Impenetrable. I know our defiance is turning everything they've been taught, everything they are supposed to do, upside down, but I don't care. Regardless of what they say, love isn't supposed to feel like this. It feels like Rani standing up for me, and even my mom sending care packages. It feels like cousins making momos to welcome Deja into the fold, and Deja, Deja . . . Deja. But not this.

I've respected and tolerated my father's rules long enough, and Van and Deja have been preaching balance to me. Balance for me tonight is accepting that nothing said here is reasonable, and I refuse to argue with someone who can't look past their own biases. Because I see my father pray every morning. I see how he gives discounts to customers of all races, the way he helps his brothers and sisters and so many others from Nepal come here. He has a heart. He needs to stop selectively using it.

"I love you both," I say, biting the inside of my lip to keep from crying. "But no, I won't accept this. I don't care what people think, but you know what *I* think? I think she's a brilliant, funny, beautiful, kind, and driven woman. And she's gonna find a way to heal her part of the world, just like her grandma, and just like Baba. She's special." I get up to walk out the door. "Call me when you're ready to accept this version of my life."

Rani follows me. "Me too," she says to my parents, then wraps her arm around my back and escorts me out the door.

Rani hops in the driver's seat of my car and takes the wheel. She drives us to my place, which has now become her home away from home too in some ways. Rani makes us tea and puts on *Encanto*, a movie that always soothes us anytime we're frustrated by our parents, and we lie out on the couch for the rest of the evening.

While the credits run, I grab an extra blanket to pass out. "I'll sleep on the couch, and you take the bed, Rani bahini—"

I turn around to my sister staring at me, tearing up.

"I'm so proud of you," she says. "You did the thing I was too afraid to do. You didn't hide anything, Raja. You were so honest. And there was nothing rude about it. You just spoke from your heart."

I sit on the couch next to her, wiping away the tears forming at the corners of my eyes. "Rani, you bossed up on our parents." She starts laughing. "You asked the hardest question of all."

"You said so much and they kept deflecting. I've been thinking a lot about it. I like her, and she reminds me of me and the girls. So if he doesn't like her and she and I share the same traits, then what *is it* exactly? He needed to know you weren't the only one that felt this way. We both needed to hold them accountable."

I grab her shoulders to embrace and kiss the crown of her head. "Appreciate you, Rani bahini."

"Anytime, kiddo," she says, tickling my rib cage like old times.

# CHAPTER THIRTY-TWO

## Raja

Deja finally calls me as I'm driving home from closing up and asks me to come over the next night.

I check in downstairs, and as Deja walks me to her room, I smell a familiar scent in the air. When she opens the door to her dorm suite, I smile.

"You're making me food? I thought you hated cooking?"

"I do," she says, laughing. "But having dinner with you and your family reminded me of home a little. I wanted to show you my version."

I laugh when I see where the aroma is coming from: a black air fryer that is clearly in violation of dorm room code.

"Don't you also have a food processor?" I ask, laughing.

"Yes, but the air fryer is Chloe's, the food processor is mine. We both like breaking the rules apparently."

"Rebels. Someone should tell on you," I retort, shaking my finger.

"Thank God my RA lives on the other side of the building," Deja says, placing a towel back under her door to mask the smell from seeping into the residence hallway. "Is that someone gonna be you?"

"What, am I crazy?" I respond. She opens the drawer to crispy, light brown pieces. She lays them out on a paper towel–lined plate, and that's when I see bits of green popping between the cooked batter. Bhindi.

"This is how we do it in North Carolina," she says, dabbing the oil off before transferring them to another plate with ranch dressing.

I bite the okra, and while the fried batter masks the flavor at first, I don't mind. The seasoning is banging. The flavor of the bhindi finally hits my taste buds, the sliminess mixed with the crispy batter feeling like a party in my mouth. It's also scorching.

"I love it," I say in between inhaling cool air, and she giggles.

"You saw the steam coming off the food, you know better!" Deja responds, gleeful.

"It's okay, the sauce cools it off," I say, refusing to wait and instead dunking the fried okra in the dipping sauce and stuffing my face some more. "Is this buttermilk ranch?"

Deja nods. "My mama is gonna be so happy I followed her recipe right!" she squeals, clasping her hands together. She leads me to the floor to eat and I happily oblige as I watch her add more okra to my plate.

"Honestly, Deja, between you learning how to make your own tea and now this, I'm content. You don't have to try anymore. I'm all in."

She grins and kisses my cheek, currently stuffed with food. My face reddens. The way she finds a way to connect the dots, to bring us together when everything around us seems to want to pull us apart. With everything that's happened over the last few weeks, when it's just us, we always seem to find our groove.

This girl has me smitten.

"So . . . ," Deja says, sitting back down with her own dish. "I found out my grandma almost had an arranged marriage."

I almost choke on a fried piece, thinking about my parents attempt with me and Bhumi. *Does she know?* "You're not second-gen African or Caribbean, are you?"

"No," she says. "My family are the descendants of enslaved Africans. But Southern Baptist tradition is sort of the same; you find a family that you think is wholesome, which means strong Christian values that you feel your kids will be safe with. They tried to set her up and my grandma dipped. Like went missing for a month."

"Whoa," I say, thinking how badass her grandma must've been, wondering if there were any women in my family's lineage who were forgotten about or ran away because they also didn't want the same. It's not like we'd ever know about it. "So your family keeps things from you too, huh?"

Deja smirks. "Only the juiciest of secrets apparently. I shouldn't be surprised, though; one of the first things people ask you in the South is *Who are your people*? Sort of like what my dad did to you. It's a way to place you."

I nod, thinking about the similarities in asking a South Asian person their surname. "We do the same with asking for last names. Sometimes it's to place you, sometimes it's to put you in your place." I roll my eyes, thinking about it all, and Deja sits there, quiet. "What are you thinking?" I ask her.

"The history of even my own last name, and how it's connected to the family that enslaved my family. I don't know what my real family name is, or even where I came from. I want to learn one day, though. But also, the Martin family name holds weight because of people like my grandma. Do you know your family history?"

"Yeah, I do," I say solemnly. "It was a story Baba would constantly repeat to me. We migrated from Persia as priests and settled in Nepal ten generations back."

"That's so cool to know!" Deja's eyes dim a bit. "Queen's stories used to stop about three generations back," she sighs, gazing at her window full of flora. I pick at my plate, not sure what to do next. "Finish your food before it gets cold."

"Yes, Aama," I say, and she chuckles, thank goodness. I go to pick up another piece, then stop myself. "I'm so sorry about what happened with my parents. I need to say it. This may not feel like the right time, but Deja, I really really *really* like you. You don't sugarcoat anything. You bring out the best in me. I know we haven't even started our freshman year yet, but . . . I'm glad I'm starting it with you as my girl."

She smiles. "All this 'cause I cooked for you?"

I stare in horror. "Nooo! No, no, no, not that." Deja howls. "I know I seem sexist saying all this because you cooked for me, but it's more that you don't like to cook, and yet you still cooked for me to make a connection during such a strange time . . . in our romance."

"Raja, I'm kidding." Deja chuckles at me. "You know the

funniest part about this? One of my uncles told me years ago I'd never find a man 'cause I always wanted to play outside in the garden and never in the kitchen. Now look at me, found one before I cooked for him," she says, leaning into me.

"Now look at you," I respond, angling my body to get closer to hers. "I think you're about to kiss me, but before you do: Is this a pity kiss or—"

"It's just a kiss I'm giving my boyfriend, no other reason," she responds. I perch my lips open, ready to receive her lips, and they're just as tasty as the last time we locked. A tingle of mint, a dash of salt. A feeling of pure nirvana overtakes me as I realize everything I felt was right. Deja felt right. She was enough to fight for every step of the way.

After my euphoria dissipates, I do as I'm ordered and finish up my plate. "But if you're never going to cook this again, can you at least share the recipe?" She chuckles and nods. "Where's Chloe?" I ask.

"Out with some boy she met at the movies the other day. She said she was having FOMO hearing about all our dates."

I chuckle, still tearing into this okra. "You got some more?" I ask, extending my plate out like a child begging for Halloween candy.

"No, sir, you cleaned me out." I give her a pout face and she laughs.

"But how about this: next date night at your place is a movie, okra, tea, and us going over what will happen at the family reunion and the . . . what's the engagement party called?"

I drop my plate in disbelief. Thank goodness it's plastic. "You want me to meet your family?! You're going to the tika-tala?!"

"Only if you want to, and only if the offer still stands . . . ," she responds, apprehensively, her voice shaking just a touch.

"Yes. Absolutely. Of course," I say, coming closer. "I just thought you weren't into this . . . us . . . after the dinner."

She sighs. "I was confused about everything. I know I'm a good person, or at least I try to be, so it was weird getting the cold shoulder from your dad. It's hard not to take it personally. And I know I've been avoiding you. I just needed to think things through."

"It's what I want," I say. "Not just for me, but for us. Not only are we official to each other, but others will have no choice but to honor our relationship."

"Oh, they have a choice," Deja responds sarcastically. "But it will be nice to know whatever happens, we have each other's backs," she says, and I silently exhale. I wanted to give her a break if that's what she needed, but those few days showed me how much I missed and wanted to be around Deja. I was concerned asking her would feel like I came on too strong. And after standing up to my dad, it was devastating to consider all this could be for nothing. My parents would never let me hear the end of my so-called careless decision. "Thank you for giving me space, and also not telling our business to my sister."

I laugh. "I know a thing or two about nosy family members." Deja's laugh is so real, I know she identifies with my struggle. "I'm just kidding, she was harmless. I could tell you hadn't talked to her yet, but it also seemed like you were talking me up to your sister, so I couldn't ruin it, ya know?"

"How did she respond?" she asks me.

"She said something like why *wouldn't* Deja want you to go?

So I told her it would be weird to accept an invitation to see your family without running it by you first."

She smiles proudly. "And what did Diamond say to that?"

"She didn't," I say, shrugging my shoulders. "She was at a loss for words."

"That doesn't happen often; Diamond's relentless," she tells me.

"So am I," I retort.

I'm playing it as cool as I can, but secretly I'm losing it at the thought of meeting all the men in Deja's life—who probably adore her ten times more than I do if that's even possible, and will probably protect her with everything they got, just like I would with my Rani bahini. There's no way I'm turning down her invitation to meet her family when I've asked her to meet mine. What would that make me look like? A coward, that's what.

She does affectionately call her uncles "cowboys" though, so let's hope I can keep this same heroism when I'm in North Carolina.

# CHAPTER THIRTY-THREE

## Deja

"Here, I brought you this," I say as I step into Raja's apartment, but this time without Raja in it. I hope he doesn't mind, but I reached out to Rani and asked if she and I could have a private conversation, woman to woman. After the housewarming party I felt we bonded, and I could use some sisterly wisdom. She seems to hold Raja up like Di holds me. And of course, not only did she agree, she had me sneak over to Raja's place while he worked the late shift.

I'm at Raja's apartment more than my own damn dorm.

Rani's eyes perk up. "My mom has been bugging me to get some more oil, so your timing is perfect!" I laugh. "Thank you!"

"Raja told me you use mustard oil on your hair weekly, so I made a hair treatment I think you'll like. I used to make it for my sister all the time. I can only imagine how often you have to re-up."

"And my mom's hair is luscious and wavy. Raja got her hair, unfortunately." She rolls her eyes.

"That he did," I utter, thinking about rubbing my own fingers through his jet-black ringlets.

"We only have a couple hours before Raja gets back, but I want to make sure we have enough time to chat. So ask me any question you want," she says as we sit on the couch, mugs in hand.

"Any?" I respond, but judging from her eager nod, she means it. This is a safe space.

"How do you really feel about arranged marriage?" I ask.

"Both good and bad. But I'll start with the good because I got to see it from someone I love and know, personally: Reya. She and her husband have an arranged marriage. Watch them at the tika-tala. You'll see them juggling their kids and being silly with them and each other, and at family functions that go late, they'll put the kids to bed and come back to party the hardest! He even sings love songs to her."

I put my hand up to my heart. "They sound perfect for each other!" I say.

"Yeah, and they never would have found each other if they didn't do it this way. He lived in Nepal. But Reya had a lot of rules, and her parents listened to her. She got to spend time with each guy and talk it through with her family. She got to decide. And she loved that she didn't have to deal with ick boys and date around. She wanted a good one."

"Whew!" I say. "That's real."

"Raja told me you watch *Indian Matchmaking*; juicy, right?"

"It's sooo interesting. My sister watches that, *Married at*

*First Sight*, *Love Is Blind* . . . all of the reality love shows," I say. "She got me hooked." And we laugh.

"I have another cousin who has terrible anxiety, so she prefers to be set up the same way. And we have Reya to thank for giving us a positive example, because not a lot of our parents are happy in their marriages. There are some, but I will say our parents have watched their kids evolve, whether they wanted to or not, and made some changes. Even with you coming to the tika-tala, changes will be made."

"They don't know what they don't know, my mama always says."

Rani smiles. "I like that! Yeah, that's it. But we're not supposed to be disobedient. I guess when it comes to negative aspects, I feel it personally with my parents in particular. They really want to choose the guy, bring him to me, and say, 'spend the rest of your life with this man!'" she says, extending her hands like a TV host revealing a prize. We both laugh.

"That sounds awful!" I say. "I'm sorry."

She shrugs. "We're fighting for choice. I know some Western ways have their flaws, but women fought and created laws here to make sure we had certain freedoms and liberties. I'd like to take advantage of that." She chuckles. "I should have a say."

"You should," I tell her, my emotions swelling. "Can I hug you?"

She snickers. "Yes!"

And I do. Just one long embrace, to say we see and feel each other.

We pull away. "Thank you for sharing that with me," I tell her. "It's already changed how I view it. Even Chloe is looking forward to meeting Raja's friends this fall and seeing if they treat their girls like Raja has been treating me. She's tryna be set up."

Rani laughs. "I know Raja would kill me for saying this, but he really likes you. He's reminded me like seven times to bring the right saree for you. He wants things to go perfect, and we both know they probably won't. But he has a good heart and wants to do the right things! And he listens because that's what the girls and I taught him to do." I smile. "My brother is smart, and he's always been our voice in the family. We check *him* on the BS and his part in it, and then he understands and checks the family." *Aww, just like Jr. with my dad and uncles!* I think.

"And as he's gotten older," she continues, "he just does it before we have to say a thing. Trust me when I tell you, he's got it in him."

I feel butterflies, learning all this about Raja. It's true, there are certain family members who've always stood up for me, and knowing Raja did that for every one of his sister-cousins is touching. And knowing he'll step in and say what needs to be said when I don't have to? It's quite sexy.

"Well, if something is gonna happen anyway . . . I feel better knowing Raja will know just what to do." And she and I sit there, just thinking of all the possibilities.

# CHAPTER THIRTY-FOUR

## Deja

From the moment we walk into the rented-out community center for the tika-tala, everything seems to go wrong.

Well, let me be clearer. Things appear to be going right for the future bride and groom (according to what Raja and the rest of the cousins are telling me at least), but as far as me and Raja? Karma is not on our side.

There was so much even Raja didn't know until the very last minute. Like, although Raja remembered I needed a saree to wear and made sure Rani picked one out for me and brought it over a few days before the event, he didn't factor in that his sister and cousins would be in different locations either getting dressed up by whoever was available or getting the bride-to-be ready.

Not only was Raja stressed about the idea of bringing me around his family, but he was also still tasked to pick up items and run errands for his cousin's big event. Because of that, I tried not to bug him about the small details, like what I was wearing, but I also didn't want to burden his sister-cousins by messaging them with questions, especially after I already snuck some time with Rani discussing the bigger issues at play. This might be a significant moment in our relationship, but it's still Lakshmi and Akhil's big day. They have their own problems to worry about.

Finding someone to wrap my saree was impossible.

Which is why Raja attempted to.

I try to bite my tongue, but Raja's false confidence in wrapping my saree has me on edge. "Raj, I don't understand why this didn't occur to you. You've seen your sister and cousins do this before, right?" I ask him as we're looking up YouTube videos in his apartment.

"I know, I know. I messed up," he says, defeat in his voice. "I just had to wake up ass-crack early to take stuff to the hall. Without fail, every family function they're calling me to do something last-minute. I hate being everyone's big little brother."

This must be how Diamond feels.

I ease up on him, my irritation softening. "I mean, you do refer to your older sister as lil sis. You manifested this life." He chuckles in spite of himself.

He pulls the saree out of a clear garment bag with gold flowers and a burgundy trim. The fabric itself is magnificent sapphire blue with gold embroidery around the hem of the garment. Based on the videos, Raja concludes that I need to put on the blouse and petticoat, and then he'll tuck and wrap the fabric around me using safety pins.

Problem number two: Raja has no safety pins. We search around his entire apartment until we're able to find three pins—a couple in his bathroom (thank goodness the sister-cousins have stayed over this summer) and one in his couch cushion. He drapes the saree over himself, attempting to fold the long fabric, his tongue sticking out in the process like he's really doing something. I'm equal parts amused at how obvious it is he doesn't know what he's doing, and petrified. But last I checked, he's still got more practice at this than I do. So I have no choice but to trust it.

Right?

He continues to tuck the chiffon around my petticoat, asking me to spin around slowly as he tucks. I'm feeling like Cinderella spinning in circles until the garment materializes as a saree for my hall debut.

"One thing I do know about draping: the women in my family gloat about only having to use a few safety pins to properly wrap a saree," he says.

"I can respect that. But Raja, safety pins are supposed to make you feel safe. I'm not feelin' that at all right now," I say matter-of-factly, walking and twisting around to see if any movement causes an issue. "This fabric looks like it's hanging on for dear life," I add, concern lines growing on my forehead.

"No, you look beautiful. Look at yourself," Raja says, leading me to the full-length mirror he has hanging on the wall next to his front door.

I check myself out. I've never had a reason to dress up in a saree, but the color is decadent, and the fabric feels soft on my skin. The simple gold sandals I brought are a great accessory to the rich navy-blue saree, gold blouse, glittery sapphire bangles, and jhumka earrings they gave me to match. Raja comes up and hugs me from behind, then kisses my cheek. He opted to wear a matching blue button-down, and seeing us hugged up in the mirror reminds me of a prom picture.

"The first time I saw you I pictured you in one of these. My imagination couldn't even do you justice."

I cheese hard. I opted for a natural look, trying to keep things simple since Raja didn't have much information to offer me; a nude lip and gold glitter eyeshadow to match my accessories. I snuggle deeper into his arms, feeling a strange sense of calm before the cyclone we must face.

"Remember, whatever happens today: it's me and you. It's always been." His pretty browns look at me through the mirror. "I got your back, okay, Deja?"

I nod, comforted. As he pulls his hand away, though, his sleeve gets caught on one of the beads, shifting the entire saree.

"Oh nooo!" I exclaim, and he greets my look of horror with one of his own.

Raja's reassurance is falling flat.

"That's it! I'm wearing a sundress and a shawl. I will not have a nip slip at the first family function I go to!" I say as I storm over to my tote, ready to pull out my backup outfit.

"Your blouse is the most secure thing you're wearing, so you'd probably be more likely to moon someone." I give Raja the look of death and he gets the hint. "Deja, it's fine! I promise!" Raja grabs his phone to make a call and Reya's face appears on the screen. "Rey, I put on my first saree. Ta-daaa!" Raja says, flailing his arms in the air while I awkwardly pose. "How does she look?"

"What?!" Reya asks, half laughing. There's chaos behind her as people are rushing around the house, scrambling to get to the venue in time. I'm sure when she anticipated all the things she had to do today, talking her brother-cousin through draping his first saree wasn't in the cards. She squints her eyes, and I can tell she senses something is off. "Raja, how many safety pins did you use?"

"Only three." He beams proudly.

"Maybe . . . you should use some more?" Reya kindly suggests.

He gives her an uneasy smile. "I don't have any more," he says, his eyes begging her not to embarrass him or reveal how catastrophic this could potentially be.

Reya just gives him a look and shakes her head. "Deja, you look beautiful."

"Thank you," I say, not sure what to do with my hands, afraid if the jewelry I'm wearing gets anywhere close to the garment the whole thing will unravel.

"Just some minor adjustments are needed," she continues. "Raja, come find me before you go into the hall. I'll fix her right up." Suddenly, Reya hears yelling in the background and she's barking orders like a wedding planner. "I have to go. Deja, you look lovely but make sure to find me, okay?" And her face disappears from the phone screen.

That can't be good.

Walking into the venue, I understand more why Raja and his family have been stressed. Your standard community center recreation hall has been turned into something much grander, with roses and linen lining the tables, gold fabric draped across white chairs, and a stage at the end of the hall, where Lakshmi and Akhil are placed for everyone to witness, with marigolds cascading behind them.

The hall has tables set up with gold tablecloths, positioned so that everyone has a clear view of the front of the room—which features the bride and groom sitting side by side, a table in front of them with a shrine of Ganesh, just like the tattoo Raja has imprinted on his arm, adorned with the same handmade rose garland currently draped around the couple. The table also includes metal trays of apples, oranges, bananas, candles, and a small metal teapot with a matching brass canister filled with grass and flowers.

"This is so nice," I whisper to Raja as we step inside, hand in hand. "What are they doing now?" I watch two older men stand near the bride and groom, one man who I assume to be the priest speaking in Nepali as the other grabs some red powder and yellow flower petals and sprinkles them over a tray, cupping the rest in his left hand.

"It looks like they're about to pray," Raja says, and on cue both gentlemen clasp their hands together and close their eyes. I stop walking and bow my head.

Raja glances at me as I honor their silence, eyes full of intrigue. "What are you doing?"

"Y'all don't stop when someone's praying?" I ask, whispering. Raja looks at me perplexed. "You know," I reiterate, "bow your head, close your eyes?"

"They'll be praying *all* day," he says, mirroring my voice's tempo.

"So y'all talk through it?" I reply in a hushed tone, then jokingly shake my head. "The disrespect."

He smirks. "Technically we aren't supposed to, but you try shushing an auntie," Raja speaks softly while the prayer continues. "Guaranteed to hear a slap to the back of the neck ricochet off these walls."

I cover my mouth with all my might to keep from laughing, but a weird sound still escapes my lips. A few people look in my direction, and I give Raja a proper stare down.

"I'm sorry, I'm sorry, I'm sorry," he whispers, suppressing his own chuckle. "I didn't think you'd laugh that hard."

"You should know by now I laugh hardest at your most inappropriate jokes," I whisper. He's glowing from that compliment. The prayer ends and the volume in the room goes up. "And what do the rose necklaces symbolize?"

"Oh, those are phool malas. It's supposed to be a symbol of, like, luck and blessings for the couple or something like that."

"Protect that at all costs. The last thing we need is to see a whole bunch of phool malas at Coachella. The new flower crown," I say. Raja is now covering his mouth with his fist to keep from laughing. "What is Nepal's national flower?" I ask.

"The rhododendron," he responds, and I nod. "But marigolds are considered our culture's festive flower." It's nice to see my genuine reaction to everything is amusing to him.

"I'm serious," I reply. "This is gorgeous. And it's not even the wedding."

He looks at me with a half smile. "This is *nothing* compared to an actual wedding. But yeah, we don't half-ass it with the decorations. Considering how much I had to help, I wish we did. My back hurts from the amount of trips I've taken the last few days."

I giggle and squeeze his hand, noticing dark circles forming around his eyes. "You didn't sleep much either, did you?"

"No," he says, touching the skin around his eyes. "My eyes telling on me again?" I nod. "Yeah, I had to drop something off at Gandira auntie's house and then got caught staying there for more projects. By the time I got home it was three, and by then I kept tossing until my alarm went off."

I squeeze his hand a little more, my optimism returning. "Things are gonna be okay today, Raja, *we* are gonna be okay."

"I hope you're right," Raja says, a slight look of defeat on his face.

Which makes me think Raja isn't being totally honest with me. He knows something that he's shielding me from. There's a part of me that wants to demand he tell me what's actually going on, but I also realize this isn't my world. I don't know what's happened behind the scenes, or what's been done to keep the peace. I've been invited to an event by a bride who is also facing backlash of her own, and so my presence must only add to the larger discussion of parent/child obedience.

Respecting your elders.

Raja introduces me to relatives and distant cousins and friends of friends and cousins he hasn't seen in years who came from Nepal, and I watch him try to recall the names of people he's met near and far, to call upon his native tongue when speaking to certain elders, and still try to check in with me along the way. He's a different person and the same person all at once—I'm watching a man who's only spoken English to me since I've known him listen to a language foreign to my own ears, answering in English, and when there's a misunderstanding, answering in broken Nepali. The best is watching him when he finds the perfect blend of both his worlds, when he cracks a joke that both a family member and I can understand, a way to bridge.

But for as much as Raja tries to do, there are just certain things we have to accept. When they talk to him in Nepali or speak to their own personal lives, I try to engage as best as I can, and when I cannot, I watch the ceremony. I watch Lakshmi and Akhil's families come up bit by bit, dropping powder and herbs into their hands, and I want to ask Raja what's happening, but he's catching up with family he hasn't seen in decades, as well as introducing them to his new . . . girl? He doesn't exactly say girlfriend when he introduces me, but just introduces me as Deja, his keti. Which seems to be statement enough in this case, since bringing me was an act of rebellion in itself—or at least I think? I try to remember that being here means I'm his girlfriend in their eyes, even if he doesn't say it out loud. Still, his not saying the word unsettles me.

My plan to conquer the day initially was to never leave Raja's sight, but that plan dissolved almost as quickly as it began because suddenly Raja is being pulled in many directions to assist with last-minute things. He does the best he can by either taking me with him or dumping me on a cousin I met and asking them to look after me, which they do without question, but everyone's busy. I'm *his* date.

Everyone's sweet, but even in a room full of vibrancy, I still feel like the most exposed, and invisible at the same time. I want to be taken seriously here by his family, just like I'm sure Raja will want to be taken seriously by mine at the family reunion.

But every time I look around, I catch someone either staring at me or quickly turning their head elsewhere when our eyes meet. Some of the aunties and uncles are staring with a smile at least, until it becomes clear that most of the family members doing the smiling are on Raja's side, and Akhil's family is giving me the cold shoulder. But then half of Raja's family is giving Akhil's family the cold shoulder because of how they feel about them. The irony in all this suddenly causes tension in my head. A migraine is the last thing I need.

I excuse myself from a conversation with Bina and a cousin I've never met when I spot Rani and her parents a few feet away and Rani waves at me. I take it as a cue to go over and say hi, but when I go over and give Rani a hug, both parents suddenly see someone they "must" talk to and jet off. I stand there a little dazed as Mrs. Sharma gives a quick apology, then gives my arm a loving tap to soften the blow as she follows her husband.

Rani looks at me in disbelief. "I'm sorry," she half whispers, embarrassment spreading across her face.

I shake my head quickly, trying to ease the awkwardness we're both feeling. If I attempt to process my emotions in real time, I'm liable to get agitated and direct it toward someone. "It's fine, Raja told me to try not to take these things personally." I smile through gritted teeth. "So I'm *tryiiiing*." I exhale.

Rani sighs as well and is about to say something else when two older women pop up.

"Hi," a middle-aged woman says, and I wave back, hyper aware of the noise my jewelry makes for the first time.

"We hear you make skin creams?" the second lady asks, and I nod with excitement.

"Yes," I say. "I'm on Etsy! My shop is Queenskincare with a number one instead of an *I*...."

"Do you sell bleaching cream?" she asks.

I stand there, a statue. Rani looks equally disturbed. "No," Rani and I both say in unison, my voice flat, Rani's curt. Unsure where to go from there. The awkward silence doesn't bother the women, though, who simply shrug and walk away.

Rani's eyes follow them. "I've never liked her."

I look at Rani in shock . . . and awe. For a girl as sweet as a rose, she doesn't strike me as someone who doesn't like people just because.

"What did she do to you?" I ask her, feeling a deeper kinship forming between us.

Already knowing what will come out of her mouth. The same things Queen and I faced.

"You see her makeup?" she asks.

"Yeah," I say, "foundation is a little lighter than it should be."

"A *little*?" Rani half smirks, an exasperated sound coming out her mouth. "Every event, every time I see her, she tells me I should start using bleaching cream if I want my complexion to look like hers one day, if I want to attract a husband. We used to be the same color," she says, looking at her arm. "Look, you can even tell with her neck." I glance at the back of her neck, visible with her hair pulled up in a clip. She definitely skipped the foundation there. "She told me I won't find a man if my skin gets any darker."

"The regular," I reply, thankful she didn't say anything about my complexion, or I might not have exhibited the same grace. But immediately afterward, I feel nothing but sadness for the lady. What would things have looked like for her if she had a granny like Queen? A wave of gratitude washes over me, thankful to have had a woman strong enough to withstand any societal pressures, who didn't need validation from a world that defined beauty by colonial standards. Queen knew she was divine and had no problem challenging anyone who tried to tell her different. We both look at each other with the same hurt faces, the same look of empathy. "That's not your people, is it?"

"A very distant relative, thank God," she says.

"I don't know why they would ask if I make bleaching cream, 'cause clearly I ain't using it." We both chuckle, and then I sigh.

"I'm sorry you had to be subjected to that," Rani says. All I can think of is how great a therapist she'll be. Maybe she can help girls like us realize their beauty and power early on too.

"I'm sorry we all are. Every culture deals with this. I want to say it doesn't make sense, but honestly it makes all the sense in the world. We know where it stems from."

"I wish it didn't," she replies.

I suddenly feel exhausted and point to a table nearby. "Do you think it's all right if I sit here? I'm starting to get a headache."

Rani nods eagerly. "Sure! Let me also get you some water. And some Tylenol?" I nod, and she rushes off to find a water bottle for me. I want to remind her how unlucky she'll probably be, seeing as Raja was tasked to buy more water twenty minutes ago, but instead I rub my temples as I continue to watch the ceremony. Lakshmi's parents light candles, and then there's more praying. Lakshmi looks opulent in a gold embroidered saree with a stunning crescent-moonlike emblem draped over her forehead, and I can't help but envision me and Raja up there instead, can't help wondering if we'll ever get past today—the stares, the awkwardness—and finally have acceptance. If we're ever acknowledged, would it happen in time, or would I have to wait until a day like this, years down the line, when the engagement ceremony is happening and the family has no choice but to accept us whether they want to or not?

It makes my nerves crank up and I catch myself picking at the sequins on the saree I'm wearing, suddenly remembering this isn't even my outfit. Nothing about that option sounds appealing, and the more I try to imagine me and Raja sitting on the makeshift stage, the less I can see it.

It's all too much, and suddenly I have the urge to go to the restroom, but when I get to the bathroom and close the stall door, I'm damn near ready to cry. How the heck do I pee in this beautiful outfit without messing it up? I hike up the fabric and underskirt as much as I can, and after I finish relieving myself, I'm feeling accomplished until I step to the sink and the heel of my sandal gets caught on the fabric. With my hands wet, my saree is unraveling before my eyes and I stand frozen, unable to figure out what to do next.

As if a guardian angel heard my prayers, I hear murmurs and run to the nearest stall, until I recognize one of the voices.

"Reya? Is that you?" I call out from the stall.

"What's wrong, Deja? You okay?" she asks, immediately hearing my panicked state. I come out and hold my half-undone saree in my hands.

Reya goes into full Olivia Pope mode. "It's an easy fix. Here." She opens her purse like a doctor opening a medical bag and places safety pins in my hand. "Now, make sure these are open and hand them to me one at a time when I ask, okay?"

I comply, twirling around as she and her cousins speak in

Nepali, adjusting the fabric, following orders to pass another safety pin when asked.

"Raja set you up for failure," she says, amused.

"I should have found you sooner, but I knew you were busy," I reply.

The familiarity makes me feel lighter—I watch in the bathroom mirror as Naima and Bina follow Reya's lead and pull out the long, glittery garment in haste, wrapping it tightly around my body this time as they pin so delicately, pleating and repleating the bottom of my saree skirt until it's just right.

"I told him it wasn't fastened enough," I mumble.

"Men," Bina says dryly, and we all howl laughing.

I feel like I'm back home again, my seven-year-old self being thrown into a chair while Mama and her two sisters take turns braiding my hair for the school year so she wouldn't have to worry about doing it while she worked.

I play around with the bangles they let me borrow to calm my nerves, and Reya looks up at me and smiles. "I do the same when I'm nervous," she says. "My wedding day was the worst. All my wedding pictures look like I wouldn't let go of my wrist, but the bangles gave me comfort." I smile, thinking of the conversation Rani and I had about Reya. I spotted her with her husband, and you wouldn't know she was nervous then by the way they interact now. They seem like such a good match.

"What's the paper on the safety pin for?" I ask, attempting to get out of my own head.

"To prevent the saree from pulling or tearing," Reya responds, a safety pin at the side of her mouth as she readjusts one part of the saree.

"Got it, though I don't think your cousin did." I chuckle to myself, and Reya looks up at me, laughing.

"He absolutely didn't. Welcome to being with Raja. We had no choice in the matter, but you did," Reya says, our laughter filling the bathroom.

After a few more minutes of pulling and tightening, she finally gets up from crouching. How she's able to kneel and move in her own saree is beyond my comprehension. "Okay, walk around so we can make sure you're okay."

I strut like I'm a model on a runway, trying to give myself a boost of confidence and filling the bathroom with laughter.

"You look gorgeous," she says, standing back, all three cousins admiring their work like they solved the crime of the century. "We've put so many reinforcements on your saree that there's no risk of you mooning anyone again." We all giggle.

"Thank you," I say, giving them all a hug. "It may seem silly to you, but if you hadn't walked in, I might have stayed in the stall for the rest of the event."

"It can be overwhelming," Reya says, and I nod.

"When I imagined coming today, I didn't think I'd have to do so much of it alone. But I get it, you all have responsibilities," I say, playing with my coils. "I just . . . I don't know what to do with myself or where to be or who to talk to."

"I'm sorry," Reya says. "We all just went right into our roles, not thinking we'd brought an entirely new dynamic into the picture."

"Yeah, I thought I was doing fine until the idea of showing my ass to half the wedding party came into play. Then I felt it all at once." The cousins chuckle.

Bina steps up. "Well, when I saw you in here, it was obvious you were scared, but out there? I can't tell you're nervous or scared or anything. And you walk in this saree like you've been walking in them your whole life!"

"Please," I say, "did you see what just happened?"

"Deja," Bina says. "Raja put on your saree. Our Raja. God bless, but he should have planned better for you."

"Tell me about it," I mumble, and Reya practically screams when Rani busts open the bathroom door like the police.

"There you are," she says, out of breath. "I got you some water . . . and Tylenol . . . and Raja's back. . . ." She hands me the water, fully gassed. "He's got more at the table."

I laugh. "Rani, you've been looking for water this entire time?"

She nods. "I had to plead with an auntie to give me one, but then I couldn't find you and I freaked out. I had one responsibility," she says.

"I got everybody stressed today," I say, leaning against the bathroom wall. None of us are ready to go back outside just yet. "Especially Raja. I feel like he might be regretting this." Rani and Reya try to reassure me that isn't the case. My phone pings, and I open it to see a message from Raja.

Did you abandon ship? Too much?

I smile.

ME: No, just hiding out in the bathroom. I almost exposed myself to the room.
RAJA: I am SO sorry. If it makes you feel better, you wouldn't be the first.

I laugh, feeling better about going back outside to enjoy the rest of the event.

We all disperse from the bathroom, and Rani, Reya, and I find Raja at a table near the entrance, four water bottles in tow. "I almost had to smuggle these in Rani's suruwal," he says, and Rani and I laugh.

"I had trouble . . . using the restroom," I half whisper, and Reya and Rani giggle a little too hard.

"Why did they put you in a kurta as your first outfit?" Reya says, looking at Raja.

"What? She said she was excited to wear a saree! I couldn't let her down!" Raja says, defending himself.

"I would have been happy wearing that. I just didn't know it was an option . . . or that it might be best to start me off slow. But he's right, my excitement was real," I reveal.

"It suits you so well," Rani says. "Aama usually wraps my saree, but I've been avoiding her and opted for the easy route today." I make a mental note to ask Raja why Rani might be dodging their mom. Raja and Rani exchange a look, and then he excuses himself while I continue to hang with Rani and a few cousins, coming back more tense than he did the last time he left.

I get up from the table and meet him halfway. "You okay?" I ask, approaching him.

It almost looks like there's steam rising from his head, he's so irate. "I asked Aama if they saw you, and she said they tried to speak but had someone else to talk to, so they made it quick. And my dad is just ignoring me." He comes in closer. "I thought you said you'd be honest if they were disrespectful?

Is this why you've been hiding in public restrooms?"

"I didn't know how to take it. Your mom said something in passing, and your dad is avoiding me altogether. It wasn't really disrespectful but more . . ."

"Passive aggressive?" he asks, and I nod, slowly. Raja's jaw goes tight and his eyes have grown cold. He's furious in a way I've never seen before. I guess the hunch I had about Rani staying away from their mom also tipped Raja off, which is why he suddenly excused himself. He needed to find out for himself.

Both the bride and the groom have red splotches on their foreheads, and I watch as people go up to place more on the same spot, the red dye spreading across their foreheads like jam on toast. I quickly try to change the subject. "What are they doing now?"

"Families are coming up now to bless the bride and groom with the tika," he responds. Voice stale. Bitter, even. "So both families go up and make promises to one another and to the bride and groom or give them well wishes, but basically this is usually when the bride and groom meet for the first time and both families approve of the marriage. Since they aren't arranged, this is like the tika-tala remixed; everyone is welcoming one another to the family. We usually do tika for big celebrations like weddings, or Dashain, which is like our Nepali version of Christmas. Stuff like that."

Now I see why I hear a trace of resentment. This is the part where the families accept each other. Maybe we were too naïve to hope all the acceptance in the air would rub off on his parents. "So what happens after this?"

"They call families up to take pictures one at a time, then move on to the next group."

I quickly scan the room, then whisper, "But it's a lot of people here."

He giggles. "This happens at the wedding, too."

"But don't, like . . . *hunnndreds* of people attend?" I ask, and Raja nods emphatically. "That sounds exhausting."

"There's nothing similar in your culture?"

I think for a second. "I mean, outside of a photo booth, no. We just go up to the bride and groom and take a selfie, but there's just not a dedicated time for it."

"Oh, we'd riot," Raja says, and I chuckle.

We both sigh, processing the day but happy to be back around each other. I wrap my arm around his and lean on his shoulder, hoping this isn't too much affection in front of his elders and also not giving a damn. He looks down at me and smiles, placing his hand over mine.

I didn't anticipate today feeling like such a solo effort, but I'm also proud of myself for the way I handled everything, and appreciative to the women in Raja's life for having my back when I almost experienced a catastrophe. And in spite of everything that happened (or didn't happen), having Raja be the one to weather this storm with makes it all worthwhile.

# CHAPTER THIRTY-FIVE

## Raja

It's been almost a month since I've had a real conversation with my dad, two weeks since the tika-tala, and no resolution.

I also haven't had the heart to tell Deja how my parents tried to set me up with Bhumi. I've been trying to find the courage to tell her, and after the tika-tala I knew it was even more important, but seeing her freak out about her own family after we loaded up my car this morning made me think that adding my family drama on top of it wouldn't help. Not right now.

And from the way she talks about her family's own cultural pride, I'm sure her parents wanted her to be bringing a Black guy to the family reunion just as much as my parents would want me to, well, let them pick my wife.

Lucky for me, between the shop and the group chat of high school friends that has somehow survived the summer even though we're in different places across the country (which I think is code for we miss one another), I got some great advice going into this weekend. The main point? *Whatever you do, be up-front with her dad about your intentions with his daughter, tell him what makes her so special to you, and above all else, always show respect.*

*But don't be no punk either.*

Oh, and the biggest piece of advice from everyone: *Don't be racist,* or I'll officially be uninvited to the cookout (aka the group chat).

*Got it,* I told them.

Pretty solid advice, but that wouldn't matter if I didn't get some advice from the source, Deja. This is her family after all.

"Tell me everything. What should I do to impress your family? How do I show signs of respect?"

Deja looks over at me and smiles sweetly. "Sorry, I'm all in my head."

"It's okay," I say, still driving. "Instead of being in your head, just think out loud. I may not have the answer, but sometimes talking it out helps. Plus, I need you to talk, Deja. We still got three more hours to go."

She laughs. "Okay, hmm, what can I teach you? Umm . . . ," she responds, still in her head.

"Ways to show a sign of respect," I remind her. "Like, in my culture, you address the elders with prayer hands and bow to their feet when you see them. Well, depends on the person but . . . I'll teach you that another time."

"Oh, yeah, right," she says, popping her knuckles.

I wait patiently for whatever advice she might have. Right now, at this moment in my life, I feel the most like myself that I've ever felt. I've finally confronted everything I've been too afraid to face until this summer—my independence, my college major, and the most pleasant surprise, going to battle for the person beside me in the passenger seat.

Deja's my girl now. This, all this, could be forever.

At least I have to fight for it like it could be.

It's new and scary and my life is in complete upheaval, yet I feel okay because I'm in a relationship with an amazing woman who is so sincere and pushes herself and doesn't need anyone *but* herself. And I somehow managed to convince her to *want* to be my girl.

"Raja, did you hear me?" Deja says.

"I'm sorry, you just look cute," I respond.

"How superficial," she snickers, rolling her eyes. She's biting on the drawstring of one of my UMD hoodies, wearing frayed shorts with her leg propped up. I should kindly remind her that the hoodie she is wearing is indeed *my* hoodie and I'd love it if she didn't damage my property . . . but she looks so stressed and cute, I can't imagine bringing up anything else right now.

"To the elders, you address them as sir and ma'am. So, like, 'yes, sir' if they call your name or 'no, ma'am' if they ask you something that you don't know."

"Okay, got it, easy one," I say.

"Yeah, about that," Deja says. "Can you explain a bhai versus a didi versus a thulo buwa?"

I start laughing and Deja gives me the side-eye. "What's so funny! I said it right. I know I did 'cause I quadruple-checked and copied the pronunciation and everything!"

"No, you said it perfectly," I say. "But you just asked me what a younger brother was versus an older sister versus an older uncle and I realize . . . this can get complicated."

"Oh! So for an uncle, it's not just Uncle James, it's my middle Uncle James versus my older Uncle Rodney versus my baby Uncle Lonny?" she asks, exasperated.

I nod my head. "You got it!"

Deja touches my arm. "Yeah, one thing at a time. How about I try to learn that on the drive back."

I chuckle. "Deal. So next question. How does one determine who is considered an elder?"

Deja takes a swig of water. "'Cause Black people age so well?"

"Look, I'm trying not to generalize. But I have seen some of your relatives in pictures you're tagged in. And I can't help but conclude that there might be a tiny bit of validity to the statement 'Black don't crack, and brown don't frown.'"

Deja practically chokes on her water. "Raja, I say this with love." She gets out, one hand on her chest and the other holding her open water bottle. "But like Queen used to say, you need Jesus."

"I've had both of my parents call on the gods in my name so it's nothing new." I shrug, arms on the wheel.

Deja begins to rub her temples. "My head hurts from laughing so much. Thank you."

"I know we just got together like a week ago," I jokingly say, "but I'll do anything for you, Deja Martin."

"Anything?" she asks, fluttering her eyelashes extra hard.

I chuckle, knowing I have a goofy smile on my face. "Anything."

"If things get tense, do this," she requests.

"Do what?" I ask.

"Be yourself. Show them why I'm so into you. I promise if you do that, they'll love you." She smiles and touches my leg. I feel like electrodes have just zapped my body. I'm happy I'm sitting or my knees would have all the way buckled.

There's so much I plan to tell her when we drive back up. That she'd be proud of me because I stood up to my parents about my degree. That I'm not talking to them, and I feel like my own man for standing up for what's right, and that gives me so much freedom. I feel invincible right now, and she has a lot to do with it.

# CHAPTER THIRTY-SIX

## Deja

Raja and I have the best time driving down I-95 South, listening to a few more SoundCloud DJs we both like, playing some question games I found to be good for road trips—anything to help with the long drive and my rising anxiety. He refused to let me drive his car down, saying he didn't want me any more stressed than I already was. I was grateful, 'cause it felt nice to let the gentle, southern wind creep into the car and wisp through my hair and face, the smell of cut grass mixed with a little cow manure, the Confederate flags slapping this country's history in our faces, the red wood barns and windmills we pass along the way—the many reminders of the things I love about home, and the things that cause me angst and anger. One month away and so much has changed me already, including the guy I chose to bring home.

But it's not my distant relatives I'm worried about, 'cause I have no problem checking anyone for my man; my siblings are going to love him and I know it. There's just one person I'm not so sure about.

My poppa.

I've tried to call him since Diamond invited Raja to the family reunion, but he still won't answer. He's supposed to be an adult here, and avoiding me is not something a father should do, especially if he's so concerned about his daughter's well-being.

He and Raja's dad are alike in one way for sure—they're stuck in their ways and take a long while to come around. Like he grilled my ex, I suspect he'll do the same to Raja and then pull me to the side to ask me if *I'm sure about this guy*. This weekend will consist of many tests to see if Raja has what it takes.

Raja's father is different. He doesn't know me; he doesn't know my family. He doesn't know if he can trust the American way. We are all taught to stay in our communities, keep one another safe. But is Raja's dad looking at my family extra critically 'cause of the color of our skin? Would he be as skeptical if I were white? And will my dad have his own preconceived notions about Raja's family or how he thinks they're treating me? Even if I can have a bit more sympathy for the ways Raja's father thinks, my dad couldn't care less. I'm his baby and I deserve to be treated right.

I consider all these things the last thirty minutes of our trip, when I tell Raja it's my turn to take the wheel and wind through these back roads like Raja drives in DC, because the roads twist and turn and can get confusing for those who've never gotten to know them intimately. I know these roads like a bird migrating for the winter; once I get off the highway and make a right at the first stop sign, I punch the gas, my body instinctively knowing each turn before I make it. Raja silently watches me in the passenger seat, impressed.

"Your dad drives for NASCAR?" Raja asked.

I laugh. "No, but he's been putting me on these roads without a license since I was a youngin."

"Deja, honey. Why are you so stressed?" my mom asks, taking me out of my thoughts and rubbing the back of my head like she did when I was a little girl.

"What do you mean why am I stressed? Uncle Roger is coming and you literally overheard him saying he doesn't know 'where the hell Nepal is,'" I reply, suds forming as I wash another plate.

"I mean, you know he doesn't know a ton of geography. And to be honest I had to look it up too," my mom says, and shrugs.

I fold, her head rub beginning to soothe me. "That's not the point. It's *how* he said it. I don't need family coming off rude just 'cause they don't understand certain things."

"Baby, that's not just our family, that's every family," my mama says, and I look out the kitchen window and watch my dad teaching Raja how to feed the chickens. As soon as we got in, my parents said their quick hellos and put us to work. Mama needed help in the kitchen and my dad had all the outdoor chores, but instead of opting for the outdoors like I usually do, I stayed inside with Mama to give Poppa and Raja much-needed quality time. Raja told me to throw him to the wolves. I would say I hope he's ready, but it looks like he's already rising to the occasion. He's smiling and charming my dad with stories of

Maryland, and I catch my dad smirking occasionally, though those cold eyes don't waver much. There's skepticism all over his face.

"That's okay, once he tastes tonight's dinner, he won't care who's saying what."

"That's how that works?" I ask, amused.

My mom shrugs. "When you've seen what I've seen, anything is possible. Breaking bread can bring people together, especially when Auntie Bertha brings her cakes." My mouth salivates just thinking about it, and Mama points to the sink. "Now finish those dishes so they're dried up by the time guests come."

"Yes, ma'am," I say, and salute.

She laughs. "It's good to have you home, Sunflower." She hugs me from behind. "Doesn't matter how many kids live here, when one leaves for good it always feels like a puzzle piece goes missing."

"Mama . . . ," I respond, feeling guilt.

"It's okay, we're resilient. We findin' ways to make it work. That's just life, we all have those feelings and whether they're temporary or permanent, we have to find ways to move along. Just like we did with your granny."

"Yeah, Queen's a hard one," I say, seeing her in every bit of this house, the grief washing back over me as memories pop up.

"Losing the glue that holds the family together is always the hardest." Mama sighs as she holds me still and lays her head on my back. "I think it's also why your dad took your move to Maryland so hard. He felt like he lost his mom, then his daughter."

I let out an exasperated sigh. "That's a lot of pressure...."

"I know, I know," my mom reassures me. "I'm not saying it's right. It's just what it is, baby."

I never thought to ask her about this thing she's been planning for a while now, the first family reunion in three years. We stopped doing them after Queen got sick. She must feel so much pressure herself to get this right. "You nervous about this weekend?" I ask her.

She pulls away from my back and stands next to me. "Can you tell?" I nod and she laughs. "I just . . . I just want this to go well. You know? The family has been so distant ever since Queen died, and she wouldn't want it this way. I thought with the anniversary and all, it would be good to get your dad's family together again."

"I think it's brilliant," I say. "But even if something comes up, that's no reflection of the amazing weekend you planned. Their own family trauma has nothing to do with you."

She nods. "We can be a wreck together."

"Thanks, Ma," I say dryly as she laughs. I go to scrub a pot out of frustration.

She rubs my back. "I'm sorry, it will be fine."

"I need you. If someone is being ridiculous, can you step in, please? Or I might be disrespecting some elders this weekend."

"Deja Martin, you know better!" my mom says, giving me a look of fake disappointment, but she also nearly chuckles. "Promise me you won't be disrespectful?"

"Yes, ma'am. I promise I won't be disrespectful . . . as long as no one is disrespectful to Raj."

She smiles, shaking her head. "That's my girl, you protect

the one you"—I give my mom a look like, *not yet*—"like a lot," she says instead, and I laugh. She squeezes my shoulders. "I already like him. I see him out there trying to impress your dad. He's genuine." I blush, thankful for the validation. She winks as she walks out of the kitchen. "And can you take the laundry off the line!" she shouts as she walks farther away.

I'm definitely home.

I stare back out the window at the garments swaying in the breeze and catch wind of some of the conversation Raja and my dad are having now that things are quiet and they've moved closer to the house.

"Mr. Martin, where do you want me to put these crates of eggs?" Raja asks, a little gassed.

City boy isn't used to this farm work.

My dad points over to our old dining room table by the car porch, which has now become his outdoor table. "Set everything on that wooden table over there. Phylicia will tell us where to put 'em. We got so much food packed in this fridge, I reckon she don't even know where to put it."

"Yes, sir," Raja says.

My dad creases his forehead, the condemnation still there with a hint of regard. As he goes to get a broom to sweep the side of the house, he looks over in the window and I give him a quick smile before I go back to washing dishes. When I look back up a few seconds later, Raja is back and grabbing a second broom to help out.

"Why don't you go sweep the car porch," Poppa requests, and Raja is on it, walking to the side of the house and whistling while he makes his way over.

My dad looks annoyed, which amuses me. He's a stickler for hard work, and Raja came with his game face on—ready to outwork my father. Dude didn't even change his Js, and with my brother Darius being a sneakerhead I *know* my dad knows how serious that is. He just looks at Raja dumbfounded as he walks away, probably perplexed at how quickly he's starting to like him, even if he doesn't want to. Welcome to the club, Pops.

I'm pulling clothes off the clothesline when Raja finds his way over to me. "My dad working you hard?" I ask, going down our line.

"This is light work," he replies, perspiration dripping off his face.

I laugh. "I don't know, you were looking a little tired . . . and moist," I respond, touching his damp white T-shirt.

"And I'm sweating balls, but at least the natural deodorant you gave me is working." He eyes the big basket of laundry I'm filling up. "No dryer in your house?"

"Yes!" I snap. "My mom says sun-dried clothes are better. Tell that to my favorite purple shirt that got sun damaged when I was thirteen. I started paying my parents to use the dryer every week."

Raja laughs. "Bartering systems are the only way."

I chuckle. "Seriously. Eventually I just started making soaps and stuff in the house and that was my payment. There were just rules for how often I could use it." Raja has a goofy smile on his face as he helps me take down clothes. "What?!" I ask.

"It's cool seeing where you grew up, your roots. I don't know, I feel connected here . . . with you."

"One with Mother Earth?" I ask.

He chuckles. "Yeah, something like that. I fed some chickens, got run down by a rooster, and now I'm helping you take down laundry. This feels so much like Nepal it's not even funny."

"I mean, not all of North Carolina is like this. My family is just a little more country."

"Same! We moved Baba to Kathmandu, and he thought he'd made it. Village boy moves to the city and gets to live like royalty."

I laugh. "That's really cute."

"But his best memories were stories of the village." He stops and looks at me. "It's kinda what you're doing. You're just exploring life and making new memories, but home will always be home."

"Amen," I say. "Is that why you stayed close for school?"

"Yeah, I'm tethered to it," he says. "Some of my friends tried to convince me to at least go one state away, but I just know. I want to be home-based. I mean, look at me, my family"—he stops suddenly, like he's withholding something—"barely talk to me day-to-day, and I still want to be close to them." He ends that sentence with almost a question mark, hoping I didn't catch the change in his voice's cadence.

I stop pulling clothes from the line and stare him down. "Raja, is there something you need to tell me?"

A loud sigh escapes his lips. "Dej, I had a . . ."

"Well, look who brought they tail back down south!" a loud voice behind me booms. Auntie Melissa, Dad's younger sister, comes sashaying her way to us, too eager to push me aside so that she can meet this South Asian man Deja's been dating that's the talk of our family chats. I have no idea what questions are about to come out of her mouth.

"Good to see you, Auntie Melissa," I say, giving her a big bear hug.

Auntie Melissa is my newly reformed, born-again aunt. A few years ago Diamond and I caught her in a local club Diamond was able to sneak me into. Auntie Melissa didn't seem to be too shocked we were there, but boy, were we shocked she was, especially all dolled up in a skintight jumpsuit that showed every single curve of her body. She swore to us she wouldn't tell if we wouldn't, then convinced her date (a former linebacker) to buy us shots, and they were off into the night before we could blink.

Now she's a devout Christian woman who works tirelessly in the church as a Sunday school teacher. But every once in a while, Diamond and I like to pry about her past . . . transgressions. She likes to say she tells us as a cautionary tale, but I honestly think Auntie Melissa wants to relive some of her wilder moments by telling us, because who doesn't love a good story?

"You too! Now introduce me to this"—she looks Raja up and down—"cute man, I must say!" she responds, practically pushing me out the way.

Raja steps up to the challenge. "Very nice to meet you. I'm Raja," he says.

"I know who you are," she responds, going in for a hug. She pulls away and gives him another look down. "Nice to meet you!"

"Deja said I should call people 'sir' or 'ma'am,' but does that apply to the youngest auntie too? You seem closer to Diamond's age."

He's doing *too* much.

"Oh, hush your mouth!" she giggles, giving Raja a love tap. "I am actually not the youngest auntie."

"Really?" Raja responds in shock. Internally I'm shaking my head, 'cause he and I literally went through my dad's sibling list in the car and his memory is so good that by the time we were done, he remembered names, where they lived, their children, and what they did for a living. Now suddenly he's an actor.

"What a charmer!" Auntie Melissa says, looking over at me and cheesing super hard. "Call me 'ma'am' so no one else thinks you're being disrespectful, but when it's just us, please don't. It makes me feel soooo old."

"Yes, ma . . . Auntie Melissa," Raja says. Auntie Melissa and I both laugh.

"At least you're already programmed to do it," I tell him, rubbing his shoulder. Auntie Melissa looks at us in wonder, and I'm glad he met her first. She's buttering him up for the storm that's brewing, because once Dad's brothers get here, I'm not sure what's liable to happen.

More of the family trickle in to stop by and pay us a visit before heading to stay with someone in the area or at a hotel downtown. Since it's Thursday and the festivities don't kick off until tomorrow, Raja is meeting our closer relatives tonight, which in some ways eases him in, but in other ways it's a very intimate space, which means more chances for snide comments to happen.

"Well, I'll be damned! Deja done moved to Chocolate City and found her a Muslim man."

Like that one.

I've just finished putting sheets on Jr.'s bed since his room has become a guest room this weekend. He's been ordered to sleep in the living room with the rest of the boys, but I have a suspicion my dad is having him sleep in the living room with Raja to watch us. Raja is also helping in the room, struggling to put a fitted sheet on the other bed. Based on the voice, I already know Uncle Lonny is at the door, but I turn around to see my dad; his other brother, Uncle Rodney; Jr.; *and* Deandre right in the doorway. Big, brawly men, coupled with my scrawny-ass brother Deandre sizing Raja up. I look to Raja with wide eyes, but the look he gives me back is like he's up to no good.

"No disrespect, sir, but I'm a different type of brown. My family is Hindu, but all love for my Muslim homies."

This man didn't miss a *BEAT*. My eyes dart from Raja to the entryway, afraid of what might happen next, prepared to throw my body in front of Raja if I need to. The dramatics of it all.

There's half a second of silence, and then Uncle Rodney chuckles. "He got some fire, I like it," he says. And just like that, it's over.

Uncle Rodney shakes his hand, and Jr. walks up to Raja next, giving him a dap to introduce himself as *my* big little brother. He's not standoffish like my dad, but he's still scoping him out. "I noticed your shoes earlier. Nice kicks," he tells Raja.

Raja smiles. "Thank you."

My dad is leaning on the doorframe. "Ya mama and sister is lookin' for y'all," he gets out, voice slightly flat.

"Thank you, sir," Raja says, nodding his head out of respect.

My dad faintly does the same and taps Uncle Lonny's shoulder before walking down the hall.

Uncle Lonny trails behind, and Jr. excuses himself to stay in allegiance with my dad (Deandre following them both) as Uncle Rodney continues to engage with Raja. For a beat I notice Raja looking at the doorway, sort of solemn, but he goes back to talking to Rodney for as long as he'll let him. I don't stop them, if Uncle Rodney's inappropriate self is taking to Raja, then I'm going to milk it, I could use his loud-ass mouth to advocate for him.

Someone needs to talk some sense into my dad because I'm not happy with him right now. Now Raja's anger at his parents' house and the tika-tala becomes all the more clear.

"It didn't feel like my dad was judging you?" I ask Raja later, swinging on the front-porch swing, dusk creeping across the sky. The night ended early with everyone exhausted from travel, and after Diamond shooed us out the kitchen when we offered to help clean (and after Auntie Bertha gave Raja another massive helping of German chocolate cake), I took Raja to my favorite spot. "I thought I heard him tell you to sweep the car porch?"

"He did. I swept the front porch too," he says, leaning back against the red swing like he leaned against his red couch the night of his housewarming.

I laugh. "Overachiever."

"Look, if your dad likes a hard worker," he says, using his fork to point for emphasis, "then I'm gonna be the hardest-working man for the next few days. And then go home and pass out from exhaustion."

He's so annoying. "You did a great job sweeping, by the way. Queen would throw this in my face if she were here."

"Why?" he asks.

"'Cause. I hated sweeping the porch. It was my protest." He chuckles, his cheeks full. "Whatever! We all have them," I declare.

"You think judgmental eyes scare me? I thrive on it," Raja says, licking his fork and then looking at it. "Auntie Bertha could cure world hunger with this recipe. This cake is so fire."

I smile. "Wait till you try her red velvet tomorrow. Also, I can't believe you kept your Js on!"

"I know! I had some crappy shoes in the car, but I didn't want to change into them. First impressions are everything."

"Yeah, my brother seemed to warm up to you a little more at dinner, so it was a smart tactic. Although he did tell me you were a dumbass for wearing those out back."

Raja laughs. "Can you ask your brother if he could help me out, then, and let me borrow some sneaker cleaner?" He looks stressed, which makes me chuckle.

It's getting late, and most of the house is winding down, so I know eventually we'll be called in to go to sleep. We're already not on the best terms, and the last thing I need is for my dad to embarrass me in front of Raja, so I let Raja know it's probably best to call it a night.

He follows me into the living room and I help him make his bed, my brothers and cousins already passed out from an active day.

"You want me to stay out here a bit longer?" I ask once the cot is made.

"Hell no," Raja whispers. "I'd like to make it back to Maryland in one piece, thank you very much." I smile, and he grabs a hand to kiss it. "Just in case they got cameras scoping us out. Night, Deja."

I chuckle. "Night, Raja."

One thing's for certain: Raja respects all the unspoken rules in this house, including not having the option to sleep in the same bed as me in the presence of family. A man with values, something my poppa should appreciate.

# CHAPTER THIRTY-SEVEN

## Raja

It's bright and early Friday morning and my stomach wakes me up to the smells of bacon and the sizzling of a pot.

Deandre starts laughing. "Man, is that your stomach?" he asks me. Darius and I are on the two couches, and Deandre and their other cousins Mason and Landon are on the floor; one's around his age and the other cousin is in middle school.

"It is," I say chuckling. They start the roasting bright and early in this house, I see.

"You eat cheese grits and biscuits?" Mason asks, and I nod.

"Mas, stop being ignorant. They serve grits at IHOP!" Darius says. Is he . . . beginning to come over to his sister's side?

I don't want to look too eager, though, so I just nod casually. "Yeah, I've been eating them almost my whole life." And I'm sure IHOP grits will taste *nothing* like these, if yesterday's dinner was any indication. The way I ate last night, I can't believe I woke up hungry. But one thing I know about most older women of color who love to cook: if you gladly eat their meals, they'll love you for life. And trust me, there was nothing hard about showing my enthusiasm for the way that the women in Deja's life cook.

Mrs. Martin walks in the room with a small box. "Mornin', you fine gentlemen! Rise and shine. Go wash up and grab a shirt on your way! Breakfast is almost ready." She drops the box of shirts on the floor and treks down the hall, on to her next task. Deja pops out of the kitchen in overalls and a sports bra, with beads of sweat gleaming from her face.

She looks hot in both senses of the word, but I need to calm down. This is not the time to be fawning over my girlfriend. Every single man in this house is watching my every move.

"Hey!" she says to her brothers and cousins as they scatter. "I got dibs on Mama and Poppa's bathroom." Then she looks at me.

"Hi," I say.

"Hi." She smiles back. "You sleep okay?" she asks, looking at the metal pull-out couch they gave me.

"Yeah," I lie. Deja giggles as soon as it comes out my mouth, and I slouch my shoulders. "I mean, my back has been better, but I sleep on the floor when I visit family in Nepal. I'm built for this." As soon as I say it, a sharp pain hits my lower back and I rub it, trying to smile my way through it.

"Honestly, the floor is probably more comfy than this couch," she says. "You can use my parents' bathroom after me—I just need to shower since I've been outside all morning."

"How's the garden?" I ask.

"It looks so good!" Deja says, her eyes perking up. "Poppa's been taking good care of it. It's his way of showing me love." She has a wounded look in her face when she says it. Equal parts love and disappointment.

"That's good to hear," I say. "Your dad looks at you with nothing but admiration, Deja. I can tell all he wants to do is protect you. I know I do, and I've only known you for a couple months."

Deja gives a half-hurt smile, then quickly squeezes my hand before anyone catches us. It's nice to know we can still steal these moments to ourselves, even when there's so much occurring around us. Dominique and Deandre cut down the hallway, chasing three-year-old Damarion, who giggles and screams at the same time. It looks like he stole one of their T-shirts. "Watch where you going!" Deja screams as Dominique almost runs right into us.

"Sorry," Dom yells as they continue around the house.

"Oh! Your mom said we all have to put those on." I point to the box, and Deja pulls out one of the many aqua-blue shirts that read MARTIN FAMILY REUNION in black lettering with a matching black tree sprouting above it.

"This is so corny," Deja says, inspecting the shirt and turning it around. She looks at the tag and passes me one shirt and finds another in her size. "Welcome to the Martin house," she adds, laughing.

"It's kinda fun here," I say.

# CHAPTER THIRTY-EIGHT

## Deja

After I wash up and set Raja up for a shower next, I go back to my old bedroom to find Diamond voguing in the mirror in her family reunion shirt.

"Why are you like this?" I say, laughing as I record her.

"Are you vlogging?" she asks me.

I roll my eyes. "I guess I am now," I say, and put the camera right up to her face.

My sister clasps her hands together. "It's ya girl Diamond, and we are at the Martin family reunion," she says, lifting the sides of her shirt to show the embroidery, "where some good barbeque, a fight, and a nasty-ass uncle trying to hit on his nieces are surely to commence." I press stop on my phone's recording so quick and shake my head.

"Di!"

She shrugs her shoulders. "What?! It literally happens at

every family reunion. Anyway, how's Raja coping? He seems to be fine to me."

"I mean, I've seen him nervous here and there, but he's been pretty laid back."

"That's 'cause you can tell he hung around some brothas and sistas," my sister says with a fist in the air, and we both cackle.

"Girl, you should have seen me asking him if he knows CP time. He was so over me." I smile. "Thank you for pushing me to do this. He's a sweet guy."

"I can tell!" she squeals. "Listen, most girls don't meet the love of their life the first night they go to college. And then sometimes the girls who least expect to do. Maybe you're that girl and we'll make fun of y'all for the rest of our lives about how y'all met your first night freshman year and how cheesy and cute it is."

I put my hand to my heart. "Aww, Di. Don't forget to say we're so cute it makes you wanna throw up," I say as I fling myself on Dominique's bed and hug a pillow to my chest.

"Literally, gag," Diamond says as she imitates pointing a finger down her throat.

I walk back to the living room to find Raja sitting on the couch next to my Great-Uncle Henry and across from my mama. They all seem to be laughing, but I can't tell if it's from *Days of Our Lives* playing on the television or Raja still on the campaign trail.

"These stories still come on?" I ask as I walk into the room and give Mama a kiss.

"Apparently," she says, and then grins. "Raja was just getting to know Uncle Henry."

"Hey, Uncle Henry," I say a little loud 'cause he has a hearing aid.

"Hey, Miss Sweet, how are you?" he yells.

"I'm doing good!" I say, patting his hand. Then I look at Raja. "What are y'all talking about?" I ask him.

Raja smiles. "Oh, I was just explaining to Mr. Henry and your mom how the South is similar to where my family's from."

"Mr. Henry?" I say, aghast.

"Me and this young fella here got to talkin' about outhouses. You know his folks got a whole movie about poop?" my great-uncle says.

"He even showed me where the holes for the outhouses used to be by Queen's house. That's when he told me to call him Mr. Henry," Raja whispers so that Uncle Henry can't hear. "First-name basis."

My mom turns her head to shield her laughter. "That's right!" Uncle Henry chimes in, zero clue as to what is happening. "We all Martins in here, it's too confusing anyhow! Fine young man right here!" he continues, slapping Raja's shoulder. "What's yo family, Mexican?"

Lord, *why?*

"No, Uncle Henry! They're from Nepal! It's in the southern region of Asia. The continent . . . sir?" I don't know why I keep trying to describe where he's from, but I feel like I'm just word vomiting right now to keep my family from saying another ignorant thing. I look over at my mom who is frozen in such an uncomfortable smile that if I wasn't so concerned about how Raja must be feeling, I would have fell out on the floor in a laughing fit.

"Okay, you ain't gotta be so loud! I reckon I woulda heard you," Uncle Henry responds, annoyed.

Raja holds my hand and nods as if to reassure me it's okay. "Your Uncle Henry is a fine young man, too. Told me how he helped give your parents the material to build this house after you were born, and how your grandmother's home housed a lot of people in the family. In my family we had an uncle who housed multiple families from Nepal while he ran a business downstairs. My parents stayed there, and that's where Rani and I were born."

"Wow, Raja."

"Right? That's so beautiful!" my mama says. "Family seems to be very important to you, Raja."

"It is," he says. "I can see how easy it would be for Deja to get homesick. She always mentions things that remind her of home."

"Home is where the heart is," my mom says, shaking her head.

"Yeah," Raja responds. "You know, I do see the similarities . . . to Maryland . . . to Nepal. Guess a little bit of my heart is here now too."

My mom beams. "Guess it is, sweetie."

After everyone in the house is fed and dressed, fifty or so Martin adults and children pile into our charter bus and head into the city to begin our first activity: the African American Heritage Trail tour. The family seems to be having a good time as we pull up to the visitor center, and Mama, Diamond, and I make a pact to keep an eye on Raja. Even Dominique trails close behind as she and Raja talk soccer. It seems to be going well.

Except I see the occasional whispers happening within the older camp, with the ringleader being my dad. As we approach Fifer's Grave, the second stop on the tour, I observe my parents' interactions, and every time Poppa tries to get close to Mama and engage with her, she pulls away. I watch as he'll creep into a conversation she's having with a family member, only to see her excuse herself or veer off without him. It's then I realize my mom has been particularly cold to my dad the last few days, but I've been so worked up about how I feel, I never noticed the silent protest going on. The house was divided, men against women. The men siding with Poppa because he's the man of the house, and the women siding with me because . . . I guess apparently we have morals.

Farther along on the tour I sneak off to look for my mom. I find her reading the plaque of the E.E. Smith Monument standing before us.

I come up behind her and wrap my arm around hers as I lean on her shoulder. She cups my cheek.

"Why didn't you tell me you and Poppa were fighting?"

"What I tell you about staying out of grown folks' business?" she says. I chuckle silently, remembering we are always being watched. Then my mom sighs. "I didn't wanna worry you. You know your dad is . . . stubborn."

"Yeah, that's an understatement," I say. "Has he told you what his deal is?"

My mom goes silent, and I stand tall, looking her in the eyes. "I can handle it, Mama. I need to know."

"Well . . ." She sighs again. "Your dad thinks he won't treat you right. That he won't be able to protect you as a Black woman.

He said it's nice and fun now, but wait until your life hits him for the first time. He wants to know you are with a man that will fight for you and knows *how* to fight for you."

My poppa makes some good points, which is scary because there's no way to know how these situations could go until we experience them together. "What do you think, Mama?" I ask, feeling small, like I need guidance.

"Diamond told me everything, how Raja's already defied his entire family for you. I told your dad I reckon he's proven himself ten times over."

I let out a yelp and then cup my hands around my mouth. "Mama, you shut him all the way down."

"*All the way down*, you hear me? I asked him what kinda Christians are we to be judging this boy before we meet him? And even if we were to judge, we should be excited to meet him since he's doing all this! I know my daughter is a catch, I made her!"

I keep laughing. I love when my mama gets feisty.

She lowers her voice. "As far as I'm concerned, Queen, Diamond, and I taught you how to fight for yourself. You were so timid when you were younger, and now look at you. Out here swingin' the most."

I give her a hug, and a tear falls from my eye.

"Raja fought to get his family to respect you, and now you're doing the same for him by bringing him here."

"It doesn't feel like I'm fighting. I'm just being honest," I say.

"Well, sweetie, it's time to go be honest with yo dad." She cups my chin. "Ya hear me?"

"Yes, ma'am," I say.

⇝ ⇝ ⇝

At the end of the walking tour, our transportation—courtesy of my cousin Jeremy's charter bus business—makes its rounds to drop everyone off at the hotel, a few more stops for the older family members, and us last. Diamond is leading the charge, making sure every relative is accounted for.

We all tear into the leftovers, and Dominique and the other younger kids crowd around the television to watch the basketball game while some of the women help put food away. Raja hangs out in the kitchen and does more labor-intensive work, like moving a few food items to the deep freezer under the car porch.

"Where do you want me to put that?" Raja asks, pointing to a tinfoil pan full of ribs.

"Lawd have mercy!" My great-aunt Gloria, Uncle Henry's wife, says. She's sitting at the kitchen table looking at Raja in disbelief, and we all turn to Raja pointing with his middle finger.

My mom fake slaps his finger as she laughs. She's so bad. "Boy, what you doin' flipping the bird to everyone in the kitchen?"

Raja quickly grabs his finger and blushes. "I'm SO sorry. My dad points with his middle finger and I guess I'm slowly becoming him." Raja looks over at my great-aunt. "I apologize once again, please forgive me," he says, instinctively bowing to my aunt, and not knowing what to do but recognizing this gesture of respect, she smiles and pats his head. She doesn't say much, so that's a plus for him.

"Well, let's put you back to work. Raja, can you help Dominique dry the dishes?"

Raja goes to the sink and I watch Dominique as she explains how she'll give him the dishes and he has to dry it with a rag and place it in the dishwasher to dry. Raja looks at me so excited.

"What is wrong with you?" I ask.

"You don't use your dishwasher either?" he says.

My mom huffs. "I don't know why they even put that thing in there. The dishwasher couldn't keep up with the amount of people in this house! That thing would be on twenty-four seven if we used it like we supposed to. As far as I'm concerned, that's a drying rack."

Raja dries his hand, walks over to Mama, and extends his arms out to hug her. "I'm home," he says, and my mom gives him the biggest hug while the room howls with laughter.

I text Raja an hour into everyone else sleeping, hoping he's up and, like me, wrapping his head around today's events. I haven't even had a moment to tell him what's going on with my dad. Turns out Raja and I have a lot in common.

> ME: You sleep?
> RAJA: Not with the way Jr. snores
> ME: LOL! Let's sneak outside
> RAJA: Hell
> RAJA: No.

Mr. Rebel doesn't seem to want to rebel, so I sneak out my room, down the hall to the living room. I crouch next to Raja and he jumps.

"My life flashed before my eyes," he whispers.

"Who's gonna hurt you, Raja?" I ask.

"Your dad," he responds, seriously.

I lean toward the open window, letting the full moon illuminate my skin and flash him my best grin. "Let's go outside and talk about it," I say, holding his hand.

"And the nominees for best actress are . . . ," he retorts.

"Raja . . . come on," I whine in a half whisper.

"You're crazy. I'm not sneaking out," he whispers back, his voice still stern. "Your dad told me he got eyes and ears all over this house. I know that at least means everyone in this living room."

I scan the room and can tell my cousins are knocked out. "It's okay, I promise," I say. "I've grown up with everyone here. Jr. only snores when he's extra tired. And look how everyone else is laid out on the floor. They haven't moved once."

"Deja, no," he says, his tone more serious. "It's one thing to have my family not talking to me, I can't have yours—" He stops cold.

So the truth comes out.

# CHAPTER THIRTY-NINE

## Raja

Her mouth is wide open. *Shit.*

Deja gives me a look, and I accept my fate. I crawl out of my cot and follow her to the front porch. The floors creak here and there and so does the door, but everyone seems so exhausted from being downtown that no one makes a peep.

We sit on the swing, rocking back and forth and holding hands as we look into the vast night sky. "Well, at least if your dad kills me, it's peaceful out here."

She snickers, and for a moment I'm thankful. I feel less bad about what I've withheld. "How long?" she asks.

I bite my lower lip. "A few weeks. I didn't want to worry you," I add. "You have enough going on here and . . ."

"Why aren't they talking to you? Was it the engagement party?"

"No, I told my dad I'm switching my major." And I close my mouth, not wanting to finish the rest. Knowing there should be a comma where I just ended that statement. I said most of it.

The other part can wait.

I finally have it in me to look her in the face, and my heart breaks a little. She looks . . . pleased.

"I'm so proud of you!" she squeals, grabs my face with both of her hands, and kisses me. She's proud of me. I don't deserve her goodness right now, so I pull away. "I reeeally wanna kiss you, but your father has put real fear in me, so can we not do this . . . here?"

She smiles, then nods. We both have the same kind of father—intimidating as shit. In their own quirky ways. "My dad is having a hard time too," Deja admits. "Like . . . a really hard time." She looks at me.

"Do you know why?" I ask her.

"He thinks . . . ," she starts. "He thinks it will be hard for me. That you won't know how to look out for me because you can't fully understand what I experience. You can't know how I'm treated unless you witness it," she continues. "And I know you've experienced your share of racism, but like you said, your family sees it as more of a caste thing, and my family sees it as a race thing. It's just different for a Black woman in America."

"But I'm American," I say. "And I'm a man, just like your dad."

"You not being Black makes my dad think you won't know my particular needs. He understands the importance of family and name and community. But he wants to make sure I'm taken care of."

"That's what he told you?" I ask, wishing I had the same clarity from my dad.

"No, that's what my mom and sister told me."

"I guess I can see his point of view. What father wouldn't want his daughter protected?" I say, ruminating on her father's fears.

"What about you? What did your dad say?"

I sigh. "Not much. He's worried about how our family will be perceived. It's not even about me, it's about the Sharmas. What will people think of Bibek Sharma and his family?"

"Is it 'cause I'm not Nepali? Or particularly 'cause I'm Black? Or customs?"

"That's the thing. It's a little bit of all of it," I say, still staring into the distance. I let out a major sigh. This is the most honest I've been with Deja, and I don't feel as afraid anymore. We both are in this relationship, facing some weighty stuff.

"This shit is hard," Deja says.

"Which part?" I say.

She pauses. "Everything. Your family not getting me. My family not getting you. I dealt with enough racism in North Carolina, will probably deal with more at UMD, and I never wanted a life where I'd have to come home and deal with it from family."

I turn to her. "Deja, I get it," I respond. "I guess, as scary as it feels for me, I always knew the day would come where I'd have to stand up to my parents for my girlfriend. I've compartmentalized my entire life, and I'm not doing that anymore. I'm Nepali, and I'm American. I can choose which customs I want to keep and which ones I want to throw away. And I choose not to buy into the idea that I can't date a girl who makes me happy and a better person. If anything, I think you'll somehow make me study more in the fall."

She giggles. Thank goodness, that means she's still in this with me.

"Deja, I can't help the family I was born into. I'm fighting to give them what they want and still do what I want, but it's a constant negotiation of boundaries. Might be for the rest of my life."

Deja looks at me with curiosity. "What inspired this?" she asks.

"Rani's been sending me these posts from this brown therapist she follows about having a girlfriend." I sigh again. "I want them to just accept me and let me be me. And being with you lets me be me. It's me and you, right?" I look at her.

She doesn't make me wait. "It's me and you," she says, and I kiss her hand, watching fireflies light up the sky.

# CHAPTER FORTY

## Deja

Saturday morning my mom and Diamond wake us at the crack of dawn to begin setting up outside for the day's festivities. My older cousins are at the grill, and Raja agreed to do face-painting for the kids, while Diamond and the rest of my teenage cousins manage the inflatable bouncy house and some of the other activities for our baby cousins. The rest of the family is doing a tradition as old as time here: softball. The kids used to play sports when they were younger, and somehow it's translated into a softball game every time enough aunts, uncles, and cousins get together. Queen umpired the games, and since her death it's been too painful for anybody to step in and be the one to coordinate them. But it's so clear as everybody gathers that we all missed this—the games themselves, but also just spending time together.

We set up tables to sit at and serving tables with trays of food and Sterno cans to keep them heated. Jeremy arrives with a busload of Martins and everyone scatters, the kids bum-rushing the bouncy house and eagerly lining up to let Raja paint their faces. I try to give him some distance to allow him to interact with my family naturally, and he's doing a pretty good job. The kids love their paintings of course, and Raja is getting so many affirmations from my cousins on how good of an artist he is, he just doesn't know what to do with himself. One thing Black people gonna do is hype up someone who's good, but I just love how he's being validated as an artist.

I guess I got more people here who are for us than against us, which is a good reminder. My dad might be a jerk about everything, but at least he's outnumbered. Raja's been getting on so many people's good side that I'm sure everyone is talking to my pops about him, whether he's ready to hear it or not.

Jr. walks up to me. "Hey, Dad wants to holla at you real quick."

That's strange. He's been avoiding me and now he wants to talk? "About what?" I ask, feeling like Jr. went back to side with the enemy.

"It's nothing, Dej," he replies, fidgeting.

"Well, if it's nothing, then you're coming with me," I demand, folding my arms. My brother is a gentle giant and hates confrontation. He knows his presence alone will cause him to get dragged into this and I couldn't care less—he should have my back here like he usually does.

"Come onnn," he says. "I don't wanna get in this." He's practically pouting.

"Let's go," I say coldly, and he leads the way, holding his head down in shame.

We go to the front porch to find the whole crew—Uncle Lonny, Uncle Rodney, and Poppa.

Darius Jr. opens the screen door and I step inside behind him. "The whole gang's here, I see," I let slip out of my mouth.

"Young lady . . . ," my dad calls out. I keep my mouth shut but stare him down. "I just want to talk to you."

"Then why is everyone else here? Why haven't you talked to me once by yourself since I've been back, Poppa? You've been avoiding me all weekend. You know how hurtful that is?"

My uncles start squirming behind my dad, not being able to take the emotional energy I'm giving everyone.

My dad's jaw tenses up. "Why don't y'all go check on the grill. Make sure them youngins doin' it right." My dad's brothers nod in agreement and file out, with Jr. trailing behind. Men are funny.

My dad pats the swing and I mosey over to him and sit on one end, giving us some distance. He leans against his legs and clasps his hands together. "Deja, I ain't tryna be difficult."

"Poppa, that sounds like '*I'm not racist but . . .*'"

"Come on. You know me betta than that," he responds sternly. He's right. "I sholl nuff didn't expect to ever have this conversation with you."

"I didn't either, sir," I say.

He eyes me. "I'm just sayin', the semester ain't even start yet. Give the brothas some time to come on campus. . . ."

"Dad!" I snap. "I like HIM." We sit in silence for a second. I appease him a bit. "I'm sure there are some fine young Black men on UMD's campus. It's not like I wouldn't have dated one. But I met Raja, and I found someone who feels like my person."

"What if he tries to convert you to Islam?"

I bury my face in my hands. "Jesus, Poppa, it's Hinduism!"

"I'm sorry, I'm sorry!" my dad responds, guilt-ridden. "What if he wants you to convert to Hinduism?"

"We know where we each stand in our faiths, and we respect each other's beliefs. If that suddenly changes, then that's a him problem, because I'm not changing who I am for anybody. As long as we're up-front with one another about what we both want for ourselves, and it goes with what we see in each other, then we're good!"

Poppa looks at me, proud. "That's a lotta insight, Night."

I heave a deep sigh. "I've learned a lot this summer. I definitely feel more like a grown woman now than I did at spring break."

"Keep on living," my dad says, and I hug his arm. "You ain't think about what if you were with a Black guy instead?"

"Sure," I say. "But I've also never felt this way about *any* guy. Black or not. And any time I need him to understand my point of view, he does a good job trying. I think he just knows my value 'cause he's a beautiful soul. It also doesn't hurt that he's cute as heck, Poppa."

He shakes his head, but I get a laugh out of him. "I'll leave that conversation to you and ya mama."

I laugh. "He's also thoughtful, he works hard, he's funny, and he's a really good artist. He wants to open a tattoo shop."

"A tattoo shop, baby? You gon get inked up all over your body next?"

I rub my temples. "*Poppa*, you're missing the point. He uses tattoos as a way to preserve stories from his family's homeland, since they don't live there anymore. Imagine if we had to leave our land and never go back." We both look around at our surroundings, thinking what that would feel like. I couldn't imagine being told I couldn't come back to this.

"I'm sorry," he says. "Let me stop being judgy. I just want to be sure he's gonna love you like I do. There might be things he just doesn't understand about my little girl . . . I mean woman. I've seen things, Dej. How folks treated your mama . . . my mama . . ." My dad's voice cracks when he mentions Queen. "The men in the family, we've always protected the women we love by any means necessary. I know you up north, but it's crazy up there, too. . . ."

I wrap my arms around my dad's shoulders, and he does something he rarely ever does: melts in my arms. He's not a protector right now; he's allowing himself to be vulnerable.

I kiss his cheek. "No one is gonna love me like you, sir," I say, and my dad smiles.

"You got that right!" Pops responds, and I chuckle.

"But he's a fast learner. Plus he's gonna come visit with me, and I got you and the uncles and my brothers to teach him, right?"

My dad nods. "It's just . . ."

"Poppa, look at me," I say, and he looks my way. "You worried about things you have no control over. I'm having fun! And I've got to make decisions for myself. If you *really* wanna be helpful, why don't you get to know him? And *then* if you see something you don't like about him, maybe tell me." He shakes his head at me, chuckling. "But this isn't about him right now; this is about me. I can also protect myself, and if a man loves me, I expect him to look after me, because I'm for sure gonna look out for him."

"That's what I'm sayin', Night. I don't want someone taking everything outta ya and not pouring back into ya. So many people do that to our Black girls and women."

I have to catch my breath. "Poppa, you've got to trust I'll make the right decision. That I'll do what Queen always taught us to do. If someone don't feel right . . ."

"Trust ya gut," my dad says, nodding his head.

"I'm so lucky I have so many men in my life willing to fight for me," I say, kissing the top of his head. "Y'all have shown me love in different ways, and guess what? I see some of your best parts in him."

My dad beams. "Queen fought for love, and you should, too," he says, and I look at him, eyes wide. Instead of saying anything more, Poppa balls up a fist. "And you got me and your brothers to remind him if he forgets."

I laugh and hug him tight again. "Don't you dare touch him!" I demand.

"Don't worry, we won't mess with the pretty boy's face."

And that makes us fall out. Glad he's coming around.

# CHAPTER FORTY-ONE

## Raja

I'm drawing my fifth Miles Morales face painting on a little cousin named Elijah when Deja walks up with her father. Thank goodness I didn't notice him, or I would have messed up the last bit of webbing on Spider-Man's mask.

"Wow, this is so cool. Thanks, Raja!"

"You're welcome, Elijah," I say, and give him a high five.

"Did you do that?" he asks, pointing to the tattoos on my arm.

"No," Deja says, bending down, "but he did draw this." She shows him our sunflower.

Elijah licks his finger and tries to rub it off. "Ooh! It's real too!" Elijah squeals.

"Eww!" Deja cries in disgust as I start laughing. Boys will be boys.

"Let me see one more 'gain?" my dad asks, and Elijah puts his hands on his hips, proudly displaying his Spider-Man face paint. My dad nods in approval.

"Lijah, go get everybody else who got a Spider-Man face tattoo. I want to take a picture," Deja requests, and Elijah darts off to grab everyone, giving Deja some alone time with me and her dad.

"Your drawings are decent," Mr. Martin says, rubbing his salt-and-pepper beard. The glare in Deja's eyes shows her annoyance to his backhanded compliment, so I try to settle things.

"Thank you, sir," I say quickly. "I've never drawn so many Miles Morales masks in my life. It's kinda cool."

"I think the face paintings were more popular than the bouncy house!" Deja says, looking around at the last bit of kids jumping about, every one of them with a piece of art on their face. "They all started coming to your line first and then going there after."

"Yeah, I reckon you made Diamond a little jealous," Mr. Martin says, and it takes a moment for me and Deja to register that her dad . . . actually made a joke? Mr. Martin gives an awkward chuckle and Deja and I follow suit. Guess I should credit the man for trying. "Well, the men are out back smoking cigars. You're welcome to come hang with us."

I sit there for a second in shock, until Deja nudges me. Bless her, she always knows the right thing to do. "Yeah . . . yeah," I say, clearing my throat and attempting to add more bass to my voice. "I'll be back there after I clean this up."

Mr. Martin snickers. "Sounds good," he says, and treads off.

"Was the voice too much?" I ask, dipping my brushes in paint water.

"Yes," Deja says, laughing as her cousins come back over

to take the picture. "Okay, everyone crowd around Raja, and I want your best Spider-Man pose!" Elijah commits with an air kick before Deja is ready and we all fall out. I watch Deja try to assemble her younger cousins to hold their poses and convince the middle schoolers to stop acting too cool to pose. In the end I throw up the spiderweb palm and a couple of her older cousins copy. I made it.

Deja and I walk toward the back of the house, and she stops me before we turn the corner, her voice showing a sense of urgency.

"I'm just letting you know, they're probably back there drinking moonshine, and my Uncle Rodney is already drunk, so he's probably gonna offer you some," she tells me.

"Okay, one, what is moonshine? And two, will I look disrespectful if I don't take it? Or will it look like I'm a... what did your auntie call your cousin earlier?"

"A heathen?" she asks, laughing.

"Yeah, that," I say.

"You can do whatever you want, Raja. Don't let anyone force you. Moonshine is illegal whiskey—well, the way they make it is."

My eyes light up. "Illegal whiskey? Hell yeah!"

"Shh!" she says. "Saying 'hell yeah' around these parts will definitely have them calling you a heathen. Raja, it's strong. That's not an exaggeration."

"Deja, I've been preparing for this since the first time I snuck an uncle's cup at a wedding," I say, trying to make her laugh, to calm her down. Maybe her dad will finally loosen up around me with alcohol in his system. I'm game for the challenge.

"Raja, don't go back there trying to prove something or you'll die drinking that stuff," she whispers. "It's no joke."

"Oh, okay. So only like a sip . . . unless I shouldn't. You still didn't answer me."

Deja thinks for a moment. "I think the only person that matters is my dad. Follow his lead."

"Done," I say. "Can I go hang with the boys now?"

"Go," she says, laughing as I kiss her on the cheek, and we part ways.

I puff up my chest as I step to the Martin men, not sure what is about to happen but excited as hell.

"Ayyy . . . look who's here! My man Raaaaja!" Deja's uncle Rodney says, words slurring slightly. Nothing I haven't experienced before so far. "Your name sounds like 'Deja,' now that I think about it."

The uncles complain about a few of the younger cousins getting caught smoking out in the woods, and I chuckle to myself, remembering how Deja held it together when my parents were bickering about this very thing. Meanwhile, everyone here's currently partaking in illicit liquor.

"So, Raja, how does your . . . family feel about Deja?" Jr. asks. There it is. He wanted to know how his sister is being treated since everyone's showing me love. I would want to know the same thing about Rani.

"A lot of them love her. She made them some beauty products and teas and I swear, every time I see them, they won't stop talking about her. I think they like your sister more than they like me."

Jr. cracks a smile. "What about the others?" he asks.

"Some will barely talk to Deja. And I've had to call them out on it."

"Like who?" Mr. Martin asks.

I look him in the eye. "Like my father, sir."

Mr. Martin's chest sinks. "How . . . how did he react?"

I pause, trying not to get emotional. "At the moment, we're not on speaking terms . . . sir."

"I'm . . . sorry," he says. And I'm not sure if it's because of my dad or because of how he acted toward me, or both, but I believe him. "Leaving the family, that's a lot to bear. My grandpa told me before he passed that Queen, my mama, ran away from home." Whoa. So he does know. "See, this why I shouldn't be drinkin' this mess," he says, and the uncles and cousins laugh a bit, but silence quickly, clearly hungry to hear more. "Pa said he found her a month earlier than when she came home. Had to negotiate with her." We all laugh. "But she taught her dad, my grandpa, somethin' that day. No matter what you do for your child, you don't get to control them forever. Either you gon learn the easy way, or in Pa's case, the hard way."

"You remind me of my buwa . . . my dad, sir," I stumble out.

"He stubborn as all get out?" he asks me.

I nod, chuckling. "Yes, sir, just what you said." Everyone around us laughs. "But also, he wants to protect us from the world. My dad has seen things I could never begin to understand. He's protective over me, and especially my sister. If I had a daughter as amazing as Deja, I'd probably be the same way," I say.

"She is something special, ain't she?" her father says, and I am filled with so much emotion. From her father's beautiful display of doting on his daughter, to men of color talking about family secrets and standing up for yourself, through the eyes of a Black woman? This is one of the most touching moments of my life, all because I got to fall for Deja. I hope my dad and I can get to a place like this. Seeing her father go from callous to caring demonstrated that maybe there's hope.

"You like whiskey?" one of the grill-master cousins asks to lighten the mood. I nod.

"Well, try this, we brew it . . . we . . . whatcha call it?" Uncle Rodney asks.

"Ferment or distill it?" I say.

"Yeah . . . smart boy! We ferment it ourselves. Just like the fancy shit they sell at the store," Uncle Rodney says as he passes me the bottle.

Deja's dad looks at me. "Now, son, you don't have to drink that if you don't wanna."

In that moment I don't know if he means "son" in an endearing way or just in a general sense, but I know what I have to do. I have to try it.

"I mean, if I don't try it here, where else can I try it? Can't be that bad if you all are drinking it."

"My man!" Uncle Lonny pops out of nowhere and smacks my back something serious. I cough. Geesh, he's strong.

Uncle Rodney passes me the bottle and I take a swig, and the burning sensation hits my throat immediately.

"Wooo!" I shout, and everyone laughs.

"You'll get a few hairs on your chest," Uncle Lonny says, puffing his cigar.

"I'm brown. I've had hairs on my chest since I was eleven," I say, and they all laugh as I take one more super tiny swig and rub my chest, feeling the burn travel down. When I pass it back to Uncle Rodney, he seems disappointed I won't drink more. It doesn't matter, though, because Mr. Martin is pleased. Plus, that's some next-level shit. I'm going to take Deja's advice and quit gracefully.

Grill-master cousin lights a bonfire, and I spend the next few moments watching the woods and the sunset glistening on their family pond. And for all the noise and laughter, there's such a serenity to it. This is what happens when I take control over my own life. It might not be one big change, but step by step, brick by brick, I'll begin to see the change I want to see.

This week my parents may disown me, but next week they'll come around. Out of want or need or guilt. But love shouldn't be control, it should be this—the uncles and fathers respecting the women in the house. The healing Deja and her father were able to do in just one weekend gives me hope that maybe I could do the same in one year. I can be just as persistent as my dad was about my report cards when I was young. I will show up. I'll pester Aama. I'll sneak Deja over while Dad is at work and get Aama to fall in love with Deja first. Then we'll gang up on Buwa until he caves. Deja's planning skills are rubbing off on me. I'll make this work.

"Anyone that can stand up to fam is my dude," Jr. says, and he and a few cousins give me a pound. This is what courage feels like. I like it.

# CHAPTER FORTY-TWO

## Raja

Deja tells the family we need to get on the road early and convinces me to let her drive the first half this time since she knows these roads, but when she pulls up to an open field not far from her parents' place and sneaks a glance my way, I'm sure I'm smiling as bright as the sunflowers in front of us.

"You wanna get your sketchpad out your backpack?"

"You know it," I say, and she pops open the trunk for me.

"Also, grab your hat and the picnic blanket," she instructs as she grabs her bucket hat and a grocery bag.

"What's in there?" I ask, leaning over to see for myself.

"Mama packed this for us," she says as she shuffles around in the bag. "Let's see, a thermos of iced tea, some turkey sandwiches, and biscuits and deer sausage." I'm in heaven. She looks back up at me and bursts out laughing. "What is it?"

"I just need you to know I will drive you up and down I-95 anytime if your mom is cooking like that."

She giggles and gives me a little hip bump as we walk to the field.

Once I pick out a few colored pencils to match the horizon, we walk hand in hand toward the rows and rows of sunflowers, the sun proudly midsky.

"Now I see why you wanted to leave early. The weather isn't so bad right now."

"Yeah, we got a couple hours to enjoy it," she says, laying the cover down.

"Deja, this is magical," I reply as I sit cross-legged, probably looking like a kid in a toy store as I take in the view.

"These aren't the dried-up sunflowers you buy at Whole Foods. This is the real thing."

I chuckle. "So are you," I say, and lean in for a deep, passionate kiss. We pull away, and I'm breathless.

"I'm just returning the favor," she says, smiling. "You took me to see cherry blossoms in DC first."

Her family came around much quicker than mine, and being around them, I see now that their only concern was making sure I was a good enough person for someone they love. I know deep down my parents feel the same, but it's all mixed in with their worries about other people's opinions and outdated values.

I clasp my fingers around her tattoo like a bracelet. "Looking at these makes me want to redo this."

"Cut it out," she says, lightly flicking my fingers. I laugh and shake my fingers like she damaged them.

"Hey, these are my moneymakers," I tell her, and we snicker.

"My bad. But no slander about my baby's art. It's perfect, look." She lifts her arm up tall like the sunflower stalks as the sun beams in her face, her eyes closed and face proud.

I'm inspired . . . and guilt-ridden. I have to tell her. I snap a picture with my phone and then grab her arm to lower it, glancing at her nervously. "Deja . . . I . . . uh . . . have something to tell you."

Deja gives me a look. "We just had a major breakthrough with my family, Raja. This is a celebration! You're making me nervous."

I clear my throat and pop my knuckles. "I didn't tell you the other thing that happened after the family dinner, but before the tika-tala."

"Okay . . . ," Deja responds, face stern.

"They, um . . ." I swallow. "There was another family there when I went home. It was this guy named Dr. Bhatta and his wife, and their daughter, Bhumi, was there."

"Huh?" Deja asks. "Am I supposed to know them . . . ?" She looks up at me, her eyes stone. She knows now, and I'd give anything to bring her joyous look back. "It was a setup?"

"Deja, it wasn't even that big of a deal! I mean, she's got a girlfriend, and I think she thinks you're hot, and . . ."

"One, if it wasn't that big of a deal why didn't you tell me?" Stumped there, I don't even bother opening my mouth because this is obviously a list of dumb-boy shit I did wrong and deserve to hear a mouthful of. "And two, Raja, don't be that guy! I already know you misinterpreted what she said!"

"No, you had to be there, she said you were a better catch than I was . . . ," I say, then shut my mouth. I'm flopping right now.

Deja refuses to look at me. This shouldn't be a big deal, and yet it feels like it could be a deal-breaker.

"You lied," Deja says, still looking off into the field.

"I didn't technically..."

"Lying by omission is lying!" she says, exasperated.

"Deja, you don't understand. I'm literally not talking to my dad for you!"

She snaps her head over to my direction, scowling. "No one asked you to do this! If your parents hate me so much that they're over here 'Nepali Matchmaking' and refusing to talk to you because we're together, then maybe we shouldn't be!"

She wraps her knees up to her chest and buries her face in them. I feel like an asshole. Then she pops her head up, her lips tight with anger. "And for the record, you don't get to compartmentalize your life like that anymore if we're together. *Especially* about something like that. I told you, Raja, I'll be honest with you, even when you may not like it. And I expect my boyfriend to be just as honest with me."

She's right. I've been desperate to push through for selfish reasons, because this can't fail. But even that is an immense amount of pressure put on her. My parents need to know that I care about her and I have a hunch this might work out. But if it doesn't, if Deja isn't my forever, I'm asking them to let me pursue love for myself, not for someone to manage my life for me.

This whole thing has to feel like a choice for her, just as much as it is for me. There's so much here—being set up, being lied to, being disrespected. "I wasn't ready to tell you . . . ," I trail off. *Own up to your faults.* Just because you experienced this growing up doesn't mean you have to continue those patterns. "I lied, and I'm sorry." I pause. "And I mean every part of it, including not telling you about the setup part. It was a lot trying to explain. And you're also right about how it makes me no different from my dad, or your uncle Lonny, when I keep stuff like that from you. A girlfriend should know this stuff."

Deja gives me a confused chuckle. "What did my Uncle Lonny do to you?"

I never got around to telling her this story. "Um. When I was face-painting, he came over. He warned me that the Martin girls are too free-spirited, and said he figured my culture has strict practices for women. So you might not be my cup of tea." Deja is clearly even more furious now, so I go on.

"I told him that's exactly why I like you. And that I had an uncle like him, one who thought the woman's job was to cook and clean and not be an equal, a partner. I never wanted that. I told him I wanted someone just like you." Deja suppresses a smile, so I hold her hand. "I said you're full of drive and full of life. If things stay this way, I'll follow you anywhere."

"Raja, you know you want to live in Maryland," she says.

"Hey, we can be bicoastal if you want," I say, and Deja smirks. "I don't mind being young and dreaming big with you. We just might do it."

She squeezes my hand tighter. "We might be crazy enough to."

I cup her cheek in my hand. "And I promise, Deja, you aren't the only reason they're being difficult right now. I'm also the reason. They want me to be someone I'm not."

I move closer to her. "I'm rebelling against literally *everything* they've asked me to do to be a good son in their eyes. As a man, I am supposed to be a provider first. He doesn't think I should make any decisions before making the most important one of all to them, my career. I hit him with everything at once . . . I might have broken him." I chuckle, and Deja rests her head on her knees.

"That doesn't change how he treated me. He tried to set you up and completely dismissed my existence."

"Yes . . . ," I say, "aaand maybe you are giving him way too much credit, and maybe he's also trying to show a level of hierarchy by enforcing something he thinks he can control onto his son."

Deja shrugs. "All these things can be true."

"It was disrespectful. And this dynamic is kinda normal in my family. So much is true, and I'm just trying to stop it. It's not fair you have to feel this burden." I hold her arm. "And I'm sorry for saying it that way. Let me rephrase. I am not talking to my dad right now because I am standing up for the things I love."

"Things?"

"Things," I say. "My dream, you, my life. I'm choosing to do this. I had to make a decision, you know? I know we don't know how long we'll be together, but I'm having the time of my life with you." She giggles. "And shit, I'm learning a lot too. And growing. Whether I am fighting with him to have you forever, or for two semesters"—Deja laughs while wiping a tear—"you've taught me what's worth fighting for. You are incredible, Deja Martin, and I'd be a damn fool not to fight for you. All I can do is try to change it, but I can't help what family I'm born into."

"Family's all you got. I get your struggle," Deja says, wiping my tears away too.

I nod, so thankful she gets me.

Deja lets out a loud sigh and closes her eyes, giving herself a mindfulness check. I smirk. Then she looks in my direction. "These mindfulness checks you do are legit," she says.

"I've been meaning to take you to a yoga studio my cousin teaches at. She met you at the tika-tala. Can I take you as your boyfriend? Or have I been downgraded to friend status?"

She laughs. "'Bout time you asked me!"

After I sketch a little and we eat some food, we lie out on my blanket and watch the clouds go by, hats on our faces to shield the sun like real cowboys. It's Deja who reminds us we need to get back, and I sulk as she walks ahead of me to the car.

"I like those shorts on you," I call out.

She looks back at me with a smirk. "Why? The only part you can see of these shorts right now is my booty."

"Mmhmm, I like it." I give her my most innocent smile.

She laughs and turns back around. "You're a butt man, Raja Sharma?"

"Always have been," I respond immediately.

She huffs. "Figures."

I come back into the tattoo shop after my vacation feeling lighter . . . at least somewhat. I'm opening, so it's just me, Van, and Vicky.

"How was it?" he asks me.

"I mean, a few ignorant statements were said, but I think if we're comparing who's got it worse in the family acceptance department? Deja's got me beat. I could honestly take a few more punches for her."

Van laughs. "Young love. 'I'll take a few hits for her honor!'" He's laughing so hard, he's practically coughing. What a dork.

"I did not say it like that." I roll my eyes. *But I would.*

"What's the funniest thing you had to do to be initiated?" Vicky asks, sitting in her chair.

"Drink moonshine. I feel like I lost my breath for a second."

"You bring any back?" they both ask in unison. We all laugh.

"We both know Raja charmed everyone's socks off," Van says, and I smile.

"You know I aim to please," I say. "Honestly, there were only a few tense moments, but everyone was so cool after they got to know me. And the jokes helped for sure." I wished *everyone* in my family greeted her the way I was greeted.

I miss my so parents badly, and I also feel like I'm taking charge of my life in a way I like—and it's not just Deja. It's the weight that's been lifted from my shoulders once I realized I could finally choose the major I want to. As much as I miss my family, I have to make my own way. I've got my sister-cousins, and my Rani bahini. They'll keep planting the seeds, and my parents are bound to come around.

"Look at young Raj turning into a man. I'm proud of you, Chora," he says, imitating my dad's voice, and Van and I can't stop laughing. Vicky just shakes her head, always over us.

I'm wiping tears from my eyes. "Bro, how do you do a perfect impression of my—Dad?!" I look up from belly laughing to find my dad standing in the seating area of the tattoo parlor, waiting for me.

"Namaste, Chora," Dad says.

For as still as I am, when I glance at Van, he's a statue. Vicky looks between us all, suppressing a laugh of her own as she waves to my dad and makes her way to the break room. Meanwhile, both of us are trying to determine how long my dad has been standing there and if he heard us, and dealing with our overall shock because my dad has *never* come to the parlor.

"Uh, hi, Bibek uncle," Van greets my dad, bowing.

"Hello, Van," my dad says. "I'd like for my son and me to have some privacy."

He has never spoken like this in his life. It's making me anxious.

"Sure, whatever you need, Uncle. I'll go in the back. Raja, call me or Vicky if a customer comes in." He gets up to walk away, and I wheel my seat around to stop him.

*Help,* I mouth.

He holds in a laugh and mumbles, "It's going to be okay, Raj." Then he looks up at my dad and smiles. "See you later! Tell Auntie I'll have to stop by for chia soon!" I swivel back around to Dad's nod of approval, his hands in his khaki pockets.

"You closed early today? What are you doing out of work?" I ask.

"I had to do something for your mom," he says, walking up to the counter. "How's today, no one's here," he says, looking around.

"We just opened," I reply dryly. Don't come in here with your judgment. This is *my* sanctuary. Suddenly, I'm less inclined to be polite. "Why are you here, Buwa? You've never visited before."

He seems more nervous than normal and is hiding something behind his back.

My dad's not one for pleasantries either, so he gets right to the point.

"What if you meet a respectable young Nepali girl on the University of Maryland's campus?"

"Dad!" I exclaim.

"Would Deja ever consider Hinduism?"

"Buwa, do *I* practice Hinduism?" Even my dad chuckles at that. "Deja is on her own spiritual journey, and so am I," I say.

He nods, then sighs. "I came to this country and all I wanted was the best for you and Rani. I followed all the rules. And then I have you, and you break them all. I don't always understand you, but I don't want to lose you. But respect is earned, Raja. Not handed to you."

I nod. "How about this: I bring home straight As, and you take me seriously. It's a business major, too. There are so many things I could do with it. And I need you to be more open to me bringing my girlfriend around," I say.

"Yes, but I need to see your report card." Some things never change. What he fails to realize is now that I'm taking business classes, I'll be applying every single thing I learn to building my tattoo venture. So As are a must. I'm ready to learn.

"Deal," I say.

This small gesture is all I need. I get up, round the counter, and give my dad the biggest embrace. He doesn't pull away. Finally, after hugging for the longest we probably ever have, I pull back to see my dad wiping a tear.

More shock waves.

"Oh, here. From me, Aama, and Rani." Dad hands me what looks like a wedding invitation—gold mandala lotuses frame the card's exterior, and the invite is handwritten with calligraphy.

*Bibek, Manit, and Rani Sharma are requesting your and Deja's presence for dinner at the Sharma residence* . . . I crack up. Rani and my parents even signed it.

"Who made this?" I ask.

"The whole thing was Aama's idea. She suggested we give Deja a proper invitation because she hasn't felt welcomed so far. It makes us look bad. Aama transcribed the invitation, and Rani bought us nice stationery."

Not Mom taking this literally. I laugh, tears welling in my eyes.

They did the right thing. It's not perfect, the gods know we have a ways to go, but damn it, if this isn't a good start, I don't know what is.

This looks like hope.

"Will you come, Babu?" Dad says with hope in his eyes.

"We wouldn't miss it for the world, Buwa."

# CHAPTER FORTY-THREE

## Deja

As soon as we walk into his house, his parents are, no lie, in the living room by the entrance waiting for us.

"Oh, hello," Raja says when he opens the door, just as shocked to see them as I am.

"Namaste," they both say, and raise their hands as if in prayer. I return the gesture and Raja smirks at me.

"What? Did I do it right?" I whisper to him.

He closes the door. "It was perfect. It's nice seeing you do it so casually now. Feels natural."

I touch his arm, forgetting for a second his family is there, and when I turn back to look at our audience, his mom is smiling.

I'm sure there's a standard of who you are supposed to address first, but I walk up to the person who showed me the most love. "Thank you for the flowers . . . and all the produce. It was very touching."

His mom takes my hand. "I'm glad. And thank you for accepting our invite," she says. "Come with me."

I pass Raja the bag of gifts I brought with my free hand and follow Mrs. Sharma to the back of the house, Raja and his dad watching me as I walk away. I haven't addressed Mr. Sharma yet, but I'm going with the flow here and can imagine Raja's mom knows best. I hope and pray Raja gets an apology, and I'm expecting one myself. But I'm also choosing to live in the moment and let his family sort things out the way they know how. If this invitation was any indication, things might be looking up.

Rani's already in the kitchen, breaking up the rice in the rice cooker.

I hug her. "Thank you for everything . . . even helping with the invite."

"All Aama's idea," she says, pulling away.

"You like it?" their mom says, and we laugh.

"It was a very nice touch," I tell her. "And it smells good in here. I'm excited."

"Just a few more things to cook and dinner will be ready," Mrs. Sharma says, then eyes me. "You cook?"

Uh-oh. Every mother's concern for her son. "I make a mean fried okra," I say, and his mom smiles.

"Oh, good!" she squeals.

"But other than that, I wouldn't call myself a cook. I'm a good sous chef, though."

Mrs. Sharma looks at Rani and Rani responds, "Like on *Top Chef*, Aama. She helps prepare the food."

"Ahh," she says, then looks around. "What can you help with here?"

I love that she's putting me to work. If a woman of color is inviting you to help in her kitchen, that means you're in her good graces. I quickly scan the room until I spot some meat seasoned with turmeric powder in a metal bowl.

"I can tenderize the meat," I say, and Mrs. Sharma nods in approval. We all get to work like we've done this before. I go to wash my hands, Raja's mom makes space at the edge of the counter, and I begin tenderizing the meat. We all get into a rhythm, and I watch Mrs. Sharma giving orders in Nepali and Rani responding with a mixture of some Nepali words and broken English. Rani and I exchange pleasantries while Mrs. Sharma comes up behind me every so often to check on my progress. She'll add more turmeric powder in the bowl every now and again, and I'm back to pounding and flipping the meat. Rani opens the fridge, and that's when I see more summer squash sitting on one of their shelves.

"Your summer squash was my favorite," I tell Mrs. Sharma.

"Oh," Mrs. Sharma says, "come! I must show you my garden!" She goes to grab my hand again until I hold it up, reminding her with my yellow palms that my hands are contaminated. She laughs and runs me some hot water in the sink.

Once I pat my hands dry and she puts the bowl of meat in the fridge to marinate, she grabs them again and rushes me to the back door.

Out back I'm mesmerized. When Raja said his family are farmers, he wasn't lying. His mom has transformed their backyard with rows and rows of crops, filled with tomatoes, peppers, cucumbers, eggplants, and yellow squash. I'm in awe.

I look to my left to see his mother beaming. "You like?" she asks simply.

"Do I like?" I respond, eyes wide. "You're hiding a whole forest behind that fence of yours. I would have never known! It's amazing," I say, scanning the perimeter again. Just to know I can make an enclave for myself like this in a city makes my heart jump. There's nothing like land of your own. Nothing like loving something from nothing and watching it grow, watching nature provide you with the very thing you need. And you can tell she pours love into her garden too. It's thriving.

I spot the okra and rush over to the vibrant plant. "You like the bhindi I sent over?" Mrs. Sharma asks. I nod my head fiercely.

I nod. "They taste so much better than the store-bought ones."

I keep walking up and down the lines of produce, pointing to plants I've never seen before.

It's nice having this shared connection with Raja's mom. A kindred spirit. "You can come over anytime to help," she tells me, smiling.

"You mean it?" I ask. "I'm no stranger to hard work."

"Yes, come! I have a lot of stuff for your business too. Buying all this is expensive, no? You come here and help me, and it's yours." She nods her head as if to decree it done, and I smile. Feeling like I have her permission, I do something I haven't done in ages: dig my hand into the soil, and pull it up, feeling it break apart in my hands. In the DMV's swamp-like August heat, the soil is pasty, dense, and rich with nutrients.

"I miss this," I say, crouched down, and Mrs. Sharma sits on the dirt, like Queen used to. "There's so much protocol at my school farm. It's not the same as doing this in your own garden."

"I don't wear gloves because this is my favorite part. Hands in the earth," she says.

"There's nothing like it," I say. I look up at Rani and she looks like the proudest big sister ever. She should be. If it wasn't for her help in bridging our worlds and advocating for us each time she came home, we might not be here today.

"The food!" Mrs. Sharma jumps, having forgotten for a moment the food still cooking for tonight's dinner. She tries to lift herself up, but Rani puts her hands on her mom's shoulders.

"No, Aama, you stay. The meat needs to sit for a bit, so I can handle the rest." Rani's mom responds in Nepali, and while I can't pinpoint what is being said, I understand her expressions immediately. Concern. "Aama, I know how to cook. Stop worrying!" We all laugh as Mrs. Sharma shrugs and turns around, not completely confident her daughter is right, but trusting her nonetheless.

Slowly learning how to let go.

"Rani is the best," I say, and she smiles.

"My chori is. You know, Rani and I had a lot of talks about you. She told me all about your business, and I fell in love. But it must be hard. What is the phrase? 'You must have money to make money.'" She's not wrong. I had to put my business on pause until my fall scholarship money hits my account. I just nod. "When we came to this country, Raja's buwa and I had to borrow money from family. It was so hard! I was pregnant with Rani and working until we could hire more people. No one took me seriously. They only saw me as some foreign woman who knew nothing. They always think women know nothing." She huffs, and I become furious for her, my hand suddenly closed into a fist, swallowing the soil in it. "Starting a new life can feel like starting at the bottom. But it's only temporary. Your business is smart, creative, and fun."

"Thank you, Mrs. Sharma. Life should be about having fun, right? You can work hard and still have fun. My granny taught me how to do both. I learned from her."

"Your hajurama seems very wise," she says.

"She was," I say, playing with the dirt. Missing her something crazy. She'd love their aama. "She taught me strong values, and how to farm. I miss her."

"I miss my aama and hajurama every day. My sadness never goes away. But I keep them here," she says, holding her heart. "And I feel them all around me, especially back here."

A teardrop falls from my eye. "Thank you," I say.

"I can tell you have love for Raja. You look at him with love. The same look you have now for your hajurama. You must understand I only want what is best for my son. I am sure even your hajurama was like that with her sons." I silently chuckle, remembering my mom telling me stories about Queen's reluctance to accept her in the beginning because she wanted to make sure she was a "good girl who came from a good home." "Then I saw you two at the tika-tala. Your eyes were full of love, and that's all I ever want for my chora." More tears fall down my face, and I wipe them with my sleeve, my hands covered in soil. "I accepted you then, but you must understand. I was expected to side with my husband. That's the way it's done."

"A tradition as old as time," I respond, not thrilled with her answer, but not surprised either. "That's why you sent over the care packages?"

She nods. "If I feed you, I show you my love. If I pick out things you need for your business, I show my support."

I smile at her. "I feel it now." And she exhales, as if the guilt she felt was released when I acknowledged her limitations as a woman in a society I don't quite understand in some ways, but do in others. We sit a little longer, swapping stories of helping our grandparents, when Rani yells from the patio door.

"Food's almost ready, Aama! Time to make the chicken." I get up quickly so that I can help lift Mrs. Sharma up.

"You got dirt all on your pretty kurta!" I say, helping pat off some dirt still on her long, floral tunic embellished with green beads around the collar and waist.

She gives me another Raja-like smirk. "In my day, we worked the field in these," she says, and I laugh again.

# CHAPTER FORTY-FOUR

## Raja

I'm alone with my dad for only the second time since the beginning of the summer, and it makes me uncomfortable, which also makes me sad. This is hard, reconciling with a parent you love dearly.

I walk up to him, popping my knuckles, then putting my hands in my pockets to show a bit more respect and a don't-I-look-like-I-grew-up-a-little stance? 'Cause I feel it. I'm just having trouble *saying* it in a way he'd understand.

"I always knew you wanted to draw, Babu. Since you were little. That's why I pushed you to be an engineer. I thought maybe you could do the thing I couldn't."

Wait, what?

Oh, so that's it. He wanted me to be a better *him*.

"Dad, I want to do something that makes me happy. I don't want to work the rest of my life. I just want to make good money and have multiple streams of income. Look at Baba: he had a farm, he grew ganja, he had . . ."

"Shh, shh, shh! Don't say that out loud," he says.

"Deja already knows, and she thinks Baba was a genius. She said it's a very lucrative herb and it should have always been legal," I say, and my dad laughs.

"Think of it like this, Buwa. You always compared me and Baba. He trusted himself and did the unthinkable—he knew exactly what to do to get you to America so you could bring everyone else. It's kinda incredible." My dad blushes. "Trust that I have that in me, too."

I give him a look. "You need to fix things with Deja. You've hurt her with how you've been acting toward her, Dad."

"Like how?" he asks.

*Lay the truth on him, Raja.* "She thinks you are a racist man who thinks your son is too good to date a Black American girl." My dad freezes, and I throw him a bone. "I explained why a career is so important and that I defied you with moving out and all." I shrug. "But I also told her there's some truth to what she feels. You have to fix that. That's the only way she'll feel welcome."

My dad sits on the couch and stares off into space. "She's a lovely girl. So nice. That's not always a guarantee," he says, looking up at me. I'm not even going to touch that right now, so I let him continue. "And driven. And so intelligent! Her ties to plants and medicine are impressive."

"And preventative, too. She's big on learning about SPF so that we can protect our skin from skin cancer. Meanwhile, she's plotting to become an agriculturist."

He pauses. "You two are the same in a lot of ways, just different."

"But it works, right?"

"Ho," Dad says. "What happens if she breaks your heart?"

My dad went from not opening up to pouring out the dam.

"Then I'll move back in with you and Aama to help me with my heartbreak."

For the first time, my dad smiles the brightest I've seen in months, and then as quickly as it comes, it fades. "She looks at you with love. Don't mess this up."

"I don't plan on it," I assure him. And it's understood. A Sharma man comes through on his promises.

"Speaking of," I say. "Follow me." I grab Deja's care package and bring it into the kitchen. My dad peeks inside. "This is for you." I reach in and grab a brown glass container with a label that says MARIGOLD OIL with a marigold flower next to it. "For your eczema."

My dad smiles. "She even drew a flower."

"No, Raja drew that," Deja says, walking back inside with Aama. "I asked him to. I figured it would be nice to have something made from both of us. Your son is quite the collaborator," she says, and I rub my hand in my hair to hide my blushing. "Also . . . that's a recyclable jar, so when you run low, Raja can bring it to me for a refill. But if you lose it, then we have to talk a payment plan for the replacement."

Rani and I giggle while Mom is over in the corner smiling with pride. She's got her family back and a girlfriend who likes to farm.

Now all I gotta do, like Buwa said, is not fuck this up.

I don't know what my mom told Deja outside, or what she told my mom, but I like this version right now. She's coming in daring my dad not to like her. My boho goddess.

My dad opens the oil and sniffs it, and it's like he's transported back in time. "You know, my aama would use this on me when I was a boy," he said.

"I had a feeling," Deja said, smiling. "You can add the oil to a bath with oatmeal, which is in there, and that should help. There's also whipped shea butter in there for you too. More soothing ingredients."

My dad barely hears a word of what Deja is saying; instead, he's sniffing like he's in heaven. He sets the jar down, and his face goes solemn. "Deja, I'm deeply ashamed of how you must view me. I have not deserved your kindness and for that I'm sorry. I worry about my children. But Raja is just different. You both are. It's why you two get along so well."

"She brings out some great parts in me," I say.

"Some of the best," Rani replies.

"Oh! One more thing. Come," my dad says, motioning to Mom, who at some point grabbed some sort of trinket.

My mom passes it to my dad and motions for him to pass it to Deja, which he does reluctantly.

Deja puts her hand over her mouth and a tear comes down. What the hell? My dad has never given me anything that would make me cry. I'm confused and happy and a little jealous all at once. Then Deja turns it around, and . . . welp, I guess it's my turn to bawl.

It's a colorful beaded frame I can tell my mom's sister made, with an image of a sunflower. The very sunflower I drew after

I met Deja. I tightened up the colors and shaded more tones into the piece, but her initials are written in one of the petals, specifically for her.

"How did you find this?" I look around.

"Guilty," Rani says. "I might have snuck your sketchbook over to show our parents how good you are."

"How did you know it was hers?" I ask them.

"We found her name in the petal," my dad says, and Deja looks confused.

Rani steps in. "There's this sweet tradition we have with mehndi where the bride puts the groom's name or initials in the design, and the groom has to find it. But in this case, Raja put your name in the petals, so I realized it was you."

"It was my idea to look for it!" Aama says while raising her hand, and we all laugh. Of course my mom would suspect her son would do something like this. Another way she shows she does understand me. "I knew you were special to Raja then."

# CHAPTER FORTY-FIVE

## Deja

It's the third week of August in College Park and the campus is slowly becoming more alive as students trickle in early to get ready for the fall semester. Raja invites me over to have some alone time before our fall schedules pick up, and I open his apartment door to incense burning, stood upright by a few bananas, and some candles lit in the kitchen. Is he trying to be romantic?

"What are you up to?" I say, walking to the kitchen, and he jumps. What has him so on edge?

I come up to hug him from behind when I notice his eyes are darting between me and the pot on the stove.

"What's going on?" I ask behind him, peeking over at the tea simmering in the pan, and from the smell, I gather it's full of cinnamon, ginger, and cloves. "Are *you* making me chia?!"

"I've never done this for a girl before . . . ," he says. "It's my first time."

I giggle with delight and hug him tighter. "This feels serious. Does this mean I can't sneak a kiss?"

"If I miss this boil, Deja . . ." And just as the pot is about to spill over, he turns off the burner and removes the pot.

"That was intense," I say, chuckling.

"This batch is about to be so good," he says, giving me a kiss. He strains the tea into two cups.

"Fine china for the win," I respond, both of us carrying our cups out the kitchen.

"Yep, courtesy of Aama's care package service. And anything to show how special this night is, even if I hate these cups." We sit facing each other on the couch.

"Cheers," we say, and I close my eyes, my shoulders rising while bringing the tea to my lips. When I open my eyes, Raja is staring.

"Why are you staring at me?" I ask.

"Okay, one, you know it's because this chia is too hot. And two, I made you a proper chia to honor you tonight." I stop midsip, setting my cup down. "I'd like to believe I must've done something pretty great in a previous life to meet someone like you. I . . ." I kiss him.

"I love you," he blurts out as soon as our lips part. My eyes go wide, and he cracks a nervous smile, seemingly just as shocked that those words escaped his lips as I am.

"Did you mean for that to come out?"

He shakes his head. "No." Then he pauses. "Not like that. But I've been trying to get the courage to say it. I guess I knew when I first met you, just like I know now, Deja," he says. "You're an amazing person and I love being with you."

I look at the sand-brown liquid in my cup. Just when I get comfortable with another step for us, he hits me with something new. We've made a lot of progress, and yet it finally feels like we can really get to know each other, with a major issue in our relationship now out the way. For the most part.

"Just 'cause I'm sure doesn't mean you have to be, though," he says, as if reading my mind. "I only want you to say it when you're ready to, okay?"

I meet his awkward gaze and nod. "Can I ask you . . . *how* did you know?"

"It wasn't just one thing; it was the whole thing. From the moment I met you, everything in me came alive, and it feels like every moment with you since has just been you proving me right."

Instinctively, we set our teacups down and I melt in his arms, letting those three words dance in my mind, and in my heart.

# EPILOGUE

## Fall

I'm pouting as I come off the elevator of Raja's apartment building, ready to share my emotions but only after he shares every single detail about Lakshmi's wedding festivities.

This weekend is not only her wedding, but Dashain, and so his days have been packed with family events. I, on the other hand, had no idea a Nepali wedding contained this many activities, and between schoolwork and my business, I couldn't afford to take off for everything. Plus we are still new in introducing him and his extended family to the concept of bringing a romantic relationship like ours into the fold, so we decided it's probably best I don't attend every event anyway, even though Lakshmi invited me to everything. So, baby steps, although he told me half his aunties are asking about the pretty girl who puts gulab jal in the essential oils she sells. I found out one of my oils, infused with rose petals, has been such a favorite, my products infiltrated the group chats. The screenshots were hilarious, and what's even better is they call my product "The Queen gulab jal." I told him I made Mary Kay status, and my heart fluttered even more when he laughed at the joke.

My baby always gets me.

The first semester of school has been a battle, but Raja and I are used to the hard stuff, so we find ways to make our lives easier and lighter. We vibe well, we daydream together, and we laugh all the time. I've even convinced him to draw outside while I plant, and he's produced some of the best flower tattoos I've seen to date.

He's become my person.

Raja's left the door unlocked for me, and as I walk right in, my phone slips out my hand right next to the fuzzy house shoes he bought for me to wear when I'm over. I smile, thinking about how Raja surprised me with them last time I was here, after he figured out how easily my feet get cold with the chillier temperatures.

He clears his throat, and I look up for the first time since I walked in and gasp. Raja has garlands of marigolds hanging from his apartment ceiling like fireworks falling from the sky, with rose petals sprinkled around tea light candles on his kitchen counter, a bronze lantern candle holder, and burning incense. And in the middle are two bohemian-style ottoman poufs with flowers floating in small clear bowls along the perimeter.

I jump when I realize Raja's hands are touching the back of mine, which have been covering my mouth this entire time.

He brings them down. "That's better, I can see your face. Hi."

"Raja, this is beauuutiful. How . . . I don't even . . ."

"I'm an artist. I get creative," Raja says, and I am overcome with so much pride, I cannot contain myself. ". . . with the help of Rani, Reya, and Kasmitha. They dropped off some leftover decorations and gave me quick instructions. I kinda did my own thing with the rest."

"You finally admitted you're an artist!" I squeal. "Ugh, it's about damn time!" And then I roll my eyes something fierce, and he laughs.

"The leftovers are from mehndi night and the sangeet, which everyone missed you at, by the way," he says. I should feel more disappointment, but it's hard to when your boyfriend has transformed his studio apartment into a florist shop.

I bite my lip instead, and Raja continues. "Lakshmi says we have to make sure everyone knows you're with the Sharmas. So, she gave me permission to tattoo you, the Nepali way."

"How's that?" I ask, excitement building.

"You know it as henna, but we call it mehndi." He motions for me to sit on one of the floor pillows, and he sits on the other, legs crossed. I can't wait until the day I get to go to a mehndi night, but Raja doesn't want to wait for that to show me this part of his world. He's bringing the experience to me instead.

"Now," he says, as he begins pulling out a cellophane sheet and wrapping it in a cone shape. "Oh, can you pass me some tape?" He smiles wide and I smile back, loving when I get to see this side of him. Being his best self.

I grab the tape off his drafting desk. "You want me to cut you a piece?" I ask, and he nods. I pull the tape until he tells me when, then watch him twist the piece around the bottom of the cone like a cotton candy spinner. We repeat this a few times, until about five are filled with paste stacked neatly on one of his art towels. "What's this supposed to be?"

"They're mehndi cones, sorta like a tattoo pen," he says, getting his station ready.

"It's so cool it's homemade," I reply, taken back to the first time I met the artist.

He grabs another pillow and places it in his lap, and once he moves his hands to the middle of the cone like a surgeon, he asks for mine. "No, the left hand," he says. With the sunflower wrist.

"You're going to snake a vine around the sunflower?" I giggle, half hoping.

"Yeah, something like that," he says. "But I need your hand as still as possible, so before we start, can you be in charge of the playlist?"

I tether my phone to his speakers and play the first song, which stops Raja in his tracks.

He smiles wide as "Simple Simple Kanchhi Ko" blasts through his speakers. "How do you know this song?" he asks.

"It was from the tika-tala, I asked Rani," I say proudly. "Issa bop."

"What else you got on there?" Raja asks, trying to peer over at my phone. I guard it closer to my chest.

"One surprise for another. You worry about my mehndi, I worry about the sangeet."

Raja's laughter fills the entire apartment as I confidently settle back into a comfortable position and pass him my left wrist.

"I'm using the phrase you always use on me: you are showing out. I take you to *one* family event and you're learning like that, huh?" He leans back, enchanted.

"Please, Raj, I still don't understand how to address half your family," I say, and we both chuckle. "Can you accept it may take me a while?"

"How long is long?" he asks, kissing my hand, then my wrist, and I feel his breath tickle the hairs on my arm. He applies pressure to the middle of his cone, and I don't know why but I hold my breath as the gooey substance glides onto my skin. Somewhat cool, but gel-like. Soothing.

It takes me back to the night we first met. That night we were both timid to touch, but now that we know each other, we don't hide our desires anymore. We feel safe with each other, even when the world around us is trying to forbid our love from forming.

He wraps his fingers around my wrist like he's familiar with my skin, because he is.

"Could be months, years even," I reply, waiting to see how he'll respond.

"Decades even" is all he says as his eyes trace down my face to my lips, and then he smirks as those big browns stare back into mine.

"Don't look at my lips and not kiss them," I demand, and he obliges. One long, sweet, tender kiss. Like nectar from a flower. God, he's such a tease.

"Okay," Raja says, clearing his throat. "You're distracting me, Deja Martin." We both nervous chuckle, the sparks still twinkling around us. He blinks a few times, and I laugh.

"You okay?" I ask him.

"Yeah, you got me over here seeing stars." He rubs his eyes, and I chuckle.

To stop myself from distracting Raja, I put on our favorite DJ and watch him create the most precious vine, lacing it around to attach to my sunflower tattoo just like he said. But when he gets to the wrist, I see what he and his dad meant. It's subtle, but he quickly writes my initials in the mehndi before I can protest. I laugh.

"No, that's tradition! You've gotta stop doing that," I declare. "First the picture, and now this."

"But I'm manifesting," Raja says, and I shake my head, grinning from ear to ear. "Plus, if we got married, someone else would tat you up, not me. Just this once. Sometimes rules are made to be broken," he says, moving the floor fan closer to us to allow the mehndi to dry.

"You're so rebellious," I say, and he chuckles.

"Only for the things that are worth it."

Unsure where to look, I turn my hand back and forth, admiring his artwork. "I love it, Raja. How do I sleep on this? How long does it last?" I ask.

"You apply lemon juice to let it set; I got some for you in the fridge. And also an extra pair of sheets, because if you really want it to pop on your skin . . ."

"Which obviously I do . . . ," I respond.

"Then . . . you let it stay on for as long as possible. Most of my cousins say it falls off while you sleep, hence the sheets."

"I think you've come up with the perfect plan, Raja Sharma," I respond, and he blushes.

The night of Lakshmi's wedding feels like something out of a Bollywood movie. I meet Padma auntie, who comes into Raja's childhood home and opens a suitcase like a hustler on the street, spilling a confetti of colors and jewels and decadence in all types of fabrics. She pulls a sunflower-gold saree out of her suitcase.

"This was requested by Raja," she says, pulling it up to my face. I was expecting a simple-colored saree, but this one feels so loud to me. Like I'll stick out. Like I'll be seen.

She and Raja's mom wrap my saree, and I can see the differences in generations, and feel a respect for women who've wrapped this fabric for years. My pleats look so sharp, it's as if the fabric were stitched that way. I watch as they take out a cookie tin with safety pins and light sewing utensils to hem my wardrobe on the spot. These women are pros. They don't use as many pins as I expected and even give me bathroom tips on how to hike up a saree. "Back in Nepal we *only* wore a saree," Auntie tells me, and I giggle, imagining myself attempting that daily.

I come out of Rani's bedroom as Raja comes out of the bathroom, almost colliding. They have him dressed in a cream daura suruwal with a sunflower-yellow vest, with gold mandalas embroidered across it. The yellow wrapped around his brown complexion glows. "You clean up nicely, Raj," I greet him.

He plays with his blouse's sleeve. "It's been a minute since I wore one, but I agree." I laugh. "I would have never worn yellow if it wasn't your favorite color."

"It makes your eyes look golden almost," I say, and cup his stubble just as his mom and auntie walk out, then quickly draw my hand away, not sure if they're ready to see this level of intimacy yet. When we look their way, their body language is rigid, but the look on their faces shows they're completely charmed. Can't help but accept love when you see it.

"He looks great in yellow, right?" I say, putting my hands behind my back. They both nod.

"I think it's my favorite color on him," his mom responds, still a bit reserved.

"And you really are a style icon," I tell Padma auntie. "I would never have picked this out myself, but the color and details are stunning."

Padma auntie blushes. "I asked him what color and he said the best sunflower-yellow saree you can find. I knew I had just the thing!" Padma auntie grins so wide, Raja and I look at each other and he winks.

We tell his aunt and mom we'll meet them at the venue and head over ourselves. Padma auntie insisted I get dressed at Raja's parents' house, and after tonight's dress-up session, Raja and I conclude it's all part of her ploy to get his parents completely on our side since she's been the ones raving about my products in the group chats. Raja opens the door and helps me out the car, determined not to repeat what happened at the tika-tala. As I grab his hand, I feel like I'm summoned out of my carriage, a princess being escorted to a ball. I chuckle.

"What's so funny?" Raja asks me.

"I feel like Princess Tiana and you're Prince Naveen . . . wait, was he South Asian? I don't know if we ever actually found that out."

"No, my sister-cousins looked it up. They made him racially ambiguous, but that name is from my people, so tonight, that's who we are." I lean my head on his shoulder as we walk into the ball.

The entrance is a walkway of lanterns of all sizes lit up by candles, leading us to a cascade of cherry blossoms framing the walkway into the ballroom, like an entryway into an enchanted forest.

We step into what feels like a magical world. Flowers, chandeliers, and fabric are interlaced and interwoven as tapestries into the ceiling, and a sea of color surrounds us—people dressed in their most decadent of outfits. The colors collide together like a patchwork quilt, all with their unique flavors, but together, it's something else completely.

"Dammmn," I say, my eyes dancing over the mosaic of colors. Raja chuckles.

"As you can see, Lakshmi also loves flowers," he says.

"If this is what the décor looks like, I know her outfit won't disappoint."

My hunch was right: Lakshmi looks like a goddess herself, her maroon and gold skirt and blouse combination saturated with beads and embellishments galore, and as she sits on her sweetheart sofa, Rani and Reya help her spread the dress out so that the videographer can get the full detail of her garment. You'd think the lehenga would stop the show, but I can't stop looking at her chandelier earrings with a matching necklace and damini, crowning her head like a tiara.

I'm eating it up and let out a hoot, which makes Lakshmi laugh and her shoulders relax. Raja squeezes my hand under the table.

The outfits are just as expressive and lively as the décor, bursting with colors and vibrancy. It's hard not to be happy surrounded by all this. People are mingling, and as Raja introduces me to someone, he's suddenly grabbed by a cousin.

"Raja dada, where have you been? We gotta go!" Nijar says as he pulls us away from each other.

"I'll be right back, just go sit at the table!" Raja says, his eyes not leaving my sight until I chuckle and nod, understanding the assignment. While Raja's sister-cousins are also pulled away, a few younger cousins introduce themselves to me and escort me to a table full of people our age, letting me know either Raja or someone in his family planned for this. The DJ asks a few times for us to sit in our seats, and the festivities begin.

After speeches and some quick announcements, the music cuts on and all the teenagers at my table, as well as some young aunties and uncles, bum-rush the dance floor.

I immediately take out my camera to record, because who is in the mix but none other than Raja. And he's been holding out. He's got moves. Why am I *just* finding this out? The cousins are clapping, dancing and lip-syncing, literally like in the Bollywood movies we've watched together. They all have parts and everything, just like a musical.

It's clear Raja didn't practice as much as he was supposed to, but he's lip-syncing his parts to Lakshmi and ad-libbing by spinning on the floor. At one point he manages to grab flowers to give away—to the bride, to Rani who's on the dance floor with him, and when I think he's done, he runs to the table next to me to give one to his aama, and the last one to me. He kisses my phone lens while I'm recording like he's kissing me, and his parents' table erupts in laughs and cheers, even his dad swelling up with pride. If there was ever any question where his love lies, he's cleared it up to five hundred people tonight.

Right after the flash mob and the undercover shots, I find out quickly what kind of party this is going to be as Raja excuses himself and suddenly he and a few other young men are grabbing Akhil by his legs and picking him up, jumping around with him on their shoulders across the dance floor. Lakshmi is up next and they twirl around as she uses her hands and shoulders to do a shimmy, Akhil fist-pumping right next to her. This wedding is LIT.

The dance floor becomes our spot for the rest of the night, me and Raja having the time of our lives, his worlds finally colliding. The tassel of my garment tickles my back as I dance, and I begin to notice it's not always the tassel, but Raja's thumb caressing the crease of my spine through the opening of my blouse. Every once in a while a cousin or auntie pulls me in and I do a two-step with them, learning a few of their moves, but it's never long before we find a way back in each other's arms.

There's even a moment where I find myself drawing closer to Mrs. Sharma and Padma auntie, who teach me a few staple twirls and I laugh, doing as I'm told.

As they leave the dance floor, Raja sweeps right back in.

"You didn't tell me you knew how to *dance* dance!" I say, and he just smirks and shrugs.

Then his forehead creases. "How was my mom?" he asks.

"Meh, following your dad's lead," I respond, mirroring his shoulder shrug while we slow dance in the midst of the wedding chaos around us.

"They're being weird 'cause they're still concerned about everybody else, but look at everyone else, no one cares. And who cares if they do!" he says.

"I mean, you ripped the Band-Aid off, right?" I say, motioning for him to look his parents' way, who are staring nonstop from their seats. His mom blushes and looks away, and unbeknownst to his dad, he has a smile on his face, watching us. I turn back to Raja. "It looks like the wound is finally beginning to heal."

He smiles. "Yeah, they'll come around. But regardless, it's me and you, right?"

"It's me and you," I reply, and he takes hold of my wrist to kiss the sunflower's center. Then he inspects his art.

"The mehndi came out super dark," he says, a look of satisfaction on his face.

"I know, I love it!" I say. "I overheard someone mentioning how dark the mehndi came out for Lakshmi, too. That's a good thing I take it?"

"Yeah, apparently the darker it becomes, the more you are . . . in love." He looks away. "At least that's what the sister-cousins tell me."

I've made him wait long enough. "Well, I guess it was good I left it on all night, then, because I do love you," I say.

He smiles. "Mero maya."

I translate "maya" in my head. Love.

I squeeze him tight and close, inhaling a whiff of—what? Rose petal oil. And while we embrace, my insides sizzle, as I know he loves me in all the ways he tells me, but most of all, in all the ways he shows me.

# Acknowledgments

Considering how long my acknowledgments were in *Love Radio*, I want to keep these simple and sweet. To everyone who had a hand in helping me get this novel out into the world, from early reads to acquisition to production, thank you. A special thank-you to Kendra for helping me shape this novel during a very difficult point in my life, and to Kristin for constantly having my back.

With *Love Radio*, I got to honor much of my paternal side, and with *This Could Be Forever*, I get to honor my maternal side. To my maternal matriarchs: My grandma Barbara-Jean, thank you for all you showed me in those summers with you down South, and my great-grandmother Leora, I channeled you in ways I could have never known in this story and am so appreciative of all that I learned while writing it. Mommy, thank you for the early confidence you gave me in my own skin, and for encouraging me to create Deja's character in this way. Hope I made you proud, Night. And to the rest of my aunts, uncles, and cousins, thank you for giving this crazy horse some fun times. ☺ To the playa from the Himalayas, we had a great run, kiddo. Much gratitude to you and your family for some wonderful moments and memories. And to the Nepali community in the DMV, I'm so appreciative of your love.

To my readers, I put my heart into this one. I hope you felt it.

## About the Author

Ebony LaDelle is a Howard University alum and the author of *Love Radio*, which was a *People* magazine best book of the summer, a 2023 Audie Award finalist, a 2023 Michigan Notable Book, an Apple Books best book of 2022, and an Amazon editors' pick, and it was featured on the *Today* show. A Baldwin Fellow, she's also the author of the forthcoming anthology *You've Got a Place Here, Too*. Prior to being an author, Ebony was a brand marketing director in book publishing and worked at Penguin Random House and HarperCollins, among others. You can visit her online at EbonyLaDelle.com and follow her on social @EbonyLaDelle.